THE VIEW FROM POMPEY'S HEAD

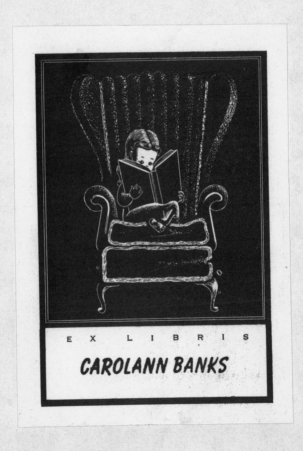

Hamilton Basso

THE VIEW
FROM
POMPEY'S
HEAD

Doubleday & Company, Inc.

Garden City, New York

Having been said so often, it must be said again—since this is a novel, none of its characters should be taken to represent any person, living or dead, and none of its incidents to be related in any way to an actual happening. It should be read as fiction throughout.

Library of Congress Catalog Card Number 54-10767

PART ONE

CHAPTER ONE

It was one of the grievances of the business element of Pompey's Head that the all-pullman train from New York to Miami reached its community at five forty-six in the morning.

Anson Page, sitting in a roomette in a car that some fanciful soul had named "The Marshes of Glynn," could understand why. Not only was the visitor compelled to rise before daylight and leave the train before the diner opened—a visitor whom the business element would naturally see as an important executive; a busy, hurried man who might well regard a poor night's sleep and an empty stomach as signs that Pompey's Head was not quite the up-and-coming place it ought to be—but along with his growling stomach and interrupted rest he would have an even larger objection. What was a man to do with himself at five forty-six in the morning?

Far removed from the commercial circles of Pompey's Head, one of the partners of the legal firm of Roberts, Guthrie, Barlowe & Paul, which represented most of the publishing houses in New York, Anson Page could afford to regard the matter lightly. Furthermore, he had not at all minded getting up before daylight, nor did he object to having to wait for his breakfast. Usually impatient for it, he was hardly aware that he had not eaten. He did not even have the slight headache that invariably bothered him whenever he had to undergo an early-morning fast. His, however, were a special set of circumstances. He could readily perceive why the more enterprising groups of Pompey's Head (the Chamber of Commerce; the Port Authority; the Industrial Committee) would prefer to have the best train that passed through town arrive at a more convenient hour; and it was no less difficult to understand why those who had to make the trip regularly, faced with the prospect of not enough sleep, no breakfast, and sitting in a deserted hotel lobby until the day's work got under way, might in time come to regard the small Southern city of twenty-five thousand inhabitants as a most annoying port of call.

These, however, were only superficial musings; Anson Page's real attention was on more personal things. Lighting a cigarette, he looked out the window and watched the gray, indefinite rush of a sweep of heavily wooded country, broken by occasional stretches of murky swampland, that was just beginning to assume form and substance in the misty light of dawn. He tried to guess where he was—just past Spur Hill; just before Acorn?—but nothing in the moss-hung woods gave him a clue. Once, fifteen years ago, he would have been able to tell by the very shape and color of the land. Now it was as if this had never been part of the country that he had claimed when he was young. But it would be a nice day, he consoled himself; it always was when the mornings came with fog. The sun would burn through, the mist would vanish, and the rest of the day would be arched over by a blue, cloudless sky—the mere promise of such weather was enough to make him forget the dejection that had plagued him in New York, still cold and miserable the end of March.

Gradually the light grew brighter. A grove of pines flashed by, each trunk showing a deep gash below which hung a metal receptacle to catch the sap that dripped from the wound, and in a small clearing amid the trees a row of ramshackle cabins with rusty tin roofs stood sealed and shuttered against the morning's chill. Thin wisps of smoke floated above them, hanging blue and intact in the mist, the sagging chimneys looking as though they must finally yield to the stronger force of gravity at any moment and collapse into meaningless heaps of homemade rubble, and in one of the front yards a solitary rooster with a loose, flopped-over comb scratched aimlessly in the forlorn earth.

At last Anson knew where he was—the turpentine camp near Acorn, a one-street village sixteen miles north of Pompey's Head. No one happening to look in on him, seeing a slender, dark-haired man with serious brown eyes and a grave expression on his thin, well-modeled face, could possibly have surmised the high pitch to which all his sensibilities had been brought—certainly not the Negro porter who a few moments later came for his bags. The porter was fat and sleepy-looking. He wore a clean white jacket and his shoes were newly shined. Several folds of evenly divided flesh rolled down the back of his neck.

"About twenty minutes now, sir," he said with more than ordinary attentiveness, knowing how long Anson Page had been awake. "Old Pompey's the next stop."

"Yes," Anson replied. "I know."

It was true; he did know. He was a stranger, but not that much of a stranger. Pompey's Head was home. He was going home for the first time in fifteen years. He started to tell the porter about it, but he could not bring himself to believe that the porter would be interested. And yet he might be. A printed card slipped into a metal frame at one end of the car said that the porter's name was Thomas McElroy, and McElroy was an old Pompey's Head name—one of "The Twenty Families of Marlborough County." It could easily be that the porter came from Pompey's Head. After emancipation many of the Negro families kept the names of their former masters, and, besides, the porter had used the casual, familiar form of "Old Pompey"—that almost certainly identified him as a native. Anson was about to ask him if he was related to any of the McElroys who lived near Mulberry, the old Blackford place on the Cassava River, having suddenly remembered a cheerful, round-faced Negro boy named Tooker McElroy with whom he and Wyeth Blackford had used to hunt and fish, but then a muffled gong sounded at the far end of the car. The porter turned away with a tired look and paddled down the corridor. The faint hiss of the air-conditioning system overrode the low rumble of the wheels, and then, in answer to some muffled query, Anson heard him say, "No sir, we's not nearly to Savannah yet. We ain't in Georgia, even. We's still this side of Pompey's Head."

By the time the porter returned to carry off his bags, Anson had made up his mind not to ask him about the McElroys—the need for identification had passed. He told the porter to leave his briefcase, crushed out his cigarette, and looked through the window again. It was almost full light now and he could make out the separate features of the landscape. He noticed that the first redbud was in bloom, saw a big hawk fly from a tulip tree that grew near the right of way, and watched the brown waters of a narrow creek ripple lazily between low-lying banks that were marked on either side by soft, muddy places where generations of fishermen had taken up their stand. Ockeesawba Creek, his mind registered; no longer any need to wonder where he was. The whole face of the land came back to him, all of a piece and in all its detail. Stretching out his legs, which were cramped from his having sat too long in one position, he picked up the thread of

9

one memory after the other, restoring the pattern of a life that seemed almost to belong to another person, and, at the same time, mused upon the chain of circumstance that had conspired to bring him back to Pompey's Head after fifteen years on what could be regarded only as a singularly curious mission.

It had been one of those cold, wet March mornings in New York City that invariably caused Anson to feel gloomy and depressed. A gray rain was driving, a high wind was blowing, and it was so dark in the apartment that Meg had turned most of the lights on. Sitting ready for work in the dining alcove and glancing through the morning paper over a second cup of coffee, Anson told himself that it was some day to have to go out in, a perfect hell of a day. Down in Pompey's Head it would already be spring. The sun would be shining, the fruit trees would be in bloom, the weakfish would be running, and somebody would be getting ready to have an oyster roast on Cassava Beach.

Anson often told himself that you could not live in one place as long as he had without being deeply attached to it, without being pledged in a way that no one in his present circle of friends and acquaintances seemed able to understand; but at times like this, in the dismal heel of a New York winter, it was more than an attachment and a pledge—it was a pull and a drain on the heart. Not that he once imagined that he could ever go back to Pompey's Head to live. The act of divorcement had been too final; the blade of separation had cut too deep. What he thought about Pompey's Head, judiciously calculated over the years, had been written, properly disguised, into his book *The Shinto Tradition of the American South*, which even the New York *Times* and *The Nation* had gone out of their way to approve. His feeling for Pompey's Head, quite a different thing from what he thought, was purely a physical attraction. Meg once said that he felt about it the way a man feels who has found it necessary to give up a mistress he was still in love with, and he guessed it was true. But this particular mistress—he had come to regard her as a sunny-tempered, laughing girl who never wore a girdle and liked to go barefoot and who greatly resembled the flower-decked maiden in Botticelli's picture about spring—had been forsworn for fifteen years. He wanted no more of Pompey's Head. Mixed though his emotions were, he was content to be where he was.

The transition had not been easy. There used to be times in New York when he asked himself what he was doing in this sooty, amorphous town where even for $375 a month you couldn't rent a decent look at the sky, but he did so no longer. The answer was woven into every act of his everyday life. He was doing a job of work; he was supporting a family; he was at last earning enough money so that money was no longer too much of a problem; he had got out of Pompey's Head at a time when he could not bear to live there any longer, and here he was.

But feeling, the old pledge and the old attachment, would still intrude. Sometimes, often when he least expected it, he would be made aware of a kind of rootlessness, especially when he discovered that some New York landmark that he had come to depend upon, like the Collegiate Reformed Church of St. Nicholas on Fifth Avenue, was in the process of being torn down. He would then tell himself, along with thinking that New York was like a blacksnake that was always shedding its skin, that if he were back in Pompey's Head he could walk in the same shadow of the same trees and houses that his father and grandfather had walked in, but that was pure nostalgia, of course. Nobody had roots any more, as Meg said, and she could argue convincingly that any person who was really adjusted, able to stand on his own two feet, didn't need an inherited background to support him like a crutch.

All that, however, did nothing to alter the fact that it was one hell of a day. Anson was thinking that down in Pompey's Head a man would hardly bother to get out of bed on a day like this, or else take his own sweet time about it, when Meg came in from the kitchen. They were without help again and she had all the work to do. She wore a red wool housecoat over her nightgown and had on a pair of brocaded mules that tapped across the floor. She had done her face and fixed her short, wavy hair, and nobody would ever guess, looking at her, that she had roused a husband, made breakfast, argued a nine-year-old boy into eating his oatmeal and getting dressed for school, and taken care of the incredibly complicated needs of a five-year-old daughter.

Meg's ability to face up to the world the moment she got out of bed never ceased to amaze Anson. He himself met the day like a Chinese coolie who has paused with his bundles by the wayside for the night—each parcel had to be laboriously picked up and loaded, just so, and even then there were times when the headstrap chafed and pulled. Meg sat down at the table and poured herself a cup of coffee.

"I forgot to tell you," she said. "You'll have to take Patrick to school this morning. Something's wrong with their station wagon."

Anson could feel his face beginning to look annoyed. "What, again? You would think that for almost what it costs to send a man to Yale that school would be able to afford something that ran occasionally. This is the fourth or fifth time in less than two weeks."

"I know," Meg said. "It's not the school's fault, though. The mechanic keeps telling them it's fixed and then it breaks down. Boojum says——"

Anson spread his hands. "Spare me what Boojum says, please. I can only take what Boojum says when I'm fully awake. Boojum and Beejum! When I went to school the principal was Mr. Roberts and his wife was Mrs. Roberts. I can just see a Boojum and a Beejum in Pompey's Head."

"Yes, darling. Everything was perfect in Pompey's Head."

It was one of Meg's useful advantages. By saying that everything was perfect in Pompey's Head, even though she knew he didn't think so, she could always cut him short. Besides, Meg didn't like the South. She had been there only once, when she and a maiden aunt went to Charleston after seeing a revival of *Porgy and Bess* and where they were made to feel cheated because there was no such place as Catfish Row, but that once was enough—it had been hot, and Charleston seemed like something preserved under glass, and why his thoughts kept returning to Pompey's Head was beyond her ability to understand.

"Isn't it a foul day?" she said.

"Don't sound so cheerful about it. This isn't a day. It's a conspiracy against the soul of man."

"Not at all," Meg said. "There's something exciting about it."

"What, for instance?"

"Oh, I don't know—the wind, the sound of the rain, the feeling that something is happening. It's exciting, that's all."

Anson started to say he knew a better excitement, fashioned of paper-whites and jonquils and the smell of tea-olives at night, but he wasn't sure that Meg knew what paper-whites and tea-olives were. He doubted that she ever had occasion to do any research about them, and, besides, he didn't want to be told again that everything was perfect in Pompey's Head. Most of the time Pompey's Head lay buried beneath the things that had happened during the past fifteen years, but on mornings like this it was different. Everything came back to him. He could see the squares that everyone was so proud of, not only for their oaks and magnolias and masses of azaleas but also because they had been laid out at least a decade before the squares in Savannah, a circumstance that Savannah was reluctant to admit but which was a matter of historical record just the same, and he could see the narrow Georgian streets that ran off from the squares, each house built close to its neighbor and the streets filled with sunlight that fell through the trees and stippled the sidewalks with a pattern of leafy shadow that shook and trembled with every current of the wind. It probably wasn't the same any more, not after fifteen years, but on mornings like this there were no fifteen years. Anson could remember everything the way it was when he was living with his family on Alwyn Street. He suspected that it had some connection with his being eight months past his thirty-ninth birthday. It was a known fact that when you approached the foreground of middle age you tended to remember only the good things in the past, and even the bad things were not nearly so bad any more—the good things had happened to you; the bad things, somehow, had happened to a person you no longer were. It was this, Anson suspected, that enabled some men to write in their autobiographies of almost unbearable things. "Look!" the implication was. "See how we have come through!"

Another, stronger gust of wind rattled the windows, and there was another slap of rain.

"There's some more excitement for you," Anson said. "It gets more and more exciting by the minute. It's too bad you had to miss the Johnstown Flood."

"The way you harp about the weather," Meg answered. "What good does it do?"

"It does me good."

"Well, it doesn't me. Besides, the weatherman on the radio said it was going to clear up. It'll probably be a nice afternoon."

"I'll bet. It has all the makings of a nice afternoon."

Meg liked living in New York. No matter what the weather, it was better on the whole than the weather she had grown up in, and were it not that she felt that they ought to move to the suburbs for the sake of the children, she would be content to live in New York the rest of her life. Meg came from a little town in southwestern Indiana, a place called Hillsdale, and as far as she was concerned it could disappear without a trace. Not, so far as Anson could tell, that she had ever been particularly unhappy there, or that anything had gone wrong—her way of explaining it was that when she was seventeen she had made up her mind that she was damned if she was going to sit and rot in the Middle West. Even at seventeen Meg's determination had been something to reckon with. After she graduated from the Hillsdale High School, one of those extroverted prairie institutions given over to basketball, football, and 4-H clubs, she persuaded her parents to send her East to college, and five weeks after graduating from Bennington she was working as a researcher for one of the newsmagazines. Anson couldn't help contrasting her with some of the girls he had known before he came to New York—Kit Robbins, Dinah Blackford, Gaby Carpenter, Margie Rhett, and Joe Ann Williams. He doubted that Meg would approve of any of them.

"What's in the paper?" Meg asked. "Anything new?"

Anson tried to remember. "The Saint's in trouble again, the Dodgers look good in spring training, Vishinsky may be coming over for another visit, some of the members of the Supreme Court seem to be at outs with each other, and Harry Vaughan's got himself mixed up in some kind of trouble with iceboxes. Other than that——"

But Meg was seeing for herself. She sipped her coffee and picked up the copy of the *Herald Tribune* that Anson had brought in from the elevator landing, where it was deposited each morning. Her intelligent face with its short upper lip and slightly turned up nose took on a sober expression as she scanned the headlines. There was something about her that reminded Anson of the day he went to her office when she was working on the newsmagazine; they had a date for lunch and she was sitting at her desk reading a newspaper with her head tilted in much the same way. Anson thought she seemed hardly a year older. She looked as though she would be getting up at any moment to track down the beef production of Texas in 1902, or the number of Basques now resident in Idaho, or the name, age, and marital status of the sheriff of Como Bluff, Wyoming.

"That Vaughan!" she said. "You would think that Truman would have sense enough to fire him. Especially with the congressional elections coming up."

Meg had worked in that department of the newsmagazine called *The National Scene*. She was very good at her job. She had no trouble generating a new burst of excitement each week regardless of the stories she happened to draw, and had she stayed on instead of getting married she would probably have realized her ambition to become a staff writer. Becoming a staff writer, at one time, had meant a great deal to her.

"A scandal like this could easily cost the Democrats the election," she went on. "Anybody as shrewd as Truman ought to see that. He's

14

going to wake up one of these days and find that he's not nearly so smart as he thinks he is."

Marriage had been a troublesome choice for Meg. Anson knew that she had moments of wishing she were back on the newsmagazine. She had been free and independent, had more admirers than she knew what to do with, and she liked the excitement of deadlines, late closings, last-minute changes in make-up caused by some dramatic break in the news, and the feeling of being close to all that was happening in the world—a false notion, perhaps, but one that the nervous atmosphere in which she worked had never given her cause to question.

"Such cheap, hick, small-town graft!" she said scornfully. "That's one of the troubles with this administration—it's so incredibly hick. I can understand Teapot Dome, but not iceboxes. It'll be interesting to see what Truman has to say."

Meg's work had often taken her to Washington and she had come to know many persons of varying degrees of consequence—congressmen, Army and Navy people, diplomats, members of the various departments, and even a couple of White House guards. Because of this, and also because one of her great-uncles had been a senator from Indiana, a powerful member of the farm bloc and one of Joe Cannon's intimate friends, Meg took more than an ordinary interest in national affairs. It showed in her face as she scanned the newspaper. Anson felt that this was one of the times when she would like to be back at work.

"You haven't said anything," she commented. "Don't you think it's disgraceful?"

Anson mumbled a noncommittal reply—yes and no, he thought. One man made off with an oil field, another man was content with an icebox. He agreed with Meg that it was hick, that even graft ought to have style, but he was surprised that she didn't see that there had been a falling off in style all along the line. It was his belief that style was one of the most important things in the world.

"It's all of a piece," he said. "It's what you have to expect."

"What must I expect?"

"The iceboxes. They're part of the new order."

"All right, I'll bite. What new order?"

"The century of the common man. There's a legal maxim——"

"No! Either you explain it without the maxims or I'll start doing the dishes. I'm running behind as it is."

Anson said what he had been thinking about style; it pleased him

15

that Meg listened so attentively. She leaned slightly forward, sipping her coffee, and her blond hair, inherited from a Scandinavian grandmother, was full of soft highlights. She was five years younger than he.

"It's too bad you're not able to do more writing," she said finally, looking genuinely unhappy about it. "Stuck in that office, nobody knows how good you are."

Anson did not answer. Nearly every woman felt at some time or other that the man to whom she was married wasn't properly appreciated; it was one of the pillars of matrimony. He was glad, however, to have her approval. Seeing that he had no special inclination to feel put upon, Meg said, "You're too darn modest, that's your trouble," and turned to the inside pages of the newspaper. Anson remembered how he started being attracted to her and how it all began with the color of her hair.

It happened the day he went to pick her up at the newsmagazine, three or four months after he had met her on a party given by the John Duncans. She was checking a story that had to close that afternoon and couldn't take too much time for lunch; since it was near her office, they went to one of those restaurants in Rockefeller Center that look out on the skating rink. It had started snowing a few hours earlier—not much of a snow; big, lazy, theatrical flakes that turned themselves on and off—and the rink was full of skaters. Anson, after the first few minutes, paid no attention to the swirl and sweep of their flaring costumes, but then, out of the corner of his eye, he happened to catch sight of a slender girl in a green outfit. Something about the way she moved reminded him of Kit Robbins down in Pompey's Head. Not wanting to be reminded of Kit, he looked back to Meg. She was having a piece of French pastry and was cutting it with a fork. She wore a gray tweed suit with a light blue blouse, and her cheeks were still rosy from the cold. He thought what a wonderfully pretty girl she was, and how her hair was the same color as the sunlight on Little Pigeon Marsh in the late fall after the frosts had turned the high, willowy grasses to almost the color of wheat, and then, to his considerable surprise, he found he was completely over Kit Robbins and magnetically drawn to the color of Meg's hair. Looking at her across the table in the dining alcove, he could still see her sitting by the big glass window with the skaters in the snow— it was hard to believe they had been married nearly twelve years.

"Well, I guess I'd better be shoving off," he said. "I've got a lot of work to do. Where's Patrick?"

"I left him reading to Debby."

"What about Debby? Isn't she going to school? Or has their station-wagon broken down too?"

"She's going to be picked up later than usual this morning. Her class is going to the museum. They're going to visit the Egyptians."

"To do what?"

"You heard me. Visit the Egyptians."

"A gang of five-year-olds? Why not Consolidated Edison? Why not Malik and the U.N.?"

"Oh, don't be like that. You're just prejudiced."

"That's right. I'm prejudiced."

Rising from the table, he started toward the bedroom he shared with Meg. She lifted her hand to catch his attention.

"Did you see this ad for Jasper Littlecoat's new book?"

"Yes, I saw it."

"It's full of quotes from the critics."

"That's the reason for the ad."

"Isn't this the book you had to read for libel?"

"It's the one."

"Was it libelous?"

"No, it was just no good."

Meg was still looking at the advertisement.

"Why don't you write a book?" she said. "I should think you'd want to."

"I have written a book. Besides, I'm a lawyer, not a writer."

"You could be both. Look what a stir you caused, despite that dreary title."

"We have different ideas of a stir. And it wasn't a dreary title. It said what it meant and it meant what it said. What did you want me to call it—Bosoms Revisited?"

Meg lifted her eyes, swallowed a smile, and gave a little laugh. "My!" she said. "What a vulgar mind!" Drinking the rest of her coffee, she folded the newspaper and followed Anson to the rear of the apartment. It was on the sixth floor of a ten-story building in the East Seventies. Besides the dining alcove and the kitchen, it included a living room from which you could catch a glimpse of the trees in the park if you pressed against the window and found just the right angle; a moderately large bedroom occupied by Anson and Meg; two cell-like chambers, also bedrooms, given over to the children; another room that Anson used for a study, the smallest of all; and two baths. It didn't seem like much of an apartment for $375 a

17

month to Anson, even with heat and water thrown in, but then he had never been able to stop thinking of New York prices in terms of prices in Pompey's Head. Everybody agreed with Meg that the apartment was a bargain, considering what rents were in New York nowadays and the neighborhood it was in and how close it was to the park. Anson supposed they were right, but at the same time he couldn't keep from thinking of what you could rent for that kind of money in Pompey's Head.

Passing the door of Patrick's room, Anson could hear the boy's self-assured voice reading the story of Jack and the Beanstalk. He thought that *Jack and the Beanstalk* was a lot closer to Debby's speed than a visit to the Egyptians, but there was no point in bringing that up again. Debby's school had been as much his choice as Meg's, and it wasn't fair to badger her about the Egyptians because the gloomy morning had caused him to feel irritable and morose. Meg followed him into their bedroom in a way that told him she wanted to talk something over. He could feel his face beginning to look annoyed again; she was going to present him with some problem or other just when he ought to be freeing his mind for the day's work. He went to the dressing table and began putting things in his pockets—his wallet, keys, a fresh handkerchief, seventy-nine cents in loose change. He could see Meg looking at him in the mirror, half frowning and preoccupied.

"Anson."

"Yes?"

"This isn't a good time to bring it up, I know——"

"I'll have no trouble agreeing with that."

"—but don't you think we ought to do something above moving to the country?"

Anson faced her squarely. "Look, Meg. It's almost nine o'clock and I've got a client coming at quarter of ten, and on top of it all I have to go fourteen blocks out of my way because your friend Boojum——"

"He's not specially my friend. I just feel that since Patrick goes to school there I ought to be nice to him."

"Well, friend or no friend, I don't have time for a long discussion about moving to the country. Why do you always bring these things up at the last minute?"

"Because I like to be difficult, darling."

"You can be. Don't ever get the idea that you can't."

"All I wanted to say was that I thought I might get in touch with the real estate people. The weather will be nice enough in a couple of weeks——"

"And what makes you think so? Will you look out the window and tell me what makes you think so?"

"Yes, darling, it's a horrible day. You mentioned it before. In another month, then, the weather may be nice enough for us to get the car out of storage——"

"That's better."

"—and there's that farm in New Milford——"

"No, there isn't that farm in New Milford. That's no farm. That's a house and six acres that is priced about nine thousand dollars too high. A farm is what my aunt Ruby has down in North Carolina. If we're so hell-bent on living on a farm, why don't we live there?"

"If you don't want to be serious——"

"But I am serious. We can move down there any day we like. If it's a farm we want, there's the farm."

"No, thank you."

"You haven't seen that farm. If you had, you'd change your tune. It's a wonderful farm—it's away back in the hills, miles and miles from everything."

"That's just it. I don't want to live away back in the hills, miles and miles from everything, and I don't want my children growing up there. And you, what would you do—milk the cows and run the tractor? Come, now! Going back to your aunt Ruby's farm is a nice, romantic notion—especially in these moods of yours when you like to wallow in romantic notions—but it wouldn't work. You know it as well as I. Why don't you face the facts of life and stop being Jean Jacques Rousseau in a Brooks Brothers suit?"

Jean Jacques Rousseau in a Brooks Brothers suit struck Anson as a very amusing idea—all his annoyance collapsed in a heap. He smiled at Meg and she smiled back and they stood looking at each other in the mirror.

"Now and then I wonder if I married the right girl," he said.

"I do too," Meg replied soberly, glancing at him in a sudden change of mood. "Not only now and then, though. I wonder all the time."

CHAPTER TWO

The day, then, except for his preoccupation with Pompey's Head, had begun almost like any other. But now, watching the countryside flow past the window of the train, Anson wondered if he should not have recognized that morning's bemusement as having been outside the average scheme of things. Seen in relation to the rest of the day, it could easily be regarded, were he of a superstitious nature, as a kind of portent—a foreshadowing of the immediate future and a sign that a higher intelligence was at work. Unable to see it in so mystical a light, he was equally unable to consign it to the realm of coincidence; try as he might, he could not rid himself of the feeling that somewhere in the taken-for-granted mechanics of that morning there had been the unheeded ticking of large, ponderous forces. He had taken his son Patrick to school in a taxi, dismissed the taxi at the nearest subway station, ridden down to his office on lower Broadway not far from Trinity Church, looked over some motion-picture contracts that had to be rushed to Doubleday, and then seen his client, an unhappy man in his late forties who wanted a divorce.

Roberts, Guthrie, Barlowe & Paul did not ordinarily handle such cases; the bulk of the firm's business was made up of the affairs of the publishing houses it represented. Occasionally, however, because of these connections, individual members of the firm were drawn into the field of domestic relations. Anson's client was an executive named Ralph Graves. Married for fifteen years, the father of three children, he now found himself caught most miserably between his established loyalties and his love for another woman—he had not wanted it to happen ("God knows I didn't," he said in a tone of helpless dejection), but it had happened nonetheless.

Anson responded with only an occasional nod; once he leaned across the desk and flicked a lighter for a cigarette that Graves was nervously fingering. He understood that what the man most wanted was a chance to talk. Graves had no priest or pastor to go to, and he was not yet ready to take his troubles to a psychiatrist. His lawyer, then, had to listen in their stead. It happened in the law more often than people realized, and it was not an easy role for a lawyer to assume—he had to be sympathetic, he had to identify himself with his client, and at the same time, merely in order to do his job, he had to maintain a certain objectivity. All Anson's natural friendliness went out to Graves, for rarely had he seen a man so at war with himself, but he could not prevent a feeling of weariness from creeping in. Graves thought his was a new story, new because it had happened to him and because no two sets of human circumstances are ever exactly alike, but in its essentials it was the same unhappy tale all over again—somewhere along the line of Graves's marriage love had died, a quiet sickening and a quiet death, alone and enfeebled in the middle of the night.

After he left, Anson wished the man had taken his problems elsewhere. The truth of the matter was that Graves had no grounds for a divorce. He simply wanted one arranged. And unless his wife stood in the way, which seemed hardly likely since she had already consulted her own lawyer about a settlement, one would be. The law, sternly committed to the sanctity of contract, had found a number of simple expediencies by which to dissolve what was once the most solemn contract of all. Anson, going to the window, found himself thinking of the bombed dwellings he had seen in London during the war—the strips of faded wallpaper; the cracked plaster; the splintered furniture; the violent, pathetic exposure of all that had once been sheltered and secret within four walls. He had yet to see a divorce action involving children and a long-established marriage that in its own fashion was not as destructive as a buzz-bomb.

It was at that moment, as he was staring out the window at the rain, that Mrs. Waggoner stepped into his office. She was the secretary of Mr. Barlowe, one of the senior partners. Anson now saw her as a kind of fateful messenger. At the time, though, she looked neither fateful nor a messenger, but just as she always did—a motherly, gray-haired widow who came from a crossroads town near Amarillo, Texas, and who each year gave him some of the bluebonnets that one of her nieces sent up by air express.

Grooved in habit, he expected her to ask about Meg and the children. Never a day passed without her inquiring about them, but on that morning they seemed to have slipped her mind completely—which should have been enough, Anson now realized, had he been sufficiently astute and had his mind not been crowded with the melancholy affairs of Ralph Graves, to warn him that this was going to be no run-of-the-mill day.

Mrs. Waggoner's departure from ordinary behavior was something a good courtroom lawyer would have spotted instantly, one of those little incidents that could alter the whole outcome of a trial. He had paid it no mind, however, and almost as little mind to the information that Mr. Barlowe wanted to see him immediately—two of the publishing houses in New York happened to be merging at the time and Mr. Barlowe was always wanting to see him immediately. He suspected that Mr. Barlowe wished to know if they had heard from London about the rental value of some real estate there on which one of the houses held a ninety-nine-year lease, which was among the various odds and ends that were holding up the final papers, and it was not until it dawned on him that Mrs. Waggoner had come to deliver the message in person, instead of merely calling him on the telephone, that he began to suspect something most unusual was afoot. Custom and usage had established a pattern of procedure in Roberts, Guthrie, Barlowe & Paul almost as rigid as that of the United States Supreme Court, and Mrs. Waggoner's having walked to his office was an unmistakable storm signal—trouble, large and unsuspected, already loomed on the horizon. Anson told himself that he could at least credit himself with that much perception, and it was hard for him to believe that even the Delphic Oracle, seeing him hurry past the library and the glass cage where Miss O'Hara was imprisoned with her switchboard, could have foretold that he had already taken the first steps along the journey that was to bring him back to Pompey's Head.

Mr. Barlowe was sitting at his desk reading the New York *Daily News*. He read the New York *Times* on the train and the *Daily News* after he reached the office. Anson had listened to him explain his newspaper habits a few days before at the Recess Club, where they were having lunch. Mr. Barlowe said that for a lawyer the news that wasn't fit to print was just as important as the news that was, and that the editorials in the *Daily News* might well be used in the law schools as models of style—not that he always agreed with them; that wasn't the point; what he was talking about was the way those

22

fellows got their ideas across; they had to appeal to a subway audience and he couldn't help admiring the way they did it. Mr. Barlowe then went on to say that one of the troubles with the law schools was that too many of them held to the theory that a brief should be a piece of literature when, instead, it was actually an editorial—a busy judge with a crowded docket wasn't interested in literature; what he wanted was a concise statement of the facts in the case, and that was where the style in which the *Daily News* editorials were written might come in handy.

Anson knew that Mr. Barlowe, who was anti-administration, also enjoyed seeing Harry Truman get his lumps, but he listened respectfully—even though he was now a partner, he still wasn't altogether comfortable in Mr. Barlowe's presence. Mr. Barlowe was St. Mark's, Princeton, and Far Hills, New Jersey, and Anson could never forget that he was Montague High, South Carolina State, and Pompey's Head. Nor could he erase the memory of the long, drudging years he had spent in one of the cubbyholes at the far end of the office where, on the principle of the survival of the fittest, Roberts, Guthrie, Barlowe & Paul gave desk room to the bright, well-connected boys out of the leading law schools who wanted to work for the firm. The distance that separated him from Mr. Barlowe might have been less had he too been a bright, well-connected boy from one of the leading law schools, but he had come into the office under circumstances so peculiar that he had been strange as a savage in church.

The faces in the cubbyholes changed with dismaying frequency, but Anson managed to survive. He didn't mind hard work, he was gifted with a retentive memory, and it was eventually discovered that he had a way of getting along with the people in publishing. A lawyer who had a feeling for books was a combination they had not often encountered, and then, when he published *The Shinto Tradition of the American South,* he came to be more or less accepted as a member of their guild. The senior partners took note of this, especially Mr. Barlowe, and at the end of five years the rest of the office began to take note of the fact that Anson was in line, though still distantly, for a partnership; it came to be understood around the Recess Club and in the corridors of the various courts that Mr. Barlowe had his eye on him and that he was Mr. Barlowe's "boy."

Always, however, there was the gap between them. Meg said it was ridiculous of him to feel inferior to such suburban buttons as Eugene Hollister and Junius Wigglesworth, both of whom entered the office about the same time he did, and it was hard for him to make her see that inferiority had nothing to do with it; what Meg didn't understand was that both Hollister and Wigglesworth were the equivalent of St. Mark's, Princeton, and Far Hills, New Jersey, and had consequently been licked into a shape that any one of the senior partners could readily recognize as being rather like his own shape when he was that age.

"They're relatively at ease in each other's presence," he said to her one night shortly after they were married, when such matters were still important enough to be discussed. "They know who scored the important touchdowns, who rowed in the winning crews, who made the *Crimson* and who didn't make the *Lit*——"

"That's important, I suppose."

"To you, no; to them, yes. But I'm talking about something else; I'm talking about me. What I'm saying is that I'm an outsider down there, almost an impostor. The curious thing is that the more I take on their kind of protective coloration—just knowing my way around the Harvard Club, for instance—the more of an impostor I feel."

Anson had got over feeling like an impostor, but he was still conscious of being an outsider. He explained his present position by saying that he was a Pawnee who for one reason and another had been adopted by the Crows; he acted, spoke, and dressed like a Crow, but he still thought like a Pawnee—lucky for him that they didn't know how often he was tempted to raid their horses. After he was made a partner, Mr. Barlowe, feeling called upon to indicate that the tribal initiation was at last complete, had several times asked Anson to call him by his first name, Charles, but Anson never even thought of accepting the invitation. You didn't address your elders by their first names in Pompey's Head and if you minded your manners you always said "sir," and he gathered that Mr. Barlowe was just as pleased.

Mr. Barlowe glanced up when Anson came into the office, said "Hullo, Anson, filthy morning, isn't it?" in a preoccupied sort of way, and lowered the *Daily News*. Anson, on the lookout for further storm signals, tried to read the expression on Mr. Barlowe's face, but there was nothing there to read; all he noticed was that Mr. Barlowe's cheeks still shone from the razor and that he was wearing a gray checked necktie with one of the double-breasted gray suits that he had had tailored in England the summer before.

"You wanted to see me, sir?" Anson said.

Mr. Barlowe folded the *Daily News* with the air of measured deliberation that characterized all his movements and dropped it into his wastepaper basket. "It's John Duncan," he said. "I've just had

24

him on the telephone." Frowning almost imperceptibly, but again with an air of measured deliberation, he opened the mahogany humidor that occupied a special place on his desk near the large, silver-framed portraits of Mrs. Barlowe and the two young women he always referred to as "the girls," and extracted a fat, rich-looking cigar.

"Duncan wants us to go uptown," he said. "Right away, of course. Something's come up in connection with that fellow who died, Phillip Greene."

Reaching into his vest pocket with two fingers, Mr. Barlowe brought out a small gold spike that folded like a pocketknife and punctured the end of his cigar—just looking at him, as Anson once said to Meg before she had met any of the senior partners, you would know that he had never been one to bite off the end of a cigar, just as you would know that he had never had to work his way up to corona coronas along the ladder of Spanish Crooks and White Owls. Meg had replied that Mr. Barlowe sounded pompous and stuffy, and without being quite so emphatic about it she still felt much the same way. Having known too many people of consequence in Washington to be impressed by Mr. Barlowe, and discovering that he reminded her of her father, she treated him from the beginning in a casual, daughterly manner that Mr. Barlowe, rather to Anson's surprise, seemed greatly to enjoy. It also turned out that as a young man he had once met her great-uncle who had been a senator and, even more to Anson's surprise, that he liked hearing the gossip about important people that Meg had picked up when she worked on the newsmagazine. Mr. Barlowe's final opinion was that Meg was a great girl and smart as a steel trap. Anson sometimes wondered how much this high estimate of her was responsible for his having been taken into partnership before either Junius Wigglesworth or Eugene Hollister. He imagined that he owed something to the senator from Indiana too.

All this was in the back of his mind as he waited for Mr. Barlowe to say why John Duncan wanted to see them, and what it was that had come up in connection with Phillip Greene. He was too busy keeping himself alert, however, to dwell on it. He knew that Mr. Barlowe might start questioning at any moment, just like a judge from the bench, and in anticipation of the eventuality he put as much of the picture together as was possible from the few scraps of information that had been let fall—John Duncan was the president of Duncan & Company, the publishing house his father had founded in the

1880s and which was one of the most respected firms in New York; Phillip Greene, until his sudden death a few months before, was the editor-in-chief of Duncan & Company, a man with more "discoveries" to his credit than any other editor in the business, with the possible exception of Maxwell Perkins over at Charles Scribner's Sons. It wasn't much of a picture so far, and Anson wished that Mr. Barlowe would get to the point—that John Duncan had called him was in itself most unusual, since Mr. Barlowe had long since extricated himself from all but the corporate affairs of Duncan & Company and had an almost ducal indifference to the routine matters that came up every day.

"What do you know about Garvin Wales?" Mr. Barlowe asked.

Anson hesitated a split instant, his mind working very fast. Garvin Wales, then, was also part of the picture—Duncan & Company's most important author and generally regarded as the country's leading novelist; a lifelong friend of Phillip Greene and now gone blind; in his early sixties; born in Alabama but a wanderer before he was twenty; a gold hunter, a seaman, a soldier; married to a woman considerably younger than himself, a Devereaux from South Carolina, and now living on Tamburlaine Island, twelve miles down the coast from Pompey's Head. Anson's thoughts went off on a tangent for a moment, finding it strange that Pompey's Head should come into it like this, along with Tamburlaine Island off the south point of which he and Wyeth Blackford used to go fishing, but Mr. Barlowe was expecting an answer and it was no time to start thinking about Wyeth Blackford and Tamburlaine Island and Pompey's Head.

"Just about what everybody knows, I guess," he said. "You don't hear much about Garvin Wales any more, now that he's blind. They tell me up at Duncan's that they've been waiting on a new novel from him for over six years and that it's never come through. He had to abandon it, I understand."

Mr. Barlowe held his cigar at a slant and frowned at it slightly. He looked more like a bank president than a lawyer, white-haired, dignified, used to authority, and Anson had always found it strange that even as a corporation lawyer he should have become involved with publishing. Take Garvin Wales, for instance—Mr. Barlowe's idea of a good, crackerjack book was Nash Buckingham's De Shootinest Gent'man, and he had never read a line of Garvin Wales in his life. He said it was hard enough for him to keep up with the things he had to keep up with, without wasting his time reading novels, and, besides, he'd rather go out for a good brisk canter any day.

26

"This Wales?" he said, holding his cigar at a new angle. "What is it that everybody knows? All I know is that I wouldn't use one of his books as a doorstop. The girls say I belong back in the days of Robert Louis Stevenson, but they weren't such bad days if you ask me, not by a damned sight. They were better than what we have now. I wrote a term paper about Stevenson once—did you know that?"

Anson didn't, and it was hard for him to believe that Mr. Barlowe had ever been young enough to write a term paper about anything. This was one of the occasions, however, when even as a partner he must try to look impressed. It wasn't such a good look, far below his usual standard, but that was because his mind was racing ahead again, trying to put more of the picture together. Garvin Wales, he surmised, was at the center of the trouble at Duncan & Company. Feeling more sure of himself, he briefed Mr. Barlowe on the principal facts of Garvin Wales's life, wondering what it was that John Duncan had said over the telephone—it was not unlike being in the theater, reading the biographies of the actors in the *Playbill* and waiting for the curtain to rise.

He hesitated only once, when he came to Garvin Wales's drinking. Everybody in publishing knew Wales's inclinations in that direction, but Anson, remembering how Phillip Greene had always dismissed it with a shrug, wasn't sure he should mention it. On the other hand, it was not his responsibility to conceal anything, especially when it was a matter of common knowledge, and the flick of interest that crossed Mr. Barlowe's face told him that he had guessed correctly—the cause of the trouble at Duncan & Company was Garvin Wales.

"What else?" Mr. Barlowe asked.

"There isn't much else," Anson replied. "Wales has become something of a man of mystery. You used to see his name everywhere, but now—well, he's dropped out of sight. My understanding is that he lives on that island of his almost like a hermit. Relations between him and the people at Duncan's don't appear to be as cordial as they might be."

"Why?" Mr. Barlowe demanded. "What's wrong between this Wales fellow and the people at Duncan's? I want you to give me your idea of the situation, and then I'd like to ask you how you think it squares with what John Duncan said over the telephone."

Anson hesitated a moment. "All I know is what I've happened to pick up. Nothing has ever been said to me officially, or even in confidence. From what I gather, though, it's not so much Wales as it is his wife."

"How does she come into it?"

"Mrs. Wales handles all her husband's affairs. She's had his power of attorney ever since he began going blind."

"How long would that be?"

"Eight or nine years, roughly."

"The instrument has never been revoked?"

"No sir, I'm sure it hasn't. Mr. Duncan was talking about it the last time I saw him, saying he wished it were possible to deal with Wales directly. It came up in connection with this new book that Wales is supposed to be writing. His blindness prevents him from attending to his correspondence, and the only communications they get from him at Duncan's come from his wife."

Mr. Barlowe brought the cigar to his lips and blew out a puff of smoke. Anson, through the window behind his desk, could see the Battery in the rain. He wondered if the weather report that Meg heard over the radio was correct and if it was going to clear up—if it was, it still had a long way to go; you could hardly see the Statue of Liberty, and the wind was driving the rain in long, ragged sheets.

"These communications from Mrs. Wales," Mr. Barlowe said. "Are they dictated by her husband? Does he sign them?"

Anson again hesitated before he spoke. "I can't say positively. It's my understanding, though, that they come from Mrs. Wales. I've been led to believe that it was when she took charge of her husband's affairs that things began to go wrong. She's not an easy person to get along with, it seems."

"You know her?"

Mr. Barlowe spoke idly, apparently intent on nothing except the enjoyment of his cigar, but Anson recognized it as one of those innocent-sounding questions that could lead a witness into a trap. He sensed that a new element had been introduced into the situation, and that he was going to be more involved than he had imagined.

"No, I don't, sir," he said. "Mrs. Wales has some distant connections, though, third or fourth cousins, who live in my town—the town I came from, that is. People named Paxton. That's beside the point, however."

Mr. Barlowe looked thoughtful. "I wouldn't be so sure," he said. "John Duncan seems to think that these associations of yours might prove valuable. He gave me the impression that you knew Mrs. Wales personally."

Anson shook his head. "No sir, Mr. Duncan is mistaken. It's a rather close-knit community down there, but not so close-knit as that. Mrs. Wales's people—her maiden name was Devereaux—come from another part of the state. They're one of our leading families. Shinto-ists of the first degree."

"Shintoists?" A frown creased Mr. Barlowe's forehead. "What do you mean by that?"

Anson chalked up an error for himself; he should have known better than to go off on such a tangent. Nor did it help, now that he had made the error, to remember that Mr. Barlowe was something of a Shintoist himself—he could see the discreetly framed square of parchment bearing the Barlowe coat of arms that hung in the foyer of the house in Far Hills. He told himself that if Mr. Barlowe had read *The Shinto Tradition of the American South* he wouldn't need to have things explained, but Mr. Barlowe, who would rather go out for a good brisk canter any day, was still frowning and waiting to hear why the Devereauxs were Shintoists of the first degree.

"They go in for ancestor worship in rather a big way," Anson said. "That's their reputation, in any case. The reason I called them Shintoists——"

"What's the matter?" Mr. Barlowe's frown deepened. "Don't you believe in ancestors?"

It was as if they were each using a separate language, Anson thought—ancestors meant one thing in Crow and another in Pawnee. Mr. Barlowe imagined that ancestors meant progenitors. He had no way of knowing that what was implied was a whole concept of thought, conduct, and social usage. Once again Anson was reminded of how much an outsider he was. It was little things like this that kept coming up to make him feel strange and foreign and out of place.

"Of course I believe in ancestors," he said. "But some of the people down where I come from——"

Mr. Barlowe, however, was not interested in the habits and customs of a distant, submerged tribe. Managing to indicate by his tone of voice that he thought Anson's views on the subject bordered danger-ously on the radical, he said, "This ancestor worship, as you call it —does it have anything to do with the strained relations that exist between Mrs. Wales and the people at Duncan's?"

"No sir. Not that I know."

For an instant, as Mr. Barlowe reached for an ash tray, Anson thought he was going to say, "Why did you bring it up, then?" but, instead, with a measured tap of his forefinger, he shattered the ash from his cigar. One of the office boys went past the door with a handful of papers, several of the stenographers began typing all at once, the phone rang in Mrs. Waggoner's office, and Miss O'Hara, in her glass cage, kept saying "Roberts, Guthrie, Barlowe & Paul" at more frequent intervals. Anson knew it was getting on toward half-past eleven—for some reason or other everything in the office always seemed to speed up just before noon. Giving his cigar a final tap, Mr. Barlowe said, "Where's the smoke coming from? Where's the fire?"

"I don't know," Anson replied. "I'm in no position to say definitely. Actually, when you come right down to it, all I've heard is nothing but gossip."

"All right." Mr. Barlowe's voice was crisp and sharp. "What's the gossip?"

Anson edited his thoughts. "Putting it simply as I can, Mrs. Wales seems determined to alienate all her husband's friends. So it's being said. Everybody at Duncan & Company is full of it, and I suppose it's being gossiped about elsewhere. How true it is, I don't know—it's never seemed important enough for me to find out. But Phillip Greene——"

Mr. Barlowe, looking suddenly interested, said, "Yes, what about Greene?" and Anson knew that the heart of the matter had finally been reached—the trouble at Duncan & Company was between Mrs. Wales and Phillip Greene; during the last months or weeks of his life, Greene must have done something that caused her to blow up the present storm. He would find out what it was in the next few minutes. Meanwhile he had some more briefing to do—it was just as it had been during the era of the cubbyhole, and he was still saving Mr. Barlowe the trouble of having to run things down.

He told Mr. Barlowe about the friendship between Garvin Wales and Phillip Greene. It began, he explained, when they were serving on the Mexican border. They were both in their twenties at the time —Greene a shy New Englander just out of Harvard, where his social position and inherited wealth automatically insured his membership in the tight fraternity of the Gold Coast, Wales a restless, hard-drinking drifter who had just returned from prospecting for gold in the jungles of Central America. The one admired the other. Greene saw in Wales the man of action he secretly dreamed of being, and Wales, ambitious to become a writer, found in Greene an understanding listener who, even as one of the editors of the Harvard *Advocate*, had developed the knack of spotting a promising author at the bottom of what others might pass over as a most unrewarding manuscript.

It was difficult for Anson to believe that the story of the friendship that joined Garvin Wales and Phillip Greene had not penetrated even the well-combed fastnesses of Far Hills. In a way, though, he was lucky it hadn't. Mr. Barlowe, busy with his large, corporate affairs, depended on him to know such things; it was part of his value to the firm. After the American troops were withdrawn from Mexico, he continued, Greene became a junior editor at Duncan & Company —old Mr. Duncan, John Duncan's father, was still alive. Garvin Wales dropped out of sight for a time, but eventually, just before the United States was drawn into the First World War, he turned up in New York with the manuscript of his first novel. Cenotaph, it was called—a frank, rather clumsily written novel about a young Southerner who served under Pershing on the border, went to live with the peons in a little village, had an affair with one of the native girls, lost her to a particularly brutal member of Villa's disbanded army, watched helplessly while she died in childbirth, and then, returning at last to the little Southern town in which he was born, got himself killed in a brawl over a mulatto girl. There was more to it than that, however. What Garvin Wales was saying was that only the so-called "primitive" peoples were in touch with their true environment; that modern man had strayed too far from his original source springs; that even if he tried to find his way back to them, as had the young Southerner with first the Mexican girl and then the mulatto one, he could not escape his doom.

To a world growing middle-aged with the century, shell-shocked by two world wars and living under the benumbing imminence of a possible third, Garvin Wales had become old-fashioned; the more he was honored as America's foremost novelist, the less he was read. But in the fall of 1917, when Cenotaph appeared in the bookstores, the sound of its explosion was heard even above the din of battle on the Western Front—it was banned in Boston, outlawed in Atlanta, burned in Baltimore, and denounced on the floor of the Senate. Garvin Wales, by then, had enlisted in the Royal Flying Corps. Instead of tempering the outcry, his presence in uniform seemed only to aggravate it—among other things, he was called a dangerous, atheistic radical who was trying to undermine all that George Washington, Thomas Jefferson, Abraham Lincoln, and the United States Constitution held dear.

The senior editors of Duncan & Company, men who had known

James Barrie, Rudyard Kipling, William Dean Howells, F. Marion Crawford, and Robert W. Chambers, agreed in general with the opinions expressed on the floor of the Senate. Had it not been for Phillip Greene, who saw in Cenotaph what the college textbooks had at last got around to seeing—the beginnings of a new, naturalistic development in American literature—the views of the senior editors might easily have prevailed. But Greene, rooted in the granite of his New England resolve, held to his original view—this was one book, he insisted, that could not be turned down.

Old Mr. Duncan, the founder of the firm, could well understand why his senior editors were shocked. He himself was shocked. It was his belief, however, that one of the obligations of a publisher was to make it possible for a young writer to be heard, and, in addition, he detected in Phillip Greene the makings of a future editor-in-chief. Eventually he voted in favor of publishing Wales's novel—the book appeared, the storm broke, sales ran to thirty-five thousand copies in three weeks, Wales shot down his first enemy aircraft, his picture appeared in the New York newspapers, and both the Atlantic Monthly and the Century confounded their readers by appearing with long reviews. Before two months were out more than seventy-five thousand copies of Cenotaph had been sold. In its customary fashion success succeeded—Garvin Wales and Phillip Greene rode into the harbor together. The friendship that began on the Mexican border was given a new dimension. In time it became one of the legends of American publishing.

Anson, not wanting to tax Mr. Barlowe's patience, gave him only the briefest outline. Men like Garvin Wales and Phillip Greene were beyond his comprehension—they fitted into no established category and were bound by no set of rules; they wore tweed coats to the city, took all afternoon for lunch, and had a cynical indifference to business; he wouldn't have either of them in his office and he deeply mistrusted their influence.

"Up to six or seven years ago," Anson continued, "no two men could have possibly been closer. They couldn't be called inseparable, since Greene was always here in New York while Wales was moving about from one place to another all over the world, but they always kept in touch. Whenever Wales came to New York alone, which wasn't often, he stayed at Greene's house. Then, about eight years ago, something began to happen."

Mr. Barlowe lifted his eyes. "What?"

"I don't know. I don't think anybody knows. Greene——"

"You knew Greene rather well, didn't you?"

"Yes sir, I did. It was he who encouraged me to write my book."

"Did he ever speak to you about Wales?"

"Often. He frequently came into the conversation. Not only was there this friendship, but Greene admired him as a writer—so do I, with a few reservations."

Mr. Barlowe nodded sagely. "I gathered as much. It's a good thing. It wouldn't do for Duncan & Company to think that we all belong back in the days of Robert Louis Stevenson down here. But let's get back to what you were saying. I take it that there was some kind of rift between Greene and Wales. What about?"

"I'm unable to say."

"But there was a rift?"

"Yes, there was—to the extent, that is, that Greene stopped hearing from Wales. It happened, however, about the time that Wales began to go blind and all his affairs were taken over by his wife. That may have had something to do with it."

"But you don't think so?"

"I don't know what to think. I have nothing but gossip to go on. However, they say at Duncan's that Wales had nothing to do with it and that it was all the fault of his wife. Greene was one of the people she is supposed to have deliberately gone out of her way to alienate."

Mr. Barlowe again tapped the ash from his cigar. "Did Greene ever mention this—this alienation to you?"

"No, never. He always spoke of Wales in the friendliest way."

"And Mrs. Wales?"

"I only remember his mentioning her once—he said she was an extremely attractive woman, still quite beautiful."

Mr. Barlowe, suddenly relaxing, leaned back in his chair.

"Well," he said, "I guess that does it. We'd better be getting uptown—we're going to have a hard time finding a cab. But one thing more. I didn't get everything John Duncan said—all these publishers are too damned excitable—but it seems that Mrs. Wales has accused Phillip Greene of stealing twenty thousand dollars of her husband's royalties. What's your reaction to that?"

Anson had been too long in the offices of Roberts, Guthrie, Barlowe & Paul to yield to his temptation to gasp. He could tell from Mr. Barlowe's expression, however, that his feeling of shocked incredulity showed through.

"It's impossible," he said.

Mr. Barlowe nodded. "Yes, I suppose it is—probably just some clerical error. But still you never know. When you've been in the law as long as I have, you come to realize that nothing is impossible. I'll meet you at the elevator. If you have any appointments, you'd better have your secretary cancel them—if I know John Duncan, this is going to take the rest of the day."

CHAPTER THREE

Whenever Anson was thrown with Mr. Barlowe for any length of time, as he was in the taxi going uptown to Duncan & Company, he could easily understand why lawyers were often looked upon as the most boring people in the world. No matter at what point a conversation began with Mr. Barlowe, it soon found its way back to the law, and once that happened it was more than likely to remain there. One case suggested another, and another still another, and though Anson always tried hard to be interested, he had never been able to discipline himself enough to keep his mind from wandering.

"On the face of it," Mr. Barlowe was saying, "I'll grant that it's impossible about Phillip Greene. From what we know—from what you know, rather—it's all out of context. But that's why there are lawyers in the world. If things didn't get out of context and everybody behaved the way society expects them to behave—well, most of us would starve."

"It's unthinkable," Anson said. "Just as unthinkable as your going out tomorrow morning and shooting your favorite mare."

Mr. Barlowe nodded as measuredly as the jouncing of the taxi would permit. Even with that handicap he managed to maintain his composure. He said:

"On the face of it, yes, as I've admitted before. I still say, though, that you never can tell. You take that fellow who got in trouble last year in Speed Colquitt's bank. Speed met him out West somewhere —Idaho, I think it was. This fellow was working in a bank out there, one of those hole-in-the-wall places, and he picked up some loose change by hiring himself out as a guide. Speed took a liking to him and brought him to New York. And what happened?"

"He showed his gratitude by embezzling a quarter of a million dollars."

Mr. Barlowe nodded again. "Yes, but that's not the point. The real question, as I see it, is this—did that fellow step out of character or didn't he? Personally, I don't think he did. Character in a man is like conformation in a horse. Either a man has it or hasn't, and if he has it he doesn't suddenly go wrong. That's basic; that's fundamental. Now what I'm saying, in connection with that fellow in Speed's bank——"

But Anson was bored. He could interest himself no longer in these transparent ramifications. What Mr. Barlowe was leading up to was that it was within the realm of possibility for Phillip Greene to have embezzled twenty thousand dollars of Garvin Wales's royalties, and Anson knew better. Glancing from the cab, he saw that they were crossing Canal Street near Worth, where all the cotton-goods establishments had their New York offices. It was like any other part of downtown Manhattan, the usual accumulation of store fronts and plate-glass windows and office buildings, but there had been a time when it represented nearly the whole of New York to him. That was when his father used to visit New York with his friend, Mr. Ed Cooper, who was vice-president and sales manager of the Arrowhead Mill, and when the family was still living in the old house in Alwyn Street. He remembered how often Worth Street used to enter his father's conversation, and once again, while Mr. Barlowe kept on talking about that fellow in Speed Colquitt's bank, he was back in Pompey's Head—that fellow in Speed's bank, he reflected, had come to New York under circumstances very much like his own.

He too had been the recipient of a rich man's favor. It happened —it began, rather—in the early winter of 1932. Because of the depression he was attending the state university instead of going to Princeton as the family had originally planned, but even in the early winter of 1932 there were some people who seemed to have heard about the depression only at second hand. As many Northern men as ever came down to the Cassava Gun Club for the duck shooting, getting off the five forty-six at Pompey's Head with their Bosses and Purdys and other fine guns, bundled expensively against the cold as they waited for the Negro porters to pile their luggage on hand trucks, and then disappearing with their guns into the new, shiny cars they had dispatched South beforehand.

John Duncan was one of them. He had been coming South for the duck shooting for twelve years. Anson had been introduced to him, as he had to most of the other members of the gun club, to which he did not belong but where he was still privileged to shoot because his grandfather had been one of the club's founders, and he knew the publisher's reputation as the poorest shot in the club. John Duncan was a long, angular man whose movements suggested the premeditated precision of a heron or a crane, with grizzled hair, high cheekbones, and rather small gray eyes, sunk deep in their sockets, that always wore a kind of puzzled expression. Anson had frequently listened to him voice his disgust over his bad luck or aim or timing or whatever it was that caused him inevitably to be low man, day after day and year after year, lapsing then into moody silence before the fire in the club's rustic, antler-hung lounge, apparently intent on nothing but drowning his sorrows in bootleg scotch while the other members held their usual post-mortem on how the flights came over, the direction of the wind, the way the ducks dropped to the decoys, and the shots that were made or missed.

But though Anson had been introduced to John Duncan and always spoke to him in passing, he would not have said he knew him. They lived in a world apart, those Northern sportsmen. Their very membership in the gun club was indicative of their wealth and power, one more symbol added to their Bosses and Purdys and tailored shooting jackets, and if you were a college student whose family was having a difficult time of it and whose father seemed more worried every time you came home, you would not presume to say you knew them. Their world was not your world, and if you happened occasionally to find yourself in their presence it was only because they were courteous enough to remember that it was your grandfather who first had the idea of starting a gun club near one of the mouths of the Cassava River.

With Wyeth Blackford, however, it was different. He knew everybody; half the time he called the members by their first names. Wyeth's status at the club was the same as Anson's, his grandfather having also been one of its founders, but he had a special, higher standing. It came from his being such a crack shot. Unlike Anson, who was only a moderately good shot at best, Wyeth was in constant demand—somebody or other was always wanting to go out to the blinds with him. Moreover, during the shooting season, Wyeth went to the club several times a week. If he had minded flunking out of Lawrenceville in his senior year and taking a job as a teller in the Merchants & Mechanics Bank, as he did not, his being able to go shooting so often would have made it up to him.

37

Anson was a much less frequent visitor. He could get home only for an occasional week end and begrudged any time spent away from Kit Robbins. He went to the gun club but once that winter, and then only because of Wyeth's urging. Looking backward, as he had done many times, he could see that if it had not been for Wyeth's insistence, added to Kit's being unable to invite him to Sunday breakfast because she had to drive her mother to a luncheon party in Beaufort, he would never have spent those few hours in a duck blind with John Duncan, and consequently never found his way to one of the cubbyholes in Roberts, Guthrie, Barlowe & Paul.

Kit Robbins was making her debut that year and her parents were giving a supper-dance at the Yacht Club. Because of it, Anson had come home for the week end. The orchestra had taken a break and Kit had gone off with some of the other girls to fix her face and hair. Anson and Wyeth Blackford were standing on the end of the wooden pier at the Yacht Club. Prohibition was still in force and they were drinking some of the white mule that the moonshiners ran down from the North Carolina mountains. Anson hated the taste of it.

"Here," Wyeth said, offering him the flask a second time. "Let's kill this off."

"Hell, no. I'd as soon drink kerosene."

Wyeth grinned. "Might well be kerosene, at that. Gets worse and worse, don't it? Man at the gun club gave me a quart of scotch —Haig & Haig, too, by God!—and I dropped it in the kitchen sink. Could have sat myself down and cried. I was saving that bottle especially for tonight. You sure you mean no?"

"I mean no."

"Guess I have to be a solitary drinker, then. Here's looking at you."

Wyeth took a swig from the flask, shuddered, made a face, and stuffed the flask into his back pocket. He was an inch under six feet and thin to the point of boniness. With his boniness, however, there went a sort of lanky grace, and he swam and rode almost as well as he shot. He brushed back the hook of sandy-colored hair that had a way of falling across his forehead, coughed, and blinked his pale blue eyes.

"Whuf!" he said. "Maybe you got the right idea. What you think they make this stuff out of nowadays—octagon soap and lye? And to think of all that fancy liquor going down the drain. Oscar Stewart gave it to me."

"Who's he?"

38

"A new member. This is his first season. He's president of some big insurance company in Philadelphia. Mighty fine man."

The music started again, drifting out into the night, and the couples on the pier began walking back to the clubhouse.

"You know what?" Wyeth said. "Let's me and you go duck shooting. We can leave for the gun club right after the dance."

"I'm taking Kit home."

"After that, then. How you figure on taking her home—by way of Omaha and St. Paul?"

"Would that I could."

"The weather is going to be just right. Calm like it is, the flocks will start feeding early. I'll meet you at your house after I drop Joe Ann. We can have something to eat at Galloway's in Bugtown and be in the blind before it's light."

"I might want to get some sleep, you know."

"Sleep? You got the rest of your life to sleep. What do you say?"

"All right, I'd like to. This may be the only chance I'll have."

"Now you're talking."

"But give me a chance to tell Kit good-by, will you? She's going to Beaufort in the morning and I probably won't be able to get home again until after my exams——"

"You got your troubles, ain't you? What you need is another drink."

"Not that stuff."

"All right. Champagne, then. They say that come midnight Mr. Robbins is going to break out with some real, for true, imported champagne. Let's go learn how to live high."

Wyeth was too open to say one thing and mean another, as Anson knew, but he was nonetheless troubled by his friend's remark about the champagne. He suspected that there would be other remarks, less forthright, aimed at Kit's father but finding their ultimate target in her. For despite Kit's popularity, her admitted beauty and acknowledged radiance, there were certain grave handicaps from which she suffered; unimportant in most places, even ridiculous, but mattering greatly in the small, confined orbit in which she happened to move—an outsider, unacquainted with the concentric structure of Pompey's Head, its dovetailed system of worlds within worlds, would find it hard to understand.

Foremost of all, there was the newness of Kit's family, the fact that she had lived in Pompey's Head only a little more than three years. All that saved her in that respect was a distant cousinship on her mother's side with the Williamses. Had it not been for that, joined to the circumstance that the Williamses went back in an unbroken line to one of "The Twenty Families," she might have foundered at the start. Anson sometimes wondered if she knew how close she had stood to peril.

Nor was the peril over. The threat still lurked in her father's money —not millions, which by their own crushing weight might have commanded that awe which passes for respect, nor even so much as a half million. With the Williams connection, Pompey's Head would have been willing to accept a half million. There would have been a substantial tidiness to the sum, impressive but not intimidating, a sign of inherited money judiciously invested. But there was neither the crush of millions, the discreetness of a half million, nor, finally, what the inner circle was best qualified to understand: "People in modest circumstances; just enough to get along on." As a consequence, the proper placement of the newcomers was puzzling in the extreme; they were not rich, they were not "family," they were not poor, they were not "Irish Channel." The only thing to do, obviously, was to wait and see—meanwhile, because of Ellen Williams, Joe Ann's mother, they had to be taken in.

The period of watchful waiting lasted for nearly a year. Then it became known that Mr. Robbins, an upcountry Georgian who had acquired the controlling interest in a fertilizer factory on the edge of town, had purchased the old Wedderburn house on St. Andrew's Square. To that, in itself, the inner circle would have had no serious objection; it was granted that he had a right to be ambitious for his only child. It was what came after—the carpenters, the plasterers, the painters, the electricians; the Negroes spading in the gardens and the other Negroes unloading antiques; the elaborate act of restoration that turned the old house into one of the show places that the tourists went out of their way to see.

But only the tourists. The tight, hard core of the inner circle, taking one look, decided to look the other way. It was done too expensively and too soon. But then, as was said across the bridge tables of the Wednesday Afternoon Ladies Society and in the leather armchairs of the Light Infantry Club, what could you expect? It was new money, wasn't it, and didn't such money always want to splash around?

And by tomorrow, if not before, they would be talking about the champagne—Anson could already hear them. But if it were Pettibone champagne, McCloud champagne, Paxton champagne, nothing would be said; Anson could feel his resentment rising. All because Kit didn't have ancestors. It sounded silly when said aloud, but it was nonetheless true. Kit's being the prettiest girl her age was not enough. Truly to dazzle, her radiance had to be looked down upon by portraits from the wall. Joe Ann Williams could afford to jest, that bright, cheerful, happy-go-lucky girl—it became part of her legend of laughter when she said, "We're just like the Japanese. All we do is worship our ancestors and eat rice." And it was granted to little Dinah Blackford, Wyeth's thirteen-year-old sister, also to question the incense and the altars. "What's so important about *ancestors?*" she demanded of a gathering of the immediate clan around the dinner table one Sunday afternoon, and then, in the midst of the astonished pause, "I think they're *dull!*" So Joe Ann and so Dinah. But not Kit. She had only that distant cousinship to sustain her; no matter how close she came to the inner circle, she could not step within that final, guarded ring—unless she married into it, of course. Anson knew this as well as she. And sometimes wondered.

This was one of the times when he wished that being in love with Kit were not so difficult. He envied Wyeth Blackford his easy relation with Joe Ann. Wyeth never had to give two seconds' thought to anything. But he, Anson—well, take this champagne. Why did he have to have it added to all his other worries; why must he be troubled with the awareness of the hurt it might do to Kit; why couldn't it just be champagne? Sometimes there seemed to be too many problems, too many things to think about. Sorry though he was that Kit could not invite him to breakfast, he was glad he was going out shooting with Wyeth. He could forget nearly everything once he was in a blind.

In later years, looking back upon that winter, Anson realized that it was Kit Robbins who caused him to subject his environment to critical examination for the first time. As part of the examination, he had to consider his own position in Pompey's Head. He had always known that he had no ancestors, not in the Pompey's Head sense of the word, and the lack had never mattered. His mother's people, the Lawrences, had been established in the small towns and villages of the western part of the state for well over a hundred and fifty years. They had contributed their share of doctors, lawyers, farmers, and merchants to the general welfare, even a minister or two, and while none of them had ever spread his name or influence beyond his immediate neighborhood, Anson knew, for what it was worth, that he stemmed from the Lawrences of Ockeelaka County. He also knew, more positively, that his father's father was David Page.

This dimly remembered progenitor could never be regarded as a proper Pompey's Head ancestor, having come South from New Hampshire at a time when all Northern men were lumped together as carpetbaggers, and his portrait would never be hung on the walls of the Pompey's Head Historical Museum. He planned no battles, pioneered no wilderness, introduced no crops to the colonial economy. However, you could find his likeness and read the story of his life in *The History of Pompey's Head*. Contained in two volumes, it was written by J. Fletcher Pearce, who was also the author of *Chronicles of Marlborough County; Genealogical History of the Twenty Founding Families*, which most people thought was a most distinguished work. The "History" was published in 1896. Its full title was *The History of Pompey's Head, From the Earliest Periods to the Present Day, Including Biographical Sketches of Representative Men*. The heavy volumes occupied a prominent place on the Page bookshelves, as they did on the bookshelves of many other families, and as a boy Anson had often taken them down.

His grandfather's likeness, a steel engraving, was in the section devoted to Trade, Commerce, and Manufactures. It showed him in a frock coat with wide lapels, wearing a pearl stickpin in his stock. His hair was white, his jaw was set, and his eyes looked straight from the page—you sensed a commanding, almost intimidating presence that was hard to reconcile with the fading recollection of the tall, kindly man who smelled of tobacco, took you boating on the river, and gave you shiny ten-cent pieces. Anson had read the passage concerning his grandfather so many times that he could recite it word for word.

David Page, one of the leading merchants and civic leaders of Pompey's Head, was born June 9, 1852, near Durham, New Hampshire, where his father was engaged in agriculture. After receiving his elementary schooling, David was employed on his father's farm until 1868 when, desiring to better his condition, he removed to Portsmouth. Finding gainful occupation in that commercial and maritime center, he remained there until 1870, when, having married the former Miss Mary Deye, the only daughter of a pious and respectable Portsmouth family, he determined to seek his fortune farther afield.

Mr. Page came to Pompey's Head in 1871, separating himself

from his bride until he had opportunity to establish himself. He had not yet reached his twentieth birthday and had but six dollars and fifteen cents in his pocket when he arrived. He is emphatically a "self-made man," whose success has been won by steadfastness of purpose, honorable dealing, untiring industry, and loyalty to the city of his adoption that has all but erased the accidental circumstance of his Northern birth. Beneath an exterior which a casual observer might deem unsympathetic is a warm, generous, and cordial nature. His sympathies are manifested by deeds rather than words, and he gives freely to every deserving charity, public and private.

Then came the part Anson liked best:

A few days after arriving in Pompey's Head, young Page, without friends or acquaintances, went to the mercantile establishment of Murdoch & Brown, and requested an interview with Mr. Brown, who consented to see him. He explained his financial condition to Brown, showed what remained of his six dollars and fifteen cents, and asked for a little credit. Brown scrutinized his visitor, and, remarking that he seemed like "a nice, honest, upright young Yankee," granted the request.

Young Page left Murdoch & Brown with a job lot of whips that he peddled about town. Within a week he returned and paid the little indebtedness, a matter of but two or three dollars. He asked for a larger supply of merchandise on credit, which Brown granted, and from these transactions there resulted a friendship that lasted until Mr. Brown's death. Mr. Page has never hesitated to say that he regards him as his greatest single benefactor.

Then came the part about young Page and the New Orleans coffee. Anson liked that too:

Having saved enough money to buy a horse and wagon, young Page's next venture was to purchase a large stock of New Orleans coffee, which he sold to the residents of Mercier's Bend, now incorporated within the city limits of Pompey's Head and generally known as the Irish Channel, and other areas far from retail stores. In this and other enterprises he also succeeded, and soon realized a sum sufficient to justify the thought of engaging regularly in business. He embarked in the retail hardware trade, and prospered to such an extent that he ventured to open a more pretentious business in what was then known as "The Green Store," on Bullis Street near the Municipal Market.

And then the conclusion:

> Mr. Page has always exhibited a warm affection for the city of his adoption, and it would be hard to select any one of her businessmen who has taken a deeper interest in every judicious scheme to advance her prosperity. One of the original investors in the Pompey's Head Spinning Company (recently incorporated as the Arrowhead Mill), Mr. Page was also identified, along with his close friend, Colonel Robert Blackford, with the re-organization of the Atlantic & Central Railroad. For eleven years he has been a director in the Merchants & Mechanics Bank, in whose prosperity he has taken great pride. Mr. Page is still in the vigor and prime of manhood, and his constant success from youth to the present time constitutes a cogent argument in favor of earnest endeavor as the pathway to high and honorable station.

It was apparent, then, even through the pages of a paid biography, that David Page, the New Hampshire Yankee who moved South, was a grandfather worth having—you bore his name, you walked in his memory, and you knew who you were.

There were certain things beyond your reach, such as future membership in the Pompey's Head Light Infantry Club, which was limited to those whose ancestors had fought in the ranks of the regiment during the Revolution, and you were aware, also, that there was considerably less money than there used to be. It had never been said so directly, or even hinted at, but you gathered that your father was not the "businessman" your grandfather had been—less ambitious; not so far-seeing; interested in books without being a scholar; content simply to run the hardware store which had been moved to the center of town on Bay Street. You suspected that there had been hurts in the past, knowing enough about your environment to imagine some of the things that must have been said about young David Page, but the hurts were not yours. Others had borne them for you, and in the bearing secured your place. It never occurred to you to question anything, so firm was the knowledge of who you were, and then, suddenly, you met a girl. You saw things differently. You examined yourself and your place more critically. And years later,

44

riding through the streets of New York with a man named Charles Barlowe, you could remember exactly how it was. You could still see the girls in their party dresses, and for an instant, as the rain drummed on the roof of the taxi, you could almost hear the music. The band was playing "Sweet Sue."

CHAPTER FOUR

A thoughtful pause on the part of Mr. Barlowe caused Anson to stop thinking about Pompey's Head. It was all right to let your attention wander during one of Mr. Barlowe's monologues, provided you were ready to return the ball if he should decide to send it into your court. Now, having followed that fellow in Speed's bank to the end of his unhappy career, and again reaching the conclusion that character in a man was like conformation in a horse, he was ready to bring the discussion another step forward.

"This Mrs. Wales," he said. "What's her story?"

It was now Anson's turn to be thoughtful. "So far as I know, it's not much of a story. Her family has always been a prominent one down in my part of the country and——"

"We've covered that," Mr. Barlowe said. "What else?"

"I don't know much else. Mrs. Wales was on the stage for a time——"

"You don't say."

The tone of Mr. Barlowe's voice, however, did say; it said, "Ah ha—so that's the way it is!" Mr. Barlowe belonged to a generation that had not been able completely to down the feeling that being on the stage was one of the more intriguing forms of immorality. He looked as though he felt that he had hit upon a significant clue.

"A chorus girl?" he asked.

It was easy to see what Mr. Barlowe had in mind—one of the editions of the *Follies*; a glitter of rhinestones in the beam of a spotlight; a powdered procession of long-legged young women descending a flight of stairs in handsome, shapely undress.

"No sir," Anson said, "Mrs. Wales wasn't a chorus girl. She was a dramatic actress. She wanted to be one, that is. Her marriage to Wales interrupted her career. She had one of the minor roles in *Caesar's Wife*."

"I saw that," Mr. Barlowe interjected with sudden interest. "Billie Burke was in it. An attractive woman, too. You say that Mrs. Wales was in that play?"

"Not very noticeably, I'm afraid. I didn't see it and all I know about it——"

"Of course you didn't see it. That was before your time. I don't suppose you saw *Lightnin'* either."

"No sir, I didn't."

"And William Gillette in *Dear Brutus?* And E. H. Sothern and Julia Marlowe in *Twelfth Night?*"

"No, but my father——"

Mr. Barlowe looked subdued. "The theater was worth going to in those days. You could count on a good evening's entertainment. But now—one of the girls dragged me to something the other night that I was ashamed to sit through. I may not be able to appreciate such things, as the girls say, but I considered it an outrage. When I think of the theater as it was in my day, Forbes-Robertson and Maude Adams and *The Chocolate Soldier* and Laurette Taylor in *Peg O' My Heart*——" He shrugged his shoulders and shook off his subdued look. "So Mrs. Wales was an actress, you say?"

"Only in that she appeared in that one play," Anson replied. "It was hardly more than a walk-on part, with only a few lines. Phillip Greene told me that she received excellent notices. It wasn't so much her talent as her appearance. She was called the most beautiful young actress on Broadway."

Mr. Barlowe meditated for an instant and then shook his head. "I've been trying to remember her but I can't. I distinctly recall Billie Burke, though. I remember discussing her with Mrs. Barlowe after the theater. I said she looked like a horsewoman—it was her carriage that made me think so—and Mrs. Barlowe didn't agree with me. We had quite a little argument, as I recall. But I can't remember this Mrs. Wales for the life of me. Are you sure she was in that play?"

"She married Wales during its run," Anson explained. "That was just after the First World War. The marriage took place in the Little Church around the Corner. It was one of the big romances of the time. The papers were full of it. Phillip Greene was best man."

Mr. Barlowe was silent for a time. There was a new, sudden burst of rain, driving against the windows of the taxi. The weatherman

Meg had heard over the radio was wrong again, Anson thought. If he knew anything about rain, this was going to be an all-day affair.

"Anson."

"Yes sir?"

"Let's go back to Phillip Greene. Do you know any reason why Mrs. Wales might want to make it difficult for him?"

"No, I don't. Besides, if she has any such reason, she certainly took her time about it. What good can it do her now that he's dead?"

Mr. Barlowe nodded gravely. "That's what has been puzzling me—that's why I say we have to approach this with open minds. The fact is that this is a deliberate charge she has made. And it seems to me that you're forgetting something important. Our client in this case is not Phillip Greene. It's Duncan & Company. Our only interest in Greene—our only legal interest, that is—lies in his being one of our client's agents. And at the moment he stands accused of a serious crime by a woman who, so far as we know, has nothing to gain by defaming his memory. My suspicion is that she must have proof—something that she regards as proof, anyway. It is inconceivable that she would have made such a charge otherwise."

Anson wished that he could think more clearly. So convinced was he of Phillip Greene's innocence that he had not once entertained the contrary possibility. Now, however, he was compelled to confront it. As Mr. Barlowe said, it was inconceivable that Mrs. Wales would have made so serious a charge unless she was in possession of something she regarded as proof. Turning to Mr. Barlowe, he said: "The way you put it, I have to agree. But how do we know what Mrs. Wales would regard as proof? It could be some bookkeeping error. If what they say about her at Duncan & Company is true——"

"You mean her—her troublesomeness?" Mr. Barlowe shook his head. "Maybe you're right, but it doesn't make sense. Not to me it doesn't. But then, of course, I don't know anything about these artistic people. They're not my stripe. I'm glad this is going to be your problem and not mine."

"You mean you want me to handle everything?"

"Everything." Mr. Barlowe nodded slowly. "You know what makes these people tick—I don't. It's what John Duncan wants too. He said as much over the telephone. After this meeting I'm going to drop out of it. I came along just as window dressing. What's the matter? You look worried."

"I was just wondering what this will do to my schedule," Anson said. "I'm pretty clear at the moment, but there's that London thing you asked me to look into, and the Maddox will is coming up for probate next week——"

"Relax," Mr. Barlowe said. "Don't let it worry you. We'll get one of the other boys to take over some of your load if we have to. And I naturally hope you're right about Phillip Greene. I never knew you felt so strongly about him."

Mr. Barlowe spoke in a benign, generous fashion, almost as if he were overlooking a transgression. Mr. Barlowe did not quite approve of strong feelings of any kind, except where horses were involved. Anson was glad that once the meeting at Duncan & Company was over Mr. Barlowe would be out of it. He did not want the guardianship of Phillip Greene's reputation to fall into Mr. Barlowe's hands.

CHAPTER FIVE

During daylight hours, whenever Anson happened to find himself in midtown Manhattan, he always felt out of place. The atmosphere of luxury that enveloped that part of the city made the more accustomed neighborhood of Wall Street and lower Broadway seem practically Spartan by contrast. No matter how serious the business that brought him there, he invariably felt like a tourist on a spree. Even the office buildings had an air of wealth and magnificence that caused the whole downtown district to appear prosaic and routine. Not only this, but some of them, such as the modernistic structure on Madison Avenue to which Duncan & Company had transferred its offices a few months before, would have been unthinkable anywhere in the financial area. Anson thought it was a handsome building, rising in a series of terraced setbacks that seemed to be made entirely of glass, but he could understand why Mr. Barlowe, who was seeing it for the first time, called it a goldfish bowl. Mr. Barlowe was expressing the downtown point of view. The building was too dramatic and unconventional. Nobody would have risked having it as an address. Mr. Barlowe, bending forward, crooked his neck in order to get a better view from the window of the cab. Like Anson, he did not get to this part of the city often enough to take its wonders for granted. He restored himself to a sitting position and gave a derogatory grunt.

"I'd just as soon do business in the shower," he said. "I wouldn't have my offices in a thing like that if they gave them to me rent-free."

Anson did not have to be told. He was fully acquainted with Mr. Barlowe's views about offices—let him have his way and they would all resemble the Victorian domain of Roberts, Guthrie, Barlowe & Paul. Mr. Barlowe was proud of his quarters. He felt that their solid, old-fashioned appearance went with the solid, old-fashioned dignity of the firm. He also felt that any concession to modernity would be an admission that Roberts, Guthrie, Barlowe & Paul was in competition with what he called those fancy boys uptown. He was not impressed by the building, and he was determined not to be impressed by the new offices of Duncan & Company. One glimpse of them as he stepped into the reception room, and his face took on a set expression that made Anson think of a senior warden being taken on a tour of a Paris bordello. He quickly observed his surroundings—a dimly lit, heavily carpeted room with deep leather armchairs and lines of bookshelves and a low, glass-topped table on which were spread all the firm's latest books—and marched toward a striking brunette who sat at the semicircular reception desk. She was so poised and decorative that Anson wondered if she had been hired through one of the model agencies. Mr. Barlowe did not seem even to see her.

"Charles Barlowe to see John Duncan," he said abruptly.

"Yes sir," the girl said. "I'll tell Mr. Duncan you're here."

She dialed a number on the inter-office telephone while Mr. Barlowe, still wearing his set expression, took deliberate note of the room; he seemed to be saying that although he had no intention of letting himself get contaminated he might just as well find out what it was all about now that he was here. The girl at the reception desk spoke softly into the telephone and almost immediately John Duncan's secretary appeared. She was a blond, businesslike young woman in a tweed suit and a pair of sensible shoes, whom Anson knew as Miss Dodge. Inclining her head to Mr. Barlowe, she gave Anson a friendly smile. "This way, gentlemen," she said, "Mr. Duncan is expecting you." She looked nothing like Mrs. Waggoner, Mr. Barlowe's secretary, and Anson wondered what it was about her that brought Mrs. Waggoner to mind. It was the expression on her face, he finally decided. She and Mrs. Waggoner both shared the same repressed look of crisis. It was another storm signal, one among many, and as Anson walked behind Mr. Barlowe, who was following Miss Dodge through a door that led to the maze of inner offices that were given over to the editorial activities of Duncan & Company, he felt a throb of excitement. It wouldn't do to let it show, however, and he made his face as expressionless as he could.

The conference was held in the board of directors' room. Looking out upon the roofs and towers of uptown Madison Avenue, it was a large, rectangular chamber with pine paneling and a heavy green carpet. The canyon of Fifty-seventh Street cut its way crosstown a few blocks away. Several English sporting prints from John Duncan's private collection hung on the walls of the room, along with a portrait of old Mr. Duncan in a heavy gold frame, and there was a long, highly polished table made of one of the light-colored woods that had come into fashion, and a set of chairs to match.

John Duncan sat at the head of the table and Mr. Barlowe sat at his right. Next to Mr. Barlowe, with a folder containing a sheaf of papers in front of him, was Paul Tarbell, a compact, square-built man in his late fifties who was one of Duncan & Company's old hands. Starting out as a salesman, he now held the title of executive vice-president and treasurer. Anson sat opposite him. Next to Anson, also with a folder, was Van Buren Bliss, the firm's editor-in-chief since the death of Phillip Greene. Bliss and Greene had entered the firm a few months apart; they had been close friends. A big man, Bliss showed the increasing heaviness of middle age. His pepper-and-salt hair was parted on the side, standing up slightly, and his jaws were clamped on a short, stubby pipe. He looked more like a retired military man than an editor, but Phillip Greene had not looked like an editor either—Phillip Greene most closely resembled a Vermont schoolmaster come to the city in his one good suit. Bliss puffed on his pipe, found that it had gone out, and reached for one of the kitchen matches that he kept himself supplied with. Turning to Anson, he said:

"This is some rain we're having. If it doesn't stop soon, my block on Eighty-first Street is going to be flooded again."

"A lot you have to worry about," Paul Tarbell said from across the table. "You should see that river that runs past my place in Connecticut. Two more feet and I'm going to have it flowing through my cellar."

"Two more feet means a lot of water," Anson put in. "It won't rise that much, will it?"

"If this weather keeps up it will," Tarbell replied. "For the past two months we've had nothing but rain—hardly any snow at all. That's why the river is so high. All that water has no place to go."

"I've never liked river property," Mr. Barlowe interjected. "You can go on for ten or fifteen years, thinking you're safe, and then one morning you wake up and find yourself under six feet of water. Shore property is just as bad. Along comes one of these hurricanes we've been having and all you're left with is a pile of matchwood."

It was like a ritual, Anson thought. Here they were confronted by a problem of such grave importance that it demanded a special meeting which was going to make everybody late for lunch, and yet it was required of them, as if by the rules of some secret society, that they first talk about something else. Not that they imagined the problem would disappear in the meantime, or that it was not occupying the whole forefront of their attentions, or that they were trying to screw up courage enough to deal with it. It was simply a kind of ceremony, reflecting an ingrained set of attitudes. Weather and rivers led to fishing, and fishing led to fishing trips, and now John Duncan was telling about the summer he packed into the Big Horn Mountains of Wyoming. Van Buren Bliss looked interested and Mr. Barlowe and Paul Tarbell looked bored. From his limited understanding of the rules and procedures of the society, and from the trace of restlessness that both Mr. Barlowe and Paul Tarbell were beginning to show, Anson surmised that John Duncan was getting close to the edge. His tone and his remarks were no longer cursory; he was genuinely interested in what he was saying; he seemed to be forgetting that there was work to be done. Mr. Barlowe made a bold show of looking at his wrist watch. The rules of the society precluded Paul Tarbell's doing this, or Van Buren Bliss, and it would have been unimaginable on the part of Anson. But Mr. Barlowe was a senior member in excellent standing. It was quite in order for him to suggest to another member that his conversation was getting beyond the prescribed latitudes. John Duncan accepted the correction in good grace.

"I suppose we'd better go to work," he said, looking around the table. "The sooner we get this over with, the better. We all know what we're here for and we all know what's happened. If we could go on from there——"

He was trying to make it easy for himself, Anson realized. It was significant that he had avoided all mention of Phillip Greene. This incredible thing had happened, this bolt had come crashing down, and although he must know that Greene's name had inevitably to be brought into the discussion, he had plainly shied away from it. Mr. Barlowe, however, was not handicapped by such compulsive behavior. Frowning ever so slightly, he said:

"Let's take our time, John. I'm afraid I don't have as much of the background as you fellows. As I understand it, from what you said over the telephone——"

"You know damn well what I said over the telephone," John Duncan burst out in a fit of impatience. "I said that Phil Greene has been accused by Lucy Wales of embezzling twenty thousand dollars of Garvin's royalties. What the hell else is there?"

Mr. Barlowe maintained his look of self-confident calm. Anson knew him well enough to know that he was thinking that it was up to him to keep the meeting in hand. Managing an indulgent smile, as if to indicate that he knew all about his old friend's short temper and profane speech, which were really quite attractive in their way, Mr. Barlowe said, "A lot else, John. This accusation, for instance? How was it made? In writing?"

"Of course it was made in writing! Do you think that woman called me up on the telephone? She hasn't spoken a word to me in nearly ten years."

"Why?"

"Because she's a bitch, that's why! A mean, poisonous, trouble-making bitch!"

Mr. Barlowe's blandness dropped for an instant, leaving his face startled and exposed. He was not used to such uncontrolled outcries. Paul Tarbell, sitting next to him, appeared only slightly less uncomfortable. Close though he had been to the chaotic world of books and authors for the larger part of his life, he was still a stray in it, out of his natural element once he left his niche in what he liked to describe as the hardheaded, practical end of the business. He seemed to Anson to be snuggling closer to Mr. Barlowe for protection. Adjusting his features, Mr. Barlowe said:

"What you say, John, may be true and it may also be relevant. That's what I'm trying to find out. Right now, though, I'd like to get a few more facts. From what you say, I take it that there was a letter from Mrs. Wales. Is that correct?"

"That's right." Paul Tarbell nodded and drew an envelope from the folder before him. "It came in the morning mail." Handing the envelope to Mr. Barlowe, he added, "You will notice that it's addressed to Van. He brought it in to John, and John brought it in to me— it was quite a bombshell, as you can imagine."

Studying the envelope, Mr. Barlowe said he could well imagine. "But there is something else I'd like to ask," he continued, lifting his eyes and looking about the table. "Is there any significance in the fact that the letter was addressed to Mr. Bliss? Purely as an outsider, coming in cold, I'd say that it seems curious that a communication such as this wouldn't be addressed to John. You understand, of course, that I'm just trying to get the background."

"The reason that letter wasn't sent to me," John Duncan said, "is because—— Oh, you tell him, Van! But make it short. Let's get this wagon to roll."

Van Buren Bliss eased his heavy frame into a more comfortable position and took the pipe from his mouth. "It's like this, Mr. Barlowe—I'm the only one here that Mrs. Wales will write to. Not that we are on very good terms. The truth is that we aren't. But she has to write to somebody and—well, I have the honor."

"I see." Mr. Barlowe touched the tips of his fingers together and looked across the manicured steeple they made. "And Mrs. Wales, as I understand it from Anson, is not above making things difficult. What I mean is that, given two interpretations, a good and a bad, she would most likely, so far as your own experience is concerned, be inclined to choose the bad. Is that correct?"

"Yes sir," Bliss said. "You put it too mildly, but that's correct."

Anson was compelled to admire Mr. Barlowe. He seemed to be proceeding in a dull, ponderous manner, and all the while he was not proceeding at all. Deliberately. John Duncan's harsh words had set him back for a moment, but he was intelligent enough to recognize them for what they were—a flash of jagged lightning in a sullen, inflamed sky. What he was now doing, along with taking his place on the side of the firm against Mrs. Wales, and so skillfully that no one around the table was aware of it, was cooling off the atmosphere.

Anson sat watching John Duncan as Mr. Barlowe asked further questions about Mrs. Wales. Since he knew that part of the story, he could afford to let his mind wander a bit. John Duncan had aged greatly since that morning in the duck blind. His grizzled sparseness had given way to a gray, almost cadaverous thinness that had drawn his cheeks into hollows and left his eyes sunk far back in their sockets. He was getting into his late sixties and looked worn and tired. Anson again remembered those hours in the duck blind, and for an instant he found it curious that he should be sitting as an equal in the same room with John Duncan, one of his associates and one of his friends. There had been almost as many ring-necks as there were mallards in the flocks that morning, and he had said to John Duncan, "I don't think you're leading them enough, sir," and because of that, and his happening to notice that John Duncan had a nervous way of jerking at the trigger, which spoiled every shot, he was now sitting in a board of directors' room in New York City with his life gone off in a direction that he would never have dreamed possible at the time.

He had not gone shooting with Wyeth Blackford following Kit

Robbins's party after all. Wyeth was seized upon by Mr. Stewart, the new member who had given him the bottle of scotch, and he, Anson, had gone out with John Duncan. He rowed him out to the blind while it was still dark, with most of the stars still shining and only the creak of the oarlocks in the lonely silence he loved so much, that and the lapping of the water against the sides of the skiff, and just before daylight he set out the decoys. The flocks started flying early, just as Wyeth had predicted, and from all across the marsh there came the firing of the guns. John Duncan had the best shooting of any day since he had joined the gun club. He made one difficult shot—bringing down a mallard that was dropping to the decoys with its wings set to brake and then, already climbing, veered off sharply to the left—and so had something to boast about that night around the fire in the lounge. He put the day's success down to the instruction he had from Anson, and when Anson sought him out to tell him good-by he pressed his hand warmly and said, "Young fellow, if ever you come to New York and I can do anything to help you, I want you to let me know." Anson thanked him, never thinking the time would come, and now, sitting in the same room with John Duncan on this rainy March day, it was still hard to realize that it was he who had sent him downtown to see Mr. Barlowe about a job. Looking at Mr. Barlowe, Anson saw that he had taken Mrs. Wales's letter from its envelope and was reading it intently.

"Well!" he said in a tone of muffled outrage. "The lady doesn't mince words, does she? Unless she receives immediate settlement she will turn the matter over to her attorneys without further notice." He lowered the letter and surveyed the faces at the table. "I now understand what you mean about her troublesomeness. Not a word about the possibility of error. Simply the flat, direct charge, and that she has her husband's consent to turn the matter over to her representative."

"That's what I can't understand," John Duncan said, "Garvin's going along with her. Except that I don't believe it—it's one of that woman's lies, I'm sure!"

Mr. Barlowe pursed his lips thoughtfully. "You may be right, John, and I hope you are. I think, however, that we ought to understand the legal technicalities. If any action is taken, it would have to be done by Wales—even with his wife's having his power of attorney she could not do it on her own. Any suit would have to be brought by him, in his own name. He would have to give his consent, in other words. And apparently, on the face of this letter, he already has."

"I still don't believe it!" John Duncan said doggedly. "Garvin wouldn't do a thing like this to Phil. It's more of that woman's troublemaking, I tell you! I know it is!"

Mr. Barlowe nodded in a consoling fashion. "If that's the case, we'll find it out in time. For the moment, though, I suggest we take the lady at her word—as matters stand, we are obliged to. But what about these dates and sums she gives? Have you been able to check them?"

"Yes, we have," John Duncan said. "Paul and Van spent the morning going through our files. They show that Phil had twenty thousand dollars of Garvin's royalties transferred to his own account. If you take only those figures into consideration—well, damn it, they make it look bad for Phil."

Anson listened with a sinking sensation. This was a scene he had not visualized. He had argued with Mr. Barlowe about how impossible it was, just as impossible as his going out and shooting his favorite mare, and already it appeared as though he might be wrong. He looked from John Duncan to Paul Tarbell and then to Van Buren Bliss; there was nothing in their expressions calculated to raise his spirits. They repeated what John Duncan had just said—it looked bad for Phil. He felt something close to gratitude for Mr. Barlowe's unruffled calm.

"Let's get the facts first," Mr. Barlowe said. "Nothing is gained by jumping to conclusions. These dates and sums that Mrs. Wales gives in her letter—I notice they go back a number of years."

"All the way to September 6, 1919," Paul Tarbell said. "That's the first one."

"And the last?"

Paul Tarbell consulted a sheet of paper on which he had made some notes. "The last one was June 12, 1940. There was a withdrawal on that date of one thousand dollars. Wales's royalty reports indicate that it was transferred from his account to Phil's. Each withdrawal was made the same way. We've found all Phil's memos to the accounting department. They show that he ordered the checks to be made out in his name."

"And you say that you have been able to check your own records as far back as 1919?" Mr. Barlowe asked.

"We could check them back to the first year of the firm if we

57

wanted to," Paul Tarbell replied with just a trace of pride. "Considering the authors we've published, our files are worth having. There is more than one university that would like to get its hands on them. Besides, in publishing you never know when the smallest scrap of paper——"

"That's true of any business," Mr. Barlowe interrupted. "Only last year we had a case in which the decisive factor was a receipted bill made out in 1898. It definitely established proof of purchase of certain disputed pieces of jewelry by a grandfather of my client. The ownership of the pieces was disputed by a half cousin who claimed that the pieces in question had been purchased after my client's grandfather's second marriage. You may remember the incident. It came up in connection with the settlement of the Dodd estate."

Anson was afraid they were in for one of Mr. Barlowe's stories, taking forever, but Mr. Barlowe brought himself back to the contents of Mrs. Wales's letter.

"The period covered by these withdrawals is how many years altogether?" he asked.

"Twenty-one," Van Buren Bliss replied. "But it seems to me—it seems to all of us—that those figures——" He cut himself short. "Excuse me, Paul, I didn't mean to interrupt."

"That's all right," Paul Tarbell said. "This isn't my party. Say what you have to say."

Van Buren Bliss stared at the table for an instant, rubbing the bowl of his pipe with his thumb. Raising his eyes, he said: "The feeling we have, Mr. Barlowe, John and Paul and I, is that these figures can't be relied upon exclusively. We all admit that they make out a damaging case against Phil. According to them, Phil was having these sums of money withdrawn from Garvin's account and transferred to his own for twenty-one years. Mrs. Wales seems to have us dead to right, but personally, knowing Phil——"

"It's been definitely established then," Mr. Barlowe broke in, "that the figures given by Mrs. Wales are correct. I want to get that straight. You have eliminated all possibility of any error in bookkeeping?"

"There's been no error," Paul Tarbell said. "We've checked and rechecked. It's easy to see what happened. Mrs. Wales copied those figures from the royalty reports we sent to Garvin. We keep a carbon of all royalty reports—several carbons, as a matter of fact—and all her figures tally with ours. But I agree with Van—there must be something behind those figures."

"You're damned right there is!" John Duncan spread his hands and put them down hard on the table. "It wouldn't take Phil five minutes to tell us what this is all about, but Phil isn't here. All we have is that woman's letter and our books. I don't care what the figures show! If Phil was drawing money from Garvin's account and having it transferred to his own, well, I say that Garvin knew about it, by God! How in the name of the Seven Tribes could he *not* know? All those withdrawals appeared on his royalty reports, didn't they? Blind as he is today, he hasn't been blind for twenty-one years! I say to hell with those figures! If that woman thinks she has me over a barrel and wants to go to some shyster lawyer——"

"Hold on, John," Paul Tarbell said in an agitated tone. "That's one of the things that we agreed upon—that she mustn't see a lawyer, I mean. I naturally go along with you and Van, of course, but, as you yourself said, if she goes to a lawyer and makes a noise about this, getting it into the newspapers——"

Anson could see why it should not get into the newspapers. The headlines would say that America's leading novelist was threatening to sue his publishers for twenty thousand dollars that had been embezzled by the most noted editor in the trade. The gossip columnists and the book sections would pick it up, along with *Publishers' Weekly*, and it would make as nice a scandal as could be imagined. It would take years for Duncan & Company to live it down.

"I've just thought of something," he heard himself say. "It seems to me that Mr. Duncan is on the right track—Wales *must* have known about these withdrawals. It goes contrary to all reason to believe that he didn't. In that case, he must have authorized them."

He was not rewarded with the more cheerful expressions that he realized he half expected. It was unwise in any conference to give the impression that you thought you had lapped the field, and it was particularly unwise in a conference with Mr. Barlowe. If he had thought about that beforehand, he might not have spoken so hastily. He waited for the troubled frown that always creased Mr. Barlowe's forehead when he was displeased—the brown badge of peevishness, Eugene Hollister once called it—only to find himself rewarded with a benevolent nod.

"There is something to what Anson says," Mr. Barlowe commented. "If he should happen to be correct, and if these withdrawals were authorized, there must be some evidence of it—something in writing from Wales. Such evidence would change the whole look of things, of course. We would have nothing to worry about. You fellows would be proved right and Mrs. Wales would be taught to mind her manners. Personally, though I don't know the lady, I'd say that what she needs is a good reining in."

"What about it, Van?" Anson said. "Have you checked to see if there were any letters from Wales to Phil—letters that bear specifically upon these withdrawals?"

Van Buren Bliss had just lit another match. Blowing it out, he said, "Not yet. So far I haven't been able to find a thing. I still have some more searching to do, but there's not much hope on that score, I'm afraid. Phil was more than careful about any dealings that involved the firm. Going through his files this morning, I came across one that he must have made himself—I recognized his lettering on the tab. It contained all his memos to the accounting department, instructing it to draw these various amounts from Garvin's account and to make the checks payable to him, but I couldn't find a scrap of paper from Garvin on the subject. Not anywhere."

"That still doesn't prove anything!" John Duncan said heatedly. "Garvin was always calling Phil on the phone. None of this had to be put in writing. Damn it, the mere fact that Phil kept that file proves that Garvin knew about it! If Phil had something to hide——"

"No one has said that he had," Mr. Barlowe observed. "That's not the question. I find it hard to believe, though, that there is nothing from Wales on the subject. We know that these withdrawals took place over a period of twenty-one years. It seems incredible to me that our friend Greene was acting solely on verbal instructions all that time. What about those periods when Wales was out of the country?"

Yes, Anson thought. What about them? How could Garvin Wales give verbal instructions to Phil Greene when he was off in all those far corners of the globe? If any of the others had ever sat through a trial, they would know that Mr. Barlowe had just asked a most damaging question. Any judge, reviewing the evidence thus far, would have to charge the jury that it demanded the defendant be found guilty as charged. But still it was impossible! There was bound to be an answer and there was one man who could provide it. Phillip Greene could no longer speak, but Garvin Wales could speak for him. Why didn't they go straight to him, then? Why all this beating around the bush? He was about to put the question when Mr. Barlowe spoke again.

"Mind you," he said, "I am not arguing that it was impossible for Greene to have been acting on verbal instructions. It could have happened. I am only pointing out that it is difficult to believe. And you say, Mr. Bliss, that you found nothing in the way of an authorization. Nothing at all?"

"Nothing," Bliss said. "It may be that a more thorough search of Garvin's correspondence will turn up something, but I am beginning to doubt it. I managed to get through all his letters to Phil from 1936 to 1940——"

"Why those particular dates?" Mr. Barlowe asked.

"The withdrawals were most frequent during those years," Bliss replied. "It occurred to me that if Garvin had been writing to Phil about them——"

"A logical conclusion," Mr. Barlowe said. "But let me ask this—during the years you have mentioned, 1936 to 1940 I believe you said they were, do we have any reason to suppose that our friend Greene was in—well, in financial trouble?"

"No, we haven't!" John Duncan said. "It so happens that Phil's mother died in 1934 and that Phil's share of the estate came to more than eighty thousand dollars—that on top of what he already had. So if you're thinking that Phil had his hand in the till because he was strapped, you're wrong! Damn it, Charlie, stop acting like a lawyer! Phil was acting on Garvin's instructions—I *know* he was!"

"But will the court?" said Mr. Barlowe. "Let's be reasonable, gentlemen. As things now stand, it would appear to the average person—and juries are composed of average persons, let me assure you—that Greene misappropriated these funds for his own use. Unless we can prove—not assume, prove—that these withdrawals were made with Wales's knowledge and consent, I'm afraid we are in a most vulnerable position."

"What about Wales?" Anson said. "Isn't he the answer? If he tells us——"

"In that event, all our troubles are over," Mr. Barlowe replied. "I will be getting to Mr. Wales and the value of his testimony soon. All I am doing now is to show what I think is clear to all of us—that our whole case rests upon what Mr. Wales has to say. But before we talk about that, I'd like to ask one more question. Did you gentlemen find any other papers that might seem to relate to the matter?"

There was a heavy pause. Anson knew that Mr. Barlowe had drilled his way to a particularly sensitive nerve, and the expression on Mr. Barlowe's face showed that he knew it too.

"Tell him about those checks you found, Van," John Duncan said. "Let's wind this up."

Van Buren Bliss reached for the folder he had brought to the meeting. Picking it up, he said, "I found this in Phil's personal files. It is ticketed only with the initials A.J., as you can see. It was clipped to the file in which we found Phil's memos to the accounting department, the ones in which he gave instructions to have those sums of money transferred from Garvin's account."

"And its contents?" Mr. Barlowe inquired.

"Sixty-four checks," Bliss replied, matching the crispness of Mr. Barlowe's tone. "They were all made out by Phil and they were all drawn against his personal account. They were made payable to someone named Anna Jones."

There was another, longer pause.

"This Anna Jones?" Mr. Barlowe asked. "Who is she?"

Van Buren Bliss shook his head. "I don't know. Neither does John or Paul. We never heard Phil mention her, and her name appears nowhere on our books. This was obviously some personal matter of Phil's. But the curious thing——"

Mr. Barlowe leaned forward on his elbows, peering across the table. "Yes?"

"Well, two things," Bliss said. "The first is that the period covered by these checks is twenty-one years—the same, you will remember, as that covered by the withdrawals. The second is that the total amount of the checks comes to twenty thousand dollars."

"But that's not all," Paul Tarbell broke in. "The number of checks tallies exactly with the number of withdrawals. I had just finished making a list of them when Van found the checks. We compared them with the list I had made and——"

"Hold on a second," Mr. Barlowe cautioned. "Let's take these jumps one at a time. Am I correct in understanding that there were sixty-four withdrawals from Garvin Wales's account and sixty-four checks made out to Anna Jones?"

"That's right," Paul Tarbell said. "Furthermore, the dates on the checks show that Phil made them out a day or two after he sent those memos to the accounting department. Here, let me show you." He opened the folder he had consulted previously and brought out first a canceled check and then a small, square sheet of paper that bore a typewritten notation. Handing the latter to Mr. Barlowe, he said, "Here is a memo from Phil to the accounting department. It is dated April 1, 1938, and is in the same form as all the others. It instructs our account people to deduct $250 from Wales's account and to make the check payable to Phil. Now here"—he handed the canceled check to Mr. Barlowe—"here is one of Phil's checks made out to Anna Jones. It is for $250 and is dated April 2, 1938, the very next day after Phil's memo. Now, if that doesn't prove——"

"Prove what?" Mr. Barlowe's tone was one of gentle rebuke. "All that is proved is that our friend Greene wrote out a number of checks totaling twenty thousand dollars to a certain Anna Jones. Beyond that it proves nothing. It would appear, I agree, that there is, or was, a close relation between the withdrawals and the checks, but proof— what could it prove?"

"That Phil was acting for Garvin!" John Duncan almost shouted. "That he was withdrawing these sums from Garvin's account and paying them over to this Anna Jones. All right!" He cut himself short, glaring at Mr. Barlowe. "Suppose that what you're thinking is true! It couldn't be, but suppose it was—suppose that Phil had this Anna Jones shacked up somewhere! Do you think he would have to rob Garvin to foot the bills! Don't be a fool! And do you think he would have kept the checks he sent her, or even sent her checks at all? If that's what you're thinking——"

"It so happens, John," Mr. Barlowe said, "that I haven't been thinking along those lines at all. I am simply trying to point out that these checks do nothing but indicate—not prove, mind you, indicate —how our friend Greene might have disposed of the twenty thousand dollars that Mrs. Wales claims he misappropriated. We are no further along than we were before. What we are required to produce, as I've said before, is concrete evidence that these sums of money were transferred from Wales's account with his knowledge and consent. What Greene did with the money need not concern us too much. Not at all, actually. The important thing is to prove that Wales knew what was going on. It is as simple as that."

Anson was not so sure. Carefully though he had listened, he found it hard to tie up all the threads. What Mr. Barlowe was saying, in his cautious way, was that unless Garvin Wales came to the rescue they didn't have a leg to stand on. But who was Anna Jones? It was easy to believe with John Duncan that Wales had authorized Greene to withdraw the various sums and that Greene, following his instructions, had then sent the money to Anna Jones, but, as Mr. Barlowe kept insisting, belief and proof were two different things. It seemed to him that Anna Jones loomed much larger than any of them imagined. What was her relation to Garvin Wales? And if he wanted to make donations to her that amounted to twenty thousand dollars over a period of twenty-one years, why had he not done so directly? Why was there nothing in Wales's correspondence to

Greene that touched on the subject? And why, most of all, had Greene permitted himself to be drawn into such an embarrassing, even damaging, position? Clearing his mind with an effort, he listened to what Mr. Barlowe was saying.

"This letter, John, from Mrs. Wales. It's your opinion, I believe, that it was sent without her husband's knowledge. We should all understand, however, that if matters stand to the contrary, then all our speculations about his being aware of these deductions would appear to be unfounded. Should that be the case——"

"Garvin knows nothing about that letter," John Duncan broke in. "I'm sure he doesn't! But where is all this getting us? We've hashed and rehashed enough. We have to decide what we are going to do. As I told you over the phone, Charlie, I think there is only one way to handle this. If you've talked it over with Anson, and if you both agree——"

Anson's name came so suddenly into the conversation that he sat up with a jerk. He was thinking that things were far more complicated than he had ever imagined they would be, with all sorts of puzzling matters that must be explained, and now, without any warning, all eyes were turned in his direction. He wondered what it was that he and Mr. Barlowe were supposed to have agreed about, and why Mr. Barlowe had not got around to mentioning it.

"I thought it best for us to go over the whole situation together," Mr. Barlowe said, addressing John Duncan but also including Anson. "Besides, I didn't get everything you said. I felt that you might like to explain it to Anson directly. He understands, however, that all this is going to be in his hands. Frankly, I'm glad it will be. I wouldn't know how to begin with these artistic people. Suppose you tell him what's on your mind."

Anson sat waiting, aware that everyone was watching him.

"This is the way it is, Anson," John Duncan said. "It's obvious that the only person who can clear this up for us is Garvin. We want you to go down and see him for us. It's not going to be as easy as it sounds. Lucy has him a prisoner on that island as much as if he were behind bars. You know the island, don't you? Tamburlaine, it's called."

"Yes sir," Anson said. "I know it."

"It's going to be up to you to get to Garvin," John Duncan continued. "We'll discuss the strategy later on. But the only way you'll be able to talk with him is by working through Lucy—you know he's blind, don't you?"

"Yes sir," Anson said.

"Unless you make friends with Lucy, or get on her good side, it's unlikely that she will let you get anywhere near Garvin," John Duncan continued. "She's become more his warden than his wife. Maybe she thinks she is protecting him from the world, or maybe, as Van and some of the others think, she's made up her mind to separate him from every friend he ever had—I don't know; it's hard to say. Anyway, this is something that none of us can take on. Things are that strained between us, as you might as well know. Not only that——"

John Duncan went on to explain in detail why it would be impossible for anyone in the firm to go down to see Garvin Wales, but Anson was not listening. He was thinking that Tamburlaine Island was only a few miles down the coast from Pompey's Head. He was thinking that he had not been there in fifteen years and that now, because Phillip Greene had caused twenty thousand dollars to be transferred from Garvin Wales's account and had written out twenty thousand dollars' worth of checks to a woman named Anna Jones, he was going home again. Meg would not like the idea, for she hated being left alone, but there was nothing he could do about it. He was aware that everyone was still looking at him and that he was expected to speak.

"Why, sure, Mr. Duncan," he said. "I'll be glad to do what I can."

"Good," John Duncan said. "We'll talk over the details after lunch. I've had all I can take on an empty stomach. Where would you fellows like to eat? We can go to my club, if you like, but the food hasn't been up to par lately. How about Louis and Armand's? It's not too late to get a table, is it, Van?"

Van Buren Bliss said he didn't think so, and Paul Tarbell suggested that they might find it more agreeable at the Ivy Room of the Drake. John Duncan agreed that the Drake might be the better idea, at that, because of the rain, and Anson hardly heard them. It had suddenly occurred to him that after fifteen years he would be almost a stranger in Pompey's Head. All the remaining members of his family had moved away. The old house on Alwyn Street would still be there, the house in which he had grown up and which he always thought of as home, but it really wasn't his home any longer and he would have to stay at the Marlborough Hotel. It was something he had never thought of before.

CHAPTER SIX

Ten days had passed since the meeting at Duncan & Company, and in ten minutes the train would be pulling into the Lafayette Street station. Anson told himself that he had better start thinking about the job in hand.

"Your being our lawyer is bound to get you off on the wrong foot," John Duncan had warned at their last meeting. "You'll have two strikes against you before you start. As our lawyer, just as our lawyer, Lucy won't let you get anywhere near Garvin. She'll probably insult you for invading what she calls their privacy. As I told you the other day when Charlie was here, she keeps Garvin on that island as though he were a prisoner. She's always had a hold on him—a damned powerful hold—and now that he is blind he is more dependent on her than ever. So being our lawyer will get you nowhere. But if you could arrange to meet her socially, through some of these connections of yours——"

"How will that help?"

"I'm not saying it will. All I say is that it may make it easier for you to get to Garvin—damn it, Anson, I know he can tell us what this is all about. All you need is half an hour with him alone. I don't know what it was he wanted to keep quiet——"

"You're thinking of those checks to Anna Jones?"

John Duncan nodded. "What's behind them, up to now, was none of our business. But with Lucy's dragging Phil into it, making these threats——" His voice changed and he gave way to one of his fits of impatience. "What the hell, Anson—who are we trying to kid! If Garvin persuaded Phil to act as some kind of pay-off man, as we think he did, he must have had something to hide—something that only he and Phil knew about. And there is one thing of which you can be sure—that Lucy didn't know about it. You can make book on that."

"It could be."

"There is no 'could' about it. I know what I'm talking about, believe me! What I don't understand is why Phil went along. If it was something—well, rotten—I know he wouldn't have. He must have been convinced that Garvin was doing the right thing—not in covering up his tracks, necessarily, but in sending that money to Anna Jones. Anyway"—he rose from his desk and began to pace the floor of his office—"this is something that we can't let come to court. Lucy is smart enough to know it, too. If you and Charlie are right, we don't stand much of a chance—without a statement from Garvin to clear him, Phil stands convicted. That's the way it is, isn't it?"

"Yes sir, I'm afraid so."

John Duncan continued walking up and down. "Not that I'm not thinking of my own skin too, mind you! Can't you see what the papers will make of it? Let's suppose, for the sake of the argument, that we can show that Phil was acting for Garvin. Let's suppose that we could prove that Anna Jones was some biddy that Garvin was laying regularly, keeping Lucy in the dark, and that Phil, knowing this—— No, it's too fantastic! Much as he was willing to do for Garvin, Phil wouldn't do that. But the important thing is that none of this gets out—we owe that much to Phil. So either you get Garvin to clear this up or Lucy wins hands down. And unless you can arrange to meet her on a friendly basis, through some of those connections of yours——"

How, though? The connections upon which John Duncan placed such importance were the very threads he had deliberately cut in two. Some of his old crowd was bound to be left, and a few of his friends, but one by one he had lost touch with them during the years he had been away. It would be awkward to ask favors, except of Wyeth Blackford, with whom he had corresponded until their lives took such different turnings that there was nothing left to correspond about, and, besides, it seemed unlikely that any of them would be on friendly terms with Mrs. Wales. How to go about it, then; what was the best way to proceed? He was considering the problem when the porter appeared again. He smiled genially as he poked his head into the roomette. Remembering that his name was Thomas McElroy, Anson was again reminded of the McElroys who lived near the old Blackford place on the Cassava River.

67

"It won't be long now, sir," the porter said. "Brush you off?"

"No, thanks. I'm all right. But there's something I've been wanting to ask—I hope you don't mind."

"No sir."

"Your name caused me to wonder about it. Do you happen to be from Pompey's Head?"

The porter nodded. "That's right. I live in Florida now—have to, account of this run—but Old Pompey is where I'm from. Just outside, that is."

"Bugtown?"

"No, now!" The porter smiled again. "You know Bugtown?"

"The S-&-S Feed Company, Galloway's Café, the Oasis, the First African Baptist Church——"

The porter began to chuckle. "The S-&-S and Mr. Galloway's—I ain't heard tell of them since I don't know when." He stopped chuckling and regarded Anson with mild puzzlement. "But that was a long time ago, my time. The S-&-S, it's closed down, and Mr. Galloway, he's dead. You don't look hardly old enough——"

"I am, though. There was a boy named Tooker McElroy——"

"Tooker? You know Tooker?" The porter focused his attention upon Anson with renewed interest. "He's my third cousin on my mother's side, my second cousin's oldest. But those McElroys, Tooker's people, they ain't from Bugtown. They come from Double Crossing."

"Frenchman's Creek, Little River, the road to the old Blackford place, Willie Randall's general store——"

The porter broke into a pleased, rumbling laugh. "That's right—that's the Crossing for sure! And here I had you figured for a Northern man. It just goes to show! But Tooker, he ain't been around for ten-twelve years. He's working in Philadelphia. If you knew Tooker——"

Anson decided to clear up the mystery for him. "It was when we were boys, a long time ago. I don't live in Pompey's Head any more. I've been away for years."

"I see, sir." The porter's voice became softer, touched with a certain commiseration; it was as if he wanted to indicate that he, too, knew what it meant to be an exile. "I reckon that's how come I took you for a Northern man."

"Yes, I reckon it is."

It was a word "reckon" that had long since been dropped from his vocabulary—you didn't say "reckon" in the chambers of Roberts,

Guthrie, Barlowe & Paul, nor in any of the places to which they happened to lead. But here it was again, coming naturally as ever; he might have been saying "reckon" right along. It was nothing to be especially pleased about, but pleased he was—at least he had not forgotten how to speak his native tongue. And he was pleased, too, that he had been correct in his surmise; "Old Pompey," the porter had said, and that was all he needed to know.

"You going home on a visit?" the porter asked.

"No, not exactly," Anson replied. "I have some business to look after."

"Yes sir, I see." The porter spoke in a more impersonal tone. Bugtown and Double Crossing were areas of shared affection, business a strange, puzzling country into which he was disinclined to venture. "Well, don't forget your overcoat when you leave. We'll be crossing the river most any time now."

Pompey's Head lay on the south side of the Cassava River, sixteen miles from the sea. Half a mile wide and providing ample draft for ocean-going vessels, the Cassava was responsible for Pompey's Head being where it was—the founding fathers, "The Twenty Families of Marlborough County" as they were generally known, had laid it out on a high bluff that overlooked the river and receded westward into a broad, fertile plain. Sir Samuel Alwyn, who in 1720 had commanded the first boatload of political exiles hustled from England to the Southern plantations in the sailing vessel *Swan*, wrote in his diary that the jutting headland of the bluff, as seen from the stretch of river where it had first been sighted, "had the plaine outline of a human countenance, witnessed in profile, and of a most noble and majestikal meine." Anson, like all the other schoolboys of his time, had been made to commit this part of Sir Samuel's diary to heart—it was because of this "plaine outline" and "most noble and majestikal meine" that the settlement had been named Pompey's Head.

Responsible for the location of Pompey's Head, the river was likewise responsible for its importance as a port—not nearly so bustling in recent times as in the great pre-Civil War days of cotton and river traffic, when hundreds of thousands of bales were brought down by steamboat from over two hundred miles inland and then shipped abroad, but still busy enough to rival Charleston and Savannah. The volume of Sir Samuel's diary always on display in the Founders' Room of the Pompey's Head Historical Museum was the one in which he stressed the value of the river. "For briefe," he summed up, "the temperature of the climate, the salubritie of the air, and the richness of the soile, and, above all else, the safe convenient harbour near the mouth of the deep river, which is called by the Indians Cassava, after an edible roote which they say used to be plentiful in the neighborhood, make this place one that affords, or can produce, whatsoever, most things affected by man, either for pleasure or profit."

For pleasure or profit—again, for no good reason, Anson felt pleased. He hadn't thought of Sir Samuel Alwyn in years, much less the faded pages of the diary that every eighth-grade class in Pompey's Head made a special visit to see. He was surprised to find that he could still remember even the irregular spelling the English nobleman had used to commit his colonizer's thoughts to paper. Sir Samuel's diary, however, was one of the points on which his life had turned—on it, as on a hinge, had swung the door of his earliest ambition.

He too was in the eighth grade when he saw the diary for the first time. Their teacher, Miss Harrigan, had taken them on what Boojum and Beejum, the husband and wife who were at the head of Patrick's school in New York, would call a field trip—to Miss Harrigan it was a visit to the museum, but to Boojum and Beejum it would be a field trip. He knew about the museum, which was in the building that had been the home of Sir Richard Montague when he was royal governor of the colony—the best example of Georgian architecture in the state, his father said, if not in all the South—but he had never visited it before. The old mansion faced on Montague Square. There was a large bronze statue of General Robert Carvell in the square, standing on a block of native granite. The inscription told how General Carvell had been the only general in the Revolutionary Army who came from Pompey's Head, and how he helped defeat the British at the Battle of Little Pigeon Marsh. Embedded in the earth on one side of the statue was a slab of rough-hewn stone to which was affixed a copper plaque. The legend on the plaque said that the square had once been occupied by a statue of Sir Richard Montague, which had been melted down for cannon balls by the patriots of Pompey's Head during the Revolution, and that the statue of General Carvell had been erected in its place by a grateful citizenry in 1825—Lafayette, it concluded, was an honored guest at the unveiling.

Miss Harrigan, their teacher, had lined them up in twos near the statue. Anson noticed that the general's hat was gray and spotted where the pigeons had been, and that his cheeks were streaked in a way that made him seem to be shedding big, thick tears. Anson started to call Ian Garrick's attention to it, Ian being his best friend next to Wyeth Blackford, who wasn't at school because he had snagged a bass plug in his lip and let it get infected, but Ian was too busy horsing around with Midge Higgins to pay him any mind. Everybody else was scrubbed and polished in his Sunday best, but Midge wore the same bright red dress she had on the day before. Midge was a new girl. She had been in the class only a few months. She lived on the far end of Hampton Street, one block away from what was called the Irish Channel, and her father was a conductor on the Marlborough Drive line. Miss Harrigan, in class that morning, had tried to impress them with the educational value of the visit they were about to make, but Midge had turned up her nose. "'That old museum," she said to Anson as they were leaving class. "Shinola! What's so wonderful about *that!*"

Midge lived the farthest away from school of any of them. If it wasn't that her father was a conductor and she could ride free, she would have had to walk eleven blocks to get to class; and if she lived just across the street from where she did, on the west, instead of the east, side of Hampton, she would have had to go to school in the Channel. Anson knew enough to realize that nearly all the mothers of the other boys and girls wished she did. They didn't think that Midge was a "good influence," citing the way that "Shinola!" had been picked up by the eighth grade, and they said that no child her age should be permitted to wear the clothes she did, particularly since she was so "well developed." One thing, though, they said they could be thankful for—at least her two older brothers had gone on to high school before her family moved to the east side of Hampton, and that the youngest one, Mico, wasn't yet old enough to attend class. They also said that maybe the Henry Pettibones knew what they were doing, turning that old house on Hampton Street into low-rent apartments, but it seemed to them that all that had been accomplished was deliberately to jump the Channel across the line that had stood as a fixed boundary for generations.

"Dear old Henry," Anson's father said one night. "What did our good friends and neighbors expect—that he would keep on paying taxes on that vacant property simply because it was where his ancestors first climbed out of the indentured-servant class? That's what they were, you know. It is one of Henry's many crosses that none of his ancestors was in the *Swan*, the *Discovery*, or the *London Merchant*—his having married an Olney hasn't helped much, either, since the first Olney, Isaac, came over as a shoemaker. And in the fifth contingent, at that." Anson's father gave an exaggerated chuckle and then began to cough. It had a dry, rasping sound.

"I do wish you'd do something about that cough," Anson's mother said. "It doesn't sound right to me. Shouldn't you see a doctor?"

"No, I shouldn't. It just comes from smoking too many cigarettes. I'll have to cut down. So our good friends and neighbors are exercised about Henry's inviting the Channel to move into that property of his, are they?" He shook his head. "Poor old Henry. He doesn't worship the Almighty Dollar—his is the shrine of the Almighty Dime. And it must be extremely trying to be a frustrated Shintoist. Henry's heaviest burden is that he wants to live up to a tradition and has no tradition to live up to—what kind of a tradition is an indentured servant and rents from the Channel and Duppytown? And so far as that property of his is concerned, history is simply repeating itself. When the first Pettibones moved in and began to act like quality—they didn't build that house, you know; it was the Archer house originally—they were in effect making the jump from the Irish Channel of their day." He coughed again, shielding his mouth with his hand. "As a matter of fact, if some of our Shinto acquaintances were even remotely honest, they would have to admit that they came from stock that was no better than these Higginses we've been hearing so much about. It may be the carpetbagger in me coming out, but I think I'll write a letter to Joe Birke on the News."

Anson's mother said he wouldn't dare—she seemed truly alarmed at the idea of his father writing a letter to the editor. Anson was surprised because he thought anyone could see that his father was only joking. He knew that his mother tried to take what she called a sensible view of the Higginses. She said that while it was unfortunate that the old Archer house could not be preserved in its original state, the Pettibones had the right to do what they wanted with the property, and the Higginses, on their part, had just as much right to want to better themselves by moving out of the Channel—there was nothing wrong in being a conductor and it was quite possible that they were nice people. Anson's sister Marion, who was in her senior year in high school, at this let out a howl. She said that if her mother knew Joe Higgins, the one who was a sophomore, and some of the things he did—— "All right, then!" Anson's father interrupted sharply. "If that's the case, you keep away from the Higgins boys! Meanwhile, live and let live."

All this conversation had the effect of making Midge doubly more attractive. Standing in line with the others in Montague Square,

Anson wished he had managed to get paired off with her instead of getting stuck with Olive Paxton, the least popular girl in class. Olive had mentioned four times already that she was General Carvell's great-great-grandniece on her mother's side, just as if she didn't talk about him nearly every day, along with her other ancestors, but if she thought that ancestors could make up for her peaked face and skinny legs and lank, mouse-colored hair, she was crazy, that's what. Besides, she had gone and let her old nurse give her another one of those vinegar rinses that the colored people thought were good for a girl's hair, and she still smelled of it faintly—Anson, feeling more and more put upon, aware that Olive liked him better than any of the other boys and that his getting stuck with her was bound to be twisted around as being his own design, just as if she were his girl, said to himself that she smelled the way the dining room did when his father was in one of his sophisticated moods, as Marion called them, and decided to mix the French dressing and dripped some of the vinegar on the table.

Midge Higgins, four couples in front of him, had none of Olive's spectacular disadvantages. Her round, animated face was set off with a bright mouth and a pair of shiny blue eyes, her blond hair was cut in a boyish bob, and her tight red dress showed all the lines of her figure. Anson noticed that her bosom was most as full as those of any of Marion's friends in high school, which was what the ladies who played bridge with his mother meant when they said she was so "well developed." Ian Garrick said that Midge was built like a brick outhouse and kissed with her mouth open the way they did in the movies, but that was just his talking big again, like the time he said he had taken so many swigs out of his father's decanter of whisky that the room went round and round—Ian was like that, always blowing off big about something, just as Wyeth Blackford said.

Anson was watching Ian fool around with Midge, saying things that made her giggle, when Miss Harrigan clapped her hands for silence. Olive Paxton straightened up, as did most of the other children, but Ian and Midge went right on giggling—"You, Ian!" Miss Harrigan said. "You, Midge! Do I have to teach you to mind!" Miss Harrigan was also dressed in her Sunday best. She wore a dove-colored dress with a lace collar that Anson had never seen before, and a gray hat with a pair of brownish wings. Anson thought that if Wyeth Blackford were there he would say it was lucky for her that he didn't have his shotgun along, and he amused himself for a moment thinking about Wyeth Blackford stalking Miss Harrigan's hat behind one of the clumps of azaleas that were still in bloom—Wyeth would get that pair of wings the first crack, too; he was the best shot of all the younger boys. Stealing another glance at Midge, Anson tried to console himself by remembering that he was the next best shot to Wyeth, and that Ian Garrick, with all that biggity talk of his, couldn't hit the side of a barn.

He was brought back to reality by another clap of Miss Harrigan's hands. "Remember what you were told," she said. "No speaking in loud voices and no touching. Not *anything*, understand! These are priceless relics you are about to see, *hundreds* of years old. All right, children, follow me."

They trooped out of the square into the street, where a few automobiles were baking in the sun along the curb and an old Negro in a battered felt hat was pushing a high-wheeled cart loaded with vegetables, on his way to peddle his produce from door to door, and then, quiet now, even Ian and Midge behaving themselves, they went up the steps of the museum. As soon as he entered the building, Anson had the feeling that he was in church—not on Sunday, when the bells were ringing and there were lots of people, but on one of those weekday afternoons when his mother, who was a member of the Altar Guild, had to change the linen and polish the brass. He found himself in a long, wide hall in which a flight of white stairs curved to the rooms above—there was a moment's confused impression of flags and charts and maps, of gold-framed portraits of men in colorful uniforms and outmoded dress, of things in cabinets and other things behind glass, and then he was off to himself reading the little printed cards that told what the various articles were. He saw a likeness of George Washington woven in silk in France, a storm flag of the Confederate cruiser *Shenandoah*, the torn and faded regimental banner the Pompey's Head Light Infantry had carried all through the War between the States, a view of the port in 1835, and, in one of the glass cases, the famous "Little Pigeon Flag." It did not look like a flag to Anson, just a piece of needlework with roses and leaves and forget-me-nots—"This square of embroidery," the card said, "was ripped from the back of an armchair in her father's plantation home by Margaret Jennor (later Mrs. John Williams) and presented to Colonel William Washington for his cavalry colors. The flag received its baptism of fire at the Battle of Little Pigeon Marsh in 1780 and was also borne at the Battle of Cowpens. It was later presented by Mrs. Williams to the Pompey's Head Light Infantry."

Anson was so absorbed in what he was reading, his mind full of martial clanging and somewhere in the smoke of battle a fearless drummer boy with a bandaged forehead who bore an astonishing resemblance to himself, that it needed a severe *"Pstt! Pstt!"* from Miss Harrigan to make him join the others. They went then into a handsome chamber just off the hall, paneled in white and lighted by two fan windows. It was identified by a little sign that hung from the doorway as the Founders' Room. Here were more portraits, twenty in all, and, spelled out in gilt letters on the walls above the portraits, so arranged that they made a kind of decoration, the names of "The Twenty Families of Marlborough County"—those who had come over with Sir Samuel Alwyn in the *Swan*. One portrait, larger than the others, was that of Sir Samuel himself—a heavy-cheeked, square-jawed man in a white wig and a snuff-colored coat with brass buttons and large turned-back cuffs. Beneath it stood a single glass case, the only piece of furniture on that side of the room—Miss Harrigan shepherded the class up to it in fours; it made Anson think of church again, the hushed, solemn time when people went up to the altar to receive communion.

At first he felt a sag of disappointment—there was nothing but some handwriting in the case, each sheet of paper weighted down by a small, oblong strip of glass, along with a copybook that was hardly different from the ones they used in school. But then, as he began to read the faded but still distinct handwriting that covered the pages of the copybook—written in metallic ink, he was later to learn—he felt a strange thing happening, beyond his ability to explain. To think that these lines had been written when Pompey's Head was nothing but a little clearing in the woods; to believe that that far time and the time of today could be brought so close together—and at that moment, beyond the awareness that Ian Garrick was trying to hold Midge Higgins's hand and that Sir Samuel Alwyn was looking down upon the cluster of heads bent over the case, he knew what he wanted to do when he grew up. He now had something with which to answer his father. When he grew up he wanted to find out all about these dusty, forgotten things and what they meant, and tell about them—didn't Miss Harrigan say he was better in Composition than anything else?

Sitting in his roomette, Anson had to shake his head. All he could show for that early ambition was *The Shinto Tradition of the American South*. He felt a certain protective tenderness for the boy he had been, much like the feeling he had for his son Patrick, and it was not the boy's fault that he did not know there was no future in being a local historian. It was just as Meg had said when he told her that if he had the time he thought he might still like to write a short social history of Pompey's Head—"Don't be silly! Who in the world would be interested? Now if it were a historical novel, instead——"

The train was going around a curve. Stretches of marshland fell away on either side, the tall, still grasses black in the early light and a few circling hawks in the sky, and then Anson caught sight of the Cassava River—the tracks followed it for a short distance before they crossed the bridge that led to the environs of Pompey's Head. Once again Anson could feel his heart beat faster; memories came with such a rush that everything was memory—the stretch of water just below the Blackford place where you could catch both fresh-water and salt-water fish; the old rice fields where the ducks settled on the ponds; the deer country between the north shore of the river and Ockeesawba Lake; the deeper swampland where he got his first wild turkey; the night when he and Wyeth Blackford and Ian Garrick were returning from Joe Ann Williams's coming-out party and wrecked Ian's brand-new car.

All his customary points of reference were in a state of flux and dissolution; even Meg and the children had receded into the distance. The roomette, like a metal, air-conditioned balloon, seemed to have drifted into the country of neither-here-nor-there. He felt momentarily suspended in space, discharged from the obligation of participation and able to regard himself as one of the proponents of his own drama—he recalled that there was something in Aristotle about this, and that there had been a reference to it in one of the books he had to read when he was taking his cram course to prepare for the New York bar examinations, but he could not remember where it was.

The train was now crossing the river. The slow-moving water, yellowish-red and silt-laden, broke into little whirlpools where it washed against the pilings of the bridge, and off to the left he could see the four or five multiple-story buildings that made up the sky-line of Pompey's Head—not much, he thought, the usual frustrated ambitions of a provincial American town. The speed of the train began to slacken after it crossed the river, and he saw that it was passing through the Negro quarter that lay on the north side of the tracks. Duppytown it was called—a random collection of sagging frame houses from which every last bit of paint had flaked and fallen, leaving them to take on the dead gray tones of ashes long forgotten in a cold, neglected hearth. The back yards were crisscrossed with lines that bellied on Mondays with the white folks' washing, there were patterns of footprints in the dust beneath the queen-of-China trees, a few skinny dogs roamed about with the ravenous lope of hunger, and in the rank weeds of an empty lot the rusty skeleton of an ancient car lay disemboweled on its side. Duppytown, Anson thought; Duppytown the Beautiful. He put on his hat, picked up his briefcase, threw his topcoat across his arm, and walked down the corridor to the end of the pullman. They were pulling into the station, and the porter was already opening the door.

"Well, sir," he said genially. "We made it."

"Yes," Anson replied. "So I see."

PART TWO

CHAPTER SEVEN

He saw, too, stepping from the train, that it was the same Lafayette Street station—this might be any one of those mornings when he had risen early and driven the family car down to the station to meet his father, who was returning from New York on the five forty-six. Handing over his baggage to a small, wizened Negro whose coffee-colored eyes peered out disconsolately from beneath the peak of a faded red cap, Anson followed him down the concrete ramp that led to the iron gates that stood at the end of the tracks. Only one other passenger had left the train. He was a portly man in a gray homburg and blue suit who strode past briskly, tagged after by a second redcap, who seemed already to be panting with the effort to keep up with him.

Anson tried to imagine what his hurry was and when he reached the waiting room he found out. A dark-haired girl who appeared to be about twenty burst through the doors that led to the street and ran up to the man, crying, "Oh, Daddy, I thought I was going to be late. Did you have a good trip?" She threw her arms about him, gave him a kiss, and they went chatting into the street—Anson, following his redcap, wondered who they were. Once he would have known and now he didn't and there never was a time when he felt so much a stranger and so alone. Here it was again—the grimy station with its waiting room of yellow brick; the rows of wooden benches divided by the brass rail demanded by Jim Crow; the two ticket windows, one on either side of the rail; the bulletin boards where the schedules of the trains used to be posted by one of Midge Higgins's many uncles; the all-night lunch counter with its lights still burning and where a stout woman in a soiled, wrinkled smock was slumped down wearily on her elbows, turning the pages of a picture magazine—here it was again, even to the smell of coal-tar disinfectant used to swab the floors, and here he was again, lonely and alien as some new drummer calling on the local trade for the first time.

"You want a cab, sir?" the redcap asked.

"Yes. Please."

"May be one." The redcap looked doubtful. "This time of morning, it's hard to say. I can phone one for you, though."

It turned out that he had to telephone. Anson stood in front of the station, listening to his high, put-upon voice speaking into a box telephone attached to the wall. He hung up the receiver and turned to Anson.

"One's coming right away," he said. "Should be one, without me having to phone, but this time of morning, they seem to figure it's too early to get up."

This business of having to telephone was plainly a deep, galling grievance—his face took on a new set of wrinkles, glum and petulant. Anson tipped him with a dollar bill, not only because he seemed to be in such need of cheering but also because he reminded him of old Henry, who used to work in the garden and who had the same kind of grievance against weeds—"Pull, pull, pull! And for what? Just to pull, pull all over again! Why is weeds, anyhow? What good is they?" Not knowing about Henry, unaware that this white stranger was offering up a sacrifice at the altar of his family gods, the redcap fingered the dollar bill gingerly—it took him several minutes to comprehend that he was not expected to make change. His face took on much the same cast as did Henry's when Anson's mother told him that the rest of the weeds could go until tomorrow, and his "Thank you, thank you," reminded Anson of Henry's "Praise be for something! Praise be!"

Anson told the redcap that he need not wait any longer. Looking dubious, the Negro said he'd better, just in case he had to phone again. Anson knew it was primarily the dollar working and possibly, behind the dollar, some momentary feeling of compassion for a solitary stranger who seemed to be a kindly man, but he was glad to have his company nonetheless—he preferred not to stand all by himself on Lafayette Street, waiting for a cab to take him to the Marlborough Hotel. Lafayette Street was where all the stores that catered to the colored trade were, where he and Joe Ann Williams used to spend hours listening to phonograph records that could be had in no other part of town, and in the new wash of memory that broke over him, bearing the fleeting figures of so many shadowy presences, it was comforting to have a living companion, even though it was a baggy, wrinkled Negro he had never seen before and would probably never see again.

"Tell me," he said. "Does Vicksburg still have his record shop?"

"Vicksburg?" The redcap twisted his face into an expression of deep concentration. "Oh, you mean the one who used to play the guitar. No sir, he don't have that shop no more. That building it was in, it was pulled down—there's a movie theater there now."

"And Vicksburg? What happened to him?"

"That I can't say, sir. He ain't been around in years. Seems like I heard that he went to live in Atlanta, but I can't rightly recollect for sure. You know how it is—so many folks coming and going, especially when the war was on, that a man can't keep them straight. But Vicksburg, I ain't seen him around in a long time—he was getting to be an old man."

Not so old, Anson started to tell him. Were Vicksburg to come walking up the street he would not be much more than sixty. And well preserved in the alcohol in which he used to steep himself night after night during the years when he played his guitar in the band at the Oasis. The affairs of the record shop were looked after by his wife. Vicksburg himself rarely appeared on Lafayette Street until late afternoon—a tall, burly man with immense white teeth and a tremendous laugh; unheard of beyond the borders of Pompey's Head, but one of the world's great natural musicians. No party was complete without Vicksburg, who besides playing in the band at the Oasis had his own quartet, and no one had a wider acquaintance among the younger white people in town. Anson was about to ask the redcap if the Oasis in Bugtown was still standing, but just then the cab arrived. The driver, a young man with a pale, narrow face and a pair of ferret-like eyes, hopped out and loaded Anson's luggage into the front seat.

"Where to?" he asked. "The Pompey Arms?"

"No, the Marlborough."

Anson found it revealing that the driver should imagine he would be going to the Pompey Arms. It was the new, modern hotel (new and modern for Pompey's Head; erected in 1923) and greatly favored above the Marlborough, that old-fashioned, high-ceilinged pile. The cab went north on Lafayette Street for several blocks, past the blank store fronts that had not yet opened for the day, and turned east on Independence Street, where the Marlborough stood, two blocks from

Monmouth Square. Independence was one of the easier streets on which to drive, Anson remembered. Taking it, you did not have to circumnavigate the various squares which, much as they contributed to the city's character, presented a bothersome traffic problem. Anson was thinking how green everything was, and how even so prosaic a street as Independence borrowed a verdant beauty from the oaks and magnolias that grew on either side, when he heard the driver speak.

"Stranger?"

"Yes, sort of."

"That's what I figured." The driver crooked his neck and looked at Anson in the rear-vision mirror. "It ain't a bad town, though—keeps picking up right along. That's why I come. I figured a man could do himself some good here, not that I call driving this cab doing me much good. But it's better than chopping cotton, even at that. You from New York?"

Anson said yes, he was, and the driver said that that was a town he sure intended to see. He spoke in the nasal twang of the upcountry, the one-crop plateau that stretched into the interior until it met the red clay hills that rose into the mountains of North Carolina, and even without the reference to chopping cotton Anson would have known him as a countryman tired of the backbreak of a tenant farm. The driver was telling about the things he wanted to see in New York—"That Music Hall theater they got there; my cousin in the Navy, he sent me a postcard with its picture on it"—when a small, neatly dressed Negro woman with gray hair, carrying a basket over one arm, stepped into the street. The driver honked his horn, and as she hurriedly regained the curb he gave a soft, throaty chuckle.

"Now what do you reckon that old nigger is out this early in the morning for?" he asked.

Anson felt himself begin to stiffen. Here it was again, that loathsome word. Here, conjured up out of nowhere by an ignorant countryman, were all the things that had caused him to leave Pompey's Head. And out of the past, set adrift by the lock's quick turning, two shadowy figures—a small, anxious, fearful boy and a tall, irate, white-haired man, himself and his grandfather. "Young sir, you ever let me hear you use that word again, just once, and I'll thrash you so that you'll still be feeling it when Gabriel blows his horn. They are colored people, understand. Colored, yes, but people. And those who use that word, those who call them nigger, make themselves out to be less, far less, than the lowliest of those they pretend to despise.

You understand what I'm saying, don't you? Remember, then. You'll not get a chance to hear me say it again!"

The driver returned to the things he wanted to see in New York—"That Empire State Building, now that must be something for sure; my cousin, he sent me a postcard of it too"—and Anson tried to shut his ears against the sharp drill of his voice. By the time they reached the Marlborough, he was holding himself so rigidly that he was reminded of Mr. Barlowe. That carrying things a bit too far, he relaxed his shoulders, paid off the driver, and stepped from the cab. There was no sign of a porter, and the driver offered to carry his bags into the hotel. Anson told him he need not bother. The man had spoiled the morning and he was glad to see him go.

The Marlborough Hotel was built in 1889. Pompey's Head at that time still had ambitions to become the leading metropolis of the southern Atlantic seaboard. Cotton and rice were firm, tobacco was bringing higher prices than ever, tar and turpentine were in brisk demand, almost any timbering operation was profitable, and the volume of ocean tonnage handled by the port continued to increase. The only blot on the picture was the railroads. The location of Pompey's Head had proved a serious handicap in that respect, and it had been by-passed by all but one of the major lines. In 1886, however, with the reorganization of the Atlantic & Central, which had never managed fully to recover from the loss of tracks, stations, rolling stock, and other equipment destroyed during Sherman's march to the sea, even this difficulty appeared to be remedied. The rejuvenated Atlantic & Central, running to Chattanooga and connecting there with other rails, would enable Pompey's Head to move its freight as far west as Louisville and Nashville, and thence eastward into Virginia. The future, consequently, had an expansive look—the Marlborough was cut to fit the dimensions of a dream.

The hotel had not changed since the last time Anson saw it. Built of native red sandstone, it was surmounted on each of its four corners by a crenelated tower that Gaby Carpenter, one of the girls in Anson's crowd, once called the Spires of Folly. There was a time when the Marlborough's reputation was exceeded in the South only by the St. Charles in New Orleans, but by Anson's day it had become the residence of so many aging aunts, uncles, and cousins that it came to be known as the Old Folks Home. It was Gaby Carpenter who christened it with that name. Gaby thought she had literary ambitions and professed to be bored with Pompey's Head—Pompey's

Dread, she called it. Anson suspected that Gaby liked to say such things because she thought they would shock people, and he never could quite see what she got out of it. More to her disadvantage, however, was the fact that, unlike the other girls, who would not be caught dead in anything that looked "Bohemian," Gaby was forever getting herself up in some outlandish creation made of red bandannas, or some print she said came from India, or even a piece of burlap. Gaby was tall and thin, with inky-black hair and small black eyes, and whenever she appeared in one of those costumes of hers Anson always felt slightly embarrassed when he met her on the street and had to stop and talk, good friends though they were. In recent years, however, especially since the day Meg came home with an outfit she bought to wear to the Duncans' for the week end and which consisted of a red bandanna shirtwaist and a voluminous burlap skirt, he had begun to suspect that the only trouble with Gaby Carpenter's ideas about dress was that they happened to be a little before their time.

He was thinking of Gaby, remembering how she persuaded her family to let her have a "studio" on the top floor of an old house the Carpenters owned on Clinton Street, only five blocks from Duppytown, when a porter came out to get his bags. He was too young for Anson to have known him in the past. Anson followed him into the hotel. The lobby was deserted and the porter's heels made a clacking sound on the tiles with which it was floored. Anson noticed that the tall columns of veined marble with their gilt pediments were still there, that a glass enclosure had been put up around the reception desk, and that a cozy fire was already burning in the hearth before which the aunts, uncles, and cousins, the widowed and the unwed, used to gather in the evening to knit, play cards, read their mail to each other, and spin the prayer wheel of old times.

The clerk was an alert, blond young man, remarkably brisk and amiable for one who had just sat through the long night shift. The way he said that he felt sure Anson would be comfortable in Room 528 identified him as a native. He made "eight" sound like a two-syllable word—"aay-ut," he said, just as did everyone who had ever grown up in Pompey's Head.

"How long will you be with us, Mr. Page?" he asked. "We have you down for a week. Is that correct?"

"So far as I know. I hope so."

"What's the matter, sir? Don't you like our town?"

For a moment Anson did not know how to reply.

"Why, sure. I like it fine."

"Oh, so you've been here before." The clerk smiled pleasantly. "We're glad you decided to stop with us this time."

It did not seem quite real to Anson, the conversation he was having —didn't he like their town and their being glad he had decided to stop with them this time. It was his town, too, and he had stopped with them because he liked the Marlborough, for which his grandfather had put up some of the money, and he suspected that his emotional investment in both the town and the Marlborough was considerably greater than theirs. But how could anyone know? He felt lonely again, reminded that he was as much a stranger as the clerk took him to be, and for an instant he thought of telling him who he was. It was even possible that he might know the younger brothers and sisters of some of his contemporaries; being a native of Pompey's Head, he would almost certainly know their names. But not now, Anson decided. He preferred not to run the risk of polite interest. He did not want to hear the clerk reply, "You don't say, sir; now think of that," and most of all he did not want to hear him say, "Fifteen years! Well, sir, welcome home." He would have found it hard to say why, but he did not want to be welcomed home by a clerk in the Marlborough Hotel.

"I wonder if I could get some breakfast," he said. "Is the dining room open?"

"Yes sir, it is," the clerk replied in his cheerful way. "We open at five forty-five for the convenience of our guests who like to get an early start. A lot of folks stop by to visit us on the way to and from Florida, you know. I suppose you've seen all our historic spots."

"Yes, I have."

"There's more to see than most folks realize," the clerk went on. "We're smaller than Savannah, and not all painted up like Charleston, but I've heard a lot of well-traveled people say that Old Pompey is a lot more interesting."

Old Pompey. It still had its hold, Anson thought; Old Pompey, we love you still. He began to feel warmly disposed toward the young man behind the desk; there was something about him that brought Wyeth Blackford to mind—Wyeth as he was when he used to be a teller in the Merchants & Mechanics Bank. The clerk seemed to be several cuts above the job he was holding down, just as Wyeth had, and he appeared no less content with what he was doing.

"If you wish, sir," he said, "I could have your bags sent up while you're having breakfast. There's the men's room if you want to wash up."

"That will be fine."

"Your key will be in your box. Anything we can do, we'll be more than glad to. We're happy to have you with us, Mr. Page."

Anson noticed a pile of fresh copies of the *Morning News* on one side of the desk. He did not have to look twice to see that the paper's page-one make-up had not changed any. Either old Joe Rawlings was still on the job, which seemed hardly possible, or else somebody was using his dummies as a model. Glancing at the headlines, which seemed to carry the same news as those he had seen in the *World-Telegram and Sun* the night before when he was boarding the train in Pennsylvania Station, Anson's attention was attracted by a small stack of thin books bound in heavy blue paper. He picked one up and looked at the cover. It was decorated with a bird's-eye view of the older part of the city, upon which was superimposed the title, *Historical Guide to the City of Pompey's Head*. A set of smaller letters, contained in a box at the bottom of the page, said that it had been compiled and published by the Pompey's Head Historical Association.

"How much is this?" he asked the clerk.

"Seventy-five cents."

"Is it any good?"

"Yes sir, I think so. It's full of interesting material, if that's what you mean."

"That's what I mean. I'll take a copy of the *News* too."

"Thank you, sir. Enjoy your breakfast. The entrance to the dining room is just past the elevators on your right."

"Yes, I know."

It was the second or third time he had said "Yes, I know," that morning and if he was not careful it could turn into a habit. But again it was true—he did know. Upon graduating from college he had written a local column for the *News* for nearly a year and a half, going to the paper after he left his office at Garrick & Leigh, and during those months Kit Robbins would often have supper with him. If it had been one of the other girls he used to date before he and Kit began going with each other, Joe Ann Williams or Gaby Carpenter or Margie Rhett, they would probably have gone to the Cassava Café, a small place near the river front that all the reporters on the *News* patronized, and where you could get a drink all through Prohibition. However, because it was Kit, they went to the Marlborough. Kit never felt comfortable in places like the Cassava Café. They made her stiff and awkward, and she seemed to be intimidated by the fellows who worked on the *News*, sitting there silently and never joining in the fun.

Anson could not find fault with Kit and he thought that the dining room of the Marlborough was a wonderful place. It was nothing like the dining rooms of most hotels, simply a long, narrow chamber with a line of glass windows that looked out upon a small garden located behind the hotel. There were many times in New York when he had wished for a dining room as pleasant as that of the Marlborough. He liked going there with Kit. He was proud of how pretty she was and of the glances that followed her, and it was pleasant to have old Watkins, the Negro headwaiter, show them always to the same table and then inquire about the health of his mother and father, or perhaps say that Wyeth Blackford had been in to have lunch that day.

During those times in New York when his thoughts drifted back to Pompey's Head, Anson often thought that the months when he and Kit Robbins used to have supper at the Marlborough were the happiest of his life. He was working as a freshman lawyer at Garrick & Leigh, he was seeing his name in print at the head of the column of historical jottings that he wrote three times a week for the *Morning News*, he fished and hunted in season, and he considered himself engaged to Kit—it would have been hard, at the time, for him to see how anyone could ask for more. He could now, wondering how it was that he had failed to notice the flaws in the structure, but even with the wisdom of hindsight it was still true—he had never known a happier time.

A Negro waiter met him at the door, wearing the uniform Anson remembered. It consisted of black trousers, black shoes, a white jacket with brass buttons, and a white shirt worn with a black bow tie. Anson looked to see if he was one of the waiters he had known, but, like the porter at the door, he was much too young. Two other waiters were standing at their stations and everything was as it used to be—the regularly spaced tables with their fresh clean cloths, the two serving stands at either end and the one in the middle, the swinging door that led to the kitchen, the line of spotless windows and the palm tree in the garden, near which stood a little fountain that sent its trickle through the early morning quiet. Anson remembered how much Kit Robbins had liked the garden, and how she and Watkins used to talk about the flowers that were in bloom, and for an instant everything began to seem unreal again, almost as if it were a dream. He could not remember having dreamed about Pompey's Head in years, not since those first months in New York when he used to wake up and not know where he was, but the configurations of a dream could easily have taken on such a shape as this— the dining room of the Marlborough in the shadowy light of early morning, the Negro waiters in their accustomed uniforms, the rustle of the palm tree in the garden, and himself walking, almost as if in a trance, toward the table that Watkins used to save for him and Kit.

It was one of the tables that stood along the line of windows, the fourth from the rear. A man drinking a glass of orange juice was sitting at the table in front of it, and two places farther along a second man was munching a piece of toast and reading the Morning News. Except for the waiters and Anson, they were the only persons in the room. It was very quiet. A sudden clatter of dishes rose and fell behind the door that led to the kitchen, and when it subsided there was nothing but the trickle of the fountain and the rustle of the palm tree and the quick bright call of a redbird. Anson recognized it immediately. It might have been only yesterday that he had last heard that cheerful call.

He saw that the waiter was not going to show him to his old table after all. Going to the table in front of the man who was reading the Morning News, he pulled back the chair and waited for Anson to seat himself. The man glanced up from his paper with a grave, slow munching and then went back to his reading. Anson ordered orange juice, bacon and eggs, and coffee. After the waiter left, he again looked around the room. Everything was the same and nothing was the same. It was like returning to a house you had rented to strangers and coming upon the changes they had made—it was the same house and the same rooms, and the clock in the hall had the same measured tick, but some of the furniture had been rearranged and the pictures were hung differently, and there was the lingering presence of alien shapes that made the house theirs, not yours.

Not wanting to think about it, Anson opened the copy of the Historical Guide. It began with several pages of advertisements and there were more advertisements toward the end. Leafing through them, he read about the Pompey's Head Candy Company, specializing in benne brittle, a famous old Southern confection; the Calico Lane Tea Shoppe, delicious lunch, afternoon tea, 12 to 3 and 3 to 6; the Pompey Arms, a Brinkler hotel, where you must be sure to serve yourself from the Plantation Hunt Board in the Sportsmen's Room; the Jolly Jim Tire Company, finest recapping in the South; and the Old Cottage Gift Shop, circa 1804, glassware, pottery, and antiques.

Out in the garden the redbird called again. Anson watched him until he flew away, and then leafed through the rest of the advertisements. He wondered how they would appear to him if he had never lived in Pompey's Head, and if he might be tempted to serve himself from the Plantation Hunt Board and buy a box of benne brittle for Meg. Somehow he doubted it. He thought he would have sense enough to stay away from the Plantation Hunt Board, and he could not see himself getting out of a taxi with a box of benne brittle for Meg. "Typical," she would say, "just typical," and she would mean by typical, not only the benne brittle, which was a hard candy full of little, flavorful seeds, but all the vexing provincialisms she disliked about the South and which the box of candy would be sure to bring to mind.

"All right, then!" he said to her one night during the third year of their marriage. "If all these things are wrong with the South, why did you latch onto me?"

"Because, darling, you caught me on the rebound," Meg answered. "Jake Sundburg was leaving to head up the Rome bureau, and I expected him to ask me to marry him before he left, and when he didn't I started to console myself with you. Besides, if you're a Southerner, you're a lapsed one—not emancipated, lapsed, the way some Catholics are lapsed. It was that that made you interesting. You'd left your church and were full of complications because of it, and I'd never known a lapsed Southerner before. Besides, if you must know, you were so darned sweet."

Anson did not answer. This was the first he had heard of Meg's coming to him on the rebound. It was fine of her to be so forthright about it, but he wished it hadn't been necessary. He would have preferred not to know that she had expected Jake Sundburg to marry her, and he did not like to think that she might have accepted him if he had. Meg noticed the expression on his face.

"But, darling! Don't be silly. That was then, not now. Jake Sundburg and me would have never worked out. Every time he shows up at a party I wonder what it was that I ever thought I saw in that big, stupid, pompous Swede. I never was really in love with him, not the way I was with you—it was the Rome bureau I was in love with— but let's suppose I was. Weren't you in love with that girl in Pompey's Head? Weren't you now? If it's our being each other's first love you want, which I will admit is a tender idea, you'll have to go back and arrange things differently. Either you'll have to get yourself born in Hillsdale, Indiana, which God forbid, or else get me born in Pompey's Head. God forbid that too."

What Meg said was true, of course. If she had ever been in love with Jake Sundburg, he himself had been no less in love with Kit. He had not gone to Meg on the rebound, however. He was completely over Kit when he began to think seriously about Meg. It did not matter any longer, nor had it ever in any vital way, but he wished that that conversation had not picked this moment to come drifting back into his thoughts. He did not like to think that when he and Meg were married Jake Sundburg was lurking somewhere in the background. But that was being silly again. Everyone had a background, and in all backgrounds there were people, and who was he to say that Kit Robbins was not present in his background on that Sunday afternoon when he and Meg were married at John Duncan's place on Long Island? He had enough to be depressed about without going out of his way.

"That old girl of yours," he could hear Meg saying as she helped him pack. "Will you be seeing her? You know, the one you ran away from."

"Why do you always keep saying that I ran away from her?" He took the pile of shirts Meg was holding and put them into his suitcase. "I didn't run away from her and I won't be seeing her. She doesn't live in Pompey's Head any more. Didn't I tell you about the time I saw her in Chicago?"

"I don't remember. Is she the one who wanted you to spend the night in Lake Forest?"

"Good lord, no!" He could not imagine anything more fantastic than his spending the night with Kit Robbins anywhere. "That was Emily Duncan. Her father asked me to call her up and I wasn't able to reach her until I got back to the hotel after five——"

"Dear me, the way you explain. I sometimes wonder how judges manage to live as long as they do. What about neckties? Don't you have any new ones? Most of these look pretty shabby."

"They look all right to me. What I was saying——"

"I heard you. What you were saying was that you wouldn't be seeing that old girl of yours because you've already seen her in Chicago. Why don't you get yourself some bow ties? I don't think you've ever worn one."

"The chances are that I never will, either. And I didn't see that old girl of mine, as you keep on calling her, in Chicago. I was window-shopping on Michigan Boulevard, hunting for something for Debby's birthday, and then, in front of the window——"

"Look, darling. I'm sure it was an interesting experience and some-day I want you to tell me all about it. Right now, though, you have forty minutes to catch your train. Are you sure you have everything? What about your toothbrush?"

He was thinking about his encounter with Kit Robbins on Michi-gan Boulevard and Meg was thinking about his toothbrush. It seemed all out of balance, even though it was not. Kit was only a name to Meg. She had no feelings about her one way or the other be-cause, as she said, it was hard to be interested in people you had never known. Whether or not he had his toothbrush was much more im-portant. In any case, whatever else lay ahead of him, seeing Kit Robbins need not be one of his worries. Not that it would have made much difference. He was sitting only a few feet from where they used to have supper together, but Kit Robbins did not matter any longer. All that was in the past. It had started being in the past the day he and Meg were watching the skaters on the rink in Rockefeller Center, and it was completely in the past the day he saw Kit on Michigan Boulevard.

"Why, Anson! It's you!"

"Oh, hello, Kit. What are you doing way out here?"

Kit was still beautiful, and with the structure of her face and frame she would continue to be beautiful until she was fifty, if not longer, but the trouble and unhappiness might never have been. Everything was over. He had often wondered what it would be like to see Kit Robbins again, and now he knew. He could even tell himself, notic-ing how the weak sunlight was being reflected in the windows of the Tribune Building, that Kit was hardly to blame. It had been too much for her, just as it had been too much for him, and Kit Robbins would never matter again.

"You're still living in New York, I hear."

"Yes, I am. And you?"

"Oh, I—we're living in Oak Park. What brings you to Chicago?"

He was still living in New York and she was living in Oak Park and all the hurt was gone. There should be more to show for all that anguish than this meaningless conversation. It made what happened so completely a waste. And now, sitting in the dining room of the

93

Marlborough Hotel, it seemed more a waste than ever. He would never have those years of his life again and be that person again, and if it mattered so little why had it ever mattered so much?

"Excuse me, sir," he heard the waiter say. "Here's your orange juice."

Drinking it, Anson leafed through the pages of the *Historical Guide*. He saw a picture of St. Paul's Church, a photograph of the old courthouse near the waterfront, an etching of one of the squares, and a pencil sketch of the J. J. Lockhart home. "This private dwelling," the guide said, "NW corner James and W. Hampton Sts., erected in 1835, is of early Classical Revival design. Strikingly designed iron grillwork ornaments the Doric portico, the balcony, and the garden fence. The living rooms are magnificent with their mahogany sliding doors, dark marble mantels, and ornate plaster medallions on the ceiling." It was an adequate description of the Lockhart house, except that it gave no idea of how oppressively sterile the place was—it was hard for him to imagine that Joe Ann Williams was Jay Lockhart's wife. It had always been assumed that Joe Ann and Wyeth Blackford would marry each other, but it had not worked out that way. According to Marion, who now lived with her husband and three children in Denver, where Anson's mother lived also, Joe Ann had grown tired of waiting for Wyeth to make up his mind and had married Jay Lockhart instead. That was about the last piece of news Anson had had from his sister about any of his old crowd. Denver was a long way off and Marion had cut her ties with Pompey's Head as completely as he had cut his.

When the waiter arrived with the rest of his breakfast, Anson saw that a helping of hominy had been served up with the bacon and eggs. It was incredible that he should have forgotten that you always had hominy for breakfast in Pompey's Head. Or, rather, that you always had hominy. Eating his breakfast with relish, he continued to look through the *Historical Guide*. It was like coming upon a pile of old snapshots at the bottom of a drawer. Things were not quite as you remembered them, and it seemed that the photographs and not your memory must be at fault, and every now and then you were confronted with some puzzling detail that brought you up short. The Hanby house, for instance, which the guide said was now an antique shop—did it have curved sandstone steps at either end of its front stairway or didn't it? The guide said it did, but he thought not. Gaby Carpenter's house had steps like that, and so had the Johnsons', but the Hanbys'——

94

Suddenly it became as unimportant as it was. Turning the page, he saw a photograph of the Blackford home on the Cassava River. It barely resembled the shabby, run-down place he remembered, but even had the name "Mulberry" not been printed beneath the photograph he would have recognized it immediately. He had no idea, however, that it could be so handsome. This was the way it must have looked a hundred years ago, when rice and cotton had brought the Blackfords to the high point of their wealth and power. He had a sudden desire to see it again; all the old affection came rushing into his throat.

But to whom in the world did it belong? Not Wyeth, surely, because when last heard of Wyeth was on the road selling ice cream in the two Carolinas. It was unlikely that he had sufficiently prospered to afford such splendor, and it was equally unlikely that he had married anybody who could afford it for him. A piece of news as big as that would somehow have found its way to Marion, or if not Marion to his mother, and it would have been surely passed along to him.

Who owned the place, though? He turned to the guide to see if it told. There was a brief sketch of the Blackford family, which related how Percy Wyeth Blackford had been Sir Samuel Alwyn's second-in-command, and an explanation of how the property had received its name. "It was the hope of the original colonists to engage in the manufacture of silk, and Percy Wyeth Blackford set out a number of mulberry trees for the culture of silkworms—hence the name 'Mulberry.'" All this, however, Anson knew. What he wanted to find out was to whom the place belonged. The guide gave no hint. The description concluded with a note that said the property was closed to visitors.

Anson felt that a door had been quietly shut in his face. He always had the run of Mulberry, just as Wyeth Blackford had of the house on Alwyn Street, and even though Wyeth's family had found it necessary to give it up before he left Pompey's Head, he always thought of it as a second home. Some of his happiest hours had been spent at Mulberry. He loved the view of the river from the room in which he always slept, the mists that rolled in with morning and the lazy shadows of late afternoon, the honk of geese in the winter midnight and the thrushes deep in the summer woods, the festive occasions when the girls appeared in their prettiest dresses and everybody sat on the steps of the porch and sang to the accompaniment of Vicksburg's guitar—it was difficult to sort them out, so fast the memories came, and it was hard to believe it was he who had figured in those almost forgotten scenes.

He lit a cigarette, trying to bring the present into some sort of relation with the past, the quiet of the morning gently invaded by the clock in the steeple of St. Paul's Church tolling seven o'clock, when he heard a shuffle of footsteps along the bare wooden floor of the dining room. He turned to see who it was. The next moment he was on his feet and the sound of his voice was booming in his ears.

"Watkins!"

He moved toward the old Negro through the awareness that the two other men who were having breakfast were watching him, that his voice was reverberating along the walls, and that the added weight of fifteen years was a burden Watkins could barely carry. A solid, heavy-set man in the old days, he was now so corpulent that he moved with difficulty. He seemed to have to pull himself along, dragging his feet. His hair had turned into a white, curly fringe, and his features, once sharply defined, had grown fleshy and indistinct. He peered into Anson's face earnestly, smiling in a bemused fashion, and then, slowly, as recognition came, his mouth widened into a big, delighted grin. He grasped Anson's outstretched hand in a huge brown paw and pressed it warmly.

"No, now! It's Mister Sonny." He wagged his head and began to chuckle, still holding Anson's hand. "Yes sir, it's Mister Sonny for sure. Where you been, young man?"

"Away, Watkins, just away."

"Yes sir, it's sure good to see you. You had your breakfast yet? They been treating you right in here?"

"Fine, Watkins, fine."

The old Negro relinquished his hand and looked at him again, chuckling deep in his throat. "Well, well. You ain't changed a bit. I'd of knowed you anywhere. Yes sir, anywhere I'd of seen you, I'd of knowed you. How you been?"

"Fine, Watkins, fine. And you?"

"I can't complain. I still get around. I don't wait any more, though —they've put me in charge of the gentlemen's hats. Eight to two I'm supposed to be on the job, but waking early like I do, five or six o'clock, I generally get here beforehand. What else do I have to do?" He checked his garrulity and began to grin again. "Yes sir, I can't tell you how glad I am to see you. I was saying to Felicity the other night, not more than a week ago, 'Felicity,' I was saying, 'I wonder what's happened to Mister Sonny Page.'"

Anson knew it was purest fiction and that it was part of the elaborate ritual that helped to govern the social conduct of the two races, but he was nonetheless grateful. He would just as soon believe that he had not been forgotten and that Watkins had wondered to Felicity about what had happened to Sonny Page. It was strange, however, to hear himself called Sonny again. It had not happened since he left Pompey's Head. The name had been invented by Marion. It was based on the last syllable of his first name, as he used to think it necessary to explain because he did not want people to think it was the diminutive of "son," and until the time he left for New York he had never been called anything else. He used to be Sonny Page, and now he was Anson Page, and somewhere along the line Sonny Page had disappeared. He could not place the time of the vanishing, nor say how it had come about, but he was not the person Watkins imagined.

"You home for good now?"

"No, Watkins. Just for a few days."

"Pshaw now! That's no way! When you coming back for good?"

"Someday maybe, Watkins. Maybe someday."

"You do that, young man. But don't make it too long. Old Pompey's the best."

For the moment Anson wished it were possible—nothing in the past could touch him any more and, given the chance, he would be tempted to risk it. But it was too impossible even to think about, and, besides, he was beginning to tire of this half-world in which he was moving. Duncan & Company was not paying his expenses in order for him to talk to an old Negro about Pompey's being the best and when was he coming back and what had happened to Sonny Page.

"Take care of yourself, Watkins. I'll see you around."

"Yes sir! And you take care too. Just wait until I tell Felicity that I saw you—it was only the other night that we were talking about where you'd gone to. And here you is! Yes sir, it sure is good to see you."

"It's good to see you too, Watkins. Give Felicity my love."

He did not know Felicity and would not have been able to remember her name. He had come home, however, and it seemed right to be sending Felicity his love.

CHAPTER EIGHT

A few minutes later, sitting on the edge of the bed with the Pompey's Head telephone directory open in his lap, Anson decided that he would have to begin with Ian Garrick. He wished he did not have to, but there seemed no way out of it. He had to find a way of getting in touch with Mrs. Wales, and Ian appeared to be his only lead. It was his original intention to first get hold of Wyeth Blackford. He had imagined them having a drink somewhere, or walking in the woods, and Wyeth's giving him what Mr. Barlowe would call the local background—who was living and who was dead, who had married and who had moved away, and eventually, who might be helpful in providing him with an introduction to Mrs. Wales. Wyeth's name, however, was not listed in the directory—Black, Blackburn, Blackdell, Blacker, but no Blackford. That ancient and honorable name, woven into the history of Pompey's Head from the very beginning, seemed to have been completely erased. Mrs. Blackford, as his mother had written him when he was stationed in London during the war, was dead. But Mr. Blackford; was he dead too? And Dinah? What about her? And what had happened to Joe Ann Williams, that sweet and happy girl?

He knew that Joe Ann had married Jay Lockhart—Mrs. J. J. Lockhart, Jr., her name would be—but Jay's name was nowhere in the directory. His mother's was included, Mrs. J. J. Lockhart, Sr., and from the address and telephone number (125 Hampton: Main 2-1006) Anson knew that she was still living in the house described in the *Historical Guide*. It was quite possible that Joe Ann and her husband were living with Mrs. Lockhart—one old lady all alone in that vast house could not readily be imagined—but if that were so it was strange that Jay's name did not have a separate listing.

Everything, however, would come straight in time. Ian Garrick could be depended upon to bring him up to date. The thought of seeing Ian, however, was no more congenial than before. He could not forget the morning when Ian had been unable to find a word for him. It was all in the past now, part of the lost, submerged world of Sonny Page, and if forgiveness was necessary the intervening years had made it easy to forgive—Ian, being Ian, could not have done otherwise. At the time, however, it had seemed a gross betrayal. The world had divided into two camps—friends and enemies—and Ian was not his friend.

Nothing, however, was to be gained by dwelling on that. He had to find a way of getting to Mrs. Wales, and Ian appeared to be his only recourse—Ian and Olive Paxton. As he adjusted himself to the idea of seeing Ian, he began to find certain advantages in it. Ian was a lawyer, whom he could bring partially into his confidence and thus give a professional emphasis to his call—there could even be a fee, if need be—and Olive, whom Ian had married, was distantly related to Mrs. Wales. Together they might be helpful; more helpful, actually, than Wyeth Blackford.

Thumbing the pages of the telephone book, Anson looked up Ian's home number. The exchange was unfamiliar to him (Bullock 2-3639) and he had never heard of Azalea Drive. He reached for the telephone, thinking to call Ian immediately, and then decided against it. Ian himself he felt able to face. The mine fields had been laid and the years had built their own defenses. He had not engineered them, planning against a time when it might be necessary to meet Ian Garrick again, but he knew they were there. He was not Sonny Page any longer—older; harder; stronger; bearing the scars of all the years he had spent in his cubbyhole at Roberts, Guthrie, Barlowe & Paul— and he had confidence in his ability to carry off a meeting with Ian without any trouble. But Ian's voice coming puzzled and disem- bodied over the wire, taking several moments to comprehend who it was and then bursting out as though they were once again meeting on terms of an old, cherished intimacy—no, that he preferred to avoid. Better simply to walk to the offices of Garrick & Leigh and announce his presence. There would be even a certain value in taking Ian by surprise. He would have no time to arrange the scenery for a sentimental meeting between two boyhood friends.

Ian, however, would be at least another hour getting to his office.

99

It was not yet eight o'clock, and the day's business in Pompey's Head rarely began until around half-past nine. What to do with himself until then? He thought of taking a walk and then rejected the idea. Sooner or later he would have to go down Alwyn Street and see their old house, but that was the one encounter for which he was not prepared. There was no way in the world he could keep himself from being hurt.

Not yet, however. For the moment he lacked the courage. Rising from the bed, he picked up his briefcase and carried it to a desk that stood near one of the windows—it would be well, while there was still time, to review all the facts he had been able to acquire relative to the affair of Phillip Greene and Garvin Wales.

First, though, he wanted a drink of water. He went into the bathroom, a high-ceilinged chamber with a marble-topped washbasin and an immense tub that stood several inches off the floor, supported by cast-iron legs fashioned to resemble lion's paws, and let the cold water run into the basin. One thing about the Marlborough, he told himself—whatever it might lack in the way of chintz, imitation maple, and framed pastels, it made up in being itself. Waking up here, you would not have to wonder where you were; you would not have to think twice to know you were not in Sioux City.

The room into which he looked from the bath was three times as large as any hotel bedroom he had ever seen. The old-fashioned furniture matched its proportions. There was a double bed, a dresser, a wooden rocker, several chairs, a bedside table on which stood a reading lamp and the telephone, the desk by the window, a floor lamp near one of the chairs, and a high, massive cabinet, made of mahogany, that reminded him of a similar one that had stood in the second-floor hall of the house on Alwyn Street. He remembered how much of a problem it had been. Well as they knew their way, somebody was always running into it in the dark. His mother kept threatening to sell it, saying that they could get something useful with the money, and once went so far as to run a three-day advertisement in the classified columns of the News. Nothing came of it, however, and they kept on colliding with the cabinet in the dark, bruising their elbows and barking their shins, and it stood there year after year until it took on almost a human presence, like some troublesome, trying member of the family whose presence everyone grudgingly had agreed to tolerate.

Staying in a room in the Marlborough was going to be more of an experience than he had imagined. It had the anonymous character of all hotel rooms, where last night's lives are bundled up and sent out with this morning's laundry, and yet, because it was the Marlborough, it represented an overlooked corner that he was coming upon for the first time—never had it occurred to him that someday he would be staying at the Marlborough, or that he would be like any other transient who passed through Pompey's Head. Not wanting to think about it any longer, he walked back into the bedroom and sat at the desk. Zipping open his briefcase, he saw that its contents were all in order—the memos that Phillip Greene had sent to the accounting department; copies of Garvin Wales's royalty reports showing the discrepancies of which Mrs. Wales had complained; several sheets of ruled yellow paper covered with notes made for his own guidance; and, finally, the sixty-four canceled checks made out to Anna Jones.

After ten days the name had taken on a certain fascination for Anson—who was this Anna Jones and what was her place in the picture? He remembered a conversation with Mr. Barlowe several days after the meeting in the offices of Duncan & Company. He had just explained to Mr. Barlowe that he had asked one of the tracing agencies to find out what it could about Anna Jones.

"We may turn up a lead," he said.

Mr. Barlowe looked at him for a moment before replying.

"I thought you had your lead," he said. "Isn't that Wales fellow lead enough? It still boils down to a question of his authorization, doesn't it? Or have you turned up something that I don't know about?"

"No, I haven't. It seems to me, though, that if we knew exactly how Anna Jones fits into this puzzle——"

"But for all practical purposes we do know," Mr. Barlowe broke in. "We know that your friend Phillip Greene wrote out twenty thousand dollars' worth of checks to her. What else is there? Her identity? Her present whereabouts?" He took a cigar from the humidor that stood on his desk and used it to make a short gesture of impatience. "I'm afraid I don't see their relevance. What's the angle?"

"I don't have any," Anson replied. "I just thought that if we could find this Anna Jones and get a deposition——"

"To what effect?" Mr. Barlowe punctured his cigar and lit it, continuing to speak the meantime. "That Phillip Greene made these donations to her as an agent of Garvin Wales? That's what you're thinking, isn't it? All right—get such a statement if you can. But what good will it do without supporting testimony from Wales? This whole thing hinges on him, remember. Suppose he chooses to deny it?"

Anson permitted himself to shrug his shoulders. "In that event we're sunk. But not any more sunk than we would be otherwise. If, that is, Wales is going to take the position that Phil Greene made those withdrawals without his knowledge and consent. Besides, as part of the background——"

"That's different." Mr. Barlowe pulled in on his cigar and glanced at its tip. "If it's background you're after, well and good. But I wouldn't let my hopes soar too high if I were you. My own opinion is that even if you do manage to locate this Miss Jones, or Mrs. Jones, or whoever she is—you don't expect me to believe that that isn't an assumed name, do you?—you won't find her particularly obliging. Why should she be?"

There was no reason that Anson could think of. Anna Jones had lent herself to a conspiracy. She had received money from Phillip Greene for twenty-one years and had managed to remain hidden throughout. So complete a concealment had to be deliberate. Yet, knowing this, he had thoughtlessly said that he thought a deposition might be had from her.

"Put it down to my going off half cocked," he said. "I hadn't thought it all the way through. You're probably correct in saying that it is foolish to imagine that this Anna Jones will talk, even if we brought her to court. And that's impossible. I had another talk with Mr. Duncan yesterday. The one thing he insists upon is that we keep this from getting any publicity. He wants it to be handled quietly."

Mr. Barlowe shrugged his shoulders. "If that's the way John wants it, that's the way it has to be—he's the one who foots the bills. I don't know that I agree with him—a lot of these loud talkers tend to quiet down when they find themselves headed for court—but he may be right, considering the people involved. Frankly, they strike me as rather a messy lot—a man doesn't slip a woman twenty thousand dollars under the barn door unless he is afraid to do it in the open. But tell me this. What's made you so curious about Anna Jones? If you've put one of the agencies on the job, you must think it important to know more about her. Why?"

Anson was facing the window. After the spell of rainy weather, the morning was clear and fine. The sun shone on the waters of the bay just off the Battery and he could see all the way across to Brooklyn.

Thinking that New York had its points after all, he shifted his position and said, "I've already explained—I went off half cocked. It may be that I'm going off half cocked all along the line. You'll say that I'm jumping to conclusions, which may be true, but I've convinced myself that it was Garvin Wales who wanted that money sent to Anna Jones—I go along with Mr. Duncan and Van Bliss on that."

"Prejudice," Mr. Barlowe said. "Rank prejudice."

"Of course it is," Anson agreed. "But you yourself will admit that in a situation like this you have to have some point of departure and that you must begin with what you know."

"I wouldn't find any quarrel with that," Mr. Barlowe replied. "But what is it, exactly, that you do know?"

"That Phillip Greene was an honest man," Anson said. "Exactly how he became involved with this Anna Jones I can't imagine. As I see it, however, Mr. Duncan is absolutely correct in believing that he was acting on instructions from Wales, and that Wales knew about those withdrawals. It's hard to believe that they would have been so carefully itemized on his royalty reports had it been otherwise—I think that you agreed to that yourself the day we were talking at lunch."

Mr. Barlowe shook his head. "Not at all. I agreed only that it was a plausible surmise, one arrangement of the few known facts. You could arrange them in several ways, as I went to some trouble to point out—it could be, for instance, that Wales regarded those various sums of money as loans."

"Yes, but——"

"Let me finish. John Duncan's error—and yours too, if I may say so—is in assuming a relation between this Wales fellow and Anna Jones. But the established relation—the established one, I repeat; not the theoretical one—is between Anna Jones and Greene. So far as the evidence indicates, there is no reason to suppose that Wales even knows of the woman's existence. But let's stop riding all over the track. You still haven't told me what caused you to become so curious about Anna Jones."

"Because I am, that's all. Aren't you?"

Mr. Barlowe was not used to being addressed in such a fashion. His face lost its composed look and a glint of displeasure shadowed his eyes. Then, taking a puff on his cigar, and with his features arranged in their habitual expression, he said, "No, not at all. It so happens that I don't like these steamy relationships. I haven't the stomach for them. If it were possible to get a deposition from Anna Jones to the effect that Wales was aware of these payments and had authorized your friend Greene to make them—well, that would be one thing. But curiosity for the sake of curiosity, who the woman is, where she lives, what she may happen to look like——" He blew out a puff of smoke and waved it away. "No, I find that I'm not at all interested. Why should I be?"

Mr. Barlowe looked friendly enough, and there was no apparent hostility in his attitude, but Anson was aware that the conversation had taken a sharply different turn. There was a note in Mr. Barlowe's voice that said very plainly that he thought Anson was implying that he was somehow at fault for not being curious about Anna Jones, and that it was up to Anson, now that he had brought it up, to show where the fault lay. It was little things like this that caused you to lose favor at Roberts, Guthrie, Barlowe & Paul and get black marks beside your name. Anson knew that the thing to do was to frame his reply carefully and to mollify Mr. Barlowe's ruffled feelings. There was a right thing to say and a right way to say it, but all of a sudden it did not seem worth the bother. He was tired of having always to edit his thoughts and he did not see why Mr. Barlowe's feelings had to be one of his major concerns. Looking across the desk behind which Mr. Barlowe sat waiting to hear why he should be curious about Anna Jones, he said:

"I don't suppose I gave your curiosity much thought. I simply assumed that you would be as curious as I am. Greene I knew and Wales I know about. I now know about Mrs. Wales too, in a general sort of way, but Anna Jones is just a name. To me, though, she is just as important as the others. It troubles me to know so little about her. It is she who is at the bottom of this—that much is plain—and I wish she were less a mystery. I think that explains my curiosity. As for yours—well, perhaps it's a little off its feed this morning."

It was a risk to end like that, much too forward and much too bold, but the look on Mr. Barlowe's face told him that he had managed to say the right thing after all. He should have been pleased but he was not. He still did not like to think that whenever he talked with Mr. Barlowe he had to edit his thoughts.

"Those checks that your friend Greene made out to Anna Jones," Mr. Barlowe said. "Have you had a good look at them?"

"No, not yet. Why?"

Mr. Barlowe considered his cigar for a moment. "If you intend to refer her to one of the agencies, you might find them helpful. I didn't look at all of them the day we went uptown, not more than four or five, but the ones I happened to see appeared to indicate that she did a certain amount of moving around—at least two of them were cashed in different parts of the country. They might bear closer examination. I don't give a damn about the woman, and I still say that even if you do turn her up you won't get anywhere, but I feel obliged to do what I can to help you satisfy this curiosity of yours."

It could have been a rebuke but it was not; when Mr. Barlowe wanted to minister a rebuke he left no question. Anson quickly ran over what he had just said. That two of the checks were cashed in different parts of the country might prove to be of no importance. The significant thing was that Mr. Barlowe, in the midst of that difficult session at Duncan & Company, had observed the clearing-house stampings on their backs and instantly comprehended their possible value. Once again Anson was driven into a kind of grudging admiration. Mr. Barlowe was not the easiest man in the world to get along with, and Meg was probably right in saying that he hadn't had a new idea in forty years, but that was beside the point. If you had to work for a living, there was always the problem of getting along with somebody, and Meg's years on the newsmagazine sometimes led her into confusing the possession of ideas with intelligence. Let there be no mistake; Charles Barlowe was nobody's fool.

"Thanks for the tip," Anson said. "I'll get to work on them right away."

Mr. Barlowe gave one of his well-bred grunts. "I wouldn't overdo it if I were you. It strikes me that you're a bit off your feed yourself this morning. Relax. It'll all come out in the wash."

What, though? It was what might come out in the wash that troubled Anson most of all. That night he went over the checks Phillip Greene had sent to Anna Jones. Meg had gone to a concert with one of the girls with whom she used to work and he was alone in the apartment with the children. He sat in his shirt sleeves in the small room he used as a study. The children were both asleep. After the shrill, romping confusion that always attended their bedtime, and Meg's hurrying to get to the concert on time, the apartment seemed very quiet.

One by one Anson examined the checks Phillip Greene had written, making notes on a sheet of ruled yellow paper. He wrote down the date on which each check had been issued, the amount of money it called for, and the place in which it had been cashed. It was not the kind of work that ordinarily appealed to him, but this time he was absorbed in it—slowly, check by check, Anna Jones was acquiring something in the way of a personal history. She herself was shadowy as ever, identified only by a labored signature that would seem to indicate only the most rudimentary kind of schooling, but gradually, as he continued to add to his notes, a few facts about her began to emerge.

It was more than two hours before Anson was through with the checks. He slipped a rubber band around them, put the bundle aside, and then considered his notes. Mr. Barlowe was correct—Anna Jones had done a certain amount of moving around. But not in the sense of traveling. What had actually happened, judging from the story told by the checks, was that she had lived, for varying lengths of time, in three parts of the country—Ransome, Alabama; Detroit, Michigan; and St. Louis, Missouri.

So much was immediately clear. The checks themselves were a little more puzzling. At first glance they seemed to have no order or pattern. It was not until Anson spent another half hour with them, making more jottings on a new sheet of paper, that they grouped themselves into three informative sequences.

The first check of the lot, drawn to the sum of $100, was dated September 6, 1919. It had been cashed eight days later, September 14, in Ransome, Alabama, and bore the endorsement of two signatures—that of Anna Jones and, below it, written in an equally uncomfortable hand, that of someone named Cleon Pyle, who apparently was the proprietor of a place called the Farmers Market. The check had been handled by the Ransome Bank & Trust Company, as had fifteen others. On none of these did the signature of Cleon Pyle reappear. Trained though he was not to jump to conclusions, Anson felt it safe to surmise that Anna Jones was at that time relatively unfamiliar with checks and that, upon its arrival, she had taken it to be cashed at a place, most likely in her own neighborhood, where she was well known. It was thirty-one years since Cleon Pyle of the Farmers Market had obliged Anna Jones, and Anson wondered if he was still alive. The tracing agency had best get on his trail immediately.

Going back to his notes, Anson saw that the fifteen other checks handled by the Ransome Bank & Trust Company were each for $250. They came to a total of $3,750 and covered a period of approximately six years. The date carried by the first in the series was January 2, 1920, and the last, September 2, 1925. Looking down his column of figures, Anson saw that Phillip Greene, during the twenty-one-year period in question, had sent a check to Anna Jones three times a year at regularly established intervals: January 2, May 2, and September 2. There were several checks mixed in for smaller amounts and one for $1,000 dated June 12, 1940, but it was plain that Greene was carrying out what he regarded as a fixed obligation.

"It's a dismal thing," Van Buren Bliss had said that afternoon in his office at Duncan & Company, where Anson had gone to pick up the checks. "Damn it, Anson, unless we clear this up, sooner or later it's bound to leak out. You know that as well as I do. There is more gossip in publishing than there is in a small town."

"You don't know small towns," Anson said.

"The hell I don't," Bliss replied, biting on his pipe. "Did I ever tell you the name of the place I came from? It's Blackwing, Minnesota. Both my grandfathers were from the East. One was born in upper New York State and the other in Pennsylvania. They couldn't make it where they were—not well enough to suit them, anyway—and when the big migration came along they went West with it. They were both doctors. One was a good doctor and the other was a drunk. A real one; an honest-to-God heller from way back. And you know what?" He bit on his pipe again. "There was a girl in the Blackwing High School I thought I was in love with. Thought? I've never loved anyone half so much in my life. I was in my senior year then, and I nearly went crazy because her family wouldn't let her go out with me—in my day, and in Blackwing, Minnesota, families had that power. And why wouldn't they? Because of my grandfather Bliss. They still remembered his bouts with the bottle and were afraid that the taint had been passed on to me. So don't tell me I don't know small towns!"

He paused for a moment and then continued: "But publishing, I say, is just as bad. It's inbred as a can of worms. I'm not worried about your talking, or Paul Tarbell, and I think I know enough to keep my mouth shut. The one I'm afraid of is John. He's going to take one drink too many someday, either at his club or at one of those parties he goes to, and surer than hell he'll blow his top. He's worried about what a scandal will do to the firm, just as we all are, and he has a tremendous loyalty to Phil. But more than that, he hates Lucy Wales. I don't mean dislike, or find distasteful, or have an aversion for; I mean hate."

"Why?"

Van Buren Bliss shrugged his shoulders. "As my fourteen-year-old says, you tell me and we'll both know. I think, however, that it involves his idea of loyalty—that among a few other things. John isn't sentimental; in some ways he can be hard as nails. He is generous, though, in that impulsive way of his, and if he happens to like you there is nothing he won't do."

Anson thought of that morning in the duck blind and of that other, later morning when John Duncan picked up the telephone and called Mr. Barlowe.

"Yes," he said, "I know."

"As John sees it," Bliss continued, "he's been unreservedly loyal to Garvin. This isn't for general publication, but there was a time when Garvin put the bite on him for sixteen thousand dollars. That was when he and Lucy decided they wanted that place in Jamaica. Garvin couldn't afford it, actually. His last two books hadn't been successful—*The Stained-Glass Window* sold less than seventy-five hundred copies—and he was pressed for cash. John didn't hesitate about advancing him that sixteen thousand. Phil was all for it too. Looking back, we can say it was the best investment we ever made—we got three best sellers from Garvin in a row, along with our share of the motion-picture money that came in from two of them, plus another cut when *The Night Watch* was made into a play. When John advanced that sixteen thousand, though, he didn't know this would happen. Sure, he was gambling that Garvin would hit the jackpot again, but at the time, with Garvin seeming to be at the end of his rope, just as he is now, sixteen grand was a lot of money to lay on the line."

The more Anson learned about publishing, the more baffling it became. No wonder Mr. Barlowe said that he wouldn't give desk room to any of those literary fellows and that he didn't see how they kept themselves alive.

"But where does Mrs. Wales fit in?" he asked. "You started to explain why John has such strong feelings about her."

Van Buren Bliss found that his pipe had gone out. Striking one of the kitchen matches he carried, he puffed a few times and said, "John is a feeling man. He feels that Lucy ought to be loyal too—it may be unreasonable of him, but he does. He also feels that he's been stabbed in the back. And that it was Lucy makes it all the worse. Garvin's real tie here was Phil; there's no need to explain that to you. It was Phil who kept him going. I mean that, literally."

A new tone had come into Bliss's voice, bearing a trace of solemnity. No one at Duncan & Company ever seemed able to discuss the friendship between Garvin Wales and Phillip Greene without becoming almost reverent. It was something Mr. Barlowe would not have understood, and Anson was not sure he understood it either. Having himself been devoted to Greene, he was not disinclined to sentiment. It did seem to him, however, that the relation between Greene and Wales had been elevated beyond the human plane to the point of sanctification and that, like one of those brittle relics to be seen under glass in the churches of Europe, it had become Duncan & Company's holiest possession—it would not surprise him, he once told Meg, if one day, walking up Madison Avenue, he found John Duncan at the head of a solemn, slow-moving procession in which papier-mâché images of Phillip Greene and Garvin Wales, six or seven times life size, were being carried down the street. "And you would be right in there with them," Meg had replied. "You'd be one of the ones holding up Phil Greene."

Van Buren Bliss was still on the subject. "It might have been possible for Garvin to bring it off without Phil's help, but I frankly don't think so. If ever you read their correspondence, you'll see what I mean. One of the few sympathetic things about Garvin—he's a pretty thorny character, you might as well know—is that he doesn't think he's worth a damn. He never has. Time after time he's threatened to chuck it."

"Who hasn't? What does that prove?"

"Nothing, probably. Unless, as Phil thought, there is a certain kind of humility involved. Writing is a queer business and writers are queer birds. Egocentricity is their principal stock in trade—that and a consciousness of their own genius. The combination occasionally produces some monstrous abnormalities, and there have been days when I've wished I never left the farm, but with anything less a writer can hardly continue. Either he is self-absorbed to the point of neurasthenia or he can't stand the gaff. Look at me. I know. I'm one of those who were shaken from the branch. The publishing offices and the universities are full of me and my kind."

"And Wales?"

Bliss collected his thoughts for a moment. "With Garvin it's the same. He wouldn't be a writer if it wasn't. According to Phil, though, he has no real belief in his talent. He doesn't think that what he has to say is important simply because he is saying it, and he has no dependable confidence in his ability to put it down. And yet, because he *is* a writer, more completely possessed than any man I know, he's caught, wholly and absolutely—all he can do is suffer."

"You make it sound pretty grim."

Bliss nodded. "For Garvin it is grim—more grim than anyone probably knows. There is not much sweetness and light to that man; don't expect to find somebody out of *Puss in Boots*. Being alive is a real torment for him, and it was Phil who made it bearable—if you think I'm exaggerating, wait till you read their letters. Garvin thought he depended upon Phil for editorial advice, of which he received plenty, God knows, but what Phil really gave him was the will to persist. If it hadn't been for Phil, always standing behind him, always encouraging, always willing to live through those suicidal moods that Garvin can work himself into—well, I don't know. It's an extravagant thing to say, but I sometimes have the feeling that it was Phil who kept him alive—what's going to happen to him now that he's blind and doesn't have Phil to depend upon any longer, I don't like to think."

Bliss had worked himself into a spell of depression. He went off into his own thoughts for a few moments and then, rousing himself, said, "But it's John and Lucy we were talking about, weren't we? That part of it is simple—simpler than Phil and Garvin, anyway. John and Lucy belong in the same social bracket and they had a lot in common. Lucy liked partying on Long Island with the Duncans and the Duncans liked visiting Lucy in all those out-of-the-way places that she and Garvin picked out to live.

"John and Garvin got along—no, let's be fair; it was more than that; a genuine friendship was involved—but the important connection there was between John and Lucy. She's not much younger than John, just by ten years or so, and she is, or was, a beautiful woman—it's been so long since I've seen her that I can't rightly say. Anyway, John was attracted to her. How much attracted, I wouldn't know—enough, though, for him to want to have her picture on the wall of his office. It hung there for years. Not, mind you, that I am implying there was anything between them—I don't think there was; I'm simply saying that John was attracted. He made no bones about it, and the bones naturally showed. And if it is a purely physical hold that Lucy has on Garvin, as he now likes to say, I venture the proposition that it is one which he was once quite able to understand."

"Is that her only hold?"

"Only?" Van Buren Bliss gave a derogatory shrug. "Is there such a thing as an only, even in this Freudian age? That she has some particularly strong hold on Garvin seems to be agreed upon by everyone. What it is, however, I'm in no position to say. The truth of the matter is that I am handicapped in talking about Garvin, since I was never part of the inner circle. The man you ought to talk to is Julian Tokar. If you want to know about Garvin, more than John or I or anybody else can tell you, he's your man. You know who he is, don't you?"

"By reputation, yes. Who doesn't?"

"Julian, as you have undoubtedly heard, was Garvin's lawyer for years. There was a break there too, though, and Lucy sent him packing. It seems to happen to everybody. But next to Phil, Julian was closer to Garvin than anyone else. I think you ought to talk to him. As a matter of fact, I'm having a drink with him this afternoon around five and I halfway promised to bring you along."

"I won't be breaking in?"

"Of course not. Julian will be glad to meet you, and he will be even gladder to talk about Garvin—the truth is that Garvin is a kind of obsession with him. You'll probably get tired listening before he is through. But let me finish what I was trying to say about Lucy and John."

"Yes, please do."

"Well, John, as I say, now feels that he has been stabbed in the back, and by a woman he might have once had boyish notions about going to bed with. So the wound is doubly deep. When he calls Lucy a bitch, it's not only because he feels she has been disloyal to the house by bringing this charge against Phil. That's why he's sure to blow off about it before long, and, when he does, Phil's name is bound to come into it. John will be half tight to begin with, and he will try to explain the details to a crowd of bored people who will only half listen, and talk will follow talk, and by the time it gets up and down Madison Avenue a few times Phil Greene will have been shacked up for twenty-one years with a woman named Anna Jones."

Anson put the conversation with Van Buren Bliss out of his mind and returned to his notes. No matter what thread was picked up, it led always in the end to Anna Jones. More and more her importance asserted itself, and the only information he had about her was what could be deduced from Phil Greene's checks. A few things, however, had made themselves clear. From September 1919 through September 1925, Anna Jones had lived in Ransome, Alabama. It was logical to suppose that she had made Ransome her residence for some time prior to 1919, but there was no evidence on that score. It could only be guessed at, not proved. But what else did he know?

Only that Anna Jones had taken her first check to a place called the Farmers Market, which was owned by someone named Cleon Pyle, and that she had herself cashed the other fifteen checks she received during that period at the Ransome Bank & Trust Company. Hers, on these, was the only endorsement.

It was not much to go on—hardly enough even to speculate. All Anson could deduce was that Phil's checks had caused some slight alteration in the manner in which Anna Jones handled her financial affairs. He knew nothing about Ransome, Alabama, other than that the latest atlas said it was a town of 2,657 people, but he suspected that during the years 1919–25 it was a place where $250 represented a considerable amount of money. Phil's first check had been for $100. Cleon Pyle of the Farmers Market could apparently oblige to that extent, particularly if part of the money had gone to wipe out a bill. However, when the second check arrived, calling for a payment of $250, it was seemingly more than Cleon could manage. Anna Jones had to go to the Ransome Bank & Trust Company and present it for payment herself.

Ransome, Alabama. Anson had never been there but he thought he knew how it was. There would be a main street, widening into a macadam highway on both ends of town, and all the business establishments would be gathered into a single block—the barbershop, the hardware store, the café with the neon sign that said EAT suspended above the sidewalk, the dry-goods emporium, the drugstore on the corner, and, on the opposite corner, the two-story building that housed the bank. The dentist and doctor would have their offices above the drugstore, their names printed on the windows in gilt block letters and perhaps under that of the dentist the single word PAINLESS, and the windows above the bank would also be lettered, though not necessarily in gilt, for behind these would be the narrow, whitewashed rooms, smelling of dust and summer, where the town's lawyers saw their clients and prepared themselves against the coming sessions in the courthouse whose red brick tower was the most noticeable landmark for miles around—and somewhere, over twenty years ago, receiving three checks a year from Phillip Greene and taking them to the bank with such regularity that it must have been commented upon (people being people and this being Ransome, Alabama), the shadowy figure of Anna Jones. The tracing agency should be instructed to check with the bank; there might be some teller who would still remember who she was.

Anson went back to his notes. The Ransome, Alabama, phase of

Anna Jones's life had seemingly ended sometime after September 1925. The next check she received from Phillip Greene, dated January 2, 1926, and bearing the cramped signature which by now he would recognize anywhere, had been presented either for payment or deposit at a branch office of the National Bank of Detroit. Once Anna Jones was in Detroit, Anson lost her completely. He could imagine her in Ransome—walking down Main Street; stopping to look at the dresses in the windows of the dry-goods emporium; having a coke in the drugstore; keeping her eyes fixed rigidly ahead as she passed within range of the stares that were turned her way by the idlers in the barbershop—but, once in Detroit, she was swallowed by the crowd.

Was that why she had gone to Detroit—because of the crowd? To be less solitary, less noticed, less marked? Had Phillip Greene's checks anything to do with her leaving Ransome—had there been talk, gossip, scandal? And why Detroit? To work as a waitress; to find employment in one of the automobile plants; to live for a time with some friend or relative?

There was no way of knowing. All he had to go on were Phil Greene's checks and on this score they told nothing. Anna Jones lived in Detroit for four years, from 1926 through 1929. During that time she received fourteen checks from Phil Greene, twelve for the usual three-times-a-year sum of $250, another for $100, and another for $450. The whole amount came to $3,550.

Then, toward the latter part of 1929, she moved again. This time she went to St. Louis. She was still living there when, on June 12, 1940, the trail ran out. On that date she deposited the last check she received from Greene. It was the largest of the lot. It called for a payment of $1,000 and had gone through the channels of the American National Bank. But why so large an amount? Had Anna Jones run into some sudden emergency, or had the $1,000 been in the nature of a final pay-off? And why the change to St. Louis? What had happened in Detroit? What was it that kept Anna Jones on the move? Restlessness? Apprehension? Fear? And if fear, what kind of fear? Who was she and how had her life become entangled with the lives of Garvin Wales and Phillip Greene?

Again there was no way of knowing. In St. Louis, Anna Jones seemed to have been able to settle down for at least eleven years. The third and last sequence of Greene's checks extended over that period. The only other information to be gained from them was that during approximately ten of those years, from January 2, 1930, to September

2, 1939, the $250 which she had been getting three times a year was raised to $350. There were thirty checks for this amount, coming to $10,500. In addition to this, Greene had sent her four others, all in 1940—one for $100, two others for $500, and the big one for $1,000. The dates borne by these were fairly close together—February 5, March 16, April 12, and June 12.

Four checks in four months; $2,100 in all. There was no question that something out of the ordinary had happened. But what? Some mad extravagance that had to be paid for? A serious operation? It was no use even trying to imagine. The checks led to their usual blank wall. The only thing of which he was certain was that no blackmail was involved. A woman doesn't blackmail a man for twenty-one years and then let her victim off the hook. Nor does she disappear. Why, then, had Anna Jones disappeared? Where had she gone and where was she now?

He could spare himself the trouble of trying to guess. Everything the checks had to tell was told already, and what they told, simply, was that it looked bad for Phillip Greene. There was not a court in the world that would not find him guilty. He had withdrawn twenty thousand dollars from Wales's account, there was no evidence that he had been authorized to do so, and he had written twenty thousand dollars' worth of checks to a woman named Anna Jones.

There was one way, though, of cutting through this fog. All that was needed was a statement from Garvin Wales. Let him declare that the withdrawals had been made according to his instructions, and they would have nothing to worry about. It was as simple as that.

CHAPTER NINE

It was actually too simple. A good position was one that could be defended in depth and maintained all along the line. Here it was vulnerable at every point, with no reserve strength anywhere and the whole outcome depending on Garvin Wales. Swayed by John Duncan, Anson had never doubted that Wales would come to the aid of his friend. He was prepared to believe, also, that Wales knew nothing of his wife's letter and that, as John Duncan kept insisting, he would readily admit, once the matter was brought before him, that Phillip Greene had acted with his knowledge and according to his instructions. That, however, was before his conversation with Julian Tokar. It now seemed that John Duncan could be wrong. The possibility had to be faced that Garvin Wales might decline to co-operate and that, instead of coming to Phillip Greene's defense, he might lend his testimony to support his wife's charges.

In which case Anson preferred not to think about it. Phillip Greene would go down as a thief. Mr. Barlowe was already more than half convinced that he was guilty, and should Wales profess ignorance of the matter, or join in his wife's denunciation, John Duncan would also be compelled to question Greene's innocence. So would the others; there would always be that cloud. Furthermore, as Van Buren Bliss had said, they could not keep it from leaking out. Mrs. Wales herself, should Julian Tokar's estimate of her character be correct, would do all the damage possible. "Don't make the mistake of thinking that you are dealing with a woman," Tokar said. "You happen to be dealing with evil in its most absolute form."

Anson, sitting in the quiet of his apartment, felt the same distaste he had felt at the time. That piece of melodrama had best be forgotten entirely. It was he who would have to deal with Mrs. Wales—not Julian Tokar; not John Duncan—and he would be placing himself under a needless handicap by accepting these outside judgments at face value. And yet——

And yet nothing! He didn't want to think about it any longer and he wished Meg would come home. That concert should be over by now. Tired of sitting in one position, he put his notes aside and rose from the table at which he had been working. It was a wooden table of the kind that people used to have in their kitchens before the advent of the porcelain age. Meg had picked it up in a secondhand furniture store on Third Avenue. They used to say that they were going to do it over, but since neither he nor Meg was the sort of person who found any pleasure in doing things over, it still wore the dingy coat of apple-green paint that had been applied by some previous, more ambitious owner.

The room was not big enough to contain much else—an unpainted wooden chair that Meg bought when she bought the table; another and more comfortable chair that used to be in the living room before Meg decided it was getting too shabby to live with; a standing lamp with an inverted bulb that reflected its light from the ceiling; and, in one corner, a metal filing cabinet that Meg had also found on Third Avenue and had been unable to resist because it was such a bargain. Anson had nothing to put in it except some copies of his university's law review and the small, flat albums in which he had pasted up the columns of historical jottings he had contributed to the Pompey's Head *Morning News*, but the metal cabinet had proved of considerable value as a place for Meg to keep her receipted bills, old checkbook stubs, bundles of the Christmas cards that came every year, and various other odds and ends.

That room of his, Meg said, was a mess. He found it hard not to agree with her, but he was unable to agree that what they ought to do was to save enough money and have it done over into a real den. Eugene Hollister had a den in his house in Larchmont, and a den was the one thing Anson was sure he could do without. A den and a plum-colored smoking jacket. The last time they had driven out to the Hollisters' for dinner, Eugene had appeared in a plum-colored smoking jacket and Anson was afraid he had not been able to conceal how dumfounded he was.

"Who let you out in that?" he asked.

It was said before he realized it and immediately he wished he had thought about it beforehand. Eugene took it the way it was intended, but Grace Hollister, who did not like him anyway, gave him a cutting look, and the rest of the evening passed off badly. On the way home in the car Meg said that it was trying enough to have to see the Hollisters even under the best of circumstances, and why he had to make a crack like that the moment he stepped into the door was more than she could understand. She wasn't angry, though, and even giggled a little.

"The look on the poor man's face," she said. "Who do you think he was trying to impress?"

"Nobody," Anson replied. "Gene's all right. He just thinks he has to live up to your friend Charles Barlowe and his idea of how a bright young lawyer should look. It's the junior esquire in him coming out."

"I'm glad you're not a junior esquire," Meg said, sliding closer on the front seat. "Give me a kiss."

Meg was inclined to regard the Hollisters more severely than he. The world of Eugene Hollister was not one in which he would choose to live, but at least it provided Eugene with the illusion of having a place. That was more than he could say for himself. There were times when he felt that he did not belong anywhere, and this was one of the times. He had not felt that he belonged anywhere since he left Pompey's Head. Nor could it be said that he had failed with his group. He had no group. Sometimes he wondered if anyone in New York had. There were circles and cliques in New York, people drawn together by the same profession or a loose collection of momentarily shared interests, as in the case of Meg and the other mothers who belonged to the Parents Club that Boojum and Beejum read papers to, but these were temporary associations at best. The interests were always changing, and the faces with them, and there was always the feeling that everybody you met in New York was just passing through, or else on an extended visit, so that there were times when you had the impression that it was not so much a city as a big, end- less game of musical chairs.

Phillip Greene once remarked to him that although New York was a collection of neighborhoods it was a place where nobody had any neighbors. "Some people say that this is one of the fine things about the city, but I don't think so," Greene went on. "A man wants neighbors. He may want to put a fence between himself and them, but he wants them just the same. The trouble with New York is that it imposes a set of unnatural conditions. Nobody knows any- body, even when they live next door to each other. You can make your home here for fifty years and still feel a stranger. I know I do."

Though Anson was barely acquainted with Phillip Greene at the time, he was surprised to hear him voice a set of feelings that were so close to his own. Greene was one of the people whom he had imagined as being completely at home in New York. It was that conversation which marked the beginning of their friendship, and Anson could never think of Phillip Greene without recalling it.

The time was October 12, 1936—bad though he was at remembering dates, he would always remember that one. He had just passed his twenty-sixth birthday and survived his first ten months at Roberts, Guthrie, Barlowe & Paul. It was a Monday. He remembered it was a Monday because Mr. Barlowe, the previous Friday, had sent for him shortly after lunch. It was only the fourth or fifth time he had been in Mr. Barlowe's office and he was nervous and ill at ease. Mr. Barlowe was signing his mail. He lifted his eyes when Anson entered, said "Oh yes, Page—I'll be with you in a minute" in that preoccupied way of his, and left Anson standing there while he affixed his signature to the rest of the letters before him. He put down his pen and picked up what looked like a box of typewriter paper.

"This thing just came down from Duncan & Company," he said. "It's one of those novels they publish. John Duncan had me on the telephone about it, but I didn't get all he said. I gathered, though, that it's a question of possible libel. Duncan tells me that it's based on the life of one of those hillbilly politicians they have down South and he wants to be sure they won't be in for a suit. He'd like to have an opinion not later than Monday noon. Do you think you know enough to handle it?"

Anson was sure he knew enough, but it would not do to say so out loud. Mr. Barlowe would expect a more tempered reply. His heart missed a beat and he told himself that here was his big chance. He was then still too new to understand that in a firm like Roberts, Guthrie, Barlowe & Paul there was no such thing as a big chance and that your whole future depended upon the skill with which you handled a number of routine chances that were deliberately thrown your way. It was just like the Army. You had a record and everything went into your record, and it was your record, at the end of a year's time, that decided whether or not you cleaned out your desk. "We school them," Mr. Barlowe once said, "and then we see how they take their jumps." Later, looking backward, Anson realized that his period of schooling had come to an end, and that Mr. Barlowe had decided it was time for him to show how he took his jumps. It was just as well that he did not know it at the time. He would have been more nervous than he was. Even so, his thinking that this was his big chance caused him to take longer to answer than Mr. Barlowe considered necessary.

"Well," Mr. Barlowe said. "Do you?"

"Yes sir. I think so."

"Good. I'm going to drop the whole thing in your lap. Mrs. Barlowe and I are going down to Virginia for a few days and I won't be back until Tuesday. You'll have to handle it direct—John Duncan knows you're going to. The man you're to see up there is a fellow named Phillip Greene. Everything straight?"

"Yes sir. I think so."

"And, Page."

"Yes sir?"

"You needn't be so damned judicious. It's not going to hurt you to speak up."

"Yes sir. I'll remember."

It embarrassed Anson to think that he had once been so gawkish in Mr. Barlowe's presence that he had to be told to speak up, and it was only slightly less embarrassing to remember how anxious he was not to miss his big chance. Nowadays, with his acquired skill, he would be able to go through a manuscript of that length in an evening; then it took him the whole week end. He went over the manuscript word by word, accumulating mountains of notes, and then pecked out a long opinion on a portable typewriter he was buying on time. It was nearly midnight on Sunday before he was through. He was then living in a one-room apartment in Waverly Place, just off Washington Square, and somebody was having a party on the floor above. He could hear voices and laughter, and above them a phonograph playing, and now that his mind was no longer occupied, he wished he had a party to go to—he also wished he had a girl. But over and above everything, even his wish for a girl, was his determination to succeed with the assignment that had been given him. His whole future seemed to be hanging in the balance and he had to make a good impression on Phillip Greene.

In Greene's office the following morning, however, just before the lunch hour, his labors of the week end appeared to have been wasted. Phillip Greene barely looked at the report, which Anson had asked one of the girls in the office to retype. "I told John he had nothing to worry about," Greene said. "This isn't *actually* based on anyone's life. You shouldn't have taken so much trouble."

Anson tried not to show his disappointment. It would have been hard for him to say what he had expected, but he had hoped for more. Phillip Greene, who had been standing when Anson entered his office, and who had remained standing throughout, dropped the report on his desk. Anson knew his reputation as a great editor, but he certainly didn't look like one. Nor had he ever seen such a small, cluttered, disorderly office; you would think that a great editor would be able to do better than a room that wasn't much larger than his own office down at Roberts, Guthrie, Barlowe & Paul. As he stood waiting to be dismissed, Greene, looking at him steadily, said:

"What did you think of it? Did you like it?"

Anson stared at him dumbly.

"Did I like what?"

"The novel. You're from the South, aren't you? Did it seem right?"

Anson had never been asked to give his opinion of a manuscript before and he was not sure if it was expected of him now. The promotion had been too sudden. A moment before he had been a young man from Roberts, Guthrie, Barlowe & Paul, hardly more than a messenger boy if the truth be known, and now, without any warning, he was being asked to tell what he thought about a novel. Something, however, had to be done—he and Phillip Greene could not stand there looking at each other forever.

"Why, yes sir. I suppose so."

"Suppose?" Greene's eyes did not move. "Don't you know? What was wrong?"

"Nothing, I guess."

"You *guess*? Something was wrong then. What was it? What didn't you like?"

This was as bad as a session with Mr. Barlowe, Anson thought. In some ways it was even worse. Mr. Barlowe didn't mind coming down on you right and left, getting you so mixed up that you could hardly think straight, but he never became this worked up and intense.

"Well," he said, "I don't want to be critical——"

He paused, hoping to hear Phillip Greene say that that was what was expected of him, to go ahead and be critical, but Greene plainly had no intention of obliging. Forcing himself to continue, he said:

"Well, that part where the hero, the politician—I suppose you'd

120

call him the hero—that part where he has dinner in the home of the girl——"

"Yes?"

"It wouldn't happen."

Phillip Greene's face took on a different expression. His eyes widened as if with surprise, and then, narrowing, became more sharply piercing than before. He leaned forward, craning his neck a little, and said:

"It wouldn't *happen?*"

"No sir." Anson shook his head. "The girl's family wouldn't have it. Not then. They would probably not object too much after he is elected governor, although they might, but before that, right in the midst of the campaign, when he's still this country redneck—well, if they are the kind of people the author says they are, that snobbish, they wouldn't have him in their house. They'd think up some excuse. It wouldn't happen, that's all."

Phillip Greene stood motionless, still with his neck craned forward, and then nodded gravely.

"You're right," he said, speaking in a low, intimate tone for which Anson was hardly prepared. "It wouldn't. That's one of the things the author will have to change. It didn't seem right to me, either. It didn't *sound* right. I'm glad to know you agree."

They stood facing each other. After his brief venture into friendliness, which Anson thought he might already be regretting, Greene seemed to have rushed back to the recesses of his own secret world, locking the doors as he went. In most cases one sees and judges a man in an instant, taking in the shape of his features, the hang of his body, and the flavor of his personality all at once, and Anson was always to remember Phillip Greene as he appeared at that moment, his tired blue eyes shining with a kind of repressed intensity, and his whole person giving off an impression of solitariness that set him apart from other men. A truly private person, Anson thought. A good man, surely.

"But you *liked* the book," Greene said doggedly. "You *did*, didn't you?"

"Yes sir, I liked it."

"And you thought it was good?"

"Yes sir, I thought so. Some parts I liked better than others——"

"Some parts?" Greene's eyes narrowed again. "What seemed to be wrong, other than what you've said about the girl's family, I mean? If you didn't like it *all*——"

Anson was about to say that that was not what he meant, that he had not said he didn't like it all, when John Duncan stepped into Greene's office. He wore a pair of gray slacks and a rust-colored tweed coat and carried a bundle of proof sheets. Except for the proof sheets, he looked as though he might be on his way to the Cassava Gun Club. He said, "Hello, Phil. Hello, Anson," speaking in the hearty, outdoor tone he sometimes affected, and then, addressing Anson directly, added, "They told me at your office that I'd find you here. Is it all right for us to publish that book? We won't get sued?"

"No sir, Mr. Duncan," Anson said. "You won't get sued. It's a good book. I enjoyed reading it."

"You hear that, Phil?"

Phillip Greene nodded and, much to Anson's surprise, sat down at his desk. John Duncan gave no sign of finding anything unusual in such behavior. Disregarding Greene, he said:

"But that's not all I wanted to talk to you about. Mrs. Duncan just called me on the telephone. She wants to know if you can join us for dinner and the theater tonight."

"Why, yes sir. I'll be glad to."

"Fine. I was afraid you might not be free. Mrs. Duncan has some fluff of a thing on her hands, the daughter of a college chum of hers, and she finds herself in need of a young man. But not just any young man. I was given specific instructions to get hold of you."

They might not have been there so far as Phillip Greene was concerned. He was absorbed in a manuscript. Trying to match John Duncan's matter-of-fact air, Anson said:

"I'll have to remember to thank Mrs. Duncan. What time, sir?"

It was plain that this was something that had come up all of a sudden and that John Duncan had not been able to give it much thought. Creasing his forehead, he said:

"Since Mrs. Duncan has tickets for the theater, we'd better get an early start. We're staying in town this week, so why don't you meet us at our place around seven? That ought to give us time. There's one other thing, though."

"Yes sir."

"Mrs. Duncan wants to know if you'd mind picking the lady up?"

Like any other young man of twenty-six, Anson had certain reservations about picking up girls he had never seen.

"No sir," he said. "I don't mind."

John Duncan looked at him and gave a knowing grunt. "There isn't much you could do about it, even if you did, is there? This is what you get for making such a good impression on my wife. Anyway, the young lady is named Margaret Whitman and she has an apartment somewhere on East Forty-eighth Street—I'll give you her address later. Mrs. Duncan tells me that she works on one of those newsmagazines and that she is exceptionally pretty—remember, though, that that's my wife's opinion, not mine. I wouldn't want you to hold anything against me."

"I won't, sir."

Anson liked seeing John Duncan. In all of New York he was his only tie with Pompey's Head and almost his only friend. At least they shared a few memories together—the Cassava Gun Club, the smell of the marshes, the way the ducks came over just after light.

"These proofs of Bob's," John Duncan said, turning to Phillip Greene. "Have you seen them? Has he any idea of how much resetting is involved?"

Greene slowly looked up from the manuscript he was reading.

"It's all right," he said in what Anson thought was a bored, almost annoyed tone. "It'll be a better book."

"But why can't he better his books in manuscript?" John Duncan demanded. "Why does he have to wait until they get in type?"

A pained look crossed Phillip Greene's face.

"It's his way, John. You can't interfere with an author's way."

There it was, Anson often thought later; there was the reason for the loyalty and devotion with which Phil was rewarded; you could not interfere with an author's way. But that was later, after a friendship of almost fourteen years; it was not the forenoon of October 12, 1936, with an unknowing young man reporting to Duncan & Company on instructions from Mr. Barlowe and listening to a conversation he did not altogether understand. He could tell, though, that John Duncan did not think much of what Phillip Greene had just said. John Duncan started to reply, decided against it, and went on wrestling with whatever it was that bothered him.

"All right, all right!" he said finally. "Far be it from me to interfere with an author's way! These changes will bring him way over his allotment, but I suppose that's all right too—just so long as we don't interfere with an author's way! Come on, Anson. I'll see if I can find that girl's address."

Anson followed him to his office, which, unlike Phillip Greene's, looked the way it should look, and waited until John Duncan found the address for which he was searching. It was written on the back of an envelope which he uncovered beneath a sheaf of letters that were apparently waiting to be answered. Since Mr. Barlowe always cleaned up his mail before eleven o'clock, Anson was surprised to see them there. It was obvious that things were arranged differently uptown, and that the procedure at Duncan & Company was not the same procedure that applied at Roberts, Guthrie, Barlowe & Paul.

"See you tonight around seven, then," John Duncan said, handing the envelope over. "Don't dress. I'm sorry I can't ask you to lunch."

"Oh, that's all right, Mr. Duncan. I have to hurry back anyway."

There was no reason for him to hurry, and he had already planned to eat somewhere in the neighborhood, but he knew that John Duncan was a busy, important man who could hardly be expected to ask him to lunch. It was nice of him just to mention it. He did not like the idea, though, of going to some drugstore alone. He had accepted the fact that his life in New York was going to be different from his life in Pompey's Head, where there was never any question of finding someone with whom to pass the time of day, but even after nearly a year in New York the lack of companionship was still hard to get used to.

Walking toward the elevator, he caught up with a slim, light-haired girl with a sensitive, well-bred face who nodded pleasantly as he went past. She was one of those young women whom he had come to associate with this part of New York, trim and confident and expensively groomed, and, nodding back, he thought how nice it would be if he could have lunch with her. The sight of Phillip Greene, who was waiting for the elevator with his thumbs hooked in the pockets of his vest, put all such notions out of his mind. It wouldn't do for it to get back downtown that he had gone to Duncan & Company and tried to make a girl there in broad open daylight. Not that Phillip Greene gave any indication that he would have noticed. He gave off such an air of absent-mindedness that he seemed almost in a trance. He looked at the girl, who had ventured to call attention to her presence by means of a faint, tentative smile, and then looked at Anson.

"Hello, Mr. Greene," Anson said. "I'm just leaving."

Greene looked at him vacantly, still with his thumbs in the pockets of his vest, and Anson wished he had not spoken. He had not meant to be forward or to pretend that he and Phillip Greene were on friendly terms, and yet that was the way it probably sounded. That girl would think he had been trying to play up to Greene and had been royally snubbed. Why didn't the man have the decency to say something, and why didn't that elevator come on down?

In the building on Fifth Avenue that the firm then occupied, the offices of Duncan & Company were serviced by a pair of small, grill-work elevators, on the order of iron baskets, from which you could see the swaying cables that dangled on both sides. The first car went by without stopping, giving off a wheezing, creaking sound, and the second dropped halfway past before its operator thought better of it and decided to return. He opened the doors with a loud "Down! Down!" a sullen-looking man with a flat, fleshy face and an untidy shock of thick gray hair, and Anson saw that the car was already crowded. The girl edged her way into it, causing the other passengers to shift their positions, and Anson waited for Phillip Greene to precede him.

"You first, Mr. Greene," Anson said. "After you."

Greene entered the elevator without replying.

"For chrisake!" the operator said to Anson. "You think I got all day!"

He spoke under his breath, out of one corner of his mouth, but Anson was sure that everyone had heard. There were no two ways about it—this was the rudest, surliest, most ill-mannered town on the face of the earth, and that fellow ought to have his face slapped. He was the one to slap it for him, too; one more unpleasant word out of him and he would get what he was asking for. Except, of course, that he knew he wouldn't. This was New York, not the Oasis in Bugtown, and a fine thing it would be if it got back to Roberts, Guthrie, Barlowe and Paul that he had punched one of Duncan & Company's elevator operators in the nose. But one thing was certain. He could be as disagreeable as any of them; if that's what they wanted, that's what they'd get! One thing, however, he failed to take into consideration—he was still in the elevator. When finally it stopped—the operator banging the doors open and calling out "Ground floor! Ground floor!" as though he loathed the sight of it—Anson moved aside to make way for its women passengers. The girl who had got on just before Greene slipped past him with a lowered sidelong glance, and then, before he knew it, everyone was hurrying out ahead of him with the exception of Phillip Greene. It was largely his own fault, since he had managed to render himself more or less helpless by getting wedged in a corner behind the operator, but there he was, just as if he had never been in an elevator before, and there Greene was, staring at him in that bemused, exasperating way. There was nothing to do but admit defeat.

"After you, Mr. Greene."

Considering how antagonistic he felt, he was surprised at how

125

meek he sounded. Greene looked at him, moved forward, stopped, gave him a second look, and stepped from the elevator. Walking into the busy corridor, he waited in a manner that Anson interpreted as an invitation to join him. He was anything but sure about it, however. More than half suspecting that he was falling into another booby trap, he said warily:

"Yes, Mr. Greene?"

"That book we were talking about——"

"Yes sir?"

"If you didn't like it all——"

"But I didn't say that, Mr. Greene. All I meant was that I liked some parts better than others. I liked the hunting and fishing parts especially. I thought they were fine."

Greene's whole expression changed. "Yes, they are fine, aren't they?" he said. "They're full of the right *feeling*. And what you said before, about the girl's family not having that fellow to dinner—that won't be hard for the author to change. It's the only really wrong thing in the book. Once the author takes care of that——"

It appeared at last to dawn upon him that this was no place for a quiet conversation. He looked around as if noticing his surroundings for the first time. He said, "I wonder——"

"Yes sir?"

"If you have nothing else to do—I mean, if we could find time to talk further about that book——"

Anson suddenly realized that he was being asked to lunch. It was not the usual sort of invitation, but he had already decided that Phillip Greene was not a usual sort of man.

"I'd like to, Mr. Greene," he said. "I'd like it fine. Where shall we go? I'm a stranger in this part of town, you know."

"I am too," Greene said. "*Everybody* is. But there's a place on Fifty-third Street——"

"It sounds fine, Mr. Greene. Thank you, sir. I was wondering what I was going to do with myself for lunch, anyway."

The place on Fifty-third Street was a small Italian restaurant where Greene lunched regularly. There was room for only a dozen or so booths, along with a small bar, and the walls were covered with those homesick murals that Anson had come to accept as part of the standard equipment of all such establishments. These little restaurants always seemed very insubstantial to him, tied to New York by the slenderest kind of mooring, and he never went into one without thinking that, if left to the pull of its own particular gravity, it would rise above the city and float back to whatever Italian town or village it was that the proprietor had come from. The present proprietor, a small, balding, voluble man in a shiny dinner jacket, hurried from his station behind the bar, which apparently he presided over, and showed Greene to his table. Greene, Anson noticed, seemed embarrassed by the effusiveness with which he was greeted; he slipped into the booth almost furtively.

"And to drink, gentlemen?" the proprietor said. "What will you have to drink?"

This being a special occasion, Anson decided to have a cocktail before lunch. It was the first time he had broken his rule against it since coming to New York. By the time coffee came around he began to realize that, whether because of the cocktail, Greene's questions, or the intimacy of his surroundings, he had done a considerable amount of talking about Pompey's Head. There was not much he could do to remedy the situation, however, and he had just started telling the story of chief Tupichichi and his daughter Mary.

"What then?" Greene said. "What happened?"

Well, Anson said, this Indian girl, Mary, who was supposed to be quite beautiful—there was an old painting in the Pompey's Head Historical Museum that was supposed to be a portrait of her, and for an Indian girl she was really quite attractive—this girl Mary, as he was saying, picked up English so readily that she became Sir Samuel Alwyn's interpreter. This didn't keep her from being a real Indian girl, though. The young men of the colony used to have foot races, and Mary always raced with them. With just a single outside garment and nothing underneath. She used to wrestle that way too. You would think that after all these years it would have stopped being a scandal, but it had not. Mary finally married one of the colonists, a man named Christian Bottomley. There were no longer any Bottomleys in Pompey's Head, but there was a family named Carpenter that was descended from them, and he knew a girl, Gaby Carpenter, who to this day had to sort of apologize because of the way Mary used to race and wrestle. Actually, it was said that Christian Bottomley *had* to marry her. The story was that Sir Samuel, after one of those wrestling matches, personally saw to it that he did. There was no proof of that, though, absolutely none, and it just went to show how long a piece of gossip was remembered in a place like Pompey's Head.

In later years Anson often wondered how he could have been that young. There were times when he was tempted to tamper with reality, and because it was so easy he sometimes did, seeing himself as more confident, more relaxed, more self-assured, but in the end he was always forced back to the truth. There was no way out of it—much as he would like to have it otherwise, he had been just that young. He did not think, however, that he had been objectionable. It was true that he had gone to Duncan & Company wanting to make a good impression, feeling that his whole future was involved, but after the first few minutes at lunch he completely forgot it. He could tell that Greene did not care one way or the other about his being a representative of Roberts, Guthrie, Barlowe & Paul, and so, with that shift in emphasis, there was no reason for him to concentrate on putting his best foot forward. He honestly did not think he had been objectionable. The worst that could be said of him was that he had talked too much and that he must have seemed extremely young.

"But how is it that you are so informed?" Greene asked. "Do you have a special interest in history?"

"Yes sir," Anson said. "I suppose you could call it that. Everybody down home has, in a family sort of way, and when you grow up hearing all those stories, like the one about Mary and Christian Bottomley, you find yourself wanting to know more about them."

Phillip Greene nodded. "Yes, I can see that you would. I used to hear stories too. None of them was as interesting as this Indian girl of yours, though. In my part of the country, they wouldn't be. Tell me—do you write?"

"Write?" Anson said. "Me? No sir. I'm trying to be a lawyer."

For an instant Greene looked as though he wanted to smile. He said, "Yes, I know. But with this interest you have, this knowledge, I would have guessed that you had been tempted to try your hand at writing. It's no vice, you know, even for a lawyer."

He again looked as though he wanted to smile. Anson, not liking to think he was being a source of amusement, said, "It all depends on what you mean by writing, Mr. Greene. I used to do a column for our local newspaper."

Greene's interest brightened, and it began to be plain to Anson that all this man really cared about was writers and writing.

"What kind of column?"

"It's hard to say. It wasn't anything like these columns you have in New York, if that's what you mean. We have this historical society down home, the one I was telling you about——"

"Yes?"

"Well, after I was old enough, by the time I went off to the uni-

128

versity, I was permitted to use its library. We had a law review, and one of my professors thought I should write for it. I was interested in colonial law at the time—pre-Revolutionary law, to be exact—and that summer, when I went home, I started going through some of the old papers in the society's library——"

Anson never once imagined that the day would come when he would be telling a New York editor about how he happened to start writing his column for the *Morning News*. He did not feel self-conscious about it, though, and he did not think Phillip Greene was simply making conversation. It was getting late, however, and he still had Mr. Barlowe to consider; if ever it was rumored that he had bored Phillip Greene all through lunch by talking about himself, there might be all sorts of adverse consequences. Against this, however, stood the fact that he was enjoying talking about himself. He would have to take his chances with Mr. Barlowe.

"One day I happened to come across three letters that Lafayette wrote to General Carvell," he continued. "The general is one of our big heroes. He was in command at the Battle of Little Pigeon Marsh, and we have a statue of him in one of our squares. Anyway, nobody knew about those letters from Lafayette. They had been tied up in a bundle of old legal papers by mistake."

"And you found them?"

"Yes sir, I did. I was pretty excited at first—I guess I naturally would be—but they turned out to be fairly unimportant. Lafayette had been given a bounty of land in our state and he wanted the general to tell him how to go about selling it. He also said he had the gout. Look, Mr. Greene—are you sure you're interested in this?"

"But of course I'm interested," Greene said. "Why shouldn't I be? Lafayette's having the gout makes him come alive, a real human being—most of these great historical figures are all so dead. And I should think that you would have been rather pleased with yourself. Did you do anything with the letters? Did you write anything, I mean?"

"Yes sir, that's what I'm coming to. I told my father about them, and the next day he happened to see his friend, Mr. Joe Birke, the editor of our local paper, the *Morning News*. That night Mr. Birke called me up and asked me to write something about the letters. He must have liked what I wrote because he printed it almost the way I sent it in. A few days later I ran into Mr. Birke on Bay Street—that's our main street—and he asked me to walk to the paper with him. He said that the historical association was probably full of things that the public didn't know about, things of general interest, and asked me if I would like to do some more stories."

"And finally it turned into a regular thing?"

"Yes sir, that's about what happened. After I graduated from the university and started practicing law, I did a column three times a week. 'Old Pompey' it was called. That's how Pompey's Head is known down home. Nobody ever calls it by its full name."

"It sounds like a fine place," Greene said. "Why did you leave?"

Here it was, the inevitable question. But much as he had come to like Phillip Greene, Anson had no intention of answering. Someday he might be able to tell why he left Pompey's Head, and even make it into something bright and entertaining, but not now. Not for a long time. Perhaps not ever.

"I guess it's the same old story," he said. "I imagine I just wanted to get away."

Phillip Greene did not seem to be convinced. For a moment Anson thought he was going to be pressed for details, but, instead:

"Those columns," Greene said. "Are they the only writing you've done? You've never tried your hand at a novel?"

"Oh, no sir. I couldn't write a novel."

"How do you know?"

"I just do, that's all. I feel that if I wanted to, or had anything like that in me, it would have made itself felt before now. All I ever wanted to be as a writer was a local historian. That would have suited me fine. I know it doesn't make me sound very ambitious, but until I came North I don't suppose I was."

"And now?"

Anson nodded. "Yes sir, I'm ambitious. I'd like to succeed in what I'm doing. And someday, if I can find time, I'd like to get back to my interest in history. I once wrote an article for the law review that I called 'The Shinto Tradition of the American South.' I know it sounds presumptuous, and I don't mean it that way, but I always thought that I would like to take some of my ideas—I guess it's all right to call them my ideas—and develop them further into a book. That's just one of those notions, though, and I don't imagine I ever will."

Phillip Greene looked at him and finished his coffee.

"I'd like to see some of your writing," he said. "Suppose you send me copies of those articles you did for the law review. And some of your columns too."

Anson didn't know what to say.

"Well, if you really mean it——"

130

Phillip Greene nodded and reached for the check.

"I really mean it. It's part of my job. I hope we can lunch together again."

Anson could never think of that day and that conversation without also thinking that under normal conditions a man's life was all of a piece. There were bound to be a few loose ends, threads that could not be fitted in anywhere, but except for these it made a whole design. He went on a visit to the museum with the rest of the eighth grade, getting himself paired off with Olive Paxton when he wanted to be paired with Midge Higgins, and his feet were set on a path that eventually would lead to a restaurant on Fifty-third Street and the beginning of his friendship with Phillip Greene.

The ancients were right to imagine the Fates as weavers, he thought. There was a warp and a woof and always some design. He knew that there were men who planned their lives, setting their sights on a determined goal, and it sometimes troubled him that his own life appeared to have been so largely governed by chance. A visit to the museum with the eighth grade and a morning with John Duncan in a duck blind—it was easy to imagine the weavers at work. Take away either the one or the other, the museum or the duck blind, and it was inconceivable that he would be where he was. He would not have been given his desk at Roberts, Guthrie, Barlowe & Paul, he would not have made friends with Phillip Greene, and he would not have married Meg. For she too was part of the pattern. He met Meg the same day he had lunch with Phillip Greene, just a few hours later—"And if you were honest," Meg once said, "you would admit that meeting Phil was more important. I was simply a chore you had to perform."

There was just enough truth in Meg's remark to make him feel uncomfortable. All that afternoon, after his lunch with Greene, he had to force himself to work. He could not forget what Greene had said about wanting to see some of the things he had written. Although he knew it might be held against him, especially since Mr. Barlowe was away, he went to Mr. Guthrie, for whom he was also doing some work at the time, and said he would like to leave early. Mr. Guthrie was a small, paunchy man with a bald head and a round pink face. According to those who hold that personality is determined by bodily structure, Mr. Guthrie should have been a jolly, twinkling man with a cheerful word for everyone. Instead, he was sour, sarcastic, and full of impatience. He said, "Do I look like a housemaster,

Page? I hope to God not. If there is something you have to do, go ahead and do it."

Long ago though it was, Anson could remember it clearly. He had to rush—riding the subway to his apartment and bundling up the things for Greene; hurrying to get the package into the mail before the branch post office on West Tenth Street closed at five—but he made it in time. Then, afterward, with the sweet taste of freedom sharpened by the knowledge that it was a weekday afternoon and New York somehow a warmer, friendlier place, he sat on one of the benches in Washington Square and read the newspaper in the late autumn sunlight before returning to his apartment to get ready for his date.

He was still thinking about Phillip Greene when he reached the building on East Forty-eighth Street in which Meg had her apartment. A uniformed doorman wanted to know if he was expected, and he still had the customary reservations about a blind date. He imagined, too, looking back on it, that before he saw Meg he had been a little put off by her being a career girl. He had been in New York long enough to have decided that career girls were not like the girls in Pompey's Head. He supposed they were brighter, and certainly they were more ambitious, but he did not think they were as much fun. He doubted that this date that John Duncan had got him into would be much fun. That, however, was before he saw Meg. The moment she answered his ring everything began to take on a more promising look.

"Hello," she said, standing framed in the doorway in a black silk dress. "I'm Meg Whitman and I suppose you're Mr. Page. Come on in. If you want a drink, there's some ice and whisky on the table. I would have mixed us a cocktail but I didn't have time."

She smiled at him and he smiled back and it was pleasant merely to be in the same room with her. She was the prettiest girl he had seen in a long time. More, though, than merely pretty. There was a fresh, intelligent look on her face, an air of alertness that was concentrated in her clear blue eyes, and he could tell that behind her smile she was coming to a cool, calculated appraisal of him, chalking up his good points and ticking off the bad. Noting that her head came hardly to his shoulder, he saw that she was standing in her stocking feet.

"Don't be alarmed," she said. "I do own a pair of slippers. It's just that I haven't put them on."

"You don't need any help, do you?"

It came out of its own volition, bubbling from the rush of well-being he felt, but immediately he wished he had not been so impulsive. He always kept forgetting he was not in Pompey's Head. Joe Ann Williams or Gaby Carpenter would have taken it for what it was, understanding that it was just a thing to say and that he was not trying to be fresh, but up here in New York it was different. Say something like that to a Northern girl, and instead of laughing it off or saying, as Joe Ann might, "All right, but just below the ankles, remember," immediately you were put in the position of making a pass. He waited to get slapped down, but, instead, dryly:

"Out in Indiana we get helped with our slippers only on the second date," Meg said.

Anson was so relieved he had to laugh. "I didn't mean to rush things," he said. "When's the second date?"

She had not expected that, he saw. It took her a little off balance. He was still playing it according to the relaxed rules of Pompey's Head, and the rules were obviously different in Indiana. What she had just said was contrary to the ones she had grown up with, most likely a sign of her determination to be emancipated from them, and he should have been perceptive enough to understand. Her face became sober for a moment, and he felt that this time he had done it for sure. Again, however, he was offered a reprieve. Gazing at him steadily, but with a different, more calculating look in her eyes, she said:

"I never have to work on Tuesday and Wednesday nights."

It was now his turn to be at a disadvantage; one thing about this girl, he thought—she was certainly quick on her feet.

"Tomorrow night is Tuesday."

"No, not tomorrow."

"Wednesday."

"No, not Wednesday either."

"Next Tuesday then?"

She leveled her eyes at him, coolly appraising as before, and then, smiling:

"Sure. Why not?"

That was the way it happened. Meg opened the door in a black silk dress and they walked into each other's lives, and it would be a long time before he ever forgot October 12, 1936.

That large milestone even marked a change in his relation with Mr. Barlowe. Toward the end of the following week, after he and

Meg had their second date, Mr. Barlowe sent for him again. Mrs. Waggoner, Mr. Barlowe's secretary, told him to go right on in. Mr. Barlowe was sitting behind his desk, and although his greeting was no more cordial than usual, he did seem less Olympian—for one thing, he asked Anson to sit down. He explained that one of the publishing houses was buying out the textbook department of another firm, and said that he wanted Anson to do the groundwork for him—sales figures, copyrights, outstanding obligations, and all the rest of it.

"I need some help around here," he grumbled. "I can't do everything myself."

There never had been a time when Mr. Barlowe did everything himself, as Anson well knew, but since Mr. Barlowe had descended far enough to the ordinary human level to pretend that he needed a moment's sympathy, it seemed advisable to go along with him—"Yes sir," Anson said. Being young and inexperienced, and almost totally ignorant of the ways of business, it was not until the interview was over and Mr. Barlowe had said in a careless fashion, "You seem to have made quite an impression the other day up at Duncan's. Keep up the good work," that he understood that Mr. Barlowe had decided to put him in the way of another chance. His feeling of elation was such that it must have showed in the way he carried himself. Mrs. Waggoner, who occupied a small office that adjoined Mr. Barlowe's, looked up from her typewriter, and then, as their eyes met, she gave him a friendly nod—Mr. Barlowe must have said something about it to her too.

Anson's elation persisted throughout the day. Wanting to share it with someone, he thought of calling Meg at her office. In the end, however, he decided against it. When put into words, it did not sound like much, and Meg might not understand. Only he could appreciate it properly. He had managed to acquit himself creditably the day he had lunch with Phillip Greene and word of it had found its way downtown—he had taken his jumps without a fault and Mr. Barlowe was not going to whistle him off the course. In retrospect it was easy to see that he owed it all to Phil, just as he owed so much else. It was Phil who had given him his first leg up, and now Phil was dead, unable to defend himself. This damnable thing had happened, coming out of nowhere, and Julian Tokar had caused the prospect to appear darker than ever before.

CHAPTER TEN

Lighting another cigarette, Anson, sitting at the desk in his room in the Marlborough, turned to the notes he made after his meeting with Julian Tokar and Van Buren Bliss. They were relatively few. Interesting though the conversation had been, it had resulted in little more than adding to the background. What stood out most clearly was that Tokar's bitterness toward Mrs. Wales was greater than that of anyone else.

Tokar was waiting for them in the men's bar of the Ritz. Van Buren Bliss, catching sight of him at a table on the far side of the room, lifted a hand in greeting as he and Anson hung their hats and topcoats on one of the old-fashioned racks that stood near the door through which you entered from Madison Avenue—so that, Anson thought, was Julian Tokar. It would not do to stare, however, and he had time to note only that Tokar had either just returned from a hot climate after an extended visit or else had an uncommonly dark complexion, when, having followed Bliss across the room, which was already crowded even though it was not yet five o'clock, he was being introduced, trying to conceal his surprise at Tokar's excessive height.

It was curious, he thought, that he had never heard it mentioned. He had been told of Tokar's library, of his small but impressive collection of modern art, and of his penthouse apartment overlooking Gracie Square and the East River. No one, however, had ever considered it worth mentioning that the man stood at least six feet four. Anson observed that it took a certain amount of ingenuity for him to fold himself back into his chair, but there was no trace of the awkwardness that is common to most people who have been overgenerously endowed in the way of height. Like his inherited fortune, it was something to which Tokar had plainly learned to adjust.

"I'm drinking rum," he said. "It sounds appalling, I know, but I've developed a taste for the stuff. Besides, I like to pretend that I'm still basking on the beach at Montego Bay."

Van Buren Bliss said, "Just don't rub it in, that's all," and then, to Anson, "What'll you have? We'd better order before the mob gets here." He passed on their wants to the waiter, a bourbon and water for Anson, a scotch old-fashioned for himself, and turned back to Tokar. "How's Molly?" he inquired. "I don't have to ask about you —you've never looked better. How was the trip?"

Anson was glad to be omitted from the conversation. It gave him a chance to fit himself into his surroundings and to have a closer look at Julian Tokar. The men's bar of the Ritz and Tokar rather complemented each other, he thought. He himself was a stranger here and always would be, despite the protective plumage that enabled him to fade effortlessly into the background, but it was plainly a part of Tokar's natural environment. It was as fitting for him to speak regretfully of the passing of the Ritz, which, it had been announced, was going to be torn down and replaced by an office building, as it was for him to mention the improvement that a new management had worked at the Metropolitan Opera. New York City was his own special place, identified with his family for five generations, and, like all born-and-bred New Yorkers of whatever station, he had developed a set of highly personalized responses to its various stimuli—Anson could not imagine him anywhere else.

"And so you got to the Caymans?" Van Buren Bliss was saying. "But why? Why the Caymans of all places?"

"Stamps," Tokar answered. "When I was a boy I used to collect stamps. Now I'm trying to collect a few of the places they made me want to see. You don't believe me? Wouldn't you like to go to a place called Grand Cayman? Or Ascension? Or the Cook Islands?"

"No, I wouldn't," Bliss said. "I think stamps are a lot of damned nonsense and I have yet to lay my eyes on Rome."

Anson regarded Tokar with renewed interest. He was sure that in his own circle Tokar had a reputation for being amusing. It went with the rest of him, part of the impression created by his long frame, his expressive hands, his simple yet elegant dress, his rather triangular head with its dark skin, narrow nose, and flat, thin mustache that emphasized the strong, firmly delineated lines of his mouth. It even went with his small, exclusive stable of clients—theatrical people, musical people, literary people, artistic people of all kinds. They would require more of their lawyer than brilliance; it would be regarded as essential that he also be amusing.

"All horsing aside, Julian," Van Buren Bliss said, "what made you go to the Caymans?"

Tokar lifted his eyebrows in mock surprise. "Why can't you believe what I say? I've wanted to visit them for as long as I can remember. We had to drive to Kingston for the day, and I went into the Myrtle Bank for a drink. There was this Englishman there, a young fellow, one of those odd-fish Britishers you sometimes run across, and he told me that he'd started an airline from Kingston to Grand Cayman—which, as you wouldn't have to be told had you ever collected stamps, is the largest of the Cayman group. Although Molly didn't think much of the idea, I said why not? I'm pushing sixty now and the chances are that what I don't do soon, I won't do."

"I feel sorry for you," Van Buren Bliss said. "You've had such a sedentary life."

"When Garvin lived in Jamaica," Tokar continued, "we always talked about going to the Caymans. A few New England whaling captains finally dropped anchor there—quite a number, as a matter of fact—and Garvin thought he'd like to do a book. We never got there, though. Garvin was all for it, but Lucy wasn't, as it should not be necessary to say, and so we never got off. Having the Caymans in my system, I decided to get them out. And I'm glad I did. It was a beautiful trip and the beach on Grand Cayman is absolutely one of the most beautiful in the world. But that's enough about me. I don't think I'm giving away any secrets, Mr. Page, when I say that I hear you are having your troubles—what can I do to help?"

The transition was so abrupt that Anson was taken unprepared. He had been thinking that the Cayman Islands sounded like a wonderfully unspoiled place, reminded of the time when he wanted to go to Burma to gather the seeds of wild plants, and his immediate impression was that already he was encountering a set of attitudes with which he had become familiar—affection for Garvin Wales, hostility toward Mrs. Wales. Wondering how much of the situation Van Buren Bliss had divulged, he said:

"I don't exactly know, Mr. Tokar. I hadn't thought."

"This is the way it is, Julian," Van Buren Bliss interjected. "Something has come up—something pretty serious, I might add—and Anson is going South to have a meeting with Lucy."

"What a pleasant prospect," Tokar said, looking at Anson. "You don't know how much I envy you."

"Of course," Bliss went on, "the matter ought to be handled by Garvin. In the end it will have to be, since it's something that only he can straighten out. You know the way things stand, though, and unless Anson manages to get to Garvin through Lucy——"

Tokar, addressing Anson, said, "They do make you earn your keep, don't they? Did they think to tell you that you were being asked to do the impossible? I hope you'll see fit to at least treble your fee."

"Never mind that," Bliss said. "The point is this—Anson, not knowing Lucy or Garvin, has been asking me questions that I don't know enough to answer. I thought it might be helpful for him to talk to you. So, if you don't mind——"

"Mind?" Tokar said. "I'm flattered. What is it, Mr. Page, that you'd like to know?"

Confronted with the question, Anson did not know how to answer. What should be done, of course, was to take Tokar wholly into his confidence. He was not yet prepared, however, to go that far.

"It's hard to say," he ventured. "Ordinarily, under normal circumstances, this whole thing could be cleaned up with a telephone call. Here, though—well, everything is being made more difficult by Mrs. Wales. It may sound unfair, but that's the way it seems."

Tokar shook his head. "No, Mr. Page, not seems—*is!* You have been hearing about Lucy from John Duncan, I imagine, and to a lesser extent from Van, and you're probably wondering if she is nearly as black as she has been painted. If it's contrary evidence you're after, I'm afraid you've come to the wrong man. You see, Mr. Page, I know Lucy Wales. John Duncan thinks he does, and Van has been able to pick up enough gossip to imagine he does——"

"That's where you're wrong," Van Buren Bliss broke in. "I know better than that."

"But with me it's different," Tokar continued. "I've seen Lucy in action. Not once, not twice, but dozens of times. May I give you a piece of advice? I don't know what's come up, and just to make everybody comfortable I'd like to say that I would prefer *not* to know, but if it's Lucy you have to contend with, as Van says, don't make the mistake of thinking that you are dealing with a woman. You happen to be dealing with evil in its most absolute form."

Anson felt a stab of annoyance. That kind of talk got you nowhere. And the fact that Tokar had neither raised nor lowered his voice from its conversational level—that he had practically thrown the line away, as they said on the stage—put a sharper edge to his displeasure. The casual, almost indolent delivery was apparently part of the technique of being amusing. Anson could see Tokar arranging his elongated frame near one of his pictures, a Léger or a Juan Gris or a Miró, standing with a cocktail in his hand and saying to a select group of guests, "Lucy Wales? Believe me, I know that woman—if, that is, woman she may be called." Under the spur of his annoyance, Anson found himself half wanting to defend Mrs. Wales. John Duncan, Van Buren Bliss, and now Julian Tokar—an outsider might easily conclude that she was being ganged up on.

"That's a pretty strong statement, isn't it?" he said.

Julian Tokar nodded affably. "Yes, a very strong statement—it was intended to be. I think you will discover for yourself, however, that Lucy Wales lends herself to strong statements. And if, as I suspect, you are thinking that there must be a considerable amount of bias involved, the answer is why yes, there is. I wouldn't like to pretend otherwise." He smiled pleasantly and finished his drink. "As I said, Mr. Page, if it's a favorable character reference you want for Lucy, I'm afraid you've come to the wrong man. She had me thrown out of her house, which was a blow to my pride, and she destroyed a friendship that I valued most highly." He crossed and uncrossed his legs, getting them out of the way. "I must say, though, lest you think that I am more prejudiced than I am, that I don't hold her entirely responsible—the real damage was done by Garvin. After seventeen years I expected more of him. Lucy, unfortunately, is not the whole story. I thought Garvin might have stood up—not for me, but for himself. Everybody else was gone. I was his last chance. But Lucy commanded and he obeyed. He didn't even want not to obey. That was the distressing thing, to see the utter coward he'd turned into."

Van Buren Bliss, who was filling his pipe, said stonily, "You do go in for strong statements, don't you?"

"Yes, I suppose I do," Tokar agreed, looking around for their waiter. "But so far as Garvin is concerned, I am not interested in evasive ones. The trouble is that you people at Duncan's have always been under the shadow of Phil Greene—you can't admit certain truths about Garvin because, if you do, they are bound to reflect on Phil. What was the point of that long-suffering selflessness of his, it would have to be asked, if Garvin turned out not to be worth it?"

"Oh, what the hell, Julian!"

"There you go again." Tokar's voice was touched with impatience. "Why do you fellows always feel that you have to run away from the fact that Garvin has turned into a moral weakling? It doesn't lessen his stature as a writer, such as it is, and it is not going to interfere with his sales. Nobody is going to write a piece for the *Saturday Review*."

"Yes, but——" Van Buren Bliss said.

"But what?" Tokar countered. "That it's all the fault of Lucy? It's there that we part company. It makes a dramatic statement to say that she is destroying Garvin, but what about Garvin himself? He didn't have to let Lucy do what she's done to him. It's not as if he had no say in the matter. Don't you see?"

"No, I don't see," Van Buren Bliss said. "I'm damned if I do. What's the mystery? What's her hold?"

Tokar, signaling their waiter, said, "How about another round?" and then, after the waiter had come and gone, speaking without haste or excitement, "It's not only *her* hold, Van," he said. "It's Garvin's hold too. The truth of the matter is that it's like a situation in one of Garvin's own books, a theme to which he has often returned—two people joined together, not by love, not by affection, not by children, not even by habit, but by hatred—a deep, abiding, mutual hatred."

"*The Night Watch*," Van Buren Bliss said.

Tokar nodded. "*The Night Watch, The Last Man Out*, the whole middle section of *The Alien Sky*. You don't have to be an analyst to know that it has preyed on Garvin's mind. What's behind it, though, I don't know. I have my own theory, since it's something I have often thought about, but I am not prepared to argue its validity. However, if you go back to the beginning——"

"How did it begin?" Van Buren Bliss asked. "All I have to go on is hearsay. I never was on the inside, you know."

The waiter returned with their drinks and Tokar reached for his glass. "Neither was I, not at the beginning. Garvin was already a rich, famous man when I became his lawyer—not so rich, though, or so famous that he had time to forget his origins. That which is generally forgotten about Garvin is that his father was a sharecropper. That which is called the destructive element in his writing stems, as I see it, directly from that—to me, if not to what I think is called the new criticism, it's a seeking of revenge. Along with being works of the imagination, his books are also exercises in hate." He took a swallow of his drink, held it for an instant in his mouth before downing it, and looked at his glass. "When I first knew Garvin, as I say, he was already rich and famous, living at those crossroads where art and money meet—there was one winter in New York, so help me, when I wondered if he and Lucy knew anyone who had less than a million. But Garvin still remembered who he was—remembered, and hated it. He'd been done some hurt—one of those hurts from which a man never recovers—and he was unable either to forget or forgive."

Anson remarked the change that had come over Julian Tokar. All the artificiality of his earlier manner was gone; he was now speaking with a quiet thoughtfulness, wholly indifferent to the effect he created. Anson did not know where he was leading, or precisely what relevance any of this had to the matter in hand, but this, in any case, was a somewhat different view of Garvin Wales. Sipping his drink, he gave his attention to what Tokar had gone on to say.

"And then Lucy—young, beautiful, touched with the glamor of the stage." He paused in contemplation. "Marriages may be made in heaven, but this one, at least in part, was made by Garvin's desire to destroy his background. We mustn't forget Lucy. She was a terrible actress, unbelievably so, but she was gorgeous to look at and she had appeal—I know; I responded to it myself; you could feel it coming across the footlights." He lifted his glass and took another swallow. "And the curious thing was that although it was a purely visceral appeal, at times downright whorehouse if I may say so, Lucy herself was unmistakably a lady. A Devereaux; one of *the* Devereauxs; the very embodiment, to Garvin, of all the social graces. You can see what a prize she seemed."

"I can also see," Van Buren Bliss said, "that you hate her through and through."

Tokar rejected the charge with a shake of his head. "No, Van, you're wrong. Not hate. There are some feelings that go deeper than hate. And you? You don't exactly love her, do you?"

"No, but when you say——"

"Say what?" Tokar asked. "That Garvin was blinded? That he was carried away? What's so farfetched about that? There was Lucy, a Devereaux, young, beautiful, eminently desirable into the bargain, and there was Garvin, riding high on that tremendous first success of his, a war hero as well, but still the son of a cropper—still hating his background; hating it all the more, perhaps, because of Lucy. Has it ever occurred to you that none of his heroes has a childhood, not one, and that there has been an act of repression all along the line? That sort of thing isn't accidental. It has to stem from something."

Van Buren Bliss, looking thoughtful, puffed several times on his pipe. "There are traces of what you say in some of his letters to Phil."

"Traces?" Tokar reached for his glass again. "I rather suspect that Garvin was more forthright with me on the subject. We had one or two conversations I shall never forget. It was apparently his assumption that I, being a Jew, might be expected to have some comprehension of those circles that lie beyond the pale." He drank, set down his glass, and untangled his legs. "One of the things I learned from my association with Garvin is that all inferiority feelings are alike. They leave the same kind of scar. With Garvin, though——"

Van Buren Bliss waited for him to continue. "Yes?"

"With Garvin they never healed," Tokar said. "They were always running wounds. And what he did not realize was the advantage he was handing over to Lucy. If she had been a French countess or an Italian princess, the cards might not have been quite so stacked against him—Lucy knew what being the son of a cropper meant. When she needed it, it gave her the whip hand."

"Why did she marry him, then?" Van Buren Bliss asked. "It doesn't case out."

"Oh, but it does," Tokar said. "For one thing, Lucy was head over heels in love with him—she was still in love when I first knew them, five or six years after their marriage. Lucy wasn't always the person she is now. Obviously, certain things were latent in her, perhaps more than merely latent, but whatever she's done to Garvin, the fact remains that he has done things to her too—not kind things, either."

Tokar paused for an instant, gathering his thoughts. "You have to remember, too, that Garvin, from any woman's point of view, was also quite a prize. Those photographs of him don't lie—he was every bit as handsome as they say. Moreover, he was at one of those high points that come in an attractive man's life. He had his success, and you could tell that it was no passing thing. It was plain that he was not going to be one of those one-shot Johnnies who make a lucky strike and then spend the rest of their lives trying to repeat. Then, too, there was that RFC uniform—let's not forget that. There was one other thing too."

"What was that?" Van Buren Bliss asked.

"Lucy's ambition," Tokar said. "Let's not forget that, either. She could have stayed down South, being Lucy Devereaux, and for most women in her station that would have been enough. Lucy, though, wanted more than that. Not only did she want what is wanted by every woman who gravitates toward the stage—applause, attention, adulation—but, and to my mind much more significant, she wanted to break away from the closed, provincial society in which she had been reared. Would you agree, Mr. Page?"

"About what?"

"That Lucy's wanting to be an actress represented a kind of wholesale break with her past?"

"Yes, I'd say it was a break. How wholesale it was, though, I wouldn't know."

Tokar gave one of his friendly nods. "You're right. Wholesale is hardly the word. For one thing, Lucy never forgot who she was, nor the people she came from, and she also found it advisable to retain at least a trace of her low-country accent. Incidentally, I find it rather charming."

It never failed to happen. Once the South came into a conversation and it was learned or remembered that you were from that part of the country, people always tried to say something agreeable. It was a commendable display of good manners, but it didn't always work. Although nobody intended to be superior, it invariably tended to sound that way, and, much as you didn't want to get your back up, you found yourself asking what it was that they had to be so superior about.

"It's just the way people talk down there," he remarked. "I suppose it's the Gullah influence."

"I'd like to talk with you about the Gullahs someday," Tokar said. "The natives who live in the back country of Jamaica speak a language which I am told greatly resembles Gullah. I made some tape recordings of it. I don't want to get started on that, however, nor do I want to bore you with a long, probably incorrect analysis of Lucy Wales."

"But you can't stop now," Van Buren Bliss said. "What's the rest of it?"

Tokar took another swallow of his drink and set down his glass. "What I was trying to say, I believe, was that Lucy was drawn to the stage, not only because she had a certain liking for glitter, but also because she wanted more than a conventional way of life—the one, I imagine, implies the other."

"Well," Van Buren Bliss commented, "if that's what she wanted, she certainly got it."

"Yes, but not on her own," Tokar said. "It was Garvin who gave it to her. Oh, I'm not saying that Lucy married him with that in mind, or that it was a piece of coldhearted calculation—as I see it, the larger part of calculation, if there was any, was most probably

143

on Garvin's side. But given a woman of Lucy's cleverness—given any woman, for that matter—and she is bound to look beyond the altar. It was Lucy's misfortune not to look far enough, that's all."

"I seem to be lost," Van Buren Bliss said. "What do you mean?"

"I mean Garvin," Tokar replied. "He wasn't that kind of man. The sort of life that appealed to Lucy was the one that suited him least. He indulged her for a time—quite a long time, actually; almost fifteen years—but eventually he'd have no more of it. He wanted out and he got out. That's when he bought his place in Jamaica. He had his work and that was enough."

"But for Lucy it wasn't?"

Tokar wrinkled his forehead. "Do you have to ask? Of course it wasn't. It so happens that Lucy is not one of Garvin's admirers. She regards his books as a malicious attack on all the things which, as a Southern lady, she holds in highest regard. And the older she gets, the more she reverts to type. She may have thought that she wanted more than the ordinary conventional life, but she doesn't think so any longer. It wasn't Garvin's idea to buy that island down South, it was hers. Is it too much to see it as a kind of returning to the womb?"

"The plot gets thicker and thicker, doesn't it?" Van Buren Bliss said. "Pretty soon it won't be able to spoon."

Tokar ignored the comment. He said, "Lucy put up with Garvin's work—or, better, she was able to control her feelings about it—as long as she was able to reap the rewards of being a great man's wife. Then almost overnight the dividends stopped. So did her patience. There is quite a lively society in Montego Bay, especially during the season. Garvin would have none of it, however, and Lucy found, possibly to her surprise, that without him she was not nearly so much in demand —an extra woman past forty rarely is."

"And now she's paying Garvin back in kind?" Van Buren Bliss said incredulously. "Since he kept her from her friends, she took her revenge by keeping him from his? Is that what you are trying to say?"

Tokar reflected for a moment. "No, I don't think so. I'd find it hard to believe that it was as deliberate as that. And again, if I may say so, you are placing the whole of the blame on Lucy. It's an easy thing to do, since she seems to have gone out of her way to invite it, but what about Garvin? Doesn't he belong in the picture? I go back to what I said before—he didn't *have* to put up with her. Plainly, he wanted to. In the beginning, before they turned against each other,

I suspect that the answer is not hard to find. Sex had its hold, along with the tenderer emotions, and there was also the fact of Lucy's being the symbol of all the social graces. But during these latter years, now, today——" Tokar spread his hands. "The only answer that I can find is that Garvin hasn't the will to break away, that he doesn't want to, that he can't." Then, turning to Anson, he said:

"But none of this has helped you very much, has it, Mr. Page? You are probably thinking that all I have said is that human nature has a disconcerting way of being human—which, as a lawyer, you already know. In Lucy's case, however, to go back to her for a moment, it has become inhuman. There is this thing that is driving her—more, certainly, than a wish to punish Garvin for denying her the fashionable world—and it has caused her to do things that even the most charitable person would have to call abnormal. Not being that person, not even wanting to be, I call them evil. Her forcing Garvin to break with Phil, for instance. Only an evil woman would have done that. But enough of me and my opinions. I'm ready to be your witness if you like. Any questions?"

Addressed so directly, Anson had to speak. "Yes, Mr. Tokar," he said. "I do have a few questions. First, though, without bothering you with any of the details, I'd like to explain that Mrs. Wales has brought certain charges against Phil Greene. They won't wash, that I can assure you, but we naturally don't want them aired in court. What I would like to know is this—did Mrs. Wales have any specific grievance against Phil, one that might cause her to want to do him damage, even though he's dead?"

Tokar hesitated before replying, weighing his thoughts. Anson felt that it had suddenly become like a game of chess. He had moved, and now it was Tokar's turn, and although theoretically they were both on the same side, neither of them wanted to take any chances.

"Let me put it this way," Tokar said. "Phil was Garvin's best friend; he was also his editor, the man to whom he looked for help and advice. That, in itself, so far as Lucy is concerned, would have been grievance enough. Whether or not there was anything else, I'm in no position to say definitely. Do you mind if I tell you a story? It might be a better answer to your question than anything else."

"No, of course not."

Tokar finished the rest of his drink. "This was a little more than seven years ago, shortly after Garvin moved to that island of his. It was just before he started having trouble with his eyes. He was all tangled up in his own feet, a usual thing when he is writing a book, and Phil had gone down there to help straighten him out. It was about this time of year, March, and I'd been fishing off the Florida keys. On the way back North, I decided to look in on Garvin. I had become his agent by then as well as his lawyer, and the movies were nibbling at that old flop of his, *The Stained-Glass Window*. Why, I don't know. That was Garvin at his fourteen-year-old worst, and I don't know any other fourteen-year-old who can be so excruciatingly bad."

Van Buren Bliss, looking solemn, said, "There were some good things in that book. You can't condemn it all."

"I don't see why not," Tokar replied. "I say it was bad, embarrassingly bad, and I am not the least bit interested in those adolescent fantasies that Garvin was having in his middle age. But have it your own way. Someday, though, you publishers are going to realize that a few 'good things' are not enough to make a book."

Seeing Bliss's worried expression, he gave a short laugh. "Cheer up, Van. Things are not that bad. But as I was saying, I decided to stop off on my way back to New York to see Garvin—it would have been easier had he been living on the West Coast. I had first to fly from Key West to Jacksonville, where it was necessary to spend the night and half the next day before I could get another plane, on one of those little hop-skip-and-jump lines, to a place called Pompey's Head."

"That's my home town," Anson said, thinking it best to make the fact known before Tokar said something that might prove embarrassing. "I grew up there."

Tokar cocked his head and looked at him. "You don't say. You must know that island of Garvin's pretty well, then?"

"Yes, I do. I used to go fishing there."

"Well, you must admit that it could be an easier place to get to," Tokar said, "especially if you're coming from the keys. It's a nice little island, though, I must say that for it. Have you seen the house that Garvin's built there?"

"No, I haven't. I've been away for nearly fifteen years."

"What do you catch down there?"

"Nothing big. None of the game fishes. Weakfish, channel bass, sheepshead——"

"But what happened?" Van Buren Bliss said. "Now that you've arrived, what happened?"

Tokar reached into the inside pocket of his coat and took out a silver cigarette case. Flicking it open, he offered a cigarette to Anson, saying in a tone of detached reminiscence, "I got there at a bad time. Phil Greene, as I've mentioned, had gone down to help Garvin with his book. I knew he was there, but it never occurred to me that I would be intruding." Taking a cigarette from the case, he slipped the silver container back into his pocket. "Garvin, who never stood on show, liked to have his friends drop in whenever they could. Besides, I was still on good terms with Lucy. I took it for granted that I would be welcome as usual."

Van Buren Bliss said, "And weren't you?"

"Hardly. I'd telephoned from Jacksonville to say that I was on my way, and it was Lucy, as a matter of fact, who took the call—looking back, I don't think she sounded particularly cordial, but, as I've mentioned, there was this nibble from Hollywood, and Lucy, daughter of the Old South though she is, was never the one to be disinterested in the possibility of a sale. I might even go so far as to say that she has a real fondness for money. She said she'd meet me at the airport."

Anson watched the play of expression on Tokar's face. A faint shift of its muscles, particularly the little ones about the eyes, had left it looking older and infinitely more grave. What he was telling, Anson realized, was being told without relish; it had never been polished into one of his "stories." What most engaged Anson's interest, however, was the fact that Phil Greene had never once mentioned his visit to Tamburlaine Island. To get there he would have had to go to Pompey's Head, and considering that he knew that it was his, Anson's, home town, it was strange that nothing had been said. Anson was convinced that it was not mere forgetfulness; it seemed more likely that the experience had been so painful that Greene wanted to suppress it. Lighting his cigarette, Tokar said:

"Since Lucy promised to meet me, I expected to find her at the airport. I should have known, after I waited half an hour, that the wind was blowing the wrong way. The thought never occurred to me, however, and so finally I hired a taxi to take me to the island. It is joined to the mainland, as Mr. Page knows, by a couple of bridges and a long causeway across those salt-water marshes that you find in that part of the country. I still remember that my bill was six dollars. There was no meter in the cab. It was a flat six dollars."

"It used to be two," Anson mentioned.

Tokar pulled in on his cigarette. "Haven't you Wall Street lawyers heard what the Democrats have done to the currency? Things are rough all over. Anyway, I reached the island and paid my six dollars. It was a fine afternoon, with a fresh breeze blowing—I remember thinking how brisk it was after the heat of the keys. But let me get on. The door, when I arrived, was opened by a Negro butler. He told me that Phil and Garvin had gone for a walk on the beach. Lucy, he said, wasn't feeling well; he said that she was in her room, lying down."

Tokar drew in on his cigarette again, letting the smoke drift from his nostrils. "Not having anything else to do, and not wanting to stay in the house, I decided to stretch my legs. I headed for the beach, which is only a few yards from the house, but then, not wanting to break in on one of those soul-searchings that Garvin used to indulge in whenever he saw Phil, I thought better of it. There is a grove of pines on the island, and I went for a walk in them, instead. I hadn't gone far, not more than fifty yards or so, when I picked up the sound of voices. Or, rather, of a voice. It was Garvin's. For all the difference it made, he might have been standing five feet away."

Pausing, Tokar turned to Van Buren Bliss. "This island of Garvin's is about a quarter of a mile long and a little less across," he said. "It comes to a point at one end, and Lucy and Garvin have built a little teahouse there, right on the beach. I imagined that Garvin and Phil had just come from it. Ordinarily I would have called out, letting them know where I was, but I immediately understood that they were having no ordinary meeting—'You've got to understand, Phil,' I heard Garvin saying. 'It's the last thing you can do for me.'"

Tokar shook his head. "My only thought was to get the hell out of there. I knew that I was listening to a conversation I was not supposed to hear and I didn't want to hear any more of it. But I couldn't get away fast enough. 'I owe more to you than I owe to anybody,' I heard Garvin say to Phil, 'but I can't see you again. Lucy says she'll leave me if I do. God help me, I can't do anything about it!'"

Tokar compressed his lips. "That was enough for me. I tiptoed away as fast as I could. If my bags were not in the house, and if I hadn't let the taxi go, I wouldn't have lingered a moment longer. I wanted no part of it. Under the circumstances, however, all I could do was to retrace my steps and start walking down the beach. I could see Phil and Garvin coming in my direction. What I wanted them to think, of course, was that I'd just arrived."

Anson could visualize it clearly. He could see the stretch of white, narrow beach, the dunes like a line of weedy breastworks, and behind them the dark trunks of the pines, and he could imagine the three men walking on the sand. Tokar said:

"I hope I'll never have to go through anything like that again.

148

They wanted to see me the way they wanted to see the hangman. We trudged back to the house in absolute silence. Phil went inside, still without saying a word, and I stood on the beach with Garvin. 'Phil has to get back to New York right away,' he said. 'Robert is off for the day, and Lucy isn't feeling well, and I wonder if you'd mind driving him to town?' I said I'd be glad to, and Garvin went into the house. I walked around the garden, looking at the various camellias that were in bloom—Lucy's made quite a collection of camellias, if that adds anything to the picture—and how long I waited, I don't exactly know. It seemed forever, but it couldn't have been more than ten or fifteen minutes. Then Phil came out alone. The Negro butler followed him, carrying his bags."

"And Garvin?" Van Buren Bliss asked.

"I didn't see him again until I drove the car—a Lincoln, Lucy's— back from the station. It was still about six or seven hours before Phil could get a train to New York, and I knew he didn't have a reservation, but the station was where he said he wanted to go. That's all he did say, too, until just before I dropped him off. Then, as you'd expect, he ran true to form. 'It's a great book that Garvin is writing,' he said. 'It will be the best thing he's ever done.' "

"Except that he never finished it," Van Buren Bliss commented glumly. "You know it's been abandoned, don't you?"

"Yes," Tokar said. "I'm not the least surprised."

"You think he's done for, then?"

"Yes, Van, I'm afraid so," Tokar said. "It hurts me to say so, but that's what I believe. I've always held that Garvin was incapable of writing a book without Phil, and I see no reason to change my mind. And don't forget Lucy, either. A more sympathetic woman might be anxious to help, but if she were a more sympathetic woman she wouldn't be Lucy. It's impossible for me to imagine her being heartbroken should Garvin never publish another line. She has all the money she needs, and feeling as she does about his work, why should she want to make it any easier for him? But let's not get off on that again. If I'd realized that I'd be windjamming this long, I wouldn't have started. I feel I ought to apologize."

Van Buren Bliss said, "I don't think any apologies are necessary, Julian. But tell me this. Why is it that you have never let on to anyone of this before?"

"For what reason?" Tokar asked. "To be objectionably knowledgeable simply because I happened to overhear a conversation that I wasn't supposed to hear? No, thank you. But now it's different. Since

Lucy is acting up again, and since Mr. Page asked me if she might have a grievance against Phil, I feel obliged to tell what I know."

Anson said, "You think she has, then?"

"Only to the extent that I have indicated," Tokar replied. "Beyond that, I know nothing. Any more questions?"

Anson said, "Yes, Mr. Tokar. Let us assume that this situation can't be straightened out; then let us further assume that Mrs. Wales insists on taking it to court. She has her husband's power of attorney, as you know, but in this instance she will not be able to proceed without his consent—the suit will have to be brought by him, not her."

"It comes to the same thing," Tokar said. "When you say him you mean her."

"That's what I'm getting at," Anson resumed. "I take it, from what you've said, that Mr. Wales will most probably go along with her, even if it could conceivably result in considerable damage to Phil. Is that correct?"

Julian Tokar, looking at him closely, said, "I'd rather not predict. I haven't seen Garvin in a long time, and what the present situation is I don't know. My feeling, however, is that Garvin is not likely to oppose her any more now than in the past. It's certainly nothing that I would count on. Anything else?"

"I'd like to know something else," Van Buren Bliss said. "What happened when you saw Garvin again?—after you drove Phil to the station, I mean."

Tokar's face again took on its detached look. He said: "I think you know that part of the story, Van. That was when Lucy kicked me out. There isn't much else to tell. I'd made up my mind, by the time I returned to the island, that I was not going to spend the night. I'd had a good vacation and I didn't want it to end on that kind of note. It had been soured enough as it was.

"When I got back to the house, Garvin was in his study, sitting near a big window that looks to the sea. The moment I stepped in I could tell that he had been drinking heavily. He didn't give me a chance even to sit down.

" 'You think I've been a bastard about Phil, don't you?' he said.

" 'Garvin,' I said. 'Please leave me out of this. What's between you and Phil is between you and Phil. I don't want to know anything about it.'

"He didn't seem to hear me. 'Bastard is a compliment,' he said. 'If I had any guts I'd shoot myself. But I had to do it, Julian. I had to.' "

Tokar was silent for an instant. Then he said, "I'd known Garvin in the good days. I could remember the way he used to be. And to see him like that, broken, split down the middle, even then going blind—well, never mind. I could tell, though, that he was beyond my reach. Beyond mine or anybody's. The best thing I could do was to get out of that house.

" 'All right, Garvin,' I said. 'If you had to, you had to. I just would prefer not to know anything about it, that's all.'

"He wouldn't let it be, however. This thing was eating him, clawing at his bowels, and he couldn't leave it alone. 'There was no other way, Julian,' he said. 'You've got to believe me. I couldn't do anything else, as Christ is my judge! Lucy would have left me if I hadn't sent Phil away.'

"Then, suddenly, I had enough—enough of his begging for sympathy, enough of his crawling to Lucy, enough of the coward he'd turned into. All that he owed to Phil, all those years of friendship, and for what! To have him turn Phil out of his house because Lucy threatened to leave him if he ever saw him again! I boiled over, I'm afraid.

" 'For God's sake, man!' I said. 'Don't you see what you are doing to yourself, what you are letting Lucy do! Doesn't anything mean anything to you any more? Do you intend to break with all your friends, one after the other, Phil above all, simply because Lucy——'

"And then Lucy came in. She had been listening all the time. Another charming trait of hers, I might explain, is that she's developed a tendency to eavesdrop. I'd often heard the expression 'to strike terror,' but that was the first time it ever became real. She looked at me in that deadly way of hers, loathing the sight of me, and I could feel the terror striking. It was like a blow on the heart.

" 'You dirty Jew,' she said. 'What do you mean, inviting yourself here and invading our privacy? Send him away, Garvin. Tell him to go away.' "

Tokar shook his head, smiling ironically. "Curiously, once my fright was over, I wasn't surprised. I knew that sooner or later it had to happen. There was a time when I too might have been a little in love with Lucy—why blink it?—but I never really trusted her. Garvin, though—from him, as I've said, I expected more. But he had been given his orders and he obeyed. She told him to send me away, and he did.

"So that was that. I'd been his friend—not nearly so good a friend as Phil, but still his friend—and that was the way it ended. I asked the butler to call a taxi and waited out front with my bags. I spent the night in Mr. Page's home town. It was the only good thing that came out of the trip. I discovered a wonderful old place called the Marlborough Hotel."

PART THREE

CHAPTER ELEVEN

Anson's thoughts had come full circle—Julian Tokar had spent the night at the Marlborough and he might have slept in this very room. Gazing through the window, Anson could see the thin white steeple of St. Paul's Church rising above the foliage of the trees that grew in Monmouth Square. As he looked at it, part of his mind still preoccupied with Tokar's account of his last meeting with Garvin Wales, and another part, less active, straying back to those scrubbed, cassocked Sunday mornings when he used to sing in the junior choir, the clock in the steeple, which he could not see from this distance, began to strike nine o'clock. Ian Garrick would be getting to his office presently and the day's work could be postponed no longer. The time had come for him to walk down Alwyn Street, to meet what had to be met, and to learn what the passing of fifteen years had done to Pompey's Head.

When he left the hotel, the morning was clear and fine. Walking toward Monmouth Square east on Independence Street, on which the Marlborough stood, he thought that this part of town looked much as it had always. Like all men who leave the places in which they are born, Anson had often imagined himself returning home. He entertained his most vivid fancies, however, long before he left Pompey's Head. There was a time during his high school days when his greatest ambition was to gather the seeds of wild plants in Burma —for over a year his mind was filled with images of shining temples, Buddhist priests in saffron robes, the riot of jungle and the glare of snow, and himself, mounted on one of those tough, shaggy ponies of the sort he had seen in photographs in the *National Geographic*, toiling up a mountainside in a dangerous region where few adventurers had ever been before. Why the seeds of wild plants in Burma, he would still find it hard to say, unless it was no more than a desire for untrammeled freedom and a vague yearning for romantic places, but in that pageant of fancy he would always see himself coming home again—five, six, seven years later—limping slightly because of an old injury suffered when his pony lost its footing and rolled over on him, tanned by the sun and burned by the wind, walking down the streets of Pompey's Head, still blinded a little by the dust of wonder that had got into his eyes.

Nothing could match that outburst. In later years he continued to think about going back to Pompey's Head, especially during the wartime stretch when he was in London, but after his return from Burma even the best of home-comings seemed pallid and tame. Whenever he imagined himself returning home, it was always much as it was now—he would be walking down one of the streets on a bright spring morning, and nothing would be greatly changed.

Taking Locust Street after he crossed Monmouth Square, where the azaleas were blooming at the base of the granite shaft that had been erected to the memory of the soldiers and sailors of Pompey's Head who had died in the War between the States, Anson walked three blocks north to Alwyn. The house where he was born, his grandfather's house and his father's, was now two blocks away. Locust Street was also as he remembered it—the same trees, the same sunlight, the same early morning stillness—and as he turned off Locust into Alwyn he could feel his heart beat faster. He deliberately maintained an even stride, ticking off the names of the families who used to live in the houses (the McCrackens, the Millers, the Jerrolds, the Whites), and when he crossed the corner of Alwyn and Myrtle, his corner, he knew that he had reached the heart and core of everything. He saw the gray limestone steps of the old house, looking rather dingy against the soft, warm color of its faded brick, and then he saw the house itself—there was a small printed sign in the window of what used to be the front parlor; Rooms, it said.

Prepared though he thought he was, he was not prepared for that. He knew it was not their house any longer and had not been for years, but he had always imagined that some other family would be living in it, keeping it up and being fond of it because it was now their home. He had not expected it to seem so run-down and shabby, although all it needed was one of those "touchings-up" his mother used to talk about to make it look good as new, and never had he thought that he would find the garden wall torn down and a tin-roofed garage, large enough to hold several cars, standing where the garden used to be.

It was not finding the garden that hurt the most. He thought of old Henry and his hatred of weeds, and of his grandmother Page who worked over her flowers until the day before she died at eighty-one, and it was useless for him to tell himself that this sort of thing happened to everybody. A garage with a tin roof stood where the garden used to be, and the wood of the trim around the door and windows was showing through the grimy, flaky paint, and a sign in the dusty window of the old front parlor said Rooms—he had come to a final uprooting and he would never be able to think of it as home again.

But at least it was over. He had a price to pay and now it was paid in full. He walked away, taking a single backward glance, and by the time he turned the corner of Malvern Street and came to the house the Blackfords had rented when they moved from Mulberry, he was able to observe his surroundings again. The solid, unbroken row of three-story brick houses reminded him of some of the streets in London, and the Blackford house looked just as it had when Wyeth and his family were living there. In those days, however, the house on Alwyn Street was always the better kept of the two, since the Blackfords were renting from the Pettibones, and Mr. Pettibone, as everyone knew, never did anything to the properties he owned unless he absolutely had to. It was still Malvern Street, however, and except for the difference between morning and afternoon, this might easily have been the time in February 1931 when he had dropped in to give Mrs. Blackford the camellias he picked at Mulberry. Mrs. Blackford was his godmother, and he thought she would like to have them. The Blackfords had moved to town only the autumn before, and Mrs. Blackford, who had gone to Mulberry as a bride of seventeen, was still unhappy over having to leave it.

With Wyeth and Mr. Blackford it was different. They enjoyed living in town. Mr. Blackford, who was not doing anything at the moment but who, according to Anson's father, hoped to get some political appointment or other, said it was a blessing no longer to have to keep pouring money into that old, drafty place, and Wyeth, who still used Mulberry whenever he went hunting or fishing overnight in that neighborhood, curling up on a blanket in one of the downstairs rooms or else bedding down in a sleeping bag if the weather had turned cold, was glad to be within walking distance of his job at the Merchants & Mechanics Bank. He also said that he was damned sick and tired of having to drive seventeen miles and back every time he wanted to go to the show.

Much as some people thought otherwise, Anson knew that both Wyeth and Mr. Blackford were being honest. Everyone was aware that the Blackfords were going through a bad time at that period. Their having to live in a rented house plainly represented a considerable decline, and it was no secret that the failure of the horse-breeding farm Mr. Blackford had tried to start in the mountains of North Carolina—the last of a long series of bizarre ventures—was causing a considerable amount of amusement among his fellow members of the Light Infantry Club. All that was true, just as it was true that the Blackfords would not have been able to move to as acceptable a neighborhood as Malvern and Alwyn if it had not been for the money that came in from a few farms Mrs. Blackford owned in her own name.

None of this, however, had any perceptible effect on Mr. Blackford and Wyeth. They did not regret having to leave Mulberry and they did not think of it as a decline. Most people might have, but most people were not the Blackfords. The Blackfords did not have to live in Mulberry to possess Mulberry, and if you were a Blackford you could not decline. The worst that could happen to you was that you had less money than you had before. Furthermore, the Blackfords, during the present generations, had never been what anyone would call rich. In later years, when time and distance enabled him to see the picture whole, Anson realized that the family had been traveling on a downward arc for as long as he could recall. Money was always a problem, this or that piece of acreage had to be sold, and Mulberry itself was mortgaged up to the hilt; the only reason the Blackfords lived there as long as they had was because the bank took the position that its investment was better safeguarded if the house was occupied. Mulberry, Mr. Blackford said, was now the bank's worry. He did not regret having to leave it, and neither did Wyeth.

Happily or unhappily, their wants were simple. Conscious though they were of belonging to what had once been a proud, influential family, neither Wyeth nor his father had any wish to reproduce in their own lives the gracious dimensions of the past. It was beyond their imaginations as it was beyond their purse. They asked no more than to be permitted to hunt and fish in season, to keep themselves in liquor, to play poker, to motor down to Savannah when one of the big-league teams was engaging the local club, to raise a few game chickens, to take in the fights at the Gates Arena in Bugtown, and, when no other entertainment was available, to read *Collier's*, the *Reader's Digest*, and the *Saturday Evening Post*. It was hard to explain about Wyeth and his father, especially to people up North, but the truth of the matter was that they were Regency bucks who had been born outside their time. Were they living when they should have lived, they would have ruined themselves at White's. That exhilaration denied them, and ruination no longer being fashionable, they satisfied their inclinations on a small-town scale. So far as Mulberry was concerned, Anson was far more regretful over its being abandoned than they.

The Blackfords moved to town in the autumn of 1930. Several times thereafter, when Anson came from the university, he borrowed the family car and drove out to Mulberry. He would use his own key to unlock the front door, going through the familiar rooms where the rain was staining the ceilings and some of the floorboards in what used to be the kitchen were already rotting away, and gradually it became his ambition to acquire enough money to purchase the old house and have it restored. It meant that much to him; there was that deep an affinity. Wyeth's mother, Mrs. Blackford, understood. "It ought to be yours, Sonny," she said the afternoon he brought her the camellias. "Except for Dinah, who is homesick for it because she has never lived anywhere else, it means more to you than anybody. It ought to be made over to you, mortgage and all."

He was back where it all had started, close to the buried source springs, and he remembered how Esther, the Blackfords' cook, grumbled because she had to let him in. Esther was the only servant the Blackfords could afford to bring from Mulberry, and it had never been one of her duties to answer the door. His being practically a member of the family gave her the right to complain aloud ("Since when you's so weak you can't turn the knob? This door ain't locked. You thought, you thought! Why didn't you turn the knob and find out!"), and it was not until he gave her news of her two sons, Junius and Julius, whom he had seen in the country, that she began to seem pleased to see him.

Little Dinah stood behind Esther in the hall, watching him with her solemn eyes that were neither brown nor gray but a dark, brindled mixture of the two. He had known Dinah since she was a baby and now she was almost thirteen years old. He had not seen her since the Christmas holidays and she looked longer and leggier and more spidery than he had remembered.

"Hey, you," he said. "How's my girl?"

Dinah did not answer. She kept on looking at him in that dreamy, far-off way of hers, a softness of expression that often caused strangers to get the wrong impression, since they had no way of knowing how that tender gaze was likely to go blazing up at any moment into one of her bursts of temper, and he wondered what the matter was. Esther went paddling up the stairs to tell Mrs. Blackford that he had called. Dinah waited until she reached the second-floor landing—deliberately, Anson thought—and then, still looking at him, said:

"Well, aren't you going to kiss me?"

It was the most natural thing in the world for him always to kiss Dinah when he returned home from the university and saw her for the first time, just as he kissed Marion, his own sister, and he was surprised to find himself thinking twice about it as she lifted up her face. He barely touched her lips. She had sat in his lap on Christmas Day, when he and his family called on the Blackfords to exchange gifts, and whenever he used to stay at Mulberry she invariably kissed him good night as she made the family rounds. In the months since Christmas, however, something had happened—there was a noticeable budding beneath her shirtwaist and she wasn't quite the same little girl any more.

"You smell good," he said. "Have you been swiping some of your mother's perfume again?"

A tiny blaze lighted up her eyes. "That was when I was a baby! You know it, too! This is my own. It's Enchantment."

"So it's Enchantment, eh? You're getting to be quite the young lady, aren't you?"

They stood looking at each other, as travelers might upon reaching the border of some new, unfamiliar country, and then, as she made a face at him, wrinkling her nose, it began to seem absurd. Any note of strangeness had been introduced by him, not Dinah. He put his arm around her shoulders and walked with her into the parlor.

"Well, how about it? Are you still my girl?"

"I'll always be your girl. Will you take me to the movies tonight?"

"I can't, honey. I've got a date."

"Who with? That sticky Kit Robbins again?"

It was only a few months before, at Christmas, that Dinah had called Kit Robbins sticky, but now, again, it was not quite the same—at Christmas it had sounded as though she wanted to use an expression she had picked up from the older girls, striving toward their status, but now, plainly, she meant it.

"Kit Robbins, Miss Impudence, is not sticky."

Dinah, who had sat down on the sofa, stared at him with her far-away look. It was not cold enough for a fire, now that the afternoon had turned off warm, but a small coal blaze was burning in the grate that was suspended in the hearth on iron hooks. Mrs. Blackford disliked the slightest chill. A head-and-shoulders portrait of Percy Wyeth Blackford hung over the hearth, he being the founder of the Blackford family in the New World and Sir Samuel Alwyn's second-in-command, and as Anson looked from the portrait to Dinah he thought he detected a vague resemblance between the handsome, be-wigged man, wearing a brilliant blue uniform emblazoned with the order he had been awarded by the King, and the silent, dreamy-look-ing child who sat on the sofa with her legs tucked under her and her bare knees showing. It was the poise of the head, he finally de-cided—generation had carried down to generation, and Dinah's head was borne on the stem of her neck in much the same imperious way; and someday, no doubt about it, she was going to be a beauty. She had all the makings and it was not too early to tell.

"You've been to Mulberry, haven't you?" Dinah broke the silence by saying. "That's where you got the camellias. Those are the ones that grow behind the house—Pink Perfection and Lady Hume's Blush."

Anson nodded. "They're still in bloom. I couldn't find any of those pure-white ones, though. I looked and looked."

"That's the Plain Jill," Dinah said. "There's just that one bush—it grows near the kitchen by the old well. It blooms early in Febru-ary. Whenever it frosts, it never does. Why didn't you take me to Mulberry?"

"I guess I didn't think about it. It never occurred to me that you'd like to go."

Dinah looked at him gravely. "I always like to go to Mulberry. I wish we still lived there. Will you take me when you go again?"

"Sure. Of course I will."

"Did you do any shooting?"

"No, I didn't. I kicked up some birds, though. And do you know where? In that old field where we used to find the arrowheads."

"I remember. I still have a shoebox nearly full."

"There were at least fifteen birds in one covey. The quail must be coming back."

"That's what Wyeth says too. I can't stand Wyeth."

"What do you mean? That's no way to talk about your brother!"

161

"I'll talk about him all I like! He's mean. But you're not. You will take me to Mulberry, won't you, Sonny?"

"I've already promised, haven't I?"

"Can we go fishing again?"

"I don't see why not."

"When? Tomorrow?"

"No, Dinah, tomorrow I can't."

"Why? Are you going to have another date with that sticky Kit Robbins?"

The date was not settled, but Anson hoped it would be—and he was beginning to be annoyed at having Kit Robbins called sticky. This was one of the times when he wished that Dinah did not stand quite so much in the relation of a younger sister. He did not know how to cope with her familiarities and, like all little girls her age, she could be a brat. She was being deliberately a brat now—he knew that glint that shone in her eyes.

"I bet you neck," she said. "That's what you do, you neck! Neck and smooch! I think it's disgusting!"

Anson lost his temper. "See here, you, if you don't shut up——"

"Make me!" Dinah flared, jumping to her feet. "I dare you to! You think you're so *big!* Just because you and that——"

She cut herself short, hearing her mother's tread on the stairs, and then, in a taunting whisper, said, "Neck and smooch, neck and smooch! Ugh! How can you be so disgusting!" knowing, as Anson knew she knew, that he would not give her away. Mrs. Blackford glanced at her sharply as she entered the parlor, however, as though she suspected something might be amiss, and Anson realized that Dinah must be getting to be quite a problem. Nobody held it against Wyeth to have all the instincts and inclinations of a red Indian, but with a girl it was different—no girl, even if her name was Blackford, could afford to be that "wild."

And Dinah actually was not. There were times when Anson thought he understood her better than anyone else, most probably because they were not kin. He had gone to her defense more than once, and it had become a standard remark in both households that he was always "taking up" for her. Because of that alignment he sometimes erred on charity's side, as he was aware, but he had come to believe that what was often charged up to Dinah as willful errancy represented not so much disobedience as a kind of tremulous reaching out—as when, against the rules, she used to steal off in one of the rowboats and paddle below the bend in the river, often to fish but most frequently simply to lie on her back and stare at the sky, invariably forgetting to appear for dinner and causing the whole household to be both fearfully and angrily certain that this time she had gone and drowned herself for sure. That soft, dreamy look of hers, in that respect, did not lie. Anson could not tell what it was that she glimpsed beyond the clouds, the shining private vision, but he had come to suspect that it was not altogether different from his own bewitchment when he wanted to go to Burma and gather the seeds of wild plants. It was a second standard saying that he and Dinah were "alike," and perhaps to that extent they were—alike, also, in that Dinah, now that the pleasures of Mulberry were lost, spent much of her time with books.

It was this, Anson knew, that troubled the Blackfords as much as anything. Mrs. Blackford said that she approved of Dinah's reading, of course, even though she had to keep a close watch on what she brought home these days, and Mr. Blackford, who had been trying to get past the second chapter of Wells's *Outline of History* for as long as Anson could remember, agreed that she certainly ought to be encouraged to improve her mind—"In our family," he once declared, "reading has always been one of the female accomplishments."

At the same time, however, over and above the mind's improvement and the proficiency of the fair, there was a whole set of expectations to which Dinah would be expected to measure up. Being a Blackford did not absolve her; it rather stressed the necessity. Kit Robbins's hard problem was fortunately not Dinah's. Even without her great-great-great-grandfather Percy, Dinah had ancestors to rent, ancestors to pawn, and ancestors to spare—one of the signers, a Chief Justice, a minister to Poland, two governors, enough of the military to form a small brigade. It would have been well, of course, had these various presences been backed by money, as in their own lifetimes they had, but the absence of money did not particularly matter. Even though the Blackfords were now living in a rented house which they would not have been able to afford were it not for the small income Mrs. Blackford had in her own name, the money, like Mulberry, like the golden days of rice and sea-island cotton that Mulberry stood for, had once been there. Dinah's handicap lay in the very burden of her name. She was a Blackford, and it was as a Blackford that she would be judged—"Rob Blackford's daughter"; "Anne's child"; "the Blackford girl." In only a few more years it would be "her" year, the time of her formal presentation to society at the Light Infantry ball, and in that colorful assembly, even as she entered on her father's arm, he in a brevet major's uniform of the old regiment and she in the billowy white demanded by tradition, the points would be added up. There could be no greater disaster than to have her put down either as a woods-waif or a bookworm. And now, despite everything, she seemed well on her way to becoming both. Plus brat, Anson thought. He couldn't take a switch to her, as she deserved, but by all rights he should tell her mother—except that he would never think of making any trouble for her, as well she knew.

"Hello, Sonny," Mrs. Blackford said. "What a nice surprise! You hadn't planned to come home this week end, had you? Does Wyeth know?"

Mrs. Blackford gave him her cheek to kiss. Her cheek was soft and smooth and she smelled of verbena, just as his mother did. She was of medium height, increasingly inclined to fullness, and had dark, wavy hair. Dinah, sitting on the sofa, watched them intently.

"I've just come from Mulberry," Anson explained. "I brought you these."

Mrs. Blackford's face seemed to cloud for an instant at the mention of Mulberry, and then it brightened. "My! Aren't the Lady Humes fine this year? I'll keep some and you can give the others to your mother. Dinah, you take these and put them in water. Use that big crinkly bowl we used to have on the sideboard."

"Do I have to?" Dinah said. "I want to hear about Mulberry."

"Oh, Dinah, please don't argue. You've tried my patience enough for one day. Put the flowers in water, as you've been told, and then go find something to do. Go visit with Esther in the kitchen if you can't think of anything else."

"Esther doesn't want me. Nobody does."

"It's just too bad about you, isn't it? But I'd rather not have to ask you to fix the flowers again. And don't forget what I said about the bowl."

"Oh, all right."

Dinah took the blossoms, looking first at her mother and then at Anson, and started reluctantly toward the hall.

"Can't you stay for supper, Sonny?" Mrs. Blackford asked. "We'd love to have you."

"No, he can't," Dinah said, stopping where she was and glancing over her shoulder. "He has a date with that sticky Kit Robbins."

Mrs. Blackford's mouth opened on a soundless gasp. "Dinah Blackford! Why, of all the——"

"It's all right," Anson put in. "She didn't mean anything."

"You stop taking up for her!" Mrs. Blackford said sharply. "That's one of the things that's the matter with her! You've gone and so spoiled her to death——"

"*Me* spoil her. *Me!*"

"Yes, you! You more than anybody! Dinah!"

"Yes, Mother."

"I want you to apologize. Now, this instant! Did you hear what I said?"

Dinah dragged one foot, outlining a circle on the floor. "Oh, all right. I apologize, Sonny. But you will take me to Mulberry the next time you go, won't you?"

She looked at him so appealingly that there was only one thing he could say.

"Sure, of course I will."

Dinah went down the hall, the dawdling sound of her footsteps mingling with the slow, steady tick of the clock, and Mrs. Blackford shook her head.

"I wish you'd tell me what good my making her apologize did," she said. "You shouldn't spoil her the way you do, Sonny. It isn't good for her and it's worse for me. I have to worry about that child. You don't."

Remembering, Anson had to smile. Hard though it was to realize, Dinah would be in her early thirties by now. He was curious to learn what had happened to her and to find out who it was she had married. He should know but he did not. When he was in London during the war he had received one of those unsatisfactory V-mail letters from his mother, who seemed to feel that it was patriotic to use them occasionally—"You didn't say anything about what I wrote about Dinah Blackford's marriage. Weren't you surprised?"

He was prepared to be as surprised as his mother apparently expected him to be, since Dinah grown was probably no more predictable than Dinah little, but even though the regularity of the mails in London in 1942 was something of a tribute to British steadiness under fire, he had not received the letter to which his mother referred. Although there were more important things than Dinah Blackford's marriage to think about at the time, he was interested enough to bring it up when next he found time to write—"Yours about Dinah Blackford must have gone astray. Who did she marry? If you know her address, I'd like to drop her a note."

Things were happening on the home front too, however, and his mother's next letter made no mention of Dinah. Marion's third child had arrived, another boy, and Willis, Marion's husband, had sufficiently recovered from the wound he had received at Midway to be back with the Marines in the Pacific—"With him so far away it's good for Marion to have the new baby to think about. We're calling him Winston, which is a family name on the Gaffney side, and I hope that people won't get the idea that we're naming him after Winston Churchill. I think that Mr. Churchill is a great man, as I'm sure your father would agree if he were alive, but I would hate for people to think that we picked out that name because it belongs to somebody important and didn't have enough good, fine names of our own."

In the weeks and months that followed, and then the years, Dinah Blackford's marriage fell back into the limbo that was Pompey's Head. She had to marry someone, and who it was did not seem of any particular consequence. Now, however, a shift in geography caused a shift of emphasis. He had always been as close to Dinah as the gap in their ages would permit, and it seemed wrong not to know what had happened to her. Soon, though, he would be able to pick up all the loose threads. Ian Garrick could be at least counted on for that.

CHAPTER TWELVE

The stretch of Malvern Street along which Anson was walking was also a familiar part of town. It was the route he used to follow to get to school and where, on the corner of Malvern and Olmstead streets, Joe Ann Williams used to live. The corner of Malvern and Olmstead marked one end of the fourteen-block square that made up the "old" part of Pompey's Head. The rows of three-story brick houses here gave way to larger dwellings that were erected in the middle of the nineteenth century, when the ante-bellum prosperity of Pompey's Head was at its height. All this part of town was then open country. The Williams house, built by Joe Ann's great-grand-father, Judge Cabell Williams, was a square white dwelling set off from the street by a picket fence. It was almost hidden by the palms, magnolias, and oaks that grew on its grounds. One of the oaks, standing behind the house, was said to be the oldest tree in Pompey's Head. A member of the staff of the Arnold Arboretum at Harvard had once handed that down as his opinion. Anson devoted a whole "Old Pompey" column to the tree's history, and both Mrs. Williams and Joe Ann called him up at Garrick & Leigh to say how much they appreciated it. "That old tree," Joe Ann called it, not because of its antiquity but because to Joe Ann everything was "old"—"that old dress," "that old tune," "that old A & P." He and Wyeth Blackford must have drawn up at the corner of Malvern and Olmstead to call for her at least a hundred times, and so close to the past it was, so little had anything changed, that he would not have been surprised to see the door open and Joe Ann come running down the steps.

The tangle of memory was like a bundle of fishhooks; pick up one, and all the others were caught in it. He could never remember Joe

Ann without remembering what a good dancer she was, and he could never think what a good dancer she was without also thinking of the Oasis in Bugtown. There was a time when Joe Ann was always asking him to take her there. He never did, since, among other things, the Oasis was regarded as being off limits to girls of good family and reputation, and he had no desire to let himself in for a lecture by Dr. Williams. Even if you were a man you risked something by being seen at the roadhouse, and Anson knew that his having gone there was bound to get him talked about, especially after the evening he fell in with Midge Higgins and some of her crowd. Eventually it got back to his family, as sooner or later everything did, and one evening Marion brought it up at supper—he knew from the tone of her voice that she had been discussing it with his mother beforehand. "What's this I hear about you and the Higgins girl?" she said. "You seem to be giving her quite a rush."

Although all the girls in Pompey's Head were frequently identified by their family names—"the Blackford girl," "the Williams girl," "the Carpenter girl"—whenever Midge was called "the Higgins girl" it had a different sound. Anson was reminded of the colored placards the Board of Health used to tack up on the doorway of a house in which somebody had an infectious illness—pink for measles, blue for diphtheria, red for scarlet fever, and yellow for mumps. "Why don't you mind your own business?" he said to Marion. "I'm not rushing Midge Higgins or anybody. Besides, if I want to, it's my own affair."

The trouble, of course, was that it wasn't. Nothing was ever entirely your own affair in Pompey's Head. If it had reached Marion's ears that he had been dancing with Midge at the Oasis, it was bound to be all over town, just as it had been all over town when Ian Garrick was meeting her secretly at the Bijou Theater. He knew what Marion was thinking, that it didn't "look right" for him to be seen at the Oasis, and it was easy to surmise from his mother's troubled expression, which she could not conceal, that she was already beginning to worry about his getting "serious" over Midge. "My God!" he thought. "Doesn't this town have anything to do but gossip? Can't you dance twice with a girl without even your own mother getting all worked up about it?"

Mothers being mothers, he guessed not—not if the girl was Midge Higgins and not if she came from the Irish Channel. The reputation that Midge had started to acquire in the eighth grade had been mounting ever since. In those days the word for her had been "well developed"; now it was "careless." But what did they mean? That

Midge had a lot of dates; that she had dropped out of high school to take a job selling in the ladies-ready-to-wear section of Cornish's Department Store; that she liked to go to the Oasis? Well, what if she did—what was so "careless" about that? Wasn't it just another way of saying that her father was still a streetcar conductor and that she had always been a Channel girl?

Annoyed with Marion for having brought the subject up, and feeling uncomfortable because his mother was trying so hard not to look uncomfortable, Anson did not find it difficult to see Midge as the victim of a snobbish conspiracy. However, even as he cast her in the role, he was aware that he was not so much obeying an impulse toward chivalry as trying to find excuses for himself. Seeing Midge at the Oasis had again reminded him how vulnerable he was; even now he could remember the way her body curved into his, and in his confusion, brought about by the unexpectedness of Marion's remark and his own guilty feelings, he felt that Midge's appeal might somehow be rendered less lawless if he could persuade himself that she was not "that kind" of a girl. One thing, however, was certain—everybody knew how Ian Garrick had dropped Midge after his father happened to see them coming out of the Bijou one afternoon and ordered Ian never to see her again, and both Marion and his mother must have had that in mind, but whoever thought he was going to knuckle under like Ian Garrick was wrong. He had graduated from high school and was going away to the university in the fall. If he wanted to visit the Oasis he intended to visit the Oasis, and if he wanted to dance with Midge he intended to do that too; besides, Midge Higgins wasn't that kind of a girl.

Marion, sitting across from him, seemed partially to guess what he was thinking. Glancing at their father, who seemed to be more than ordinarily preoccupied that evening, she said, "It's not that I'm criticizing Midge, you understand. I guess there's a lot to be said on her side, considering her disadvantages and all. But you hanging around with her at the Oasis——"

"Who says I've been hanging around?"

"Weren't you out there two nights last week?"

"What if I was? Whose business is it? I like to listen to Vicksburg and the band. And just because I happened to dance a couple of times with Midge——"

Marion lifted her eyes to the ceiling. "Happened! A couple! That's not what I hear."

Anson could endure it no longer. He was trying not to think of

Midge in a certain way, troubled by the thoughts he was having, and Marion's insinuations caused those very thoughts to burn all the more vividly in his mind.

"What do you hear! That I've been taking Midge out to the woods! That we sneak into one of those tourist cabins! Is that it? Is that what you hear?"

"Oh, Sonny, please." His mother lifted both hands in an alarmed gesture, glancing in the direction of her husband for support. "You must know that we don't think—that Marion didn't mean——" But it was impossible for her to continue; the threat and danger were too near. Her eyes traveled back to her husband, begging for help, while Marion, turning up her nose, said scornfully, "Evil to him who evil thinks!"

"And who thinks it, I'd like to know!" Anson said. "Who starts all those stories about Midge? That crowd you run around with, that's who! Just because she comes from the Channel and works at Cornish's——"

"Oh, Sonny, I wish you wouldn't say that," his mother said. "That's not it. It's not that we think we're any better than the Higginses——"

An impatient sound from Anson's father caused them to look toward the head of the table.

"Of course not," he said in a tone of kindly scorn. "How could anyone ever get the idea that we thought we were any better than the Higginses? You, Marion, you leave your brother alone. And you, Anson, you show your sister some respect. And so far as the Higginses are concerned——"

The rest of the sentence was choked off by a spasm of coughing. His face became flushed for a moment and then went pale. His skin had a yellow look.

"You must do something about that cough," Anson's mother said. "It worries me. I don't like the way it sounds. I'm going to make an appointment for you to see Fred Williams tomorrow."

Anson's father drank a glass of water. "I've already been to see Fred Williams. How many times do you want me to go? He says that this is nothing but a tobacco cough and that it will clear itself up."

"It hasn't cleared up in five years. It keeps on getting worse, if you ask me. If Fred can't help you——"

"Please, Maria, please. I hate to deprive you of the pleasure, but I won't have you fussing over me. It's nothing but a tobacco cough, I tell you. I refuse to keep on running to doctors."

170

"One visit to Fred Williams over six months ago and you call it running!"

"Please, Maria, I beg you."

"You'll be sorry someday."

"Yes, I daresay I will. I wouldn't be surprised. It's beginning to be my experience that sooner or later we find ourselves being sorry for nearly everything. Right now, though——" He coughed again. "Right now I'd like to have my coffee. This is our week to take inventory and I have to get back to the store."

Another bundle of fishhooks. Had it not been for that episode at the supper table Anson did not think he would ever have called Midge and asked her for a date. He knew what the rules were, and that one of the most inflexible of these was that you shouldn't get mixed up with a Channel girl, and until that evening he never had any desire to go against them. It was Marion and his mother who forced him into opposition.

Even then, however, he knew that his flare of rebellion had nothing to do with principle. It seemed unfair to him that the circumstances of Midge's origin should be held against her, and that it should be accepted as a proven fact that she was that kind of a girl, but his asking her for a date was in no way related to the reformer's desire to change things or, defiantly, to take up a position on her side. Though it would be years before he saw it clearly, what he most wanted to do was to get Midge out of his system. He had been drawn to her the first day she walked into the eighth grade and the pull had been there ever since. He had been afraid to admit it even to himself, always mindful of the dictum that it was unwise to get mixed up with a Channel girl, but now he was prepared to accept the attraction for what it was. Had he ever heard of it, he might have understood that it was the principle of sexual selection which had taken hold, and had he been truly honest he might have admitted that he wanted to find out for himself if Midge was that kind of a girl. So it was more, then, than an ordinary date. Driving through the summer evening on his way to Frenchman Street, where Midge was living with her family, he was lifted by a feeling of special adventure. He had a date in the Channel and he was on his own.

The Channel was hard to explain. "What you mean," Meg said once, "is that it's the other side of the railroad tracks. What's so unusual about that? Why do you have to insist on its being something special simply because it's in Pompey's Head?" Meg, however, was wrong—the Channel was special. It was impossible to grow up in Pompey's Head without its becoming part of your consciousness, and it was difficult to believe that it would have acquired its particular meaning anywhere else. Unlike the old lower East Side in New York City during the years of the great immigrations, it was not a ghetto, nor, like the French Quarter in New Orleans or Chinatown in San Francisco, had it ever been a city within a city, separate to itself. The Channel could not be called the poor part of town, since the section south of the depot was considerably poorer (Meg's other side of the railroad tracks), and it was not even exclusively Irish—not unless the Scotch-Irish migrants who drifted down from the hill country to work in the thread factory and the four or five other industries that provided employment in Pompey's Head, most of whom also lived in the Channel, were given an identification which they themselves would have denied.

The first inhabitants of the Channel were a handful of French immigrants. Bound for Louisiana in the winter of 1801, the sailing vessel on which they had embarked, partially disabled by the great storm which swept the Atlantic in December of that year, limped for safety to Pompey's Head. Either out of gratitude or fear of another passage, the French wayfarers, led by their priest, a certain Father Mercier, decided to settle where the winds of Providence had apparently been instructed to blow them. They built their church and then their dwellings in an outlying section two miles north and east of what was then the center of town. Part of the settlement ran along the Cassava River and it was reached by a single muddy lane that eventually became known as Frenchman's Road. The colony, planted along a curve in the river, was called, after the leader of the group, Mercier's Bend.

Thirty-three years later, in 1834, the population of the Bend was increased by a contingent of Germans, forerunners of those who were to leave their homeland after the revolutionary disturbances of 1848. These, however, by 1861, had been sufficiently worked upon by opinion and environment to overcome their libertarian impulses and march off almost en masse to the Civil War. In this adventure they were joined by their equally acclimatized French neighbors, with whom they had intermarried to produce a type which Pompey's Head had already identified as "Black Dutchmen."

It was in no sense a term of disdain. Indeed, by the turn of the century, to be able to include a Black Dutchman among one's ancestors was almost as advantageous as to claim a member of one of the original Twenty Founding Families. Gaby Carpenter's maternal grandfather, Herman Schermerhorn, was a Black Dutchman, as had been one of Olive Paxton's great-grandmothers, a famous beauty whose maiden name was Josephine Cloinpêtre, the last being a Gallicized version of Kleinpeter, and few local heroes were more revered than Major Wolfgang Webber, a member of Longstreet's staff who was killed in the Battle of the Wilderness.

It was the misfortune of the Irish to be relatively late arrivals. Their first outriders did not get to Pompey's Head until 1856. Too poor to establish themselves in trade, neither could they turn to the land. All the available land had been brought into the large plantations. Even as field hands the Irish could find no room. The plantations were worked by slaves. It fell to the newcomers to perform the lowly, backbreaking tasks made necessary by the growth of the city—draining the malarial bog at the south end of Bay Street, digging the ditches for the first waterworks, and filling in the shallow, dirty lake, known as Jennie's Basin, which spread over a large part of the Negro section now called Duppytown.

Anson's father said that in those days this was enough to cause the Irish to be set apart; by the sweat of their brow, he said, they earned the mark of Cain. "Don't you see, Sonny? They worked with their hands. It was beneath the color of a white man's skin. That was all that was necessary. Almost a hundred of those Irishmen died of yellow fever before Jennie's Basin was filled in. Think of that for a minute. What did it mean?"

"I don't know," Anson said. "What did it mean?"

"It meant this," his father replied, "that in those days an immigrant Irishman's life was held cheaper than a slave's. Both that bog on Bay Street and Jennie's Basin should have been cleaned up years before. They had been a breeding place for the fever, and Lord only knows what else besides—cottonmouths and swamp rattlers, for one thing—since the first days of the colony. Why wasn't something done about it then? Why did it have to wait until the Irish arrived?"

"Because the work was too dangerous for slaves?"

"Of course." His father nodded. "Once you stop to think about it, it's obvious. A slave was worth a good thousand dollars or more. It represented too great a capital risk. You take that swampy land that used to be around Jennie's Basin—do you know to whom most of it belonged originally?"

"No sir, I don't, I guess. Who did it belong to?"

"The Pettibones," his father said. "It was the best that dear Henry's great-great-grandfather could do for himself after he climbed out of the indentured-servant class. And the Pettibones, I'm afraid, tend to discredit the theory of evolution. It is hard for me to imagine that old Peter was much different from our own Henry. You don't think that a Pettibone, any Pettibone, was going to risk sending a gang of slaves into that fever-ridden muck, do you? But when the Irish arrived, willing to work for fifteen cents a day——"

Anson, who liked hearing about the old days, was interested in what his father was saying, but he could not understand why Mr. Henry Pettibone had to come into it. It seemed to him that Mr. Pettibone was always coming into something. He knew that Mr. Pettibone had the reputation of being extremely careful with money, and Mr. Blackford was always saying that he was tighter than a tick, but whereas Mr. Blackford passed over it lightly, in a tone of jovial disdain, his father, who ordinarily was much more charitable than Mr. Blackford, never touched upon the subject without seeming to take a sort of pleasure out of exposing some skeleton or other in the Pettibone past. It was not hard to guess that his father did not like Mr. Pettibone, and that Mr. Pettibone most probably did not like him.

"And then the yellow fever," his father was saying. "It wasn't enough that those poor homesick Irishmen had dropped to the bottom of the scale. The fever had to hit them as well. A cordon of armed guards was thrown about the Channel. Only the doctors were permitted to leave or enter, and even the funerals were accompanied by men with guns. Don't you see the effect it had?"

"No sir, I don't, I guess."

"Sonny, I do wish you would stop putting 'I guess' at the end of everything. Either you see a connection or you don't. You don't have to guess."

"It's just a habit."

"I hope so. And I also hope that you will break yourself of it soon. What I was trying to make you see, in connection with that epidemic of yellow fever when the Channel was sealed off, was that it created an attitude that has lasted ever since. A keep-out sign went up that has never been taken down. The Channel became something like that Casbah you read about."

"What Casbah?"

"Never mind what Casbah. We'll talk about the Casbah some other time. The point I am trying to make is that some of the people in this town still think about the Channel as it was thought about nearly a hundred years ago. They don't seem to realize that the old Channel doesn't even exist any more—that it was burned to the ground in the big fire we had in '72. That's another thing—the fire of '72 began in the Channel, and even that has been held against it. You'd think that those people wanted to be homeless. All I'm getting at, Sonny, is that the Channel has acquired a reputation that it doesn't quite deserve."

"Like giving a dog a bad name?" Anson said.

"Yes, Sonny, that's it exactly. Like giving a dog a bad name. I'm not saying, mind you, that the Channel in the old days was everything it might have been. I daresay it wasn't. But now, today—well, the truth of the matter is that the Channel is simply another neighborhood; not the best neighborhood in town, perhaps, but not the worst one either. And to hold it against the people who live there, without any thought of the individual person—no, Sonny, that we mustn't do."

This conversation had taken place a short time before and Anson could remember every word of it. He knew better than to imagine, however, that his father would be altogether happy if he knew about his date with Midge. The generosity of his view would have made it hard for him to disapprove (a view undoubtedly conditioned by those whips and bags of New Orleans coffee that young David Page once hawked through the streets of Pompey's Head, Anson had come to realize) and certainly he would never go so far as to forbid him to see Midge. But still, if he knew about the date, he would not be altogether happy. He would say that with a boy of eighteen there was always the danger of some entangling alliance and that it had to be recognized, for the sake of everyone concerned, that the danger was probably a little greater if the young lady in question happened to be a Channel girl.

CHAPTER THIRTEEN

Midge Higgins no longer lived in the old house on the corner of Hampton and Wentworth streets that Mr. Henry Pettibone had turned into low-rent apartments. After several years there, she and her family moved back to the Channel, where Mr. Higgins had purchased a cottage on Frenchman Street. This took place shortly after Midge dropped out of high school and went to work in Cornish's Department Store. Her two older brothers were also working, one as a traveling salesman and the other as a member of a construction crew, and the youngest Higgins, fourteen-year-old Mico, along with selling the *Saturday Evening Post*, had a paper route that took in the whole of the Channel. It was said that it was their combined earnings that enabled Mr. Higgins to buy the cottage on Frenchman Street, but this, obviously, could not be true—there had not been time enough for them to accumulate that much money.

Anson got the straight of the story from Wyeth Blackford, who was then working as a teller in the Merchants & Mechanics Bank. Wyeth said that when Mr. Higgins went to the bank to arrange the mortgage, he put down two thirds of the $5,500 purchase price and held another $500 in reserve to paint and improve the property. Wyeth added that Mr. Murdoch, the president of the bank, was greatly impressed with the soundness of Mr. Higgins's financial position. He had no debts and seemed to have put everything on a cash-and-carry basis. But what really surprised Mr. Murdoch, according to Wyeth, was why Mr. Higgins wanted to buy in Frenchman Street when, for that kind of money, he could have found something in another and more desirable part of town—the new development out on the north end of Bullis Street, for instance, in which the bank was interested. Mr.

Murdoch, Wyeth reported, took the liberty of asking him about it. "Well, Mr. Murdoch," Mr. Higgins said, "I'll tell you. It's each man to his own taste, and my taste is for the Channel. This development out on Bullis Street is everything you say it is, I know, and it's fine that Old Pompey is growing. But the wife and myself, we like the Channel. It's where we want to live."

Were it not for Midge, none of this would have been of any interest. It was she who caused the return of the Higginses to the Channel to assume the proportions of an event. The swath she had cut through the eighth grade had not been forgotten, nor had "Shinola!" which was now permanently embedded in the vocabulary of the slightly younger generation represented by Dinah Blackford, and though no visible damage had been done to the boys with whom she had associated, the boys were older now, as was she, and it was only prudent to realize that it was always possible for things to happen. Midge's moving back to the Channel did not necessarily mean that she would be removed from circulation, any more than had her leaving high school, but taken together they had the effect of placing her in a slightly more distant orbit—at least the dangers inherent in proximity had been eliminated. Nothing, now, could just come about. Any boy who wanted to interest himself in Midge would have to go out of his way.

The geography of Pompey's Head, in relation to the Channel, might have been arranged to stress the fact—to get to the Channel from Alwyn Street one had to go downtown to the business district, negotiating four of the squares, and then cut across town. Anson, coming to Frenchman Street, had to slow down. This was new territory; in all the years he had lived in Pompey's Head he had never been in the Channel after dark before. Frenchman Street, he knew, was the old Frenchman's Road. It was badly paved, with large cracks and potholes, and the street lamps appeared to be dimmer than in other parts of town.

Anson went along at a crawl. Midge said she lived at 702, between Fremaux and Austerlitz, which was the street he had just crossed, but it was too dark to read any of the house numbers. The row of one-story frame dwellings all looked alike. Each had a narrow porch, a small front yard set off from the street by an iron picket fence, and a slightly larger yard to the side. They were of a type known in Pompey's Head as shotgun cottages. Each room was coupled to its neighbor in a straight, unbroken line, and it was said that if a shotgun were fired

177

through the front door, the charge would whistle through the whole house without damage and spend itself through the back door.

That, Anson thought, must be 702—the one just ahead where the light was burning on the porch and in which a phonograph was playing. He drew up before it and stopped the car. The front door was open, letting a splash of light fall across the vine-covered porch, and he could see Midge sitting on a sofa in the front room. She was wearing a white dress and listening to the music, with her loose blond hair coming down to her shoulders. She rose when she heard him close the gate, which creaked on its iron hinges, and disappeared for a moment, turning off the phonograph. She came to the door as he walked up the steps, opening the screen; the faint scent of her perfume merged for an instant with the heavier odor of moonflowers blooming on the porch.

"Hello, Sonny. Come on in."

She showed him into a kind of double parlor, two doors thrown open into one, with high ceilings and cream-colored woodwork and too much furniture; new furniture, as if it had just recently arrived —overstuffed chairs and other chairs of golden oak; the phonograph; a cabinet for records; the sofa on which she had been sitting; two small tables, each with a lamp; a number of photographs on the mantel, propped up amid a clutter of china ornaments—and, in the second of the two rooms, a complete dining-room suite, also of golden oak, with a corner cupboard filled with bric-a-brac, and a large oval table about which the chairs were ranged as if guests were coming to supper. Anson's impressions, however, were fleeting and hazy; he was too busy looking at Midge.

She appeared older somehow—even older than when he had seen her at the Oasis. And she looked different, too; it was hard to recognize her as the same Midge with whom he had gone to school. He had never known what some of the girls meant when they said she was tacky (nothing but cattiness, he used to call it), but now he could see that those tight skirts and tighter sweaters represented an earlier idea about attractiveness in dress. Perhaps it was working in Cornish's Department Store that had done it—instinctively he guessed it was—but none of those girls would be able to call Midge tacky now. He didn't see how anyone could look any nicer.

"Did you have any trouble finding your way?" she asked.

"No, Midge, not at all. The directions you gave me were fine."

"I was afraid you might get lost."

"In Old Pompey? It's not big enough for that."

He could think of nothing else to say, and neither, apparently, could Midge. A large gray moth, circling and diving about the light on the porch, batted against the screen. Anson said:

"It's a pretty evening, isn't it?"

"Pretty as can be. There's going to be a moon. I thought it was going to rain this afternoon, but it didn't."

"I thought so too. I went fishing for a couple of hours and while I was out on Little River——"

Midge laughed. "As if I couldn't have guessed that you had been fishing. You and Wyeth Blackford, I'll bet. Isn't that what you always do?"

"No, Midge, not always." For some reason he did not want her to think that all he did was to go fishing. "I've had to study for my entrance exams, and sometimes, when my father needs me at the store——"

Midge regarded him soberly. The color of her hair reminded him of a brand-new penny and he thought that her eyes were the same shade as cornflowers that had been wet by rain. She said:

"I was just teasing, Sonny. Do you think I've forgotten how serious you are?" She glanced at him and smiled. "Not that I've ever held it against you, though."

"I'm not that serious, am I?"

"Yes, you are. You're the most serious boy I know."

"There's nothing I can do about it, I guess. Would you like to go to a show? It's too early to drive out to the Oasis."

"What's playing?"

"*Seventh Heaven* is at the Bijou and *Wings* is at the Strand."

"I've seen both of those. Janet Gaynor was wonderful in *Seventh Heaven*—I nearly cried my eyes out. I'll tell you. Why don't we just sit on the porch for a while? Or we can play some records if you like. I brought some new ones home from the store. First, though——"

An automobile passed before the house, its horn giving off a blare. Midge turned quickly and waved. Her hair tossed gently and an amused look came into her eyes.

"That's my uncle Ned," she explained. "He lives in the next block. He has the late shift at the thread factory and he always honks when he goes to work." The look of amusement still hovered in her eyes; she glanced up and giggled; it was the same giggle that Anson remembered from the eighth grade. "I guess it's lucky that we weren't in a clutch or something."

Anson could feel himself going away from her; all the warm feelings he had been having were suddenly chilled—so that's the way it was; a clutch or something! Here he had been, building up a lot of fine notions and thinking how nice she looked, when all the while, night after night after night—but no! What she said did not mean what he thought; she would not have been so open about it—his eyes met hers and they laughed together.

"Yes," he said, "I guess it was lucky. I wouldn't like to have Uncle Ned get after me. It might be worth it, though."

Midge was ready to laugh again. She said, "You take it easy, Sonny Page—I don't like that look in your eyes. Before you get any more notions, I want you to meet my folks. They've been hearing about you ever since the eighth grade and they want to meet you—in case you haven't guessed it, it's a pretty big build-up you've had." She started to lead him through the rest of the house and then turned on her heel. "I guess we'd better go through the yard. Ma wouldn't like my taking you into the bedrooms—you don't know us well enough yet. They're all in the kitchen playing cards."

Anson had not considered the possibility that he would have to meet her family. Walking with Midge through the side yard, where the smells of night and summer mingled with the darker smells of earth, he was overtaken by a feeling of awkwardness which only later, in retrospect, would he be able to recognize as having been compounded partly of nervousness, partly of trepidation, and partly of the wish to please. A magnolia grew in the yard, full of blossoms, and they passed through a still, heavy scent of roses hanging in the dark. Midge reached for his hand, gave it a little squeeze, and ran up the steps of a screened side porch. He followed her into the kitchen, where a group of cardplayers, six in all, sat around a table in a gleam of light and porcelain; the Higginses' kitchen, Anson thought, looked newer and shinier than the one at home. "Hey," Midge said. "Who's winning? This, everybody, is Sonny Page."

Anson forced himself to meet the scrutiny of the upturned faces; in later years, whenever he heard one of Meg's friends talk about a person moving out of his group, he would always remember himself standing by the table in the Higginses' kitchen. Midge began to introduce him.

"This is my mother, Mrs. Higgins——". (Anson smiled and nodded to a small, stout, middle-aged woman with a tired, kindly face and Midge's cornflower eyes) "—and this is my father, Mr. Higgins——"

Midge's father sat back in his chair and held out his hand. He was in his shirt sleeves, bull-chested and slow-moving; he had a short, blunt nose, a jutting chin, and had apparently just shaved. "*Mister* Higgins, indeed!" he said. "And who do you think the young man would be imagining I was—Jay Gould?"

"No, Pa, not Jay Gould. Old man Vanastorbilt."

It was Mico, Midge's youngest brother. He grinned at Midge and then at Anson. He gave the impression of being older than his fourteen years. His face was thin and rather narrow, and his thick black hair was brushed back from his forehead in a loose, plumelike wave. He continued to grin, looking at Anson steadily, and then:

"I know a friend of yours," he said.

"You do? Who?"

"Dinah Blackford."

Anson was caught off balance; of all names, that of Dinah Blackford was the last he expected to hear.

"Is that so?"

Mico's eyes had not moved. He said:

"I deliver the *Saturday Evening Post*."

"Way out there in the country?"

"I've got all that territory. I've got all of Bugtown too. I go to Bugtown on the bus and a kid out there lends me his bike—he's my cousin. I ride the bike out to Mulberry. That's where I see Dinah."

"Oh, that's how it is."

"She says she's your girl."

Anson did not know whether to be angry or not—the arrogant impudence of the little monkey! And how often did he see Dinah; how often and under what circumstances? He was aware that all eyes were on him, that Mico was grinning again, and that they were waiting to hear what he would say—wisps of tension floated about the room.

"Well," he said, "don't let me beat your time."

A murmur of laughter—not laughter really; a way of easing the tension—rose from the table. Mico glared at him hotly. He did not like being laughed at and he would not be put in his place; the others might feel constrained because Midge had a date with this Alwyn Street stranger, but not him; he was as good as anybody. A flush of anger darkened his face.

"Come on!" he said. "Let's play cards!"

Midge continued with the introductions—her brother Ed, a heavyset young man in his mid-twenties; her aunt Frances, a large-bosomed woman with a pair of restless eyes, dark like Mico's; her middle brother, Joe, in whom Mrs. Higgins's fair hair and blue eyes had run down into a kind of vapid, washed-out blondness; and finally a young man of approximately Anson's own age, thin and frail-looking, whom she introduced as Bill Dillon. The way Midge spoke his name, and the quick light that came into his eyes when he looked at her, made Anson understand that he was one of her admirers—a neighborhood boy, probably; one who had the run of the house. Mr. Higgins said:

"Pull up a chair and join the game, why don't you? We're playing blackjack, two cents' limit."

"Sure," Ed said, moving his chair to make room. "We can always use some fresh meat."

"Oh, Sonny doesn't care about playing blackjack," Midge put in. "We'll just watch for a while."

Mr. Higgins looked displeased. "I think you might let the young man speak for himself, Midge Higgins," he said. "Why don't you get him a bottle of beer?"

"That old home-brew!" Midge wrinkled her nose. "Sonny doesn't want——"

"I told you, Midge Higgins, that you might be letting the young man speak for himself."

There was an undercurrent of resentment in Mr. Higgins's voice that made Anson uncomfortable. He did not want Midge's father to get the impression that he thought he was too good for the home-brew that everybody was making during prohibition, nor did he want anyone to think that Midge thought he was too good.

"I'd like a bottle of beer, Mr. Higgins," he said, "and I'd like to sit in the game for a while. Midge and I can play together."

"A lot of good she'll be doing you," Mr. Higgins replied. "You be smart and play your own game. That girl has no more card sense than you can put in a thimble."

But if Midge hadn't, Mico had—the pile of pennies before him mounted steadily. Five times in a row he collected while his aunt Frances was dealing ("It's not the luck of the Irish you have," she said at one point. "You're the kind who would fall into a pigpen and come out smelling like jasmine"), and on the sixth hand he turned up with a blackjack, getting a queen on the deal and then drawing an ace. He gathered in the cards and shuffled them briskly.

"O.K.," he said. "All the ribbon clerks go home!"

Who the other ribbon clerks were Anson could not imagine, but there was no mistaking that he was included in the category. Mico played every card with the same kind of nervous intensity, seeming, in the way he won, to possess some extrasensory perception, but when the time came for him to deal against Anson, a hard, cold look came into his eyes; it was plain that he did not intend either to forgive or forget. On the first hand of the deal, Anson, drawing a nine and then an eight, stood on seventeen—Mico, with two face cards, each of which counted as ten points, beat him with twenty. He reached for the pennies and grinned. "Chicken!"

"We'll chicken you!" Midge said. "Just you wait and see!"

The next time round Anson was dealt first a three and then a nine. He asked Mico for another card, hoping for an eight, which would have given him twenty, or a nine, which would have added up to an almost-impossible-to-beat twenty-one. A four fell instead, making the count sixteen. "Hit me again."

"O.K., mister," Mico said. "You asked for it!"

He flicked another card across the table, a nine.

"Shinola!" Midge said. "We're bust again! Why didn't we bluff and stand on sixteen?"

"A lot of good it would have done you," Mico replied, dealing himself a card. "Two kings, back to back. Twenty pays twenty-one. Who collects besides me?"

"I do," Bill Dillon said. "I've got twenty-one."

"Luck," Mico said. "Nothing but luck!"

"What do you call what you have?" Dillon asked. "Skill?"

"Listen, plumber," Mico said. "Name any game you want, any game at all, and I'll bet you——"

"Pipe down, for God's sake!" Ed said. "Someday you're going to gas your jaw off. Turn the crank and deal."

"Aw, stop chewing on the kid," Joe said. "Just because he's taking you to the cleaner's——"

"That's right, Joe," Mico broke in. "When *he* hits a streak it's all right—sure, sure, everything's dandy!—but just let somebody else get hot and what happens? Right off the bat he starts getting sore, the chinchy piker! What's the matter, Ed? Can't you take it?"

"Listen, you little shrimp! You start riding me and——"

"Oh-ho!" Mico said. "Now he's getting tough. Look at those muscles! Boy, am I scared!"

"O.K., Mico—I warned you. You keep it up and——"

"*Deal!*" Mr. Higgins exploded. "Let's have done with this jabbering, the whole kit and caboodle of you! I'm eighty-nine cents in the hole. Deal, Mico, or pass the cards!"

"Hot like I am?" said Mico. "In a pig's eye, I will!"

His run of luck continued—only Bill Dillon seemed able to win from him consistently. Whether it was because of that, or because of Dillon's friendly, open look, Anson took a liking to him—he found it hard to conceal his pleasure when Dillon came up with a blackjack, an ace and a king, and collected double from Mico. And once, when in her absorption Midge unconsciously leaned against his shoulder, resting there a moment, he saw a troubled look come into Dillon's quiet brown eyes—he moved away from Midge and poured the rest of his beer.

"Be careful you don't stir up the yeast," Mr. Higgins said. "You have to pour it gentle-like. Midge, get the young man another bottle."

"Thank you, Mr. Higgins, but I think I'll stand on this. It's wonderful beer, though."

Mr. Higgins seemed pleased with the compliment. "It's all in the mixing and straining, I reckon," he said. "I do think I have a hand for it, even if I do seem to be patting myself on the back—it's something like having the green thumb of a gardener, you might say. Are you sure you won't have another? The icebox is full."

The game was resumed and Midge and Anson played for nearly an hour. Anson, who had bought a half dollar's worth of pennies, lost the last of his stack to Ed. "Oh, damn!" Midge exclaimed. "That was my fault. We should have stayed."

"You had fair warning," Mr. Higgins said to Anson. "I told you not to be paying any attention to Midge. She has no more card sense than a newborn rabbit."

"Oh, who cares!" Midge said. "Come on, Sonny, it's time for us to go."

Rising from the table, Anson began to say good night—first to Mrs. Higgins, next to Aunt Frances, and then to the men. Bill Dillon and Ed stood up to shake hands; Joe simply nodded from his chair. Mr. Higgins said:

"You'll be coming around to sit in with us again, I hope. We owe you some revenge."

"Absolutely," Mico said. "Drop in any time."

"Good night, Mico."

"So long, mister. Don't take any wooden nickels."

"My," Midge said, "aren't we funny! Good night, you all."

She stood near Anson, her soft bright hair coming just above his shoulder, and for an instant her mother looked at her in a way that reminded him of the expression that sometimes crossed his own mother's face when she glanced at his sister Marion and young Dr. Gaffney. Dr. Gaffney, who came from Denver, was interning at the municipal hospital, and Anson knew that his mother was wondering if he and Marion were going to get married. Mrs. Higgins, noticing that he was watching her, turned her eyes from Midge and gave him a warm, approving smile. He had seen that smile before, too. Mothers, he guessed, were all alike.

A few minutes later, on the way to the Oasis with Midge, it began to dawn on Anson that there would be talk—talk, that is, of a different kind. Ordinary talk, of the usual variety, he had been fully prepared for. What he had not foreseen was the new turn that talk would take, linking his name and Midge's in a way that he had not anticipated. It needed only the look on Mrs. Higgins's face to make him understand that gossip would now have something fresh to seize upon, and that, like Mrs. Higgins's parting smile, it would be related to the fact that Midge, though only eighteen, had reached what was called a marriageable age. This was not true of the other girls with whom he went around, Joe Ann Williams and Gaby Carpenter, for instance, both of whom were also eighteen, and why it was true in one case and not the other, he did not know.

"A penny, Sonny. What are you so quiet about?"

"I didn't know I was being quiet. I was thinking what a nice night this is."

"Yes, isn't it? And I was right, too. There's going to be a moon."

Glancing from the car, Anson saw that a glow of whiteness was already beginning to brighten the sky. And even the moon, he thought, would find a way of coming home to roost—somebody else would be out tonight and inevitably it would be remembered, when the time came, that he and Midge Higgins, on the night of Saturday, June 16, 1928, had been favored with a moon. There was no way to prevent the events of the evening from becoming common property. One of the Higginses would be bound to mention that he had played cards with them and pretty soon it would be all over town. Everybody would know that he had played blackjack in the Higginses' kitchen and come away the loser by fifty cents.

"Another penny, Sonny. You are quiet."

"It's not worth a penny, Midge. I was thinking what a small town this is."

"No, now! You're not just finding that out, are you?"

"Not exactly. It's beginning to seem smaller and smaller, that's all."

So small, indeed, that it was the game of blackjack which would make the difference. If he had picked Midge up at her home and gone to a movie, or even to the Oasis, it would have been simply another date—a few eyebrows would be lifted, a few insinuating glances would be exchanged, and in certain quarters it might be wondered, when it was learned that he had again been seen at the Oasis with Midge, if Sonny Page, who had always seemed like such a nice, well-behaved boy, was beginning to run wild. But the game of blackjack was something else again. It implied an intimacy, an introduction into the bosom of the family, a more meaningful evening than if he had merely called and taken Midge out. Because of the blackjack game it would be speculated if he had become serious about her—serious, in that sense, being the first step on the road to matrimony.

"Sonny."

"Yes, Midge."

"I like your tie."

"Do you?"

"Yes. Dark red goes well with your eyes. You look nice in blue too."

"Well, you don't look so bad in white yourself."

Him and Midge get married? Him and anybody get married? Marriage was something in the future, after he graduated from college and established himself as a lawyer. He knew that all the girls were thinking about marriage, and that Midge must sometimes think of it too, and all you had to do was to look around to see that nearly everybody got married someday, bewilderingly intimate though that state would appear to be. He was aware, also, that every pairing off, now that they were older, was looked upon in a different way. Going steady with a girl was colored in everybody's mind with the thought of marriage, especially those of the parents involved, even though they would insist that their sons and daughters, unlike Midge, were not of a marriageable age.

"Want a cigarette, Midge?"

"Yes, Sonny, thanks. Do you want me to light yours?"

"No, I'll get it."

"Do you have a match?"

"Yes, here's one here."

Parents were hard to understand. The subject of marriage was always coming up with them, sometimes when you least expected it, and the general idea seemed to be to make you understand that it was something that should never be rushed into. And yet, despite their words of caution, they were not above doing a little nudging here and there—his own parents and Gaby Carpenter, for example; they didn't want him to rush into anything, and he was far too young to be thinking seriously of any girl, but still he did not think they would be displeased if he and Gaby became what they would call interested in each other. Nor was this only because Gaby was their favorite. He and Gaby were supposed to have the same interests, a conclusion he found hard to follow. Gaby, who was going to Newcomb College in the fall, had outgrown her literary ambitions and now said she wanted to paint; the reason she picked out Newcomb was because it and the French Quarter were both in New Orleans.

"What I'd really like to do," she confessed to Anson one evening, "is to go to New York and study at the Art Students League and live in the Village. I don't have a chance, though! Can you imagine the family consenting to *that?*"

Knowing her father and mother, Anson could not, and even to himself the idea of wanting to go to New York and live in the Village seemed rather daringly emancipated. What puzzled him most, however, was how his parents ever came to imagine that he and Gaby had so much in common—he liked to shoot and fish and Gaby didn't; he liked to dance and listen to jazz music and Gaby said it was a waste of time; he liked to interest himself in the history of Pompey's Head and Gaby thought it was dull. "I'd think you'd want something *bigger,*" she said. "I don't see how you can be so *confined.*" Now that he thought about it, it seemed that much as he liked Gaby he had less in common with her than any girl he knew—certainly he found that cousin of Joe Ann's who had just moved to town, Kit Robbins, far more attractive.

"There's your moon, Midge," he said. "Over that stand of pines."

"I was watching it. It's most at the full."

"All the stars are out too."

Midge drew in on her cigarette. "Are you going to be around all summer, Sonny?"

"All except for a few weeks at my aunt Ruby's farm in North Carolina, I am. Why?"

"I was just wondering. The Williamses have a farm in the mountains too, don't they?"

"Not a farm, a place. It's next to my aunt Ruby's. Old Dr. Williams and my grandfather bought some land up there together and then split it up."

"Oh?"

"The Williams place isn't as big as it used to be. They sold all of their bottom land to my aunt Ruby and her husband. He's my uncle Ralph. The Williamses just use their place in the summer, but it's a real working farm my aunt and uncle have."

"I think I'd like that, a farm in the mountains."

"Would you?"

"Uh-huh. I think so. Wouldn't you like it?"

"I don't know. Maybe. I've never thought. I guess I'd rather be a lawyer, though."

"You would? Somehow I don't see you as a lawyer. It seems— I don't know—too kind of stuffy for you. Don't you want to be an explorer any more?"

Anson felt slightly embarrassed. Midge was thinking about the time he wanted to go to Burma and gather the seeds of wild plants, and that was years and years ago. Flicking the ash of his cigarette out of the window, he said:

"Sure, Midge, I'd like to be an explorer. It would be wonderful to go to all those faraway places—I guess that's what I'd like to do most of all; just seeing the world, I mean—but I'm afraid that was kid stuff."

Midge nodded. "I know. It's like me wanting to be a movie star —the way I used to dream and dream! Sometimes I didn't know which was the real me, I really didn't—that tacky little kid in the tenth grade or that wonderful creature lying in the sun at Palm Springs. You would have loved me, Sonny. You would have positively swooned at my feet. And do you know what?"

"No, Midge, what?"

"I was always awfully nice to you when I was in the movies. I used to be hateful to all my other slaves—you know, cold and icy and sneery like Garbo—but you——" She looked at him and giggled. "I used to let you go to my private soda fountain and make us banana splits. I spent most of my time when I was a great star eating banana splits."

Anson laughed. "And now you say that you'd like a farm in the mountains?"

"No, not really. I just like the idea. It's what standing on your feet from nine to five and getting fallen arches does, I guess. When are you leaving?"

"I don't know exactly. I promised to drive up with Joe Ann and that cousin of hers who lives here now, Kit Robbins——"

"Oh, is that her name—Kit Robbins? She's beautiful, isn't she? I saw her with Joe Ann in the store the other day. I think she's the most beautiful girl I've ever seen."

That was what everybody was saying. Kit Robbins had been in town only a short time but already she had established a place for herself. Margie Rhett and one or two of the other girls said that she was too cold-looking really to be beautiful, but theirs was a minority opinion. The general agreement was that Kit Robbins was the most beautiful girl who had ever lived in Pompey's Head. Anson thought so too. He was glad he was going to drive to the mountains with her. He said:

"You really mean that?"

"Absolutely. She's—I don't know—not just attractive, not just pretty, but *beautiful*. She looks the way I wanted to look when I was in the movies."

"I thought you looked sneery like Garbo."

"That's the way I looked all right, but that's not the way I *wanted* to look—I'm talking about me now, the real me, and not who I was in the movies. And I wanted to look the way she does. She looks *exactly* the way—so, so—I don't know—so queenly, I guess—so aristocratic. I used to practice by the hour."

"Practice?"

"All the time, especially after I saw one of those movies about old plantation days before the Civil War." She gave a little sniff of self-depreciation. "I guess I knew I was common, coming from the Channel and all, and I always wanted to be a lady."

It was one of the most forthright statements that Anson had ever heard; he was not used to that kind of honesty. He took his eyes off the road for a moment and glanced at Midge. She was sitting with her hands in her lap, staring straight ahead, and he thought that a kind of fineness was showing through.

"But, Midge," he said. "You are a lady. How could you be more of one?"

"By not living in the Channel," she said. "By having grown up differently. By feeling—not looking, *feeling*—in a way I don't. You're a nice man, Sonny Page, and I'll always remember what you said, but——"

"Yes?"

"Oh, Shinola, Sonny!" She sat up straight. "I don't give a damn any more. I'm me, Midge Higgins, a snub-nose blonde who works in Cornish's ready-to-wear, and all that was kid stuff too—first I'd be Garbo and then I'd be a lady; sometimes I'd be Garbo and a lady *both*. But now——"

"Now you're just a lady."

"Oh, Sonny, you mean that, don't you?" The tone of her voice changed and she reached for his hand. "Stop the car for a minute. I want you to kiss me."

Their lips barely touched. Midge closed her eyes and ran her fingers across his cheek. He kissed her again, harder. Then:

"That wasn't very ladylike, was it?" Midge said. "You're all over lipstick. And don't think that it was because of what you said. I just wanted to."

"Do you want to often?"

She glanced at him through lowered lids. "Would it make any difference?"

"Maybe."

"No, Sonny, not often." She gave a little laugh and leaned her cheek against his. "Give me your handkerchief. We'd better get rid of some of this jam."

The Oasis was a large wooden structure that stood just outside the limits of a small community, known as Bugtown, that had grown up around the Arrowhead Mill. Originally spelled Buggtown in honor of the first white settler in that part of the country, a man named Josiah Bugg who owned and operated a raft on which he ferried passengers and freight across the nearby Little River, one of the branches of the Cassava, the settlement lay nine miles south and east of Pompey's Head.

Serving, because of the Arrowhead Mill, as one of the town's principal sources of income, Bugtown had also become established as the center of its sporting life. Close by the Oasis was a smaller wooden building in which boxing contests were staged every other Friday night. It was called the Gates Arena. Boys from as far away as Jacksonville and Columbia were matched against the local club fighters and more ambitious mill hands, and now and then one of the marines would come down from the sleepy, peacetime boot camp at Parris Island, accompanied by a sergeant who acted as his second. Wyeth Blackford, who frequently attended the fights with his father, told Anson that purses for the main event never came to more than twenty-five dollars. Wyeth never went to Bugtown at night alone, however, and seemed to accept the prevailing opinion that it was a good place to stay away from. There was hardly a card at the arena that was not followed by one or two unscheduled bouts, especially after the crowd broke up and went either to the Oasis, which would then be going full swing, or to a combination pinball parlor and juke-joint, draped in neon and reportedly a bootleg establishment, that stood across the road and was called the Golden Horseshoe—somebody or other, judging from what appeared in the News, was always getting beaten up.

"Let's ride some more," Midge said when they drew up before the Oasis. "The place looks dead. It never gets going till after eleven o'clock."

There was nothing in the tone of her voice to warrant Anson's taking her remark as anything more than a statement of fact, but he felt rather huffed. True though it was that he had been to the Oasis only twice before, he did not want her to think that he was an absolute greenhorn—didn't she remember that he had suggested that they go to a movie beforehand, as they might have done had she not seen everything in town? "Yes," he said. "I guess we are a little early."

Midge was sizing up the situation. "It looks like the Horseshoe is getting a play. The crowd must be tanking up. You don't want to go there, do you?"

"I don't know, Midge. I've never been. Do I?"

She glanced at him—differently, he thought—and shook her head. "No, I don't think so. It's nothing but a joint. Why don't we ride some more?"

It struck Anson, as he put the car into gear, that she was completely at home—there was nothing about the Oasis and the Golden Horseshoe she did not seem to know. It was a different vocabulary she was using, and, as language will, it caused her to be reflected in a different light. Once again, as when they were standing in the parlor and she mentioned that it was lucky that her uncle had not caught them in a clutch, he found himself being put off. Apparently sensing his change of mood, Midge said:

"You don't mind riding some more, do you?"

"No, of course not."

"We can go to the Oasis now if you like."

"No, it's too early, as you say."

Bugtown, when they passed through it, was in the midst of the little festival with which it celebrated Saturday night. All the establishments strung along its one commercial block were open for business, and on the sidewalk, where the illumination from the windows and the glare of the neon signs merged into a dim, multicolored glow, knots of men and women stood about, talking and visiting. The women wore thin cotton dresses and most of the men were in overalls, and a troop of barefooted boys raced up and down, sometimes darting into the street. A few wagons and buckboards were mixed in with the mud-splashed cars that were parked against the curb, the horses and mules standing with drooping heads and half-closed eyes in a kind of forlorn patience, and farther along, across the Atlantic & Central tracks, the windows of the Arrowhead Mill shone blue upon the dark. Driving across the tracks, where the street ended, Anson noticed that an itinerant preacher had pitched his tent along the side of the road: *Old Time Hymns*, said a crudely lettered sign in front of the tent, *Biblical Prophecies for Today*. The flap of the tent was open, showing a patch of flame-colored light in the shape of an inverted V, and Anson caught a glimpse of crowded benches, a cluster of gasoline torches attached to the pole of the tent, and a man on a platform of raw yellow lumber waving his arms—his hoarse, ranting voice sounded above the noises of the car.

"Old Brother Bixby sure is whooping it up tonight," Midge said. "He's got himself a real crowd."

"Is that who he is—Brother Bixby?"

"That's what he calls himself," Midge said. "I don't know what his full name is. He's been here for two weeks. I went to hear him the other night."

Anson thought it a curious way to spend an evening. "You did?"

"One of Joe's friends took me—a fellow called Sailor Greer. Sailor isn't his real name. His real name is Erwin. Sailor's the name he fights under."

"Fights under?"

Midge nodded absently. "He works in the mill but he doesn't want to—he wants to be a fighter. He fights at the arena now and then. He calls himself Sailor because he was in the Navy."

"Original, isn't it?"

Midge did not seem to hear the note of sarcasm. She said, "My brother Joe and he are old friends. That's how I came to meet him. Joe brought him to the house. He always shows up at the Oasis too. I see him all the time."

Yes, Anson thought, I wouldn't be surprised—some jerk of a fighter and you go out with him! And who else? Anybody who comes along, most probably. For a few moments he was torn between solicitude and outrage, one occupant of his mind protesting that she was inherently too fine to throw herself away so thoughtlessly and another crossly insisting that if that was the way she was going to behave what else could she expect but a reputation for carelessness, and then, while still a third voice was saying that someone ought to take her in hand, he himself was brought up short by the realization that what he was going through was an attack of jealousy, the severest he had ever known. He said:

"This Sailor fellow. Is he a special friend?"

"Special?" Midge thought for a second. "I don't know. He's been giving me a rush. Is that what you mean?"

"No, not exactly. I was just wondering——"

"If I was in love with him?" Midge shook her head. "No, I'm not. He's nice to me, and tries to show me a good time, but that's as far as it goes. Where does this road lead to?"

"Haven't you been out this way before? This is the road to Mulberry."

He had swung into it out of habit after they left Bugtown, where, one mile beyond the Arrowhead Mill, four roads came together at a little hamlet, consisting of but a few Negro cabins and a general store, that was known as Double Crossing. The woods grew thicker as they went along, dense tangles that seemed to stretch endlessly behind the curtain of moonlight that fell from the trees that bordered on the road, with now and then an open, marshy place to tell that they were approaching the tidal swamps—rice fields in the old days—that lay along the Cassava River. They rode along in silence until Midge, who had been staring from the window, said:

"Hold my hand, Sonny. I always feel lonesome in the country in the dark."

She slipped her fingers into his, and then, as if in need of closer contact, she moved toward him and leaned her head upon his shoulder—he turned and kissed her on the cheek. Midge came closer.

"I don't care if we never get to the Oasis," she said. "This is nice."

"I think so too."

"It's funny, Sonny, isn't it?"

"What's funny?"

"Me and you being out here in the country together. Back in the eighth grade, when I was a famous movie star——"

"Yes?"

"I had an awful crush on you. Didn't you know?"

"No, I didn't. I thought it was Ian Garrick."

"Ian?" She thought for a moment. "Yes, I had a crush on Ian too —I couldn't make up my mind. You were dark and Ian was fair and one week it would be you and the next week it would be Ian. One thing, though——"

"What?"

"I never let Ian make any banana splits. That proves something, doesn't it?" She paused briefly, staring ahead. "They say that it was Mr. Garrick who made Ian stop seeing me, don't they?"

"Honestly, Midge——"

"Honestly nothing! You don't have to pretend. But it's not true about Mr. Garrick. The day he saw me and Ian coming out of the Bijou—I'd stopped meeting Ian weeks before that. I got tired of his being ashamed of me. I told him that if he wanted another date he would have to come to my house. I knew he wouldn't and he never did. The day Mr. Garrick saw us—I didn't meet Ian that day; I didn't even know he was in the show; we just happened to meet coming out. But what are we talking about that for? Are you glad that you're going away to the university in the fall? I would be. I'd love to get out of Old Pompey for a while."

At that moment they passed the entrance to Mulberry. Except for the line of oaks that grew on either side of the drive, it looked like any other dirt road. The branches of the trees arched across the drive, and the pale moonlight, dripping through the leaves, spilled down in splashes that collected in little pools. A single light was burning at the end of the drive, and as the road curved toward the Cassava River, where the old rice fields used to be, the house came briefly into view, a moment's whiteness in the dark. Whether because of Midge's nearness or because it had been lying just beneath the surface of his mind all evening, Anson thought of Mico Higgins delivering the *Saturday Evening Post*—once again he wondered how often he saw Dinah and under what circumstances. There was an incongruity—a wrongness, even—that he could not define. He told himself that if it was all right for him to be out riding with Midge Higgins it was by that same token all right for Midge's brother to strike up an intimacy with Dinah, but even in the midst of the telling, as he confronted and admitted the charge of snobbery, forced to agree that he was being ruled by the same set of prejudices that in relation to Midge he refused to accept, he brushed the argument aside—it was not all right; it was all wrong; he could not say why, but it was.

"Now you're quiet again," Midge said.

"I was thinking about something."

"Me, I hope."

"Yes, in a way."

194

He swung the car off the road into a smaller lane that led toward the river. The land was very flat now and only sparsely woded. The lane was one of several narrow wagon tracks that used to run to the rice fields from which, in the time of Anthony Blackford, Percy Wyeth's grandson, the family had reaped a series of fortunes. But that was the glittering zenith; the dawn of emancipation had been the setting sun of the rice planter. Colonel Blackford, the grandfather of Dinah and Wyeth, was forced to abandon the fields in the early years of the present century when the mechanized competition of the new growers in Texas and Louisiana made the cultivation of tidewater rice ruinously unprofitable. The weedy ditches and rotting sluice gates, part of the old irrigation system, stood like markers along the slow incline that led to less land, less money, less indulgence. Bereft of its golden touch, the Midas land lay under water in the spring when the river was in flood, and even now, in June, there were long stretches of swampy places, the home of mosquitoes, snakes, fiddler crabs, waterfowl, and frogs—the frogs were in full voice everywhere, calling all over the marsh.

"Where are we going?" Midge said.

"There's something I want you to see."

That, however, was not quite true; it was more something that he wanted to see himself—the white herons that roosted in the trees that grew along the river. He had been taken, again, by the same necessity that always gripped him whenever he was in the neighborhood of Mulberry; a wanting to see it whole, an anxious desire to know that everything was in its right place—he stopped the car, turned off the motor, and blackened the lights. The herons, he saw, were still there. He made out four of them in the lower branches of one of the trees. Midge saw them too.

"Look!" she cried. "What are they?"

There was no need to explain. One of the birds slowly took flight, gathering itself in a moment of exquisite tension and then soaring into the moonlight on wide, luminous, astonishing wings.

"They're herons, Sonny! White herons!"

"They roost here. If you look over there——"

"Yes, I see! Oh, Sonny, they're beautiful! Thank you for showing them to me."

Her face, like her voice, quivered with delight. Their eyes met, searching in the dark, and they moved toward each other with the same compelling swiftness; he kissed her, not gently as before, feeling the shiver that swept over her as she came into his arms, and then he was in stunned, trembling possession of all that the night had promised in the moon-struck darkness of its deepest folds—he had never kissed anyone, nor been kissed like that, before; he had never imagined; he had not once dreamed.

"Oh, Sonny."

"Midge, Midge."

It was then that the night should have ended, he often thought later; they should never have gone to the Oasis. It was in full swing when they returned, and as they walked into the blare of jazz he realized that he was in possession no longer—the final chorus of "Bugle Call Rag" carried away the last recollection of the herons on a brassy, tumbling flood, and he could see why Midge had thought that they didn't want to stop by the Golden Horseshoe—on this summer evening most of the men were in shirt sleeves, and the blue suit that he wore to dances at the Yacht Club was all wrong. Even on the two previous occasions when he had dropped in at the Oasis he felt out of place—once late at night when he was going home from Mulberry and once after he had taken Gaby Carpenter home from a picnic—but that sense of being an intruder was nothing compared to this. Midge, following a waiter to one of the tables ranged against the walls of the large, barnlike room, waved gaily to some friends.

"What'll it be?" the waiter said, looking sullen and impatient.

The waiter was also in his shirt sleeves, a thin, undersized man with a splotch of reddish freckles and a milky cast in one eye. There was no reason to suppose that he was not speaking in his normal tone, and certainly it was impossible to imagine any note of grace or courtesy ever invading that lantern-jawed drawl, but Anson thought he detected a deliberate rudeness. Midge, however, seemed not to notice. She said that she would like a coke and Anson said that he guessed he'd have a coke too.

It was then, as the waiter turned away and the band crashed into silence, that Anson remembered that it was part of Bugtown custom, when you brought a date to the Oasis and sat at a table, to carry a bottle of liquor along. A quick glance confirmed his oversight. Bottles were in display on all the nearby tables, or, if not bottles, the mason jars that moonshine whisky came in—white mule or white lightning, it was called; a colorless, violent potion on which, two summers before in the mountains, he had been made deathly ill. It was his first and only experience with moonshine; the mere smell of it now made him want to gag. Had he remembered, however, he could have gone to that place on Liberty Street and got a pint of bourbon, even though

196

Wyeth Blackford said it was no more bourbon than white mule was and probably more dangerous to drink, but at least it didn't smell and taste so bad; if you had to, you could manage to get it down. The band started playing again, picking up the introduction to "Me and My Shadow," and Anson saw Vicksburg grinning from the platform, twanging away at the bull fiddle which, when he sat in with the band at the Oasis, he exchanged for the guitar he played in his quartet.

"You know what, Midge? I forgot to bring something to drink."

"Oh, that's all right."

"Couldn't I get something at the Golden Horseshoe?"

"Yes, you could, but there's no need to. Not for me, anyway. But if you want something——"

"No, I don't specially care either."

"Why don't we dance, then? And, Sonny, don't let anybody cut in. This is our night—I only want to dance with you."

Anson was overtaken by a new fit of self-consciousness as he and Midge made their way to the dance floor. He was aware that he was being stared at, and for the first half minute or so, as Midge came into his arms and leaned her temple against his cheek, he was too aware of himself to be able to dance. But then it was better. Midge was a natural dancer, moving with easy, instinctive grace, and his awkwardness soon fell away—he became lost to everything but the pleasure of nearness, the sound of the music, and the rippling flow of her body beneath her thin white dress.

"Gee but you're good," Midge said.

"It's not me, it's you. You're wonderful."

They danced closer to the platform on which the band was grouped. Anson, looking up, saw Vicksburg watching him, bulking massively behind his bull fiddle. He wondered what lay behind the bemused expression on his face, so different from its usual animation, and then, as Vicksburg gave him a welcoming nod, he thought he understood. It was that blue suit again; Vicksburg was remembering Margie Rhett's party the week before for which he and his quartet had provided the music; Vicksburg had been seeing him at parties for years and he was wondering what an Alwyn Street boy was doing this far away from home. But then a tap on the shoulder caused him to stop thinking about Vicksburg. Turning, he saw a lanky, towheaded boy of about his own age who wanted to cut in.

"Sorry," he said. "We're not breaking."

The boy looked bewildered. "Not breaking?"

"That's right, Orrin," Midge said. "This is a private party."

Vicksburg had witnessed the incident, Anson saw, as had several of the dancers. This does it, he said to himself; this rips it for sure—before tomorrow evening the whole town would know, not only that he had played blackjack in Midge Higgins's kitchen and had a date with her at the Oasis, but also that they had not let anyone cut in. There was another tap on his shoulder, almost a blow. The severity of it caused him to miss several steps. Offended, he looked to see who it was—a short, flushed man with small blue eyes set close together and a broken nose was staring at him belligerently; his shirt collar was unbuttoned and he wore one of those tight-waisted sports coats that fell nearly to his knees. "Oh," Midge said in a troubled tone. "Sailor."

So that's who it was, Anson thought—Sailor Greer. He should have known by that nose. "Sorry," he said. "We're not breaking."

"Ahhh——"

"It's true, Sailor," Midge said. "We're not."

"Ahhh——"

It was more a snarl than anything else, all the more unnerving because it was so unexpected—the man was drunk, too. Anson did not want to be intimidated but he was. Sailor Greer's broken nose and hostile glare, the pack of muscle that lay piled on either shoulder gave him the same cold feeling as did those slouching, furtive figures who hung around the alleys on lower Liberty Street, south of the railroad tracks. He forced himself to smile, moved by an instinctive desire to placate the enemy and also because one part of his mind was still active enough to remind him that for Midge's sake he must not let it be said that he had got into a brawl over her at the Oasis, and then, with the dry, empty grin glued to his face, he found his shoulder being seized roughly and himself pulled from Midge's arms. He heard Midge say, "Don't start anything, Sailor. Don't make any trouble. Please."

Already some of the dancers had fallen back; the wires of animal communication flashed out the news of impending conflict. Sailor Greer was trying to get Midge into his grip and Midge, squirming, was trying to break away. Anson moved toward them, sick with the awareness that this was a professional fighter he was being compelled to square away against, blindly reasoning that drunkenness might work to his advantage and that, if he could get in quick enough, he might be able to land at least one lucky blow—Midge, seeing him advance, tore herself from Sailor's grasp.

"No, Sonny, don't!"

Sailor, rocking slightly, glared at him. "Ahhh, this jelly-bean punk wants to start something, I'll——"

Midge stepped between them.

"Go back to the table, Sonny. I'll meet you there."

It was she now who took the initiative, forcing herself into Sailor's unwilling embrace and dancing him away. Anson stared at them, knowing that through the flow of jazz the crowd was waiting to see if he was going to take it, and then, trembling, weak with rage and shattered pride, he turned away and took it. But Christ! Why had she ever let herself become involved with such a man—the bullying hulk of him, the look of proprietorship that oiled his eyes, the cheapness of his person and the foulness of his tongue—oh, to be called such a name and do nothing about it! Walking blindly to his table, he passed the towheaded boy who had first tapped him on the shoulder. "What's the matter?" he heard him ask, grinning. "The Sailor stole your girl?" Pretending that he had not heard, he walked past and sat down at his table—one more insult did not matter.

The waiter had brought their cokes. Anson was emptying his glass, sitting in his cave of shame and solitude, when Midge returned. Somehow or other she had managed to get rid of Sailor Greer. She slipped into her chair and tried to smile—"I'm sorry, Sonny. He was drunk."

"That's all right, Midge. I know he was."

The evening was too shattered, however, for him to want even to try to pick up the pieces. When the band started playing again he did not ask Midge to dance. That made it all the worse, however, for now he had put himself in the position of seeming to have been too humiliated, and possibly too frightened, to want to show his face— finally, not caring about anything any longer, he suggested that they leave. "Sure, Sonny, if you want to," Midge said. "It's getting late, anyway." Nor was it any better driving back to town. They rode in unbroken silence until Midge, who sat over in the corner with her hands in her lap, said, "Look there's the last of our moon." She need not have gone to the trouble. It was not their moon any longer, and it was hard to remember that it ever had been. It was a different moon and she was a different person and he was thinking different thoughts. He was thinking that it was not always a good idea to go against the rules, and that it was true what they said about getting mixed up with a Channel girl.

CHAPTER FOURTEEN

More and more fishhooks. He was approaching St. Andrew's Square, where Kit Robbins used to live, and though a whole new set of memories came tumbling into his mind he brushed them aside, telling himself that he ought to be thinking of what he was going to say to Ian Garrick. Were it someone other than Ian, Wyeth Blackford or Joe Ann Williams, he need not be bothered with such considerations. He could tell them the story of Garvin Wales from beginning to end, leaving out nothing. They could be depended upon in a way that he did not think he could depend upon Ian. It had all receded into the past, which could not touch him any longer, but the past, so distant in New York, was here constantly invading the present. He was Anson Page, one of the partners of Roberts, Guthrie, Barlowe & Paul, a successful New York lawyer on a business trip, and yet, walking down Olmstead Street toward the center of town, he was still Sonny Page, returning to the same place where he had come to the harsh discovery that Ian Garrick was not his friend.

It was May 10, 1935. If he would never forget October 12, 1936, the day when he and Phil Greene had lunch together for the first time and when, later, Meg opened the door of her apartment in her black silk dress, neither would he ever forget May 10, 1935. It was then that everything had come to a climax. He did not know it at the time, but later he could see it clearly. It marked the end of one phase of his life and the beginning of another. It could not be said that there had been a sudden break, since one thing went into another and there were never any such convenient definitions, but it was now easy to see that most of his subsequent actions had been determined in large part by the events of May 10, 1935.

He and Ian Garrick had been working at Garrick & Leigh for nearly two years. They entered the firm after they graduated from law school, he at the state university and Ian at the University of Virginia. The offices of Garrick & Leigh were on the second floor of the old McCracken Building, a three-story brick structure that stood on the north corner of Bay and Olmstead streets. He and Ian shared the same room. It was on the corner and had a large bay window from which you could look down upon the lower stretch of Bay Street and across the whole of Cemetery Square. Once a parade ground and then a burial place, the square had been set aside as a public park a few years after the Civil War. The chipped, worn headstones had never been removed. Most prominent of all the markers was a small granite shaft which the ladies of the Daughters of the Confederacy had erected over the grave of Major Wolfgang Webber, the Black Dutchman who was killed at the Wilderness while serving on Longstreet's staff. Major Webber was the last person to be buried in the square. The monument to his memory rose from a square base on which were carved a broken sword and a shattered harp. The harp, Anson knew, having written an "Old Pompey" column about the major, was because he had founded the Pompey's Head Choral Society.

That morning, however, Anson hardly saw what lay beneath him. Ian was sitting at his desk pretending to be busy, going through a file of papers relative to the Gogarty property, and he, Anson, who should have been in the office of the Recorder of Deeds, looking up one of the titles involved, was standing by the window. Bay Street was crowded with its usual midmorning traffic and the sidewalks were full of shoppers. Cemetery Square, which Bay Street here had to circumnavigate, was much more peaceful. A few old men were sitting on the wooden benches that stood amid the graves, a stray pigeon scratched hopefully in the shade of a clump of oleander, and off in the distance, beyond the trees, the spire of St. Paul's rose white and slender on the sky.

Like truth, Anson thought. Like truth and honor and goodness and justice. Like the supreme majesty of the law soaring above the everyday grubbiness of it. Like the way things ought to be. A hundred times he had seen the spire, and never had it appeared to him in such a light before. This was a morning, however, when all things were beginning to appear in a new and different light. Within the next hour or so his father would be called upon to testify in court against Mr. Henry Pettibone on behalf of Clifford Small—Mr. Pettibone,

one of the town's most eminent citizens, a cotton broker, and Clifford Small, an old, shiftless, good-for-nothing Negro who couldn't ever be depended upon for anything.

Truth, honor, goodness, justice. The words were all mixed up with what Kit Robbins had said the night before, and his mother's distracted look at breakfast, and Marion coming out of the bathroom with a drawn, sleepless face, putting her hand to her mouth when she saw him, wanting to speak and not being able to, reminding him of some helpless creature trapped and tormented beyond all bearing. And why? Because his father had caused Mr. Pettibone to be brought into court; because he felt responsible for Clifford Small and wanted to see justice done.

Anson knew, however, that it was not nearly so simple as that. He sensed that more than his father and Mr. Pettibone and Clifford Small was involved, that there was a deep, devious interlocking, with roots that went back far into the past, and that somewhere near the center of the scheme, since it was he who had first begun the tracing of the design, lay the person and memory of his grandfather, the ambitious young man from New Hampshire who had come South. It was impossible, however, for him to find his way through the maze. He could not get beyond the realization that nothing would ever be the same again. All his life he had lived in Pompey's Head, taking his place for granted, and now, standing by the window and looking down at Cemetery Square, he had a sense of being dispossessed, of standing alone and isolated and wholly cut off—and there was Ian pretending to be busy, too afraid even to look up, and saying, merely by the hunch of his shoulders, that he had taken his place on Mr. Pettibone's side.

It did not matter any longer, nor had it for years, and it was plain that Ian could not have done otherwise. To call Ian a snob, as most people did, was not enough; it was Ian's cross to be a social coward. He was afraid of knowing the wrong people and of doing the wrong thing. Although the Garricks were as respected as any family in Pompey's Head, and Mr. Garrick was known to have made an imposing financial success, for Ian it was not enough—it could not make up for Mr. Garrick's having had to work his way through school and college, an orphan farm boy who had been raised by a succession of impoverished relatives. Every now and then one of these connections, in Pompey's Head for the day, would walk up the stairs to see Mr. Garrick—silent, sunburned men dressed in patched overalls and faded blue shirts that spoke of cotton fields and fertilizer and bad-tempered mules—and Ian, apparently able to divine their presence from the sound of their footfalls, would visibly cringe. "What do they want to come here for?" he would say to Anson. "It doesn't look good, having them hang around."

Anson, remembering, shrugged his shoulders. Ian, in that time of trouble with Mr. Pettibone, had to turn aside. He was too fearful of having it suspected that he had cast his lot with one whose father had transgressed a solemn unwritten law and thereby fallen to the position of an enemy of society—guilt by association, it would later be called. Once he hated Ian, but now he did not even dislike him. He simply wished that he had been able to think of someone else who might be able to put him in touch with Mrs. Garvin Wales.

Now that he again confronted the matter which had brought him to Pompey's Head, Anson saw it as a most disagreeable business. "As our lawyer, just as our lawyer, Lucy won't let you get anywhere near Garvin," John Duncan had said. "But if you could meet her socially, through some of those connections of yours——" All right, Anson said to himself; what then? Would he not eventually have to reveal his identity and explain his mission? Nor could he imagine Mrs. Wales approving of him; it was too much to expect that she would forgive him for having sailed under false colors. Assume, however, that she did. Could it further be assumed that she would consent to his having a private conversation with her husband? Originally, when he and Mr. Barlowe had gone up to Duncan & Company, he thought there was a chance, but now it began to seem like wishful thinking. But still he must give it a try. Only Garvin Wales could explain the checks that Phillip Greene had sent to Anna Jones. But would he?— that was the further, more depressing question. Could it be true, as Julian Tokar seemed ready to believe, that he would be disinclined to oppose his wife, regardless of the damage it might do to Greene?

None of the questions could be answered beforehand. Meanwhile, in talking with Ian Garrick, he must remember to be careful. Under no circumstances must the name of Anna Jones be permitted to come into it. Unless Ian had gone through a complete transformation he would have a hard time keeping his mouth shut. Tamburlaine Island was just far enough away from Pompey's Head to have the appeal of distance, and Wales, as an author and a recluse, was by now certain to have become a "character." It must then be realized that whatever was said to Ian would immediately be repeated to Olive, and that Olive would naturally pass it on in turn. Let him explain to Ian that the business at hand was of such a delicate nature as to make it advantageous for him to meet Mrs. Wales socially, an explanation he did not see how he could avoid, and in forty-eight hours it would be common property. It was conceivable that it might even reach the ears of Mrs. Wales herself, in which case the game would be over before it started. Nonetheless, he still had to do what he could. It was not only the clearing of Phillip Greene's name and John Duncan's twenty thousand dollars which were at stake. His own reputation had become involved. More and more it was beginning to appear that he had been asked to do the impossible, but if he failed it would not be remembered that he had been asked to do the impossible. It would only be remembered that he had failed.

By the time he reached Cemetery Square, Anson had managed to make himself feel most unfairly treated. He was not cut out to be a conspirator and he did not see why he should be required to act like one. Crossing over into the square, which reminded him of Trinity Churchyard in New York, he could detect no difference in its appearance. Bay Street, however, had undergone a few changes. Sears Roebuck had modernized itself with a line of plate-glass windows that ran the length of the store, a cafeteria stood on the corner where Spier's Drugstore used to be, and the five-and-ten, probably in an effort to live up to Sears across the way, faced the world with a new, lifted face and a small loud-speaker above its entrance which at that moment was filling the street with one of the tunes from *South Pacific*. But it was unmistakably Bay Street. The Merchants & Mechanics Bank stood on the corner of Bay and Constitution, a young Negro in a purple shirt was absorbed in the billboards which advertised the current attraction at the Bijou Theater, the windows of Johnson's sporting-goods store were filled with a display of fishing equipment and baseball paraphernalia, and when Anson turned into the narrow doorway next to Cohen's shoe store, mounting the flight of wooden stairs that led to the offices of Garrick & Leigh, the years in between might not have been. The clock in the steeple of St. Paul's Church struck ten o'clock, the spaced notes drifting above the tune from *South Pacific*, and for an instant he was Sonny Page again, getting to work a little later than usual.

So much was everything as he remembered that he would not have been surprised, upon opening the door, to find Mrs. Telfair sitting at her typewriter in the reception room. He half expected to see her look up with the cross expression that resulted not from disagreeableness, since Mrs. Telfair was one of the most amiable people imaginable, but from her extreme nearsightedness and a refusal to wear glasses.

But Mrs. Telfair naturally was not there. Her place had been taken by a plump young woman in high heels, nylon stockings, and a thin cotton dress who wanted to know if he had an appointment. No, he said, he hadn't, thinking that Mrs. Telfair would not have approved of her successor. She would have regarded high heels and nylon stockings and a thin cotton dress as beneath the dignity of the office. The plump young woman explained that Mr. Garrick was busy with a client. She did not think he would be long, though, and told Anson that, if he wanted to, he could wait.

Seating himself on one of the wooden chairs in the reception room, Anson thought that Mr. Barlowe would have appreciated the offices of Garrick & Leigh. He would have been quick to detect their air of drowsiness, stained with the smell of the law books that stood on the open shelves that covered one of the walls, but he would have recognized and commended the same indifference to show that prevailed at Roberts, Guthrie, Barlowe & Paul. A good, solid firm, Mr. Barlowe would have decided—small-town, to be sure, but when you got down to cases there was much to be said in favor of small towns. Give him his own way and he would just as soon have a limited practice somewhere down in Maryland or Virginia where a man wouldn't have to work himself to death and could give some time to his horses—yes sir, if he were a young man just starting out and had to do it all over again, that was what he would shoot at; a modest practice in some small, neighborly town.

Mr. Barlowe could be so persuasive about it that there were times when Anson was inclined to agree. Not now, however. He was thankful from the bottom of his heart that he had got out of Garrick & Leigh. That much, in any case, he had been able to accomplish. He had not set the world on fire but at least he managed to escape. And once again, as when he stood before the house on Alwyn Street, he was back where it all had started. He had imagined that nothing in the past could touch him any more, protected as he was by the armor of fifteen years, and it was disquieting to discover the number of chinks and cracks there were. It was here, on May 10, 1935, that he knew he would not be able to live in Pompey's Head any longer, already oppressed with a sense of exile and thinking that he had crossed over into a hostile country that was like no country he had ever known, the streets different, the houses different, the faces different, and over everything, like some sentence already decided upon but not yet pronounced, the relentless inch of time as it crept toward the moment when his father would be called upon to testify against Mr. Henry Pettibone on behalf of Clifford Small.

His father put it simply. "I saw it happen," he said. "Do you expect me to stand by and do nothing? Henry didn't do it intentionally—nobody's claiming that—but he did it. Clifford lost a hand and it was Henry's fault. Any other man would admit it and do the right thing. But Henry, a Pettibone?" He had to stop and cough. "And it's not that Henry's a scoundrel, either. It's simply that he can't bear to part with a dime."

Actually, however, it was more than a dime. Clifford Small was suing Mr. Pettibone for ten thousand dollars damages. Nothing like it had ever happened in Pompey's Head before—an old, shiftless Negro suing one of the town's leading citizens—and everyone knew that it was Anson's father who had brought it about. Clifford would never have done it on his own. He lacked both the courage to take such action and the money to initiate it. Had it not been for Anson's father, who went to Mr. Jake Brewer and persuaded him to act as Clifford's lawyer, the matter would never have gone to court.

Clifford, at the time of the incident, was working at the store. He had been employed there for nearly a year. Why Anson's father ever gave him the job of handy man was more than anyone could understand, since Clifford was about as unreliable as anyone could be and occasionally did not even bother to show up. Anson's mother explained it by saying that Clifford was one of his father's charities. She said that now that Clifford had lost his job in the maintenance department of the thread factory he felt obliged to do what he could to keep him off the streets. But Marion, who had been married to Dr. Gaffney the previous winter, was not satisfied. "Why *him?*" she demanded. "Why does Daddy feel that it has to be *his* responsibility? I passed the store with one of the girls the other day, and there was Clifford standing on the sidewalk leaning on his broom—he was *drunk*, that's what!"

"Oh, I'm sure you're mistaken," Anson's mother replied. "Your father keeps a careful eye on Clifford. He wouldn't permit anything like that at the store, I'm sure."

"All right, then!" Marion said. "Maybe Clifford wasn't drunk! Maybe he just smelled to high heaven. I still don't see why Daddy doesn't get rid of him. What will people think?"

Marion had always been inclined to examine everything from the standpoint of what people would think, and Anson felt that her marriage to Dr. Gaffney had emphasized the tendency. She was exaggerating about Clifford, too. He might take a little nip now and then, but that was all. Marion said, "It isn't as if Clifford was the only one Daddy could have hired. I don't see why he did it. Does he want to embarrass us before the whole town?"

Anson's mother shot her a censorious look. "It seems to me, Marion, that it doesn't become you to criticize your father. As I told you, he feels that Clifford is his responsibility. Clifford's father used to work for your grandfather and so did Clifford. Years and years ago, before I ever came to Pompey's Head, he used to run errands at the store."

"Did he?" Anson said. "I didn't know that."

"It was when Clifford was a boy," his mother said. "Your father and Clifford sort of grew up together. And now, since they won't have him at the thread factory any longer——"

"That's it!" Marion exclaimed. "Of course they won't have him! Nobody will have him! Only Daddy will put up with that trifling good-for-nothing! And why? Because he used to work for Grandpa! Is that any reason why we should be saddled with a public disgrace?"

"Oh, come on," Anson said. "What do you mean, a public disgrace? Sure, Clifford takes a swig at the bottle once in a while, but all you can really say against him is that he doesn't specially like to work. If Father feels that he wants to help him, though, and if he used to work for Grandpa——"

"Grandpa, Grandpa!" Marion threw up her hands. "There are times when I get sick of hearing about Grandpa—you'd think he came over on the *Swan* with Sir Samuel or something! Do you want to know the real reason why Daddy keeps Clifford on at the store? Because he's stubborn, that's why! He says to himself, 'All right, if nobody else will have him, I will.' He's as stubborn about Clifford as he is about that cough! Why doesn't he go to the hospital and have some X rays taken, the way Willis says he should? And do you know what he said to Willis last night? He said that he thought people spent too much of their time running to doctors. Imagine! And Grandpa had to come into it, naturally. 'My father,' he told Willis, 'never set foot in a doctor's office in all the days of his life.' Grandpa, Grandpa! What's so special about Grandpa?"

"He just helped to build this town, that's all," Anson said.

"Oh, who cares about that?" Marion replied. "Who even remembers? Daddy just uses him as an excuse for that stubbornness of his. Grandpa never went to a doctor so *he* isn't going to go to a doctor!

Grandpa never wore an overcoat in winter so he doesn't wear an overcoat! Oh, I give up! I'm glad that Willis has decided to move back to Denver and practice there. I'm looking forward to having some of my own worries for a change."

Poor Marion, Anson thought, standing by the window in the office he shared with Ian—she had not been able to get away to Denver in time. Now she had this to go through, and she pregnant besides. And it was only natural for her to blame their father. Pulled by her affections on one side, and by her anxiety over what people were going to think on the other, she was bound to say that none of this would have happened were it not for their father's loyalty to Clifford Small. Nor would it have, of course. Clifford would not have swept that pile of dust into Mr. Pettibone's path as he was passing the store, Mr. Pettibone would not have lost his temper and pushed him, and Clifford, who may or may not have had a couple of drinks that morning, would not have gone crashing into the window, slashing his right hand so severely that Dr. Williams had to cut it off. And had that not happened, there would have been no suit—it all went back, as Marion could say, to their father's loyalty to Clifford Small.

Their father, who was in the store at the time, saw everything that happened. He rushed Clifford to the hospital, and the next day, after Dr. Williams said that Clifford's hand would have to come off, he called on Mr. Pettibone at his office. Though Anson had only his father's version of the interview to go on, it seemed to him that he had been reasonable enough. He told Mr. Pettibone that he thought he should take care of Clifford's medical expenses until he was ready to work again. He himself, he said, would keep Clifford on the pay roll, since all he had to support himself and his wife was his salary, and that he would naturally take Clifford back at the store.

It did not surprise Anson that Mr. Pettibone had refused. He thought that his father should have anticipated his refusal in advance. He found it curious, also, that his father should lay it solely to Mr. Pettibone's closeness with money. Perhaps even more important, as he saw it, was the fact that had Mr. Pettibone consented to the plan it would have amounted to a kind of public humiliation. It would have meant not only an outlay of cash, which Mr. Pettibone could be expected to resist, but a much more uncomfortable outlay of face. One of the tacit assumptions of Pompey's Head was that a person of consequence like Mr. Pettibone, in relation to a Negro like Clifford Small—in relation, indeed, to almost any Negro—could do no wrong. For Mr. Pettibone to have accepted the responsibility of Clifford's care on his own initiative would have been an entirely different matter, a gain of prestige rather than a loss. The tacit assumption, in that instance, would have been waived by his consent. It would then be said that hot-tempered though Mr. Pettibone was, and a hot temper always being understood to be one of the proper possessions of a Southern gentleman, he had realized that he had overstepped himself and that it showed his innate quality to do such a decent, generous thing. This way, however, when the whole town knew that he had taken the position that Clifford was drunk and had got just what was coming to him—this way he had to refuse. He could not let it be said that Will Page had compelled him to backtrack and forced him into doing what he would not have done on his own. "I'm damned if I'm going to let you hold me up this way, Page," he said. "Any money you get out of me you'll have to get on a court order. That nigger of yours was drunk. If he needs help, you help him. He's your nigger, not mine."

Anson felt that his father should have known Mr. Pettibone would take that position. And he should have known, too, that once the matter became a public issue the weight of general opinion would lean toward Mr. Pettibone's side. Privately it might be admitted that Mr. Pettibone had been in the wrong, but publicly, when the time came to stand up and be counted, it was bound to be said that Will Page, kindly and generous though he was, had in this instance gone a little too far. There was always that tacit assumption. Deny it once, and it might be denied forever, with who could say what disastrous consequences.

Why, then, in the possession of this knowledge, since he could not have lived the whole of his life in Pompey's Head without having acquired it, had his father brought the suit? Because he could not stand by, he said; because Mr. Pettibone was at fault. Yes, of course he was, but could it be imagined that opinion in a jury box was going to be different from opinion on the streets? Then why had his father persisted? There must be a reason. Was it more of what Marion would call stubbornness, a new reflection of the same hardheaded streak that had caused him to neglect his health for years? Was it that, was it principle, or was it a combination of that and principle and something else besides?

Anson, looking from the window at the steeple of St. Paul's, was beginning to think it was. He was remembering all those times that Mr. Pettibone's name had come up in family conversations, and he was thinking, in particular, of a talk that he and his father had had one afternoon a few years before. He was then still at the university but had managed to get to Pompey's Head for the week end. There was to be a party that night and he had a date with Kit Robbins. His father had come home as usual for dinner, which they always had at half-past one, and Anson accepted his invitation to walk back to the store. As they went past St. Andrew's Square, Anson looked over to the south side, hoping to catch a glimpse of Kit. There was no sign of life at her house, but Mr. Pettibone, who lived two doors away from her, was hobbling down the steps on crutches. He was being assisted by Abel, his houseboy, and wore a white sock pulled over his left foot. Anson turned to his father.

"Whatever happened to Mr. Pettibone?"

His father was also looking across the square.

"Haven't you heard? The poor fellow broke his toe."

"Broke his toe? How?"

"I don't know, exactly. The story is that he went to a party in Savannah, where one of his friends has a daughter who's coming out, and worked up enough ambition to try to dance the Paul Jones. Something gave way, apparently." Anson's father shook his head and chuckled. "Poor old Henry. He always used to fancy himself as the debutante's delight and I suppose he still does. I wonder if he's going to send those friends of his the bill. If I know Henry, I wouldn't be surprised."

"Father," Anson said, "what do you have against Mr. Pettibone?"

He had not intended to ask. He was talking to himself, saying, "What makes him take all these pokes at Mr. Pettibone, I wonder?" and then, before he realized what was happening, he had spoken out loud. Immediately he regretted the slip of his tongue. His father looked upset, breaking his stride for an instant, and Anson did not like to think that it was he who had placed him at this disadvantage.

"Why, Sonny," his father said, forcing a smile. "What makes you think that I have anything against Henry Pettibone?"

Anson was embarrassed. "I don't know. It's the way you sometimes talk about him, I suppose."

"You mean that I don't seem always to regard Henry as the most admirable person in the world?" His father looked at him with the same forced smile. "Is that it? Well, in case it is, I'm afraid you have me. It seems to be one of those unfortunate antagonisms that you can't do much about. Henry and I haven't been able to get along ever since we were boys."

Anson was still embarrassed. "Yes sir, I see."

"So I gather," his father said dryly. "It never occurred to me, though, that I was letting my feelings about Henry show through. We're never as clever as we think we are, are we? But it's true what I said, that I don't have anything against him. 'Against,' Sonny, implies a grudge, a chip on the shoulder, and it's not like that at all. It may have begun that way—Henry had a fondness for being lord of the manor even in the fourth grade and I was always the carpetbagger's son—but I do hope, at sixty-three, that I'm not still living in the fourth grade. No, Sonny, I don't have anything against him, not in the sense of a grudge. If I don't altogether admire Henry, as I'm forced to admit——"

"You don't have to explain."

"I'm not sure that I can, Sonny. It's something I've never tried to put into words. But suppose—well, suppose I said that to me Henry Pettibone represents just about everything that is wrong with this town. Would it make any sense?"

"I didn't know you thought there was anything wrong with Old Pompey," Anson rejoined. "You've always said——"

"Don't look so shocked, Sonny." His father smiled again, normally and naturally this time. "I haven't committed a felony. Whatever I said, I'm prepared to repeat. And what I said, if I remember correctly, is more or less what I understand they say about Dartmouth College —something about its being a small, dear place that we shall love eternally, or words to that effect. That doesn't mean, though, that this little garden spot of ours is altogether the Eden that the prevailing sentiment among our friends and neighbors would have us believe." His father paused and looked at him, shaking his head. "I'm afraid your mother wouldn't like this, Sonny. She'd say that I was putting notions in your head."

"I'm old enough, I guess."

His father nodded. "Yes, I guess you are. Besides, what I have to say probably won't make much sense to you, anyway. Certainly it's never made much sense to your mother. And then, again, your mother may be right. It *is* a notion and I wouldn't be surprised if it bordered on the heretical. I'm not sure that I should risk it."

This was one of the times when his father was amusing himself, as Anson was aware, but his eyes were warm and kind. Across the square, Abel was helping Mr. Pettibone into his car. Anson said:

"Why don't you take a chance?"

"All right, Sonny, why not? You're old enough, as you say. Have you ever heard of Shintoism, by any chance?"

Anson had to think for a moment. "I've heard you mention it. Isn't it something they have in Japan?"

"Yes, it most definitely is. Not in the same sense, though, that they 'have' dwarf trees and geisha girls and paper houses. Shintoism is the ancient Japanese religion and it is based in large part on ancestor worship."

Anson watched Abel get Mr. Pettibone settled into the back seat of the shiny new Buick the Pettibones had just acquired. He kept hoping that Kit would come out of her house, even though she said over the telephone that she had to go shopping with her mother. He said:

"Yes sir, I remember now."

"Good." His father gave a kind of grunt. "Since you'll be graduating from law school this year, I'm glad to know that it's not coming as a complete surprise. But where were we? You were saying that Shintoism was something they had in Japan and I agreed that it was. What I was getting at, however, is that we have a form of Shintoism here in Old Pompey. It's not one of the sanctified forms of worship, but it's my notion that it has a more powerful hold than even the Methodist Church."

They had come to the end of St. Andrew's Square and Anson relinquished his hope of seeing Kit. Watching Abel and Mr. Pettibone drive off, he said, "Has it?"

His father caught the note of preoccupation. "I don't happen to be boring you, am I?"

"No sir, you're not boring me."

"But do you know what I'm talking about?"

"Yes sir, I think so. You mean the way people go on about their ancestors, don't you?"

His father nodded. " 'Go on' is a good way of putting it. That's all that it amounts to nowadays. The Japanese, as I understand it, are not quite so trivial. Their form of ancestor worship appears to be a vital, positive force."

"And ours isn't?"

"What do you think?"

"I don't know what I think. I've never paid any mind to it before. What's your idea?"

"My idea?" His father thought for a moment. "My idea is this—I think that it is a lot of damned nonsense. Its principal effect, as I see it, has been to produce that enervated, run-down condition that is commonly known as Southern gentility. You've heard of Southern gentility, I suppose?"

"It's what we mean when we say that somebody is too poor to paint and too proud to whitewash, isn't it?"

"Why, Sonny, you surprise me." His father gave him a look of exaggerated approval. "That's it exactly, the whole philosophy in a nutshell. And I don't like it. I couldn't disagree with anything more."

Anson was surprised at the vigor with which his father spoke. He had assumed that he was simply making conversation, but it was obvious that this way of looking at things was something he had been bringing into focus for years. He said, "Why do you disagree with it? What's wrong, I mean?"

"What's wrong?" His father spoke in the same vigorous tone. "This is what's wrong—it's based on a fallacy. It depends wholly on the assumption that pride and whitewash won't mix—that that kind of pride, indeed, is something of which to be proud."

"And it isn't?"

His father shook his head. "Not to me it isn't. I always keep remembering that up in your grandfather Page's part of the country, up in New England, the very reverse about pride and whitewash would once have been held to be true. Pride, there, would have been equated with the willingness to whitewash. It would have been held a collapse of pride not to. And that, to me, is much the healthier view. However, I must confess that I often find myself wondering, out of my own brand of Shintoism, if the old New England strain wasn't a considerably hardier, more durable breed."

"Yankees, you mean?"

"My God, Sonny!" He fixed Anson with a sharp look of impatience and reproof. "Don't say 'Yankees' as though it were an ugly word. You can't help being a Southerner, but you might try to steer clear of being a professional one. And you might remember, also, that your grandfather——"

"I didn't mean anything about Grandpa."

"Of course you didn't," his father said. "I know that. And it wasn't your grandfather we were talking about. Where were we, anyway? Somewhere along the line I seem to have run off the track."

"We began with Mr. Pettibone."

"Yes, of course. Dear old Henry." His father wagged his head in a pretense of despair. "The truth is that I feel sorry for him at times. As I've said before, it's his misfortune to want to live up to a tradition without having a tradition to live up to. I don't mind the Blackfords' almost total immersion in ancestor worship, and I grant the Williams family its right to burn incense night and day, but our friend Henry, the Pettibones——" He wagged his head again. "None of those ancestors of his was ever first-rate, not one, and in all the years they've been here the Pettibones have failed to produce a single member of any real consequence. But Henry, because of the Blackfords and Williamses, because of the state religion, has to go on pretending that he too is quality—that that indentured-servant great-great-grandfather of his was no less important than old Tobias Williams, the first rice planter in the colony, and that Jennie's Basin, which was the Pettibones' only holding, was equal to Mulberry."

Anson could see that what his father was saying was true. It struck him that "Shintoism" was a most revealing word. One could use it as a key to explain much that was peculiar not only to Pompey's Head but to the whole South. The ancestor worship to which his father was alluding was directly related to the aristocratic principle inherent in the structure of Southern society from earliest times, and which much of the early colonial legislation, about which he was writing a paper for the law review, was intended to affirm. Thinking that his father's observations would give his essay a much larger dimension, he said, "Yes sir, I see what you mean."

"Do you? And you don't think that I have anything against Henry Pettibone?"

"No sir, I don't."

His father gave a casual shrug. "Well, that's something, in any case. I wouldn't want you to believe that I was still bogged down in the fourth grade. And, Sonny——"

"Yes sir?"

"I see no reason why any of this conversation should be repeated to your mother. She would probably say that I was confusing you unnecessarily. You don't feel any more confused than you were when we began this little visit, do you?"

"No sir, anything but."

"I'm glad to hear it," his father said. "I have enough on my conscience without wanting to burden it with that."

Sitting on the hard wooden chair in the reception room of Garrick & Leigh, Anson wished that Ian would hurry with his client. He wanted to put their meeting behind him. A month before, had he seen Ian walking on one of the streets of New York, or had Ian been invited to lunch at the Recess Club by one of the members, he would have gone out of his way to avoid him. And Ian, he imagined, would have done likewise. It was too much to expect that Ian had ever regretted his behavior during the time of the trouble with Mr. Pettibone, and yet, because of his involvement in it, by virtue of their having shared the same office, he would find it uncomfortable to have the episode brought back to mind. If Anson knew Pompey's Head, the trouble between Will Page and Henry Pettibone had receded to a point in time almost as distant as the Battle of Little Pigeon Marsh. None of the principals was alive any longer and it was most unlikely that a bystander like Ian would be able to remember all the details. Any discomfort he felt would not be for himself, since he could truthfully say that it had been none of his doing, but for this boyhood associate who, appearing out of nowhere, practically a ghost from the grave, had had to leave town. For that, certainly, was what it would have boiled down to—Sonny Page, in the unlikely event of his name ever coming up in conversation, was the boy who had to leave town.

And of course it was true. Not, however, in that intonation. He could have stayed in Pompey's Head had he wanted to. It was not as if he had got a girl into trouble, or absconded with funds, or been involved in some other personal disgrace. As things turned out, even the affair of Clifford Small need not have warranted his departure. The Page family lost a certain amount of caste because of it, for reasons which no outsider could be expected to understand—a breach of custom; a disloyalty to one's class; a thoughtless alignment with those revolutionary forces which threatened the whole social order— but since most of the Pages' acquaintances would have preferred to ignore the whole affair, again for reasons which no outsider could ever comprehend—a sense of form and good manners; an ingrained tendency to overlook the disagreeable; a recognition of the position which the Pages had enjoyed for years in Pompey's Head—he could easily, and in time perhaps comfortably, have gone along with the pretense that nothing had happened. There was no question about it; had he wanted to, he could have stayed in Pompey's Head. It was pride that caused him to leave. Kit Robbins hurt him beyond all bearing and he was too proud to stay.

To put it that way, however, was probably to make it simpler than it was. Motive in his case was no less obscure than in the case of others. Nothing could be truer than that he had left Pompey's Head because of Kit, and yet it stood to reason that there must have been other motives, less clear, less forceful, and it was conceivable that

215

among them there might have been a desire to justify his father. Somewhere in his resolve to get away there must have been the thought that if he went elsewhere and made a success it would reflect to his father's credit; at least part of his psychology must have been related to that of one whose father is a failure and who feels that he has to make up for it. And in part he had. He refined his father's ideas about Shintoism in the paper he wrote for the law review, and he developed them further in the book Phillip Greene encouraged him to write. It was not much, but it was something. He could say that he had at least given his father a chance to state his case.

The real spur, however, was Kit. It always came back to that. She had hurt him and he wanted to hurt her. He wanted her to be sorry someday and to realize how unfair she had been. There could hardly be a more embarrassing kind of pettiness, but one of the things you learned from the law was that most human motives are petty in the extreme, and, uncomfortable though it was, your own pettiness had to be faced. He had always objected to Meg's saying that he had run away, which implied a kind of cowardice, but hers was manifestly the correct version of what happened—he had run as fast as his legs could carry him. It was not so much a flight from Pompey's Head, however, as from a galling humiliation that he did not see how he could live with. He had built up an image of Kit, and that was destroyed, and he thought he loved her more than he had ever loved anyone, and that was destroyed too. The aloneness he felt was not because of Ian Garrick's defection, nor because of what people might say, nor because, overnight, the Page family had been injured in its position in the social scale. It was Kit who was responsible; from her came the damage that could never be undone. It was the night before his father was supposed to testify against Mr. Pettibone, and he and Kit stood facing each other in the living room of her home on St. Andrew's Square.

"Your father isn't doing this because of that old Negro!" she cried. "It's because he hates Mr. Pettibone. Oh, don't think I don't know! Mr. Pettibone told us everything. Your father hates him because the Pettibones have ancestors and you haven't! Oh, why did you let him do it? Why didn't you stop him? Don't you see that I can't think of marrying you now? I wouldn't ever be able to hold up my head in public."

Anson was too stunned to say anything at first. He stood looking at her with a curious numbness at the base of his skull. He found it impossible to believe that it was she who was saying these things, that

216

this was the girl who had caused him so many anxious moments and whom he had tried so hard to please, and then, suddenly, in a way he would never forget, it was not. The whole of their relationship passed before him, as all the details of a drowning man's life are supposed to appear in that last convulsive instant between struggle and surrender, and when the moment was over, he staring at her and she giving way to a burst of tears, she might have been someone whom he was seeing for the first time.

"Don't cry, Kit," he said finally. "It's not true what you think about my father, but it's not your fault. You can't help it. There's no reason to cry."

Anson did not know how many times he had gone over that last meeting with Kit. It was years before he could think of it without some of the numbness returning, and that he was eventually able to remember it calmly, almost as though it were an incident in the life of another person, was because it might well have been someone else who stood in that room with Kit, asking her not to cry and saying that it was not her fault. He was glad, however, that he had spoken as he had, without giving way to the bitterness he felt, and he thought it was to his credit that he could see even then that it was not her fault—it must have been then, stunned though he was, that he first began to comprehend that Pompey's Head had worked on her as a crippling, stultifying force.

Meg, with whom he once tried to discuss it, brushed aside his attempts to explain. "Oh, be reasonable!" she said. "I don't see why you can't even have an ordinary love affair without trying to make it into something unique simply because of Pompey's Head. Things like that happen in Indiana too, you know. All I get out of what you've been saying is that she was one of those silly, shallow Southern girls. What happened, if I have to spell it out for you, is that she threw you over. Why don't you relax and admit it?"

Whenever Meg spoke in that vein, Anson knew it was pointless to continue. Besides, what she thought of Kit was not that important. Nobody was hurt by her seeing Kit as a silly, shallow Southern girl, which had to be recognized as one way of reading her character, and it was possible that he was being overgenerous in thinking that she might have been a different person had she not had to live in Pompey's Head. However, after taking everything into consideration, he always returned to his original conclusion. It was not Kit's fault. She was as much sinned against as sinning and could not be held wholly to blame.

Much of the blame, as he saw it now, went back to her parents. It had always been a source of trouble to him that he did not like them. Mr. Robbins was a big, heavy, yet soft-looking man who always seemed uncomfortable in the tight shirt collars he wore, especially in warm weather, and it may have been this that caused Anson to imagine that he was uncomfortable in other ways also—his habit, for example, of never letting a chance go by to say what a fine place Pompey's Head was. "It's a great town," he would announce. "There's no other place in the country that can touch it. To live here is a privilege, that's what it is." Such appreciation was not unusual, for it was what everybody in Pompey's Head felt to some degree or other, but there was no one else in Anson's acquaintance who ever became quite that oratorical. He soon realized that Mr. Robbins felt under an obligation to say such things, as though he were afraid that his loyalty to Pompey's Head might be questioned, and he came to suspect that it was because Mr. Robbins was an outsider whose right to reside in the old Wedderburn place had never been completely accepted.

The notion of falsity was planted in Anson's head and the notion continued to grow. Mr. Robbins made a special point of being extremely cordial to him whenever he called on Kit, but Anson could not believe in his sincerity. There was a kind of hollowness to Mr. Robbins's geniality that made it impossible for him to respond. He became tongue-tied and ill at ease, wishing he could be as relaxed with Mr. Robbins as with most of the other men he knew—Mr. Blackford, for instance, who now admitted his and Wyeth's having reached man's estate by sprinkling his conversation with off-color anecdotes about the town's departed worthies, or Mr. Carpenter, Gaby's father, who was a student of the Civil War and liked to discuss the smallest details of all the battles and campaigns.

However, numerous though his reservations were about Mr. Robbins, Anson was even more strongly put off by Kit's mother. She could not have been more than fifty at the time, but she looked considerably older, a tall, angular woman with well-defined features, iron-gray hair, and a vexed expression that might have resulted from the sick headaches that caused her to take to her bed for days at a time. Proud of her home on St. Andrew's Square, she had so exaggerated an interest in housekeeping that some of the ladies in Pompey's Head called it a mania. Anson, used to his mother's more casual approach and Mrs. Blackford's downright slap-dashness, found it rather intimidating. Everything in the Robbins house was so perfectly in order, so polished and dusted and in-its-right-place, that it seemed almost a defilement to use even an ash tray—several times the thought crossed his mind, when he was sitting in the living room with Kit, that it was like having a date in the Founders' Room of the historical museum.

Mrs. Robbins's excessive tidiness, however, could readily have been overlooked. It was her hovering over Kit that got in the way. It did not take Anson long to perceive that she was reliving her own girlhood in Kit, making up for its disappointments, and though it was understandable it was also disconcerting. Her concern exceeded a mother's normal interest and passed over into anxiety. What Anson did not realize, and what he was not astute enough to understand until many years later, was that Mrs. Robbins's whole life was pitched on an anxious plane. She was not a happy woman and hers was not a happy household. Anson did not think she could have been happy anywhere. He felt that any household that sheltered both her and Mr. Robbins would be subject to considerable strain, and he could see that moving to Pompey's Head was the worst thing that could have happened to her. In the small South Carolina town in which she had been born and raised, she at least had a place. Her family had been native to the community for several generations and her father, a grain merchant, was one of the wealthiest men around. In Pompey's Head, however, she was nobody. It recognized no standards but its own, and its iron laws made no provisions for strangers. They could either sink or swim, and were more likely to win approval if they showed their good manners by choosing not to swim.

The mistake of the Robbinses was in staying so noticeably afloat. Mrs. Robbins would have been determined to do so even without her ambitions for Kit, resentful at being placed in an inferior position, but it was her aspirations for her daughter that were most in her mind—thus the expensive restoration of the house on St. Andrew's Square; thus the pretense to a social inheritance equal to that of the Blackfords, Carpenters, Paxtons, and other long-established natives; thus the frequent references to family silver, family furniture, family portraits, and to that distant progenitor who stood in some obscure kinship to old Tobias Williams, he who had introduced the cultivation of rice to the colony and through whom Mrs. Robbins was related, no less obscurely, to Joe Ann's father, Dr. Williams.

On the surface it appeared to work. Even more than the Blackfords, the Williamses were regarded as the first family in Pompey's Head, their past being only slightly less brilliant and their present grounded in a financial stability of which the Blackfords had not been able to boast for years, and because of the Williamses the newcomers had to be taken in. There was a difference, however, between being taken in and being accepted. Moreover, that which Mr. and Mrs. Robbins had hoped would seal their acceptance, the turning of the house on St. Andrew's Square into one of the handsomest residences in town, worked to their disfavor—the general opinion was that they should have waited at least another ten years; it showed a lack of respect for the local proprieties.

Under the surface, then, with the Robbinses in the position of permanent probationers, there was a set of tensions which could have but one result—Mr. and Mrs. Robbins became more royalist than the king. The standards they set up for Kit, and which Kit seemed predisposed to accept, were far more severe than those that the Carpenters, to take only one example, would ever have thought of raising for Gaby. Kit, however, did not have Gaby's secure footing. That Indian girl Mary, Tupichichi's daughter, may have behaved scandalously, but at least she bestowed upon the Carpenters a patent of priority—Gaby lay under her protection; she excused even those extravagant costumes that Gaby got herself up in. Kit, however, walked alone. As her parents saw it, she could take no chances. And Kit, wrapped in bandages as confining as the strips of silk with which the Chinese used to bind the feet of their female infants, was turned into a kind of cripple.

Freed from the obligations of loyalty, Anson was able in time to see it clearly. Kit could have rebelled, of course, but rebellion was contrary to her nature—Gaby was a flaming revolutionary by contrast. He never appreciated this side of Kit until one night shortly after he went to work at Garrick & Leigh. Some of the crowd had congregated at the Williamses'—he and Kit; Wyeth Blackford and Joe Ann; Jay Lockhart and Margie Rhett—and Joe Ann suggested that they drive out to the Oasis. Although the proscription against the roadhouse had not been lifted, Joe Ann and Margie, along with Gaby Carpenter, had joined against convention and sometimes got their dates to take them there. Their parents did not approve, but since the girls were now old enough to vote they could not well object.

Everybody was eager to go but Kit. She said her mother was not feeling well and that she promised to get in early. Anson knew it was true about her mother, but this was the first he had heard about her having to get in early. He felt let down. He would have liked to listen to Vicksburg and the band. His disappointment must have showed itself when, later, after they said good night to the others, who had already piled into Jay's car, he walked Kit home.

"You wanted to go with them, didn't you?" she said.

"Yes, sort of."

Kit seemed annoyed by the admission. "Well, I didn't! I wouldn't be caught dead in such a place! It seems to me, too, now that you're a lawyer——"

This was something new. "What in the world does being a lawyer have to do with it?"

"Do with it?" Her chin went up and she tossed her head. "Isn't it like you to ask! Don't you see that there are some things you can't do any more? It's all right for you to spend most of your spare time in the woods with Wyeth—nobody's going to mind that, I guess—but how do you expect people to have any confidence in you if you hang around with a lot of mill hands and Irish Channel toughs?"

This was also something new. Anson thought he could see Mr. and Mrs. Robbins hovering in the background. Nor did the picture that Kit was drawing coincide with reality—certainly one evening spent at the Oasis in the company of his friends would not get him accused of hanging around. Only the Robbinses would think so. Their idea of how a young man just starting out should behave was Marlin Fowler, a recent arrival who came from Montgomery and worked in the local office of Fenner & Beane. Fowler would agree with Kit that the Oasis wasn't a place fit to be caught dead in. Anson was not jealous of him —not that prematurely balding sissified male!—and he could understand why the Robbinses were pleased over his interest in Kit. Fowler was correct, his mother was a Bartlett from Pompey's Head, and he was supposed to have that vague thing called a future—in some ways, Anson thought, it was more than could be said of himself. He more than once had disregarded correctness, his grandfather was a New Hampshire man who had moved South at a time when all Northerners were looked upon as carpetbaggers, and the best future he could anticipate was that of a lawyer in a small Southern city of limited opportunity. He said, "You don't really believe, do you, that if we'd gone to the Oasis——"

Kit did not let him finish. "If it means that much to you, why didn't you go! You needn't have let me stand in the way. You can still go if you want to. You'll just have to go alone, that's all, or else find one of your Channel friends!"

His Channel friends. You would think that the gossip generated by his almost getting into a brawl over Midge at the Oasis would have died down by now, but it hadn't. Merely his stopping to visit with her when they happened to pass each other on Bay Street, and his buying her a Coca-Cola a few times in Spier's Drugstore, had been enough to keep it alive. Sly references were always being passed, especially by Ian Garrick, and as a consequence he found that Midge was more in his thoughts than she might have been ordinarily. He was certainly not in love with her and never had been—what happened that night in the country could have happened to anybody—and yet whenever her name entered into the conversation, which was not often, since her path and that of the Alwyn Street crowd rarely crossed any longer, he found himself taking up for her. Joe Ann and Gaby had always been fond of Midge and so said nothing unpleasant. Gaby, indeed, upon hearing that Midge had been made assistant head of the ready-to-wear department at Cornish's, said that if she went to New York and got a job in one of the better stores she could make a real career for herself, just as she, Gaby, intended to do as a portrait painter as soon as she could get her benighted family to consent to her going back to New Orleans, which, when she was attending Newcomb College, she had come "simply to adore," but with Margie Rhett it was different. She had never liked Midge, possibly because she had had a hankering in high school for the popularity that seemed naturally to come Midge's way, and was always going out of her way to make ugly remarks. Anson would have objected to them in any case, based as they were on Midge's Channel origins and the broad implication that she was no better than she had to be, and since they came from Margie, who had got the popularity she was after by turning into one of the worst neckers in town, they seemed all the more unfair. Anson could never fully speak his mind, bound on the one hand by the circumstance that he could not give Margie away and on the other by the sometimes embarrassing fact that his knowledge of her behavior had been gained partially from personal experience, but whenever she became particularly unpleasant he boldly stood up for Midge.

All this Kit knew. It had never occurred to Anson that she might be jealous of Midge, however, and he did not believe that she was jealous now. Her animosity, he felt, went deeper than that—Midge, like the Oasis, was beyond the pale. Only that could account for the way her body went stiff with disdain. She reminded him of her mother and he wished she were less concerned with the proprieties. It was all right to want to be nice, but there was such a thing as carrying niceness too far—a girl could end by being a stick. The first real difference between them, the Oasis made Anson suspect that there might be other differences. He was far too much in love, however, to want even to confront the possibility. What, he decided, if Kit did not like the Oasis? He certainly had no intention of holding it against her; as a matter of fact, it probably reflected to her credit.

It did not occur to Anson, not until years later, that Kit was frightened of the Oasis. He was not perceptive enough to realize that the circumstances of her upbringing caused her to recoil almost in trembling against all that the roadhouse stood for, but even then he suspected that her antipathy stemmed from a feeling of insecurity. If she would not consider going to the Oasis, it was because it lay too far beyond the genteel pattern. The other girls might be willing to run the risk of being seen there, but not she. Better by far to have it known that you wouldn't be caught dead in such a place; better to sit at home and play bridge with Mildred Bridges, Julia Pettibone, and Betsy Follinsbee. Sticks they were, but safe. And of the best, nicest people. Playing at cards with them would get no black marks beside your name; you moved in the shelter of their familial correctness; and you proved, to your further advantage, that you knew better how to behave, even though you were a "new" girl, than Joe Ann Williams or Gaby Carpenter.

Everything came clear in time. The only trouble, Anson thought, sitting in the reception room of Garrick & Leigh, was that understanding had a habit of arriving much too late. If he had known then what he knew now, the whole story might have been different. He had not known, however, and neither had he known, as he stood looking at the spire of St. Paul's, that anyone could be that sick with pain. "I'm going to the courthouse," he said to Ian, speaking in an unnaturally loud voice. "Tell your father and Mr. Leigh that I won't be in for the rest of the day." Ian gave him a frightened glance and Anson did not have to be told what he was thinking. Among the various rules you were expected to obey, one of the most important was that you did not walk out of the office without permission when there was work to be done—not unless you wanted to throw everything up and burn your bridges behind you. What Ian had no way of knowing was that to burn his bridges was precisely what he did want. Already they had been put to the torch and he would never be traveling by that road again. He was not going to live in Pompey's Head any longer. He was going to draw out all of his savings and go to New York. He never wanted to see Kit Robbins again.

CHAPTER FIFTEEN

Anson's long thoughts were broken into by a busy duet of voices coming from the narrow corridor along which were strung the individual offices of Garrick & Leigh. One of the voices, high-pitched and querulous, sounded as though it belonged to an old man, and the other, placating yet slightly impatient, belonged to Ian Garrick—Anson recognized it immediately. The plump young woman who had taken Mrs. Telfair's place looked up from her typewriter, nodding in the direction of the voices to indicate that Ian would soon be ready to receive him, and then Ian and a thin, leathery little man, old as his voice had proclaimed him, came through the door that led into the reception room. The old man was a stranger to Anson, but Ian he would have known anywhere. Though his blond hair was thinner and beginning to turn gray, the grayness was not especially noticeable, and while he looked older and heavier, broader in the shoulders than Anson had remembered, the extra weight was distributed evenly over his frame.

Neither Ian nor the old man noticed his presence. The old man was stubbornly trying to continue some discussion, and Ian, no less stubbornly, was trying to break it off. He kept bobbing his head in short, impatient jerks, vainly seeking to interrupt the old man's flow of talk, and there was an irritable expression around his eyes that reminded Anson of the times when he used to be annoyed by the visits of his father's country kinsmen. Nothing could be more obvious than that he wanted to get rid of his caller, but the old man refused to be hurried. Planting his feet firmly, he said doggedly, "Dammit, I know there's a deed telling about that boundary somewheres. It says that the line goes to the middle of the creek, not just to the edge of it! I know what I'm talking about! It ain't something that I went and dreamed up, by God!"

Ian tried to quiet him, saying, "Yes sir, Mr. Hauslauer, I'm sure you're right. That's the way most of those old deeds used to read. Until we find it, though——" And then, as in his restlessness he glanced about the room, he saw Anson sitting on the chair. A look of incredulity froze his face, as though he found it impossible to credit his senses, and his eyes went blank with surprise. His jaw dropped for an instant—"For God's sake!" he managed to say—and both the old man and the plump young woman who sat at Mrs. Telfair's desk followed the direction of his stare until they too were looking at Anson. Rising, Anson stepped forward and held out his hand.

"Remember me?" he said. "I used to work here."

He hoped that Ian would be willing to let it go at that. He did not want to pretend to any emotions he did not have, and he did not feel up to a scene. Ian, however, was more spontaneous. He said, "Sonny! Of all people! Where did you come from?" and rushed forward to shake Anson's hand. "I can't believe it!" he said. "You haven't changed a bit! Am I glad to see you!"

Anson regretted his own lack of warmth. He could not believe, however, that Ian was truly that glad to see him. There was always that anxiety of Ian's about knowing only the right people and doing the right thing, and it did not seem likely that he would have overcome it. He may have dropped his guard for a moment, taken by surprise, but already, as Anson saw him looking at him in a different way, the barricades were being thrown up again. Ian Garrick had always been one of the most transparent people he knew, and it was obvious that already he was beginning to wonder what Sonny Page was doing back in town.

"How are you, Ian?" Anson said. "You're looking well."

"You too," Ian replied. "You look fine. I still can't believe it's you."

"It's me, all right. I hope you don't mind my just walking in."

Ian had a hundred questions to ask, but the old man was silently clamoring for attention. He knew that something out of the ordinary was afoot, and so did the plump young woman who sat at Mrs. Telfair's desk. Ian introduced Anson to them—"You remember Sonny Page, don't you, Mr. Hauslauer? He used to be here in the office, but Old Pompey was too small to hold him. He's a big New York lawyer now. Millie, this is the Mr. Page you've heard so much about. Sonny, we used to call him. And don't let his looks fool you. He's as old as I am."

Anson, shaking Mr. Hauslauer's hand and nodding in what he hoped was a pleasant fashion to Mrs. Telfair's successor, thought that this was Pompey's Head again—the bland assumption that Mr. Hauslauer must surely remember him; the casual identification of himself as a "big" New York lawyer; the implication that Millie was already working up a set of designs on him. There was not a word of truth in any of it, as they were all aware, and yet, because of the demands of custom, they must adjust themselves to the pretense that Ian could not have come closer to gospel had he tried—Mr. Hauslauer saying let him see now, mebbe he *did* recollect him and wasn't he Will Page's boy, the one who used to have the hardware store down on Bay Street, while Millie, now that she had been called upon to introduce the female element, smiled plumply and lowered her eyes.

But much as Anson wanted to play the part to which he had been assigned—the local boy who made good; the big New York lawyer still at ease in the world of his childhood—he could tell that he was falling short. He tried to make conversation with Mr. Hauslauer, or, rather, to listen to Mr. Hauslauer's conversation, since the old man was rattling away about how he remembered when there used to be a saddle maker in the rear part of the hardware store, which would be back in Anson's granddaddy's time, he reckoned, and all Anson could think of was that this sort of thing could never happen at Roberts, Guthrie, Barlowe & Paul. Were Ian Garrick to put in an appearance there, it would not turn into a social occasion.

He had plainly lost touch. He had again been put in the position of being an outsider. The feeling still weighed heavily upon him when, a few minutes later, he and Ian faced each other across the desk in Ian's office. It was the same room that he and Ian used to share, the one with the bay window that looked down on Bay Street and Cemetery Square, and Anson recognized some of the furniture. The office, however, was considerably larger. The wall that had separated it from the office which formerly adjoined and which used to be occupied by Mr. Leigh had been removed. There were marks on the ceiling that told where the partition had been.

"You've changed the office," Anson said.

"What?" Ian looked puzzled for an instant. "Oh, the office. It's been fixed up like this going on nine years. We had it done over when Mr. Leigh died—you knew he was dead, didn't you? Funny way it happened, too. He was out hunting rabbits—you remember how crazy he was about hunting rabbits—and he must have had a heart attack. That's what Doc Williams said it was. They found him in the woods. It was Mr. Leigh's going like that, all of a sudden, that caused the old man to make up his mind to retire. He's past seventy now, you know. He and Mother spend most of their time in Florida. They have a place just outside of Fort Lauderdale. The old man likes to fish, and Mother's all crippled up with arthritis, and——"

"You're here alone, then?"

Ian's expression changed and Anson realized that it was the wrong thing to say. Ian wanted him to understand that he was no one-horse lawyer struggling to get along. Anson expected him to utter a sharp denial, but, instead, regaining his composure, "No," Ian said, "Luke Elliot's in with me. I don't suppose you remember Luke. He's some years younger than we are—Mr. Leigh's grandson. You remember the Paul Elliots who used to live on Independence Street, don't you? Well, Luke started taking over some of Mr. Leigh's practice before Mr. Leigh died, and then, after the old man retired, we formed a new partnership. It's Garrick & Elliot now."

"I see. You must have to carry quite a load."

That was better. Ian, now that he had corrected any possible misconception, could afford to relax. Leaning back in his chair, he said, "A load is right. As a matter of fact, we're not taking on any new clients any more. We can't, not unless we get another man. It's more of a problem than it sounds. We can't take in just anybody, not in a firm like this, and, besides, we need more than some kid fresh out of law school."

"Why don't you make me a proposition?"

"All right." Ian smiled genially. "Name your own terms. Seriously, though, it's getting to the point where we are almost obliged to take in someone else. Just looking after Consolidated Enterprises alone takes up practically all of my time. And Luke's too. He's over there at a meeting now."

Schooled though he was, Anson found it hard to look interested. He was not impressed by Consolidated Enterprises, which was apparently a holding company of sorts, nor by Consolidated's president, who appeared to be known as Mickey, and he wished that Ian had not thought it necessary to bowl him over. He could pretend to be as bowled over as the next man, however, having had schooling in that direction as well, and Ian seemed finally satisfied.

"So you can see why we could use another man," he said. "The way it is now, Luke and I are being run ragged."

"That's fine, Ian. I'm glad things have gone so well. How's Olive?"

Some of Ian's enthusiasm began to fade. "Olive's all right, I reckon. She's got a back that keeps bothering her, and now and then she runs into a spell of sick headaches, but all the doctors say there's nothing wrong. It's mostly nerves, I reckon. Olive always was a high-strung girl."

Anson could remember that she was. It seemed a more mismated union than ever, Olive Paxton and Ian Garrick, but that was not for him to decide. He nodded sympathetically, and Ian, who had been looking thoughtful, said, in the cordial tone which he had apparently decided to adopt, "Wait till Olive hears that you're in town! She won't be able to wait to see you."

"I want to see her too."

"I'd call her up right now," Ian went on, "but she's not home. This is her day to have the Wednesday Afternoon Club and she had to come to town to buy some flowers. You'd think, though, that with all the flowers we have growing out there on the Drive, and the money we spend on them——"

"The Drive?"

No sooner was it said than he knew that Ian's had been a baited remark. He had been wrong, too, in thinking that Ian had finished trying to bowl him over—he had simply moved to another alley.

"Azalea Drive," Ian said. "It's where we live now, out on the water. Nobody lives in town any more unless they have to. They'd all live out on the Drive if they could. It's out on Paradise Isle."

This time the bait was plainly visible. It was not an attractive way for either of them to behave, Anson thought, but he was not going to give Ian the satisfaction of hooking him again.

"Paradise Isle?" he said. "It sounds like an amusement park."

Ian had not expected anything like that. He looked worried, and there was a short, uncomfortable silence before he spoke.

"I don't reckon you would know it by that name," he said cautiously. "There have been a lot of changes in Old Pompey since you left. Paradise is the one we used to call Boogooloo. It's all built up now. You remember Boogooloo, don't you?"

Anson thought it strange that Ian should ask. Why shouldn't he remember Boogooloo? It was one of the places where he and Wyeth Blackford used to go shooting when they were boys. The island was known as Boogooloo because that was what the colored people called it. There was a small cemetery on the island, one that went back to colonial times, and because of it, the island was supposed to be haunted by boogooloos, or ghosts. It used to be Boogooloo and now it was Paradise and Ian Garrick was right about one thing, at least—there had been a lot of changes in Old Pompey since he left.

"It still sounds like an amusement park."

Ian forced a laugh. "Yes, I suppose so, if you want to look at it that way. To us, though—well, we think the name fits. Wait till you see the place we have out there. Everybody says it's one of the prettiest places on the water."

Anson expected him to go into details, making it clear how much the place on the water had cost, but, with a new show of cordiality, somewhat less convincing, Ian said, "When can you come to supper? I'd ask you for this evening but I'm all tied up. There's a meeting of the social committee at the Light Infantry Club. I wish there was some way that I could get out of it, but I can't. The Easter Assembly will be coming up before long and——"

"I didn't know you were in the club, Ian," Anson said. "I always thought——"

What he thought was that membership in the Light Infantry Club was limited to those whose ancestors had fought in the regiment during the Revolution, as none of Ian's people had. Ian tried to shake off a new look of worry and Anson wished that he had been more circumspect. Ian's membership in the Light Infantry Club was plainly his proudest possession; fired off at the proper time, it could always be counted upon to impress people. Now, however, because he and Ian had grown up together, because his memory was longer than it should have been, and because they knew all about each other, it had backfired in Ian's hand.

"It's a little different about the club now," Ian said warily. "With so many of the old members dying off, and the admittance rules being as strict as they were, the Board of Governors decided that they'd have to make a few changes. Now, if anybody you can lay claim to was a member of the Light Infantry, like, say, your wife's ancestors, the way Olive's were, like her great-great-granduncle General Carvell——"

"Sure, Ian," Anson said. "I know."

And there was something else he knew. He knew that beneath whatever changes lay upon the surface, beneath the transformation of Boogooloo Island into Paradise Isle and the greater leniency of the Light Infantry Club, nothing in Pompey's Head had changed. It was still the place he had to get away from, and he was more than ever thankful that he had. Those years in the cubbyhole were worth it; everything he had gone through was worth it. He was freer in a way than, had he stayed in Pompey's Head, he ever could have been. All he needed was to look at Ian Garrick to know it.

Remembering his wife's ancestors seemed to have restored some of Ian's self-confidence. He said, "Of course we don't admit just anybody into the club. It's just as hard to get in as ever. We have a waiting list two blocks long. And you'd be surprised at the claims people make. It got to be so bad that we had to appoint a special committee on ancestors."

"What does the committee do?" Anson said. "Give a Wassermann?"

Ian tried to force another laugh, but this time it was too much for him. He said, "That's right, you never did think much of the club, did you? I remember all those remarks you used to make. But if you live here like we do, and have a daughter who will be making her debut someday——"

In which case, if you lived in Pompey's Head and had a daughter who would be making her debut someday, you would naturally want to belong to the club. For one thing, you would not want your daughter to miss the supper given by the club on the night before the Light Infantry Ball—anyone who lived in Pompey's Head could tell you that the club supper, with dancing afterward, was the highwater mark of a girl's social career. All the year's debutantes were sent invitations to the Light Infantry Ball, whether or not any of their male connections belonged to the club, but the club supper, along with several other intimate functions, was restricted to those who were known as Light Infantry Girls. So if you lived in Pompey's Head and had a daughter who would be making her debut someday, you would not want to have her left out.

But what, as it happened, of the daughters who were—as Kit Robbins had been; as any number of girls had been; even as his own sister Marion had been? That was a Marion, he remembered, whose existence he had never suspected. Eunice Pettibone was going to the Light Infantry supper, and Marion was not, and Eunice had just called her on the telephone—deliberately to remind her, it seemed, of what she was going to miss. Marion came running into the library with blazing eyes. Anson did not know his sister could feel that deadly about anyone. "I despise that dirty little sneak!" she cried. "I could cut her heart out! I hate, hate, *hate* her!" But what Marion really hated, as Anson knew even then, was not being one of the Light Infantry Girls. Everything was different and nothing was different and it was all as dry as dust.

Ian had gone back to being cordial again. "How are you fixed for tomorrow night?" he said. "Can you make it for supper? Olive will want to give you a party, I know. It will be a fine excuse to round up all the old gang. What about it?"

Anson did not want Olive to give him a party, and neither did he want her to round up all the old gang. It would not do to seem indifferent, however, or superior, and, besides, there was still the possibility that Olive might be able to help him get in touch with Mrs. Garvin Wales.

"That will be fine, Ian," he said. "I'd love to come."

"How can we get hold of you? Where are you staying?"

"I'm at the Marlborough."

The change of expression that crossed Ian's face, hurriedly dissembled and masked, told Anson that he too had finally got around to remembering. It needed only his mentioning the Marlborough to bring it about. He might be Anson Page, one of the partners of Roberts, Guthrie, Barlowe & Paul, but to Ian Garrick, now that he had said he was staying at the Marlborough, he was still Sonny Page, the boy who had to leave town—the closet doors were open and the ghosts were streaming out.

"Let's count on tomorrow night, then," Ian said. "I'm sure it will be all right with Olive. If we had another date, she would have told me about it. How long are you going to be in town?"

"Only a few days, I imagine. I had to come down on a little job."

Now that everything else had been disposed of, Ian was able to bring his curiosity into the open.

"Business?"

"Yes, in a way. One of our clients is Duncan & Company, the publishing house, and they have an author by the name of Garvin Wales. Probably you've heard of him. He lives on Tamburlaine Island."

Ian nodded solemnly. "I don't suppose you remember it, but his wife is one of Olive's cousins. Mrs. Wales was Lucy Devereaux before she married, and one of Olive's grandmothers, her grandmother on her mother's side, was a Devereaux too."

Anson lit a cigarette. One of the things that the law had taught him was that it was better not to tell everything you knew. Not all at once, anyway.

"Now that you mention it," he said, "I do remember something about Olive and Mrs. Wales being related. Do you and Olive see them often? Mr. and Mrs. Wales, I mean?"

Ian looked worried again. He said, "No, we don't," and then, after a pause, "We tried to be friendly when they first came down here, more because Olive thought we ought to than anything else, seeing as how she and Mrs. Wales are kin, but——"

Anson shrugged off the details. Those "connections" of his that John Duncan imagined would be so valuable had proved worthless already. Olive Garrick had been his only hope, and the Garricks, as he should have known beforehand, were the sort of people Garvin and Lucy Wales would naturally avoid. Olive and Ian, it seemed, had driven to Tamburlaine Island to call—that cousinship, in Olive's mind, gave her the right. But apparently the meeting had not gone off well. Mrs. Wales was polite, but only polite, and her husband did not even appear.

"One thing I can tell you," Ian said coldly. "We didn't try to be friendly after that. I don't suppose you know it, since it's naturally something he'd want to hide, but that Wales fellow——"

Anson looked up. "Yes?"

"He's a drunk! I mean that—a real soak! The way I hear it, he hasn't drawn a sober breath in years. I read somewhere that he prefers to live like a hermit, never seeing anybody, but do you expect me to believe that? The truth is that he is never in any condition fit to be seen. That's why he's gone and hid himself on Tamburlaine. Why else would he?"

Anson hardly listened. With his own problems in front of his mind, he could not be bothered to explain that Garvin Wales's drinking was a matter of common knowledge, and that the reports which Ian had heard were probably exaggerated. Under different circumstances it might be amusing, the comeuppance Ian got, but he had no time to be amused. The way things had turned out, he seemed to have come to a dead end.

"No wonder he's blind," Ian was saying, still on the subject of Garvin Wales. "Blind drunk, if you ask me! I don't know what your business with him is——"

"It's not especially important," Anson said, crushing out his cigarette in a tray that stood on Ian's desk. "We just need his signature on a few papers, that's all. It could have been handled through the mails as easily as not, but I didn't take a vacation last summer and this looked like a good chance to get away from the office for a day or two. Tell me this, Ian—are Mr. and Mrs. Wales friendly with anybody in town? Anybody I might know, that is."

"Friends?" Ian looked determinedly scornful. "With him? Anybody who'd write the books that he does, with all that rape and incest and somebody catting around on every page, making it seem like that was all we did down South——"

Weary though he was beginning to feel, Anson forced a smile. "Let's not get off on that, Ian. The truth is that I have a little problem on my hands. I decided to make this trip on the spur of the moment and I didn't have time to write the Waleses beforehand. I've never met either of them and they don't know that I'm in town. So, rather than just barge in on them, I thought that if we happened to know someone in common, someone who could introduce me, it might put everything on a friendlier basis. Not that it's very important. It's just a notion I had, that's all."

He sounded exactly as he wanted to sound. One used the social gambit whenever possible in Pompey's Head and he had said nothing that should cause Ian to become suspicious. He could not have improved on it had he rehearsed it for hours.

"Well, I don't know," Ian said. "Nobody knows him, like I said, and I wouldn't say that anyone knew her, either, with maybe the exception of Dinah Higgins. One thing, though—you don't hear people saying things against her the way they do him. Why did she marry him, coming from a fine old family like the Devereauxs?"

"I've no idea, Ian. I know practically nothing about them."

"That woman must have a hard life," Ian said. "She hardly ever gets off that island. It's no wonder, either, considering the shape that fellow is in. One of their servants told the cook who works for the Fowlers——"

"But Mrs. Wales does appear now and then?"

"Not very often," Ian said. "Like I told you, she hardly gets off Tamburlaine. Olive, though, sees her now and then at the Camellia Club. She says that she's a wonderful person. All she does, it seems, is to take care of that husband of hers. That's a job I wouldn't wish on any woman. Did you know that she used to be on the stage?"

Anson was glad to find that his thoughts were running smoothly again—Olive, if she had concluded that Mrs. Wales was a wonderful person, must have been won over. She must have decided to overlook that initial snub. Nor was it hard to understand. Lucy Wales had much in her favor. She was a Devereaux, she had been on the stage, she was one of the elect who owned an island, and she was married to a famous man. What it all added up to was that she had a name worth dropping. It could do Olive no harm, when she visited in Charleston or Savannah, to let it tinkle into the conversation at just the right time. It was a small piece of artillery, not in the same class with the Light Infantry Club, but at close quarters it had its advantages.

"You know she used to be on the stage, don't you?" Ian asked.

Anson brought his thoughts back into focus. "Yes, I do," he said. "I gather that she caused quite a stir. She wasn't much of an actress, as I get it, but I'm told she made a striking appearance. I've yet to meet a person who knew her who doesn't still talk about how beautiful she was."

"That I can understand," Ian said solemnly. "I just saw her that one time, when we went to call, and it's easy to believe what you say. You can tell she used to be beautiful. She doesn't look nearly as old as Olive says she is. Olive says that she's past fifty. Is that right?"

"I think so."

"It just goes to show," Ian said. "Me, I'd have put her down as being just on the far side of forty-five. And I don't know—she still looks like an actress. But what I don't understand is why she married that fellow. She must have known what he'd turn into."

When you were after information, Anson reminded himself, you sometimes had to be patient. He said, "As I get it, it had something to do with love."

"Well, maybe." Ian did his best to sound cynical. "That's what Olive says too. Olive says——"

"She and Olive sound as though they were on pretty good terms."

Ian looked suddenly wary, as though he had had enough powder burns for one day. "Oh, I guess they get along all right. I wouldn't exactly call them friends, though, and I don't think Olive would feel that she knew Mrs. Wales well enough to introduce you. The only time they see each other is when they go to the Camellia Club."

"How often is that?"

Ian still kept his look of wariness. "The club meets every month, but Mrs. Wales isn't a very good member. She only shows up about once or twice a year. She's made a big collection of camellias, though, and so has Dinah Higgins. Dinah probably knows her best of anybody. The Camellia Club generally meets at Dinah's——"

Anson found himself stiffening in his chair. Something about that name, Dinah Higgins, now that Ian had mentioned it again, had a different sound. He was sitting bolt upright before he knew it.

"Dinah who?" he said.

"Dinah Higgins. Wyeth's sister, Dinah Blackford. She and Mickey Higgins——"

"Wait a minute," Anson said. "Are you trying to tell me that Dinah Blackford and Mico Higgins——"

234

Ian stared at him in amazement. "Didn't you know? You have been out of touch, haven't you? It happened during the war. Dinah was getting on, working in the bank and living with her father in that house they moved into on Upton Street, and Olive says——"

Anson heard him through a new tumbling of his own thoughts, centering about the V-mail letter he had received in London from his mother: "You didn't say anything about what I wrote about Dinah Blackford. Weren't you surprised?" He could not be surprised because he had not received the letter to which his mother referred, and neither had he received an announcement of Dinah's marriage—that, too, must have gone astray. It was a small, quiet wedding, Ian was explaining, with only the two families present and a few intimate friends, but no matter how small or quiet or intimate it was, he was sure that Dinah would have wanted him to know.

"What were the Blackfords doing on Upton Street?" he asked, remembering that Upton Street was one of the meanest and shabbiest streets in town. "When did they move there?"

"It was after Mrs. Blackford died," Ian said. "You know she passed away, I suppose? Well, Mr. Blackford got his hands on most of her money—she didn't leave a will, for one thing—and you don't need me to tell you what happened. What do you think he did this time?"

"I wouldn't know, Ian. What did he do?"

"He went into turkey-raising. Not just the way anybody would go into turkey-raising who was just starting out, not like you or me, but on that big, grand scale he always went in for, like the time he had that horse ranch in the mountains. He took that little farm that Mrs. Blackford had out on Little River and poured money into it like he'd come into a million dollars. He had himself a time, all right. It was a dilly while it lasted! You should have seen some of those turkey houses he built. They were damn near good enough for people to live in! But it didn't last long, naturally. In a couple of years he was broke again, just like he always was."

Ian's manner and tone of voice were causing Anson to become impatient again, and he had to remind himself that there was nothing to be impatient about. What Ian was saying was nothing new. Everybody in Pompey's Head knew that Mr. Blackford had gone through a lot of money, thousands and thousands of dollars, and it was not surprising that he had gone through Mrs. Blackford's money too. It was easy for Anson to understand his wanting to have a turkey farm —a "model" farm, he probably called it; one that would have done credit to Mulberry in the old days—and it was certainly not surprising that it had failed. Just as success is expected of some men, failure was expected of Mr. Blackford. He wore his withered laurels well. The turkey farm, however, leading as it did to Upton Street, must have been the end. It was not surprising and yet it was hard to believe.

"And Wyeth?" he asked. "What's happened to Wyeth?"

"You mean to say that you've lost track of him too?"

"Is he still around?"

"Yes, he's still around." Ian's tone of voice gave Anson to understand that Wyeth Blackford was one of the people with whom he no longer associated. "I hardly ever see him, though, except when I happen to run into him on Bay Street."

"What's he doing?"

Ian seemed reluctant to answer. "He has some kind of job at the Cassava Gun Club—caretaker, I reckon you'd call it. He married a girl from up in Collingwood County whose father trains bird dogs. Her name was Ivy Mapes. They live in one of those cabins on the gun-club grounds. I don't know that you'd recognize Wyeth. He's turned into a regular boomer."

Boomer was a rather special word in Pompey's Head, confined to the small group which spent its summers in the North Carolina mountains. It meant a confined backwoodsman, one who rarely emerged from the hills. Anson could tell that Ian expected him to be taken aback, and even to be a little contemptuous—not so much because Wyeth was a caretaker at the Cassava Gun Club, little more than a servant, but because he had marrried a girl named Ivy Mapes whose father trained bird dogs. And yet, as in the case of Mr. Blackford, there was a kind of preordained correctness. The Cassava Gun Club had always been the center of Wyeth Blackford's universe and it was only proper that he should end up there. He was indeed a servant, as Ian had gone out of his way to imply, but the chances were that he had never given it a thought. Wyeth had always been mildly hypnotized by the Northern men who came down to the gun club in winter, taken by their guns, their cars, their aura of wealth and position, and now, finally, at least in his own mind, he was one of them. That he was really their servant would never occur to him. He would call them by their first names, he would be much in demand as a shooting companion, and he would have all that he ever wanted. For what Wyeth wanted—perhaps an inherited want; conceivably a want so deeply buried that it had never been fully articulated—was to enjoy the kind of life that had once been lived at Mulberry. Not the life but the *kind* of life; the indolent privileges and

236

indulgences. Unable to achieve it for himself, he now had it achieved for him by others. He might be a servant, but he would never think of it. He would still be mildly hypnotized by those glittering visitors from the North.

There was something depressing about it, if one wanted to get depressed, and Anson knew that he did not want to see Wyeth. Too many years had passed and too much had happened. At the same time, however, without being anxious to put too fine a point on it, he wanted Ian to understand that he was still loyal to his friend, Ivy Mapes and all. It was only natural for Ian to be horrified of a girl whose father trained bird dogs, and yet it was that, Anson thought, that probably made her a good wife for Wyeth—a girl whose father trained bird dogs would have been conditioned to live in a climate that knew but two seasons, open and closed.

"That sounds like a fine job Wyeth has," he said. "I'd like to give it a try myself."

"Sure!" Ian snorted scornfully. "I'll bet! All in all, though, Wyeth's lucky to have that job—God knows he's run through enough of them! Both of those Blackfords are alike. What they've always wanted is a free ride. And that's what they're getting—Wyeth at the gun club and Mr. Blackford spending the winter in California on the allowance he gets from Mickey. The truth is that neither Wyeth nor his father has ever done a lick. If their name hadn't been Blackford they would never have been able to get away with it."

Everything that Ian was saying was true, but once again Anson had to control his impatience. It seemed to him that Ian was being extremely free and easy. Back in the days of Mulberry, or even in the days when the Blackfords lived on Malvern Street, few people would have dared to be so openly critical. Only one deduction was possible—anybody who wanted to could now be as outspoken about the Blackfords as he liked and not run any risk. Some enormous offense had been done to gentility and there had been a wholesale fall from grace.

How, though, had it happened? It was impossible for Anson to believe that it was because Mr. Blackford had come to a final characteristic failure, or because Wyeth was now working as a caretaker at the Cassava Gun Club, married to a girl named Ivy Mapes whose father trained bird dogs. Leniency might have been stretched to the breaking point, but it would not have snapped. The Blackfords would still have been protected by those towering shadows from the past. Even Ivy Mapes would have found shelter.

It had to be Dinah, then—sure as he was sitting there, it was she who had caused the roof to fall in. There was one thing, however, he did not understand. Ian had said that Olive sometimes saw Lucy Wales at the meetings of the Camellia Club; he also said that the club met generally at Dinah's. Anson could not speak for Lucy Wales, who was as much an enigma as ever, but he was sure that Olive would never enter Dinah's door were it attended by any social risk.

"And Dinah?" he asked. "Where is she living these days?"

Ian looked at him in such a cool, penetrating way that he had to use all his self-control to keep from looking away. For no reason at all, unless it was because his thoughts were in more of a turmoil than he realized, he recalled what Mr. Barlowe said about the advantage, if you had to see a man, of making him come to your office—"It puts you in the saddle. You hold the reins. It gives you the advantage."

"Dinah?" Ian said, plainly enjoying his advantage. "She's back at Mulberry."

Dimly, as though it were something that happened a long time ago, Anson remembered the picture of Mulberry he saw that morning in the *Historical Guide*.

"Well!" he said. "This is a surprise!"

"Mickey's poured thousands into that old place," Ian volunteered. "I don't have to tell you the shape it was in. It was more Dinah's idea than Mickey's, naturally. Oh, I'm not saying that Mickey doesn't like the idea of living at Mulberry, having a show place, but if it hadn't been for Dinah——"

Anson did not bother to listen. At last he knew how the Blackfords had tumbled from grace. Gentility had its own set of commandments and Dinah had broken them all. Because of her the Irish Channel had bridged the distance between Frenchman Street and Mulberry. Had the leap been accomplished without her help it would have been bad enough, but, as when Kit Robbins's father had rushed ahead too fast by buying and restoring the old Wedderburn house on St. Andrew's Square, the situation could have been dealt with. This way, however, with Dinah's right to live in Mulberry established by generations of occupancy, with a Blackford in residence where the Blackfords had always resided—what could they do except stand back and shudder? "To marry a Channel man; deliberately to marry him for his money——" But that, Anson knew, was not the whole story; there was bound to be more to it than that. He said:

"Tell me this, Ian. How did Mico—or Mickey, as he now seems to be known—make his pile? Where did the money come from?"

Instead of becoming disdainful, as Anson expected, Ian leaned forward on his desk. He said, "I thought I told you. You must not have been listening. Mickey's the head of Consolidated Enterprises. Actually, he *is* Consolidated Enterprises. What he says goes. There's no telling how much money Mickey has made. Well over a million, anyway."

Anson was only moderately surprised. He realized that he had always known that Mico Higgins would make a lot of money. Not well over a million, perhaps, since to think in terms of millions you had to be used to millions, but a lot of money just the same.

"Somebody ought to write him up," Ian said, looking at Anson as though he thought that he might be the somebody required. "He'd make a good story for *Time*. You know how he got started, don't you?"

"Yes, just like all those fellows who get into *Time*," Anson replied. "By selling the *Saturday Evening Post*."

Ian glanced at him reproachfully. "I don't mean that. I mean after that."

"Tell me about it, Ian," Anson said. "I find myself rather fascinated, as a matter of fact."

Ian looked at him distrustfully for a second, and then, "It started with that little pop factory that old man Milliken had in Duppytown," he said. "You remember old man Milliken, don't you, the one who set himself up in that old blacksmith shop that used to be on Liberty Street. Well, when he died——"

Anson had not thought of old man Milliken in years and years, but here, big as life, he was again—a tall, bearded, rawboned countryman who drifted down to Pompey's Head from the Georgia hills with the gleam of a fanatic in his eyes. Always dressed in his Sunday best, wearing a high stiff collar and a shiny black suit mended and darned with his own needle, he looked like one of those itinerant preachers who sometimes passed through Pompey's Head, churning down Bay Street generally in a battered T-model Ford on which, in white paint or calcimine, was lettered, inevitably, JESUS SAVES and ARE YOU READY FOR SALVATION? Old man Milliken, however, was made of less transcendental stuff. The gospel he preached was that of a non-alcoholic beverage, compounded of water and the extract of several native herbs, which he himself mixed in open barrels in a one-story shack in the Negro section on the other side of the railroad tracks, working always in his black suit and high stiff collar, and looking, with his bearded face and possessed eyes, like a man of God who had unaccountably strayed into moonshining. It was his belief that his brew possessed health-giving properties. He called his product Sassafras Wine, and his, truly, was a local industry—if ever a bottle of Sassafras Wine was sold outside of Duppytown, no one ever heard of it; the word among the colored people was that it was an aid to manliness. And when old man Milliken died——

"Who would have thought that any money could be made out of that stuff?" Ian said. "Mickey, though—well, you have to hand it to him. He bought all the rights from Milliken's only survivor, a sister the old man hadn't seen in thirty years. I know how much he paid for them, two hundred and fifty dollars, because he came and asked me to represent him. That's how he started being our client. You may have been wondering how I came to take him on——"

"No, Ian, of course not. Why should I wonder? A client is a client, isn't he?"

Ian, who had started to look distrustful again, warmed to his story. "Two hundred and fifty dollars is just like chicken feed to Mickey today, but back then, back when he was starting—you want to know something? He had to pay me off in stock; that's how tight things were. I have to admit that I didn't much like the idea, but it was either that or nothing. Pretty soon, though, after I saw the way things were going——"

"You put up some of your own money?"

"Yes, and I wish I'd had sense enough to put up more. Why, if I wanted to sell out now, after the number of times the stock has been split, I could practically retire if I wanted to. That's how good an investment it was. You don't get a chance to get in on the ground floor of anything like that very often these days."

"No, I don't suppose you do. And that's how the money was made? With Sassafras Wine?"

Ian shook his head. "Not exactly. It wasn't as easy as that. Mickey knew he couldn't buck the market with a new soft drink, not with Pepsi and Coca-Cola and Dr. Pepper entrenched the way they are, and he was smart enough not to try. He knew, though, that old man Milliken really had something with that hillbilly recipe of his——"

"What do you mean? *Had* something?"

Ian shifted his eyes for a moment. "Well, something—something that would do what old man Milliken said it would do. Build people up. Mickey figured that if he changed the formula and bottled it as a tonic——"

"Oh my God!" Anson burst out. "You mean he turned it into a patent medicine? Is that how he made his money?"

"All right, call it a patent medicine!" Ian was being pressed a little too far. "But what's wrong with a patent medicine, I'd like to know? Some of the best remedies in the country are patent medicines. Just because we sell Peppo mostly in the South and don't advertise in all those fancy magazines——"

"Peppo? Is that what you call it? Peppo?"

He did not want to sound scornful, but he was afraid he did. It was almost too much to take in. Gradually, however, as Ian explained that Peppo was only partially responsible for Mico's success, and that it was now merely one of a number of operations controlled by Consolidated Enterprises, everything began to fall into place. He knew why Olive went to meetings of the Camellia Club at Dinah's and why Mico had compelled Ian's envious respect—and, if Ian's, that of all Pompey's Head. Money still talked and more than a million would have found a way of making itself heard. Then, too, there must be a number of people in town who, like Ian, had greatly profited from Mico Higgins's energy; Peppo, once the first swallow was stomached, could not have been too hard to take.

Nor was he himself beyond being impressed. Even now Mico Higgins must still be in his middle thirties—a boy genius, no less—and Ian had not overstated the case when he said that he would make a good story for *Time*. Peppo might be a patent medicine with a rather high alcoholic content, and consequently beneath notice, but the other holdings of Consolidated Enterprises—three dairies, several thousand acres of timberland, a string of filling stations, a couple of portable sawmills, a few independent utilities—these must surely be recognized as the substantial possessions of a not inconsequential tycoondoom.

"A lot of people looked down on Mickey when he first started out," Ian was saying. "When he showed what he could do, though—well, if there is one thing you can't argue with, it's success. And not only that. Mickey's a good citizen. He has the welfare of Old Pompey at heart. He wants to see it grow and prosper. Right now, for instance, he's working on a deal to bring a big cellophane factory to town. He has an ideal building site for it and naturally he wants to sell, but, more than that, he's interested in the number of jobs it will create. Should it go through——"

Anson no longer listened. If Lucy Wales occasionally put in an appearance at the meetings of the Camellia Club, and if the club generally forgathered at Mulberry, it might be that Dinah was the person for whom he was looking.

"What happened to Midge, Ian?" he said. "Does she still live in town?"

He was thinking of the part Midge had played during the trouble with Mr. Pettibone, and how throughout the turnings of his life he seemed to have met the Higginses at almost every turn, but Ian must have thought that he was remembering those meetings at the Bijou, deliberately bringing them up. Ian's face became set, and Anson knew that he would have preferred not to be reminded of Midge—nor did he want it assumed, merely because he had got in on the ground floor of Peppo and valued Consolidated Enterprises as his most important client, that he was on intimate terms with Mico Higgins's Channel relatives. He said:

"Yes, Midge is still around."

"She's married, of course."

Ian nodded. "Her husband's a plumber. Some fellow by the name of Bill Dillon. They live out in that development at the end of Bullis Street. We never see them, though. They naturally don't run with our crowd."

Anson found it hard to believe that he had heard correctly. "My God!" he could imagine Meg exclaiming. "What a cheap, insecure, ten-cent snob! I thought Hillsdale was bad, but this Pompey's Head of yours——" And for a moment, as he looked across the desk at Ian, he was extremely glad about Meg. He did not think that he had ever been this glad about Meg before.

"Well," he said, "I guess I'll be shoving off. I've taken up enough of your time as it is. Thanks for letting me visit. So far as Mr. and Mrs. Wales are concerned——"

"Why don't you call Dinah?" Ian suggested. "I think that she would be your best bet."

"Yes, I was thinking the same thing."

Ian looked enormously relieved. His face brightened and he said, "Don't forget about tomorrow night. I'll pick you up after work."

"Thanks, Ian. That will be fine."

It wasn't fine, but he had to say so; everything he did would be talked about and he couldn't be too careful. He rose to go and Ian rose with him.

"I'm sorry about tonight," Ian said. "If it wasn't for this meeting at the club——"

"That's all right, Ian. Forget it."

242

"You wouldn't like to use the club while you're in town, would you?"

"No, thanks, Ian. I'm doing fine at the hotel. Do you have time for one more question?"

"Sure. What is it?"

"Is Mickey Higgins a member of the club too?"

He was sure he knew the answer, but he wanted to hear it from Ian.

"No, he isn't," Ian said, looking warier than ever. "His name is on the list, though. I was one of his sponsors."

Ian walked to the reception room with him, saying that he was sorry they couldn't have lunch together, and when Anson descended the stairs to the sidewalk, the loud-speaker above the main entrance of the five-and-ten was filling the street with the words of one of those hillbilly tunes that Joe Ann Williams used to like so much—nine tenths of the Tennessee River, the tune said, are the tears that I shed over you. Anson was sorry that he had not remembered to ask Ian about Joe Ann, and Gaby Carpenter as well, but chiefly his thoughts were occupied with Mico Higgins. Mico had made a fortune and married a Blackford, he was now installed in Mulberry, and he was on the waiting list of the Light Infantry Club. It did not please Anson to think that Mico Higgins was going to have an extremely long wait. That, however, must have been made plain to Mico a long time ago. It must have been made plain to Dinah too.

CHAPTER SIXTEEN

Walking down Bay Street in the direction of the Merchants &
Mechanics Bank, the street crowded, the sun shining, the music from
the loud-speaker at the five-and-ten blown by a gentle breeze, Anson
tried to decide what to do next. He knew that if he had any real initiative he would find the nearest telephone and get hold of Dinah. Getting hold of Dinah, however, was something he wanted to postpone.
Sooner or later he would have to face up to the situation, and the
sooner the better, but at the moment, drained as he was by his session
with Ian Garrick, he did not feel up to it. He had known that Dinah
was married, and he certainly understood that she would no longer be
the troublesome child who was so often underfoot, but in a vague way
he had imagined, as he had imagined in the case of Wyeth, that they
would be able to take up approximately where they had left off. Never
would it have occurred to him that Dinah would be married to Mico
Higgins.

All the rest of it he could understand—Wyeth's being a caretaker
at the Cassava Gun Club, Mr. Blackford having a last fling with Mrs.
Blackford's money, the descent to the shabbiness of Upton Street.
Everything hung together and was all of a piece. Dinah, though,
Dinah married to Mico Higgins—that was going to take a certain
amount of getting used to. He was sure that it was not Mico's money
that Dinah had married, as every loose tongue in town must have
gone out of its way to say, but, if Mico's money was not the explanation, what was? And why had they waited so long? Ian had said that
they were married during the war—putting it at its earliest, say 1942,
that meant that Dinah had been around twenty-five. One could hardly
call twenty-five "getting on," as Ian had done, but Ian's remark was

enough to show that it had been wondered if Dinah was going to wither on the vine.

But what to do with himself? He did not like the idea of going back to the hotel and neither did he want simply to roam the streets. Here was one of those days off that, back in New York, he wished he could have. Why not get in a car and drive—not with any destination in mind, but aimlessly and leisurely; just get in a car and drive?

He noticed that a Rexall drugstore occupied the corner opposite the Merchants & Mechanics Bank, which was where Gregory's Bookstore used to be, Gaby Carpenter's favorite hangout, and it was as good a place as any to look up the local U-Drive-It in the telephone directory. He crossed the street, entered the store, walked past a double line of counters heaped with the usual glut of colorful merchandise, and sat down in one of the booths, leaving the door open. He was riffling the pages of the directory, which hung on a small brass chain attached to the side of the booth, when he wondered if it might not be wise to call Dinah then and there—if she was married to Mico Higgins she was married to Mico Higgins; he could not postpone seeing her forever and he might as well get it over; nothing was to be gained by putting it off.

According to the directory, it was now possible to dial Mulberry. The number was County 7-5525. He could remember when Mulberry's number was 3—just that, 3—and when you had to give it to the operator. In those days you had to give the operator any number you wanted to call. The dial system was undoubtedly more efficient, but the old method had its advantages. He never knew how many operators were employed in the small brick exchange that stood on Harmony Street, and though it was possible that he might have sometimes passed them on the streets he did not know any of them by sight. They were something like mediums, existing for no other reason than to put your voice within sound of other voices, and one of them was named Miss Minnie Simms. It was she who invariably handled the calls to Mulberry. Incorporeal though their relationship was, she and Anson were on the best of terms. She called him Sonny and he called her Miss Minnie. He doubted that it had ever brought her any great advancement, or even called her to the attention of her employers, but Miss Minnie made it part of her job to be informed. "If it's Mrs. Blackford you want," she would say, "she's not at home. Mrs. Blackford and Mrs. Williams went up to Summerville this morning to see Mrs. Williams's aunt. Miss Joe Ann went with them to drive the automobile. Mr. Blackford ain't home neither. He's off in

245

town somewheres and Wyeth is at the bank. There's nobody home at Mulberry except that little Dinah girl. Maybe you'd better call later on. Mrs. Blackford said she'd be home around five."

Noting Mulberry's number again, Anson dialed it carefully—County 7-5525. He could hear the buzz at the other end of the line, punctuated at the end of each ring with an instant of silence, and after it had rung three or four times he concluded that he must have made a mistake—Mulberry, under the present regime, would not be without someone to answer the phone. He was about to hang up and dial again when a voice answered. It was unmistakably a Negro's voice, but a trained one; a careful, correct voice saying, "Mulberry. Mrs. Higgins's residence." One did not often hear such precise enunciation in Pompey's Head, and Anson was briefly put off—it wasn't anything at all like Esther, the Blackfords' cook, crossly demanding, "Who's dare! Ho, hit's you agin! You got nothing better to do but fool around on the telephone all day long? Well, *I* has!"

"Mulberry," the voice repeated. "Mrs. Higgins's residence."

"Is Mrs. Higgins there?"

"No sir, Mrs. Higgins is not at home. She is not expected back until late afternoon. Would you care to leave a message?"

Anson couldn't think. "No, I don't think so. I'll call back later. No, wait a second."

"Yes sir."

"Will you say that Mr. Page called?"

"Mr. Page?"

"That's right. Anson Page."

"May I have the first name again, please?"

"Anson. A-n-s-o-n."

"Mr. Anson Page. Thank you, sir."

"You've got it straight, haven't you?"

"Yes sir, I think so. Mr. Anson Page."

"That's right. And will you tell Mrs. Higgins—— No, never mind. Just say that I called."

He was halfway to the street before he remembered about the U-Drive-It. There was now no question in his mind. He could do nothing further until he saw Dinah and he had no intention of just hanging around. Going back to the directory, he found that the U-Drive-It agency was two blocks away, close to the Pompey Arms. He had to pass the store to get there. Glancing through the entrance as he walked by, he could see that the interior of the store was just as he remembered it, even to the bamboo rakes that were always displayed

246

up front in the spring. He liked its general appearance. It looked the way he would have wanted it to look, clean and well kept and prosperous, and he had none of the feelings that had troubled him on Alwyn Street. For an instant he thought of dropping in to see Mr. Meekim, to whom his father had given his first job and who, with the bank's help, had been able to buy the store when his father died, and though he would have liked to see Mr. Meekim, he decided to put it off—what he still most wanted to do was to get in a car and drive.

He hired the car for three days. It was beginning to be apparent that he could not get out of going to Mulberry, since Dinah would surely insist on it, and, in addition, he would need a way of getting to Tamburlaine Island when the time came for him to call on Mrs. Wales—this regardless of how helpful Dinah might or might not prove to be. It was more complicated to rent a car than he realized, with various papers to be signed and a deposit to be handed over and his driver's license to be looked at, but eventually it was brought around, a serviceable enough looking vehicle that had been newly washed and polished. He negotiated his way around several of the squares, went crosstown on Olmstead Street until he reached the east end of town, and took the old road to Bugtown and Double Crossing.

The road was now a paved highway, built up on both sides with rows of small frame cottages and some of those ranch houses that were cropping up all over the country. Except for the flat landscape and an occasional stand of pines, it could have been anywhere. Bugtown he hardly recognized. The Oasis was gone, as was the Gates Arena and the Golden Horseshoe. A machine shop and two filling stations had sprung up where they used to be. The Arrowhead Mill was still there, standing on the other side of the Atlantic & Central tracks, and beyond the mill, between Bugtown and Double Crossing, it was as thickly wooded as ever. He drove on to Double Crossing, which looked as dusty and sleepy as ever, and then, instead of following the road to Mulberry, he took the fork that led in a northerly direction to Yemassee and Charleston—the road to Mulberry, he noticed, was still unpaved.

He had lunch at a combination service station and restaurant about thirty miles past Double Crossing, dining off a hamburger, which he washed down with two cups of coffee. It was the kind of meal that Meg deplored, but he felt better for it. Driving on again, he turned off the main road into a smaller one which, by means of a series of causeways, traversed the salt marshes that stretched all along that part of the coast.

In a few minutes he was away from everything. He stopped the car and sat looking across the marsh. The long grasses shone in the sun, and the air was heavy with the salt, brackish smell that the marshes always had. There were a few stretches of open water in the near distance, not much larger than ponds, and on one of them a flock of ducks were feeding. They looked like mallards, but he could not be sure. He sat watching the ducks and a half dozen or so small hawks that were circling overhead. Every now and then one of the hawks would break its flight and dive down to the marsh with its wings folded tight against its body and its claws held ready to strike.

Anson sat in the car for some time longer and then started back to Pompey's Head. It was a few minutes past five when he reached town. Pompey's Head was knocking off for the day, and the sidewalks were full of people in that light, holiday mood that briefly takes hold of a city when another session of work is over, and though he did not recognize anyone and was driving a rented car, he did not feel like a stranger any longer. His mood was cheerful enough, when he walked into the lobby of the hotel, for him to be able to appreciate a stunning-looking girl who sat in one of the chairs before the hearth where already a new generation of aunts, uncles, and cousins, gray and tottering, were beginning to forgather. The girl, who was reading a magazine, was determinedly, almost belligerently aloof—her head was bent forward and her eyes were glued to the page; too tightly glued for her to be reading; she gave the impression of trying not to be noticed by any of the elders, lest she be drawn into conversation.

Something, however, was wrong. She did not look as though she could have any possible connection with that fussy domestic scene, those talkative old ladies and brittle old men, and yet, were she some stranger who happened to be passing through, perhaps on her way to Florida for the last weeks of the winter season at one of those places like Hobe Sound, why had she gone and shut herself off like that?

Because of the forward tilt of her head, Anson could see only the bridge of her nose, a pair of dark lashes, and the curve of her cheeks—it was the way she was dressed that set her apart; the blue jersey dress worn with a blue-and-white tweed jacket; the little flat hat; the hand-stitched shoes; the thin chain bracelet with a dangling bangle made from some heavy foreign coin—he quickly averted his eyes as she glanced up from her magazine. He thought that her gaze might be following him but he could not be sure. One of the old ladies said to a companion in a thin, shrill voice, "Annie Lou took me for a drive today. It was such a pretty afternoon——"

"Sonny."

Anson stopped and looked behind him. It was Dinah Blackford who was sitting in the chair. She had lowered the magazine and was looking at him with a shadow of uncertainty on her face. He moved toward her hurriedly.

"Dinah! For heaven's sake!"

"I heard you were here. Olive Garrick told me. Where have you been?"

"Out in the country. I didn't know what to do with myself, so I hired a car. What are you doing here?"

Dinah looked at him steadily. "What do you think? I've been waiting for you. I came here from Olive's. I had to go to a meeting of that damned old club."

"I called you this morning. You weren't home."

"I had a date for lunch."

Anson had always known that she would turn into a beauty—she was already a beauty before he went away—but now that it had happened, now that he could see the proof before him, it was not easy to take it in. He had not expected the promise to be so abundantly fulfilled. She was still looking at him steadily, trying to see what the years had done, and as he looked back he noticed that her eyes had changed—they still held their glint of mockery, and he didn't have to be told that she hadn't lost her temper, but there was a softness, perhaps even a sadness, that had not been there before. The glint struck fire and she said, as though she wanted deliberately to be a brat again, "Well, aren't you going to kiss me?"

He started to reply, "What? And have it all over town by morning?" but instead, as on the day when he stopped to give Mrs. Blackford some of the camellias he had picked at Mulberry, he bent over and brushed her cheek.

"Hmm," he said. "You smell good as ever. Is it still Enchantment?"

For a moment she did not remember—then, laughing, she held out her hand; he caught it in his and they looked at each other again. She said, "Oh, it's wonderful to see you, Sonny! I can't tell you how glad I am. There's so much I want to know. Won't you buy me a drink?"

Everyone had heard and everyone was watching—by this time tomorrow it would be all over town that he had kissed Dinah Blackford in the lobby of the Marlborough and that she had asked him to buy her a drink.

"Sure. Where do you do your drinking these days? Is there a bar anywhere around?"

"There's one here in the hotel. It's down where that place they called the Cave used to be. Is that all right?"

"Anything would be all right. I'm that happy to see you."

It would have been difficult for him to say how happy he was. Not only was there the pleasure of her presence, and knowing that she had been anxious enough to see him to wait in the lobby of the hotel, but now, for the first time, he could feel that someone cared that he was here. They walked down the flight of carpeted stairs that led to the basement of the Marlborough. Dinah carried her head, he noticed, in the same high, aloof way—he remembered the portrait of Percy Wyeth Blackford wearing the order of his King.

"Olive says you're going to be here only for a few days."

"That's right."

"You don't want to go to her for supper tomorrow night, do you?"

"Not if I can get out of it."

"That's what I thought. I'm going to give the party instead."

"But see here——"

"See here yourself! You don't think I'm going to let Olive Garrick give you your first party, do you? I've talked to her and it's all arranged. Here—this is the way to the bar."

"My, haven't we got fancy?"

Back in the old days, the very old days around the turn of the century, the Cave of the Marlborough was the most fashionable dining place in town. Originally christened the Grotto, which was instantly dropped in favor of the Cave, it was a large, subterranean room, always pervaded with a closed, dampish smell, that was festooned with green plaster-of-Paris stalactites which, hanging from the ceiling, reminded Anson the first time he saw them of evil-looking ice-cream cones. The turn-of-the-century generation, however, found the Cave greatly to its liking. Everyone of any consequence always went there to celebrate New Year's Eve, and it was the scene of the Light Infantry suppers. The popularity of the Cave continued until the First World War, when, with a new generation in command, it went out of fashion. By the time Anson saw it, a few months after the Armistice (the streets, he remembered, were still full of recruiting posters and advertisements for Liberty Bonds), it was ready to close its doors. His father took the family there for dinner one night because, as he expressed it, there were not many places like the Cave, and he wanted Marion and Sonny to be able to remember it.

The dripping stalactites, the evil-looking ice-cream cones, were no longer there—the Cave had been transformed into the Marlborough Room; a hand-lettered sign just outside the door, resting on a wooden easel, said that there was dancing every Wednesday and Saturday nights with music provided by Ziggy Zorach and his Dixieland Five. There was a glossy photograph of Ziggy, and, within the room, which still seemed to be hung with the same suggestion of dampness, a small bandstand over which Ziggy presumably presided. There was also a horseshoe bar, a polished dance floor of yellow wood, and a number of shadowy booths. The white bartender began suddenly to busy himself as Anson and Dinah entered, and a colored waiter in a white jacket with brass buttons showed them to a booth on the far side of the room; a small lamp stood on it, burning dimly.

Dinah wanted an old-fashioned and Anson said that he would have some bourbon and water.

"I would have known you anywhere, Sonny. You've hardly changed at all."

"You have."

"Have I?"

"Yes, you're all grown up."

"Is that all?"

"Oh, stop fishing. You don't need me to tell you anything."

The waiter brought their drinks; the bartender continued to busy himself; a lonely-looking man drifted in, surveyed his surroundings, and sat on one of the stools at the bar. Anson could feel sorry for him. All day long he had been at loose ends, and he was no longer, and it was Dinah who made the difference. He saw the stranger at the bar steal a glance at her; admiration, even from this distance, showed in his eyes.

"Why didn't you let me know?" Dinah said. "Why didn't you call me first thing?"

"I would have, I wanted to, but I didn't know how to reach you. I have this business to attend to, it's what I came down for, and I went to Ian, thinking he might be able to help."

"Olive told me. She says you want somebody to introduce you to Lucy Wales."

"Yes, I do, but I don't want to talk about it now. What I meant to say was that had I known you were back at Mulberry——"

"Olive told me about that too. She said that Ian said——"

"Nothing's changed, has it?"

"What do you mean?"

"Olive said and Ian said and she said and they said——"

"Oh, that." She took a sip of her drink and lifted her dark, luminous eyes. "What did you expect? You didn't know that I'd married Mickey, did you?"

Now that it was there, spread out on the table before them, it was no longer possible to ignore it.

"No, I didn't. I suppose Olive told you that too. I know it's hard to believe, but when I was in London during the war, just after I got there, I received a letter from my mother——"

Dinah interrupted but once, to ask for a cigarette.

"So that's it," she said as he came to an end. "I kept wondering why you never wrote. I thought——"

"You thought what?"

"Never mind. It's all right now." She took another sip of her drink. "Tell me about yourself. How many children have you?"

"Two, a boy and a girl. The boy is nine and the girl is five. His name is Patrick and her name is Deborah. And you?"

"Three, all girls—Cecily, Julia, and Wrenn. Cecily is the oldest and Wrenn is the baby. They're delicious."

They dealt out the cards of their lives, arranging them in neat little piles—there were no cubbyholes, no anxieties, no grubby rooms on Upton Street.

"Gracious, Sonny, it's almost six. I have to run."

"Do you really?"

"Yes, I must. Some of those cellophane people are in town—the ones who are thinking of building the mill—and Mickey's asked them to supper. If you'd like to join us——"

"No, Dinah, I think not."

"But what are you going to do with yourself? I can't just go and leave you alone."

"It will be good for me. I have some work to do."

Dinah looked dissatisfied. "Don't you want to move in with us? You can even have your old room. Won't you?"

She must have known that he could not accept, that nothing could be more impossible, but the invitation had to be made.

"No, Dinah, thanks."

"Well, all right, then. I don't like it but I don't suppose I can do anything about it. You won't forget about tomorrow night."

"I won't forget."

252

"Is there anyone special you want me to ask?"

"I don't know. Why don't I leave everything up to you?"

"All right. I'll see what I can do. And Sonny——"

"Yes?"

"I almost forgot. I can introduce you to Lucy Wales tomorrow afternoon if you want me to."

"You can?"

"Yes. I'm having the Camellia Club again and she's coming to lunch. If you could get there beforehand——"

"What time?"

"Ten, eleven? Any old time. We can walk around the place and you can see the girls. Lucy's coming for lunch at one-thirty. I can give you a bite to eat, and then, when she arrives—— What's the matter? What are you looking so strange about?"

Anson was thinking that it was much too simple. There had to be a catch somewhere.

"What will I be supposed to be doing at Mulberry?"

"Seeing me, you goose! What's wrong with that? If I can't have you to Mulberry——"

Her eyes had lighted up and she appeared to be more exasperated than was necessary. Immediately he understood why. It would soon become known that he had been to Mulberry, seeing her alone, and in a place like Pompey's Head——

"I'll be there," he said. "I want to see Mulberry and I want to see your girls."

"And not me?"

"I told you to stop fishing, didn't I? You're big enough now to know better. What I'd like to ask, if I may——"

"What is it?"

"It's this. How did you and Lucy Wales happen to become such friends?"

Dinah began gathering up her purse and gloves. "Friends? Who said we were friends?"

"But if she's coming to lunch, if you and she are on such good terms——"

"We're not on 'such good terms,'" she said. "What gave you that notion? She wants something I have. Do you remember the Plain Jill?"

He was not quick enough to suit her.

"The camellia," she said impatiently. "The Plain Jill. The all-white one."

"Yes, I remember. What about it?"

"There are two of them at Mulberry," Dinah said. "There's the one you know about, the one that grows near the old well, and another, which nobody even knew was there, behind that little brick building where Grandpa had his office. I found it when we cleaned up the old garden that used to be there. It's where Wyeth and Papa used to keep their game chickens."

"But what has this to do with Lucy Wales?"

"She wants one of my Plain Jills for that collection she's made," Dinah said. "She's been after me to sell the bush behind Grandpa's office ever since those pictures of Mulberry came out in *Harper's Bazaar*. Didn't you see them?"

"A man in my business doesn't have much time for *Harper's Bazaar*."

Dinah looked at him through a long silence.

"Do you like what you are doing," she asked, "being a lawyer in New York?"

Anson did not know how to reply. "Never mind about that. Not now. The answer is yes and no. But what happened? Did Mrs. Wales come and knock on your door?"

Dinah was still looking at him in her disturbing, level way. "No, it wasn't that bad. Do you remember Nan Schulkens?"

Nan Schulkens was a contemporary of Dinah's, the daughter of one of the Black Dutchmen families.

"Yes, I remember Nan. She was that shy one."

"Shy my foot! Not so shy that she couldn't land one of those rich Yankees who belong to the gun club; not so shy that she couldn't face the prospect of being his third wife! His name is Jerome Barbour and he owns that little island next to Tamburlaine—the one they call Mungo. Nan and Lucy got to know each other, and Nan introduced me to her one week end."

"So that's how you met her?"

Dinah nodded. "She'd seen the pictures of Mulberry, and since I love to show it off—I *do* love to; I think it's glorious to have it looking the way it should look, instead of falling to pieces with nobody ever caring what happened—and so, as I started to say, I asked her to call. That's when she saw the Plain Jill. She's been after me to sell it ever since. As if I'd dream of selling anything that belonged to Mulberry!"

"And that's the basis for your beautiful friendship?"

"That's it," Dinah said, pressing her little flat hat more firmly on her head. "But now I do have to run. I'm neglecting my children on account of you. Walk to the car with me, Sonny, won't you?"

The evening had turned off cool. Dinah gave a shiver as they left the hotel and started walking to the place where she had parked her car. Anson did not know enough about cars to distinguish the make that she was driving, but it was one of those long, expensive-looking models—he opened the door and she slipped under the wheel.

"It still doesn't seem right," Dinah said, "your staying at the hotel. I wish——"

"I'm doing fine, I tell you."

He closed the door and bent over so that he could look through the open window.

"So long. I'll see you in the morning."

"Come as early as you can. I'll be waiting."

"Don't drive too fast."

"I won't."

Anson stood on the curb and watched the blink of the car's taillights as they went down the street. He watched them until they disappeared around the corner and then returned to the bar. The booth at which he and Dinah had been sitting had already been cleared away. Four or five men were lined up at the bar, including the lonely-looking stranger, and though Anson could tell that he wanted to strike up a conversation, he gave him no encouragement. He was not enjoying his solitariness but he no longer minded it. He found it rather pleasant in the bar.

PART FOUR

CHAPTER SEVENTEEN

May 10, 1935, was a Friday, and the trial of Small vs. Pettibone, Honorable Martin T. McMasters presiding, had been in progress for four days. Once the jury was selected, the trial had moved along speedily enough. Toward the middle of the session of Friday morning, by which time Anson's father had been called to the stand by Mr. Jake Brewer, who was acting as Clifford Small's attorney, and then been cross-examined by Mr. Arthur Kennon, who was representing Mr. Pettibone, it began to be apparent to Anson that the whole case being built up by Mr. Kennon was going to hinge in large part upon a single issue—was Clifford under the influence of liquor when he swept that pile of dust into Mr. Pettibone's face, or was he not? Anson's father, under Mr. Kennon's cross-examination, earnestly maintained that Clifford was not.

"Sir," Mr. Kennon said at one point, looking very imposing with his robust frame, ruddy face, and soft white hair, "would you go so far as to say that you are positive in this regard?"

"Yes, I would."

Mr. Kennon looked thoughtful, pursing his lips. "Then, sir, let me put this question, or, with the permission of the court, this series of questions. It is my intention, your honor, in order to bring to the attention of the jury——"

"Proceed, Mr. Kennon," Judge McMasters said sharply, giving one more indication that his reputation for irritability had not been acquired gratuitously; a small, almost tiny man, nearly bald, peering out of a pair of steel-rimmed spectacles. "If necessary, the court will rule on your intentions when your intentions are clear."

Mr. Kennon went back to his cross-examination. His deep voice rumbled through the courtroom, and Anson, who had never seen him in action before, understood why Mr. Leigh always spoke of him as the Organ Master. Mr. Kennon said, "As I understand it, sir, from your testimony under direct examination, you saw our friend Clifford"—he turned slightly toward the jury when he said "our friend Clifford"—"at nine forty-five on the day in question. Is that correct?"

"It is."

"I now ask you," Mr. Kennon continued, "to recall the two hours from nine forty-five to eleven forty-five. Was our friend Clifford under your observation throughout that time—your direct observation?"

"Well, if you mean——"

"I mean, sir, your direct observation."

"No, he was not."

"Let me now ask this question." Mr. Kennon's voice took on a new and different rumble, and Anson could see the jury responding to it. "Since, as you have admitted, the plaintiff was not under your direct observation—that you did not keep your eye on him all the time, in other words—would it not have been possible for him, during the two-hour period from nine forty-five to eleven forty-five— in short, would it not have been possible for him to take a couple of quick snorts, as I believe they say around the poker table? More than a couple? A whole pintful of quick snorts?"

A wave of laughter rolled across the courtroom and Anson could feel himself cringe—it was Mr. Kennon at whom they were laughing, not his father, but Mr. Kennon's theatrical triumph had been gained at his father's expense. And it had been extremely adroit of him to drop that reference to the poker table. He was proving to the jury that he, too, was one of the boys. Judge McMasters rapped angrily with his gavel, drumming a tattoo through the aroused voice of one of the clerks crying "Quiet in the courtroom, quiet in the court-room!" and Mr. Brewer jumped to his feet with an objection, saying that counsel was trying to force the witness into an expression of opinion and demanding that the jury be instructed to ignore the question, which should be struck from the record, but Anson neither saw nor heard. He looked at his father on the witness stand, wearing his best blue suit and sitting very straight, and he was so knotted up that he thought he was going to be sick—oh, if only he could believe that his father might be vindicated; if only the jury would return in favor of Clifford Small!

It was too much to hope for. In theory the case was only now being argued, but Anson felt that its decision had already been reached —there was Clifford, sitting at a table in front of the courtroom with Mr. Brewer's empty chair beside him, looking so frightened that his eyes were as white as the dressing on the stump of his severed hand— an old, shiftless Negro who, as Mr. Kennon had taken great care to establish, had been locked up no less than nineteen times on charges of being drunk in the public streets—and there, at a second table, wearing an air of composed assurance, was Mr. Henry Pettibone. The look on Mr. Pettibone's face said, "How dare this coon do a thing like this to me!" and Anson, even though it had been drummed into him in law school that you could never tell what a jury was thinking until it brought in its verdict, was certain that the twelve men who sat in the jury box were beginning to share, under the shrewd manipulation of Mr. Kennon, some of the same indignation.

Whether or not Clifford had been drinking continued to be an issue. Mr. Kennon, by putting his questions in a different manner, was able to establish that Anson's father could not be certain that Clifford, at some time or other during that morning, might not have had a few drinks.

"But he was not drunk," Anson's father said. "Of that I'm certain."

Mr. Kennon slumped his shoulders in what could be taken for a little bow. Turning to the bench, he said, "If it please the court, I would like to point out that the exact state, or amount, of intoxication is not the issue. I merely wish to show——"

It was a clever maneuver, Mr. Kennon's pretending to address the bench when actually he was speaking to the jury, but Judge McMasters was an old hand at clever maneuvers. He said, "Proceed, Mr. Kennon! I think we can follow your argument without these unnecessary interpolations."

What Mr. Kennon wished to show was what had already been shown—that although Anson's father had said that he was positive that Clifford had not been under the influence of liquor, all he could really be positive about was that Clifford had not been noticeably drunk. Mr. Brewer rose to his feet with another objection, saying that Mr. Kennon's questions were irrelevant and immaterial, and, after a lengthy exchange with Mr. Kennon, who even here gained an advantage by maintaining his composure while Mr. Brewer lost his, was overruled by Judge McMasters. Even without the dispirited look on Mr. Brewer's face as he returned to his seat, Anson would have known that considerable damage had been done; Clifford's having swept that pile of dust over Mr. Pettibone was bad enough, but to have done it when he was all likkered up—well, as Mr. Kennon was implying to the jury, how could anyone be sure that he had not done it deliberately, fired by alcohol and, since you never could tell when a Negro was involved, spite?

Mr. Kennon excused Anson's father from the stand and went through the formality of asking the court's permission to call his first witness. A thickset man of advanced middle age lumbered to the stand and was sworn in. He had a gray, tired face, deeply lined. He swallowed nervously after he took the oath and began fingering the ends of his necktie when he sat down—there was something about him, the dull look in his eyes, the melancholy aura of lethargy and defeat, that told of a man, not very resilient to begin with, who had gone to pieces a long time ago. Answering Mr. Kennon's questions, he said that his name was Phineas Bell and that he was employed as an orderly at the Community Hospital—his responses were delivered in such a listless monotone that Judge McMasters at one time had to ask him to speak up. He testified, aided by more questions, that he had helped Clifford out of his coat when Anson's father brought him to the hospital. He identified Clifford, who was asked to rise, and then went on to say that, while helping Clifford out of the coat, he had found a pint bottle in one of its pockets—at the mention of a bottle the courtroom became stiller than usual; Anson saw two of the jurors lean forward.

"And this bottle?" Mr. Kennon said. "Will you describe its contents?"

"You mean what was in it?"

"Yes."

"Moonshine. Corn likker."

"And how much of this—this moonshine—was there? Was the bottle full, half full, nearly empty, or what?"

"It was nearly empty."

"Will you explain to the court how you came to discover that it was nearly empty?"

"Well, I——"

"Please continue, Mr. Bell," Mr. Kennon said. "Please tell the court in your own words exactly what happened."

Phineas Bell shifted uneasily; an expression of trouble darkened his lined, defeated face. "Well, I—I felt that I could use a drink myself—I've never been much at standing the sight of blood—and after they took the patient into Emergency——"

262

"Yes, go on." Mr. Kennon was beginning to show signs of impatience. "What happened then?"

"Well, I——"

"You will have to speak up," Judge McMasters commanded. "You are delaying proceedings. I must ask you, Mr. Kennon, to secure the co-operation of your witness!"

"Very well, your honor." Mr. Kennon again slumped his big shoulders in his approximation of a bow. "Mr. Bell, if you will tell the court, in your own words——"

"I started to take a swallow," Phineas Bell said. "I started to, but I didn't."

A bang of Judge McMasters's gavel silenced the laughter before it had time to get started. Mr. Kennon put another question.

"And it was then, was it not, that you discovered that the bottle was nearly empty?"

"I object, your honor!" Mr. Brewer, in his agitation, began waving a sheet of paper. "I object on the ground that the witness is being told what to say!"

Judge McMasters sustained the objection. "You will put your questions more properly, Mr. Kennon. Permit the witness to give his own testimony. Let him speak for himself."

Anson thought that Mr. Brewer might have saved himself the trouble. No matter how the questions were asked, it had been established that Clifford had had an almost empty pint bottle on his person. Mr. Brewer, when the time came, would undoubtedly point out that it was nothing but circumstantial evidence, and so would Judge McMasters in his final charge to the jury, but Anson, in the mood he was in, could not persuade himself that the jury would pay much heed—an almost empty bottle in a man's pocket was proof that he had been drinking, especially if, again, that man happened to be a Negro. There was something, however, more troubling even than that. Anson could not rid himself of the feeling, after Mr. Kennon gave another slump to his shoulders, saying "Your witness, Mr. Brewer," and Mr. Brewer began his cross-examination, that Clifford's lawyer—he almost said his father's lawyer—was working in the dark. The issue of Clifford's drinking had taken on far too great an importance. Mr. Kennon was not going to all this trouble because he hoped to convince the jury that it gave Mr. Pettibone the right to shove him through the window. Anyone could see that he was laying the groundwork for something much more damaging. But Mr. Brewer, even though he understood this, was apparently unable to discern, even as Anson was, Mr. Kennon's ultimate purpose. Consequently, in order to disrupt at least partially any plan that Mr. Kennon might have in mind, he could merely try to undermine Phineas Bell's reliability as a witness; to persuade the jury that he was not the sort of man who could be believed even under oath. Following this course—the only course that was open to him—Mr. Brewer made much of the fact that the orderly had been tempted to sneak a drink. Too much of it, Anson thought. The whole courtroom was beginning to feel that the witness was being hounded—Phineas's very hangdog look worked in his favor.

"And you say you did not take a drink?"

"No, I didn't."

"But you admit you wanted a drink."

"Yes, I wanted one."

"You openly admit it?"

"Yes, I admit it. I needed something to settle my stomach. I was sick to my stomach at the sight of all that blood."

"But you didn't take a drink?"

"No."

"Even though the bottle was in your possession?"

"No."

"No what?"

"No, I didn't take a drink."

"You were alone at the time, were you not?"

"Yes."

"You could have easily helped yourself, couldn't you?"

"Yes."

"But you didn't?"

"I said I didn't, didn't I?"

"But if you wanted a drink that much, if, as you say, you needed it, then why——"

Phineas Bell showed his first sign of spirit; a tremble of animosity flickered beneath the pallor of his face. "It was *his* bottle, weren't it? I wasn't going to take no drink after *him!*"

Him—Clifford; this impudent colored man, locked up nineteen times for being drunk, and now suing one of the town's leading citizens for ten thousand dollars! Anson always thought, whenever in later years he happened to remember the trial, that had Phineas Bell been permitted to continue he would have said that he had his pride —that, broken and defeated though he was, homeless, living in a dank room in the hospital basement next to the coal bunkers, he was not so humbled and shattered, so finally brought to ruin, as to have forgotten the color of his skin; he was a white man, and no white man—no white man worthy of calling himself white—would think of drinking from the bottle of a nigger like Clifford Small.

Already Mr. Brewer's ill-considered attack was rolling back on him —there was not a man in the courtroom, or on the jury, who had not gone over to Bell's side. Mr. Brewer pretended to mount a new offensive, firing another round of questions, but it was only a covering action; the best he could hope for was to disguise the fact that he had been driven from the field—"That is all, your honor. I have no further questions."

"Prejudice! Rank prejudice!" Meg said when Anson, telling her the story for the first time, reached this point in the trial. "But it was a splendid thing for your father to do. It shows what a fine person he was."

Both statements were true and Anson did not want to contradict them. However, unless Meg was to get a wrong impression, he had to modify them slightly. Meg, who took what was called a liberal view of things, was thinking of his father's action as a kind of social protest. It pleased her to imagine that what he had done was what she would have done, and Anson felt that she would have been even more pleased were he able to tell her that his own departure from Pompey's Head had been a similar act of protest, a way of refusing to have anything more to do with a society that judged a man by the color of his skin. Nothing, however, could be farther from the truth. He could not pretend to that degree of high-mindedness and neither could he believe that his father would have wanted it credited to him. They were not reformers. He had left Pompey's Head because Kit Robbins had hurt him beyond all bearing, and his father had caused Mr. Pettibone to be brought into court because something had snapped.

Seen at its simplest, his father's action was an attempt on his part to see that justice was done. Never could that be doubted, and neither could it be doubted that his father was honest in saying that he did not have anything against Mr. Pettibone, not in the sense of a grudge. Anson could see, however, now that over a year had passed, that his father's feelings about Mr. Pettibone went deeper than a grudge. There had always been that latent hostility between them, going back to the time they were boys, and Mr. Pettibone's hot-tempered refusal to do anything about Clifford must have been the end. Had Mr. Pettibone been more courteous, or merely more temperate in his language, Anson was sure that his father would never have brought the matter to court. He would have looked after Clifford out of his own pocket, thinking less of Mr. Pettibone than ever before, but he would not have acted so drastically. "If he needs help, you help him," Mr. Pettibone had said. "He's your nigger, not mine," and in that moment, even as he spoke, Anson thought that something must have snapped—his father had had his fill.

"But it amounts to the same thing," Meg said. "He was fighting prejudice."

Yes, but not directly; not with that in mind—it was more complicated than this charming, high-spirited girl who sat across from him at a table in a little Greenwich Village restaurant seemed willing to believe. For what was on trial in Judge McMasters's courtroom was not Mr. Pettibone or, conversely, Clifford Small's right to sue him, but a tacit assumption—deny it once and it might be denied forever, along with everything that lay behind it, the whole structure of a society.

"That's just the point," Meg said. "It *should* be denied."

"Ah, but it's not that easy. You are asking people to deny what they value most, that which they regard as their identity. Would you? You say that that is why you came to New York—to establish your identity. You say that you want to insist upon it. Well, that's what my old friend Mr. Pettibone was doing. That's what that fellow Phineas Bell was doing. They were insisting on their identity."

"But at someone else's expense!" Meg cried. "At the expense of a whole people!"

Anson admitted the charge. They were getting more deeply into the subject than he had intended, but he was not especially anxious to change it. He was working on one of the sections of *The Shinto Tradition of the American South*, the chapter in which the issue of prejudice had directly to be confronted, and he welcomed the opportunity to test his ideas.

"True enough," he said, "but it's something that ought to be understood. It's not enough to call it prejudice. What you have in the South is not prejudice—or not only prejudice; let me put it that way, lest you think that I don't know about such things as segregation— but a kind of mortal combat. Not over 'rights,' as some of those magazines you read keep saying—not rights alone, since certain rights are involved—but something that goes much deeper."

"What? What *can* go deeper?"

"Identity—the question of identity. On the one hand you have the white man trying to protect his identity—or so he imagines—and on the other you have the Negro trying to establish his. That's what it's all about. That's what it has been about for years—for generations, ever since the first boatload of slaves arrived. The white man could not bring himself to accept the Negro as an equal—he simply could not—and yet, since there the Negro was, breathing, walking, talking, living, he could not deny his reality as a human being. The white man tried to, drawing on Gospel and ancient law, building up his theory of a Greek republic, but nothing really worked. The best he could do was to pretend that it worked. For no matter where he turned, regardless of the arguments he built up, always there was the Negro, another person, another human being—and determined, even in those early days when he was most inarticulate, even from the depths of bondage, to insist that he was a human being, to establish his own identity."

Meg fastened him with her clear blue eyes and shook her head. "I don't understand about you. You're beyond me completely. Why is it that you want to keep on being a lawyer? Why?"

"The biggest reason is you."

"What do you mean, me?"

"It's the only way I can afford you. I don't know any other way to make a living. How else can I ask you to marry me?"

Meg tilted her nose. "I wish you'd ask me for a change instead of just talking about asking. And the first time you do I'm supposed to say yes, I suppose?"

"That's the rough idea."

"I thought so. And I probably will, too, fool that I am. I'll tell you this, though—I'd feel a lot happier about it if I didn't think you were wasting yourself. And don't say that you're doing it for me, either! I don't want that thrown up to me when I'm old and gray. Don't say it's my fault that you've wasted your life at Boring, Barlowe, Tedious & Impossible, and never did any of the things you really wanted to do. Don't blame me!"

"I won't. Did I ever tell you of the time I wanted to go to Burma and gather the seeds of wild plants?"

"That's nothing. Me, I wanted to disguise myself as a man and do another Lawrence of Arabia. And what happens? Do we? No! I end up as one of those downtrodden females at that place where I work, and you end up at Boring, Barlowe, Tedious & Impossible. But let's trade our broken blossoms another time, shall we? I want to hear the rest of the trial. What happened next, after that obnoxious Phineas Bell?"

What happened next, when court resumed following the noon recess, was that Mr. Pettibone was called to the stand. He nodded briefly to Judge McMasters, took the oath in a firm voice, and settled himself in his chair. Anson saw that he too was wearing his best suit. Mr. Pettibone looked as he did in church on Sunday. His thin black hair was combed back straight from his forehead, the loose skin of his neck was being pinched by his starched collar, and his deliberately remote expression was the same, Anson thought, as when he dropped his envelope into the collection plate. The preliminaries were soon disposed of; Mr. Pettibone gave his name, his occupation, and his address. Mr. Kennon then said:

"Mr. Pettibone, I now ask you to recall the morning of Wednesday, March 6, 1935. You do recall it, do you not?"

"I do."

"On the morning in question, between approximately eleven-forty and eleven forty-five, where were you?"

"I was walking down Bay Street. I was going from my office to the Merchants & Mechanics Bank."

"You are certain of the time?"

"I am. I had an appointment with Mr. Robert Miller, the president of the bank, and I was running a little late. I looked at my watch to check the hour."

"Now, sir, at the time of which we are speaking, between approximately eleven-forty and eleven forty-five on the morning of Wednesday, March 6, where were you on Bay Street?"

"I was passing the Page Hardware Company."

"On the sidewalk?"

"Yes, on the sidewalk."

"Were you accompanied by anyone?"

"No, I was not."

"You were alone, in other words."

"Yes, I was alone."

Anson wished that Mr. Kennon would get along with it—courtroom procedure required that he ask these questions, but he needn't be so pompous about it, playing on that organ voice of his. Knowing that it would be some minutes before Mr. Kennon showed his hand, in which the possibility that Clifford had been drinking was plainly intended to be the trump card, Anson permitted his attention to wander. This was the time of day, just before two o'clock, when, in the kind of warm weather they were having, all of Pompey's Head would have liked to succumb to an attack of drowsiness. The windows were open, and though the sun was not shining through them any longer, having started to drop toward the river, its reflected glare poured into the courtroom. The spectators sat in a kind of torpid quiet, the rows of seats separated from the forward part of the courtroom by a wooden rail, and on the bench, his forehead resting on the knuckles of his left hand, Judge McMasters was making notes on a sheet of paper that lay before him. Occasionally he lifted his eyes, glancing from Mr. Kennon to Mr. Pettibone and then to the jury, and once, as he leaned back in his chair, he put his pencil between his teeth and bit down upon it. Below him, sitting at the defense's table, which stood to the right of the bench, Jay Lockhart seemed to be trying to outdo the court stenographer. His blond head was bowed and he never stopped writing. Anson watched him as Mr. Kennon's voice reverberated through the courtroom. Standing slightly to one side of the stand, from which position he was able to face the jury, Mr. Kennon said, "Mr. Pettibone, when you noticed that the plaintiff was sweeping the sidewalk—or, to be more precise, sweeping a pile of dust through the doorway of the Page Hardware Company onto the sidewalk—what did you do?"

"I tried to get out of his way."

"You changed your course, in other words."

"Yes, that is correct."

"In what manner did you change your course?"

"I moved closer to the street."

Anson thought that Jay Lockhart must be trying to take down everything that was being said. Like Anson and Ian Garrick, Jay was one of the youngest members of the bar—the most promising of the whole new crop, it was generally said, and the one with the most brilliant future; if, that is, he wouldn't drink so much. Anson thought it ironic that Jay, who must have agreed with Mr. Kennon that Clifford's tippling should be made into an issue, for whatever reason Mr. Kennon had in mind—if, indeed, it was not Jay who had thought of it originally—should himself be one of the hardest drinkers among the younger men in town.

So isolated did Anson feel, tied only to his father among all the people in that courtroom, that he began to think that perhaps his sister Marion was right—it might have been better had his father not so stubbornly persisted. Anson was reluctant to side with his sister, believing it disloyal to judge their father's action in the light of what people might think and say, but he needed to look no farther than the courtroom to understand why Marion felt as she did. The people whom Marion was prone to admire—the "nice" people, she would say —all seemed to have gathered on the other side.

Even the opposing lawyers pointed up the fact. Mr. Leigh might call Mr. Kennon the Organ Master, and there might be others who whispered that it was more than business that took him to Atlanta once a month, but he was a member of the Light Infantry Club, he was the attorney for the Arrowhead Mill and several other corporations, and he was on the board of directors of the Atlantic & Central Railway. Success and affluence stood out all over him, whereas Mr. Brewer, sitting at the table next to Clifford Small, looked almost seedy by contrast. "More stubbornness!" Marion had said. "If Papa wanted to get Clifford a lawyer, why didn't he get a good one? Why didn't he get either Mr. Garrick or Mr. Leigh? Why that old Jake Brewer? Why *him*?"

Marion, however, must have known the answers. She must have been aware that their father had not wanted to embarrass Mr. Garrick and Mr. Leigh by asking them to take a case from which they would have instinctively shied away—an embarrassment that would have been all the greater because he, Anson, was now working for the firm—and she must also have known that he wanted to save himself the awkwardness of being refused. But even were none of this involved, there was still the fact, as Marion also knew, that their father and Mr. Brewer had been close friends ever since they went to grade school together, and that Mr. Brewer had always handled the legal matters that came up in connection with the store.

Marion's grudge against Mr. Brewer was not because he was not a very good lawyer. For her, as for any number of people in Pompey's Head, his lack of ability was less important than his lack of standing. What Marion was thinking was that Mr. Brewer's hill-born father, a dogged Republican, had been a foreman at the thread factory, and that Mr. Brewer had grown up on the edges of Duppytown. She was thinking that when he finally returned from the state university, already in his late twenties, since he had had to take time out to work at various jobs in order to finance himself, he brought with him a mountain bride of seventeen—Birdie Dell Smith, her name was—who ran away with a linesman from the power company less than twelve months after she arrived in Pompey's Head. She was thinking that Mr. Brewer, driven to the borders of ostracism by his public humiliation and turning gradually into a morose, tight-lipped man whose mask of bitterness became more gaunt and hollow with each passing year, had then seemed willfully to put himself beyond the pale by becoming the county chairman of the Republican party.

Marion's disdain was nothing new. Ever since she was old enough to understand the shadow that Mr. Brewer walked in, she had professed bewilderment over his handling the infrequent bits of legal business that came up in connection with the store, nor would she see it as another example of their father's loyalty. "Loyalty, loyalty! That's all I hear around here! But who pays for it? We do! So he and Papa went to school together! He and Papa used to be friends! Is that any reason why that Black Republican should always be hanging around the store?"

And already it was being said, as Anson knew, that it was that which prompted Mr. Brewer to take Clifford's case, that Black Republicanism of his, together with a desire to hit back at those who, in the distant but still galling days of his disgrace, had seen fit to interpret Birdie Dell's errancy as the sign of a lack of manhood, and though none of it could ever be proved wholly or even partially true —though Mr. Brewer's presence in the courtroom might be more charitably regarded as a token of his misanthropic regard for the one man whom he was still willing to acknowledge as a friend—it did not either alter the fact that the general interpretation of his motive had become part of the climate of the trial or undermine the soundness of Marion's basic complaint.

For the truth was that Mr. Brewer was indeed not a very good lawyer. Despite his inexperience, Anson could tell that Mr. Kennon was running circles around him. Witness by witness, under cross and now direct examination, Mr. Kennon had established that Clifford might well have been drinking, that he had virtually the whole of the sidewalk to do his sweeping upon when he lifted that pile of dust into Mr. Pettibone's face, and that the jury had before it the choice of choosing between Mr. Pettibone's story and that of this frightened-looking colored man, practically a public nuisance, who had been prevailed upon to drag Mr. Pettibone into court. Mr. Kennon could not ask, "And at whose instance? For what reason?" nor could he let drop even a hint in that direction, since Judge McMasters would not have tolerated it, but Mr. Kennon did not have either to hint or ask —that too was part of the climate of the trial; the whole courtroom knew that Clifford was only incidental to the action and that the contest, at bottom, was one between Henry Pettibone and Will Page.

It seemed to Anson that Mr. Kennon commanded every advantage; even the best of lawyers would have found himself in a difficult position. Mr. Brewer, however, ever since Mr. Pettibone took the stand, did not seem even to be trying—even now, when Mr. Kennon was at last beginning to show his hand, laying it down with the confidence of one who knows that he holds the top cards and wants to prolong his pleasure as long as he can, he barely lifted his eyes, scratching listlessly on a sheet of paper.

Anson had expected some bold stroke from Mr. Kennon, and he could now see what it was going to be—Mr. Pettibone was preparing to claim that he thought he had a drunk Negro on his hands and had acted in self-defense. Mr. Kennon said, "Let me ask you this, Mr. Pettibone. Have you ever seen a man under the influence of liquor?"

Mr. Pettibone smiled before replying. "Yes, I would say that I have. My experience has been pretty considerable along that line."

"And when you saw the plaintiff, what impression did you have?"

"I thought he was drunk."

"For what reason?"

"The way he looked. He *looked* drunk."

"Was there anything else?"

"Yes, the way he was sweeping. The way he was using that broom."

"And what way was that, Mr. Pettibone? I wonder if you could explain to the court."

Mr. Pettibone knotted his brows. "He was just sort of waving it around. He didn't seem able to make it do what he wanted it to do."

"And this confirmed your impression that he was under the influence of liquor?"

"Yes."

Mr. Brewer at last gathered himself together and came to his feet. "I object to this line of questioning, your honor. What the witness thought or did not think is not evidence, or, if it is, of an immaterial nature."

"Just a moment, your honor," Mr. Kennon said. "I submit that what the witness thought is material—not tangible, perhaps, but most definitely material. What the witness thought had a direct bearing, as I intend to show, upon what the witness did."

Judge McMasters nodded, peering through his steel spectacles. "You are overruled, Mr. Brewer. You may have an exception if you want one."

"Thank you, your honor. I do."

Mr. Kennon, turning again to Mr. Pettibone, said, "Let's go back a little. You have testified that you thought the plaintiff was drunk. You have said that he gave you this impression because of the way he looked and the way he was using his broom. Do you think that you could have been mistaken?"

"No, I don't. I've seen too many drunks in my time."

"It comes down to this, then—in your own mind you were convinced that the plaintiff was drunk. Is that correct?"

"That is correct."

"What happened next, Mr. Pettibone? When you saw the condition that the plaintiff was in——"

Mr. Brewer rose to his feet. "Again I object, your honor. It has not been proved that the plaintiff was in any condition of any kind. All we are getting from the present line of questioning is what the witness thought."

"We will sustain you, Mr. Brewer. Let the last question be struck. Proceed, Mr. Kennon."

"What happened next, Mr. Pettibone? Tell the court in your own words."

"My first thought was to protect myself. When I saw the end of the broom coming at me, I grabbed hold of it."

"And what happened then?"

Mr. Pettibone's face took on an aggrieved expression. "He began trying to wrestle it away, and since I thought that he might be after me——"

"I don't want to keep on holding up proceedings, your honor," Mr. Brewer said, "but here we are again on the subject of what the witness thought. First he thinks that the plaintiff was drunk, and now he thinks that he was coming after him. I again object on the ground that it is not evidence."

"We will have to continue to overrule you, Mr. Brewer," Judge McMasters said. "I think it is fairly clear that what the witness thought, in so far as it is related to his actions, has to be admitted as material."

Mr. Kennon said, "Please continue, Mr. Pettibone."

"Like I said, I thought he might be after me. He wasn't too steady on his feet to begin with——"

"So you thought!" Mr. Brewer interrupted.

"Yes, so he thought!" Mr. Kennon shot back, looking angry for the first time. "Please continue, Mr. Pettibone."

Mr. Pettibone, glancing coldly in Mr. Brewer's direction, said, "He wasn't too steady on his feet to begin with, and the next thing I knew he was going through that window."

"Did you push him?"

"No."

"Did you exert any form of force or pressure that might have caused him to go through the window?"

"No."

"Was there any action on your part that might have caused him to go through the window?"

"No."

"Exactly what happened?"

"Well, like I said, we were wrestling with that broom and he just kind of stumbled back. That's when he broke through the glass. If he hadn't been drunk, he wouldn't have."

Anson, in his identification with Mr. Brewer, said under his breath, "I object, your honor. That I do object to!" but Mr. Brewer, scribbling on the slip of paper before him, made no move to protest. Even Judge McMasters seemed surprised. Mr. Kennon said, "One last question, Mr. Pettibone. What was your motive throughout this unfortunate incident?"

"I've already said. I wanted to protect myself. I was acting in self-defense."

"Thank you, sir. Your witness, Mr. Brewer."

After Mr. Brewer's clumsy handling of Phineas Bell, Anson was prepared to have him bungle his cross-examination of Mr. Pettibone as well. Jay Lockhart, he noticed, was whispering to Mr. Kennon, who had bent his head toward him so that the part in his soft white hair could be seen clearly, and Judge McMasters, up on the bench, was making a few more notes, holding his pencil close to the point. Mr. Brewer, rising from his table in the new hush that had come over the courtroom, took up his position near the witness chair and said:

"You have testified, Mr. Pettibone, that on the morning of Wednesday, March 6, you were passing the Page Hardware Company on Bay Street. That is correct, is it not?"

"It is."

"And you have said that the time was somewhere between eleven-forty and eleven forty-five. Do you recall making that statement?"

"I do."

"You also said, as I believe you will remember, that you were certain of the time because you had reason to look at your watch. Is that also correct?"

"It is."

"You are still certain that that was the time?"

"I am."

Anson could not imagine why Mr. Brewer was rehashing all that again—the time had been clearly established, and what difference did it make, anyway? Jay Lockhart and Mr. Kennon, sitting at their table, appeared to be just as puzzled as he—Jay wrote something on his yellow pad and slid the pad toward Mr. Kennon, who looked at it and nodded. Mr. Brewer, standing with one hand in his pocket, said, "As I recall, Mr. Pettibone, coming to the final part of your testimony, you said that it was your firm conviction that the plaintiff was drunk."

"I object, your honor," Mr. Kennon broke in. "Nothing was said about a firm conviction."

"I think there was," Mr. Brewer replied, walking back to the plaintiff's table, where Clifford Small was now sitting alone. He picked up the slip of paper on which he had been scribbling and read from it. "Question: *In your own mind you were convinced that the plaintiff was drunk. Is that correct?* Answer: *That is correct.* I submit, your honor, that what we have here is a firm conviction, or something so close to it that nobody would be able to tell the difference."

"But there *is* a difference," Mr. Kennon insisted.

"Yes," Judge McMasters said, "I suppose there is. Very well, Mr. Kennon. You are sustained."

Mr. Brewer, turning back to Mr. Pettibone, said, "All right, then. It was merely something of which you were convinced in your own mind—in your own mind you were convinced that the plaintiff was drunk. Is *that* correct?"

"Yes, it is." Mr. Pettibone's voice had an undertone of anger and he was beginning to show signs of restiveness. "I don't see why I have to keep on repeating what I've said before."

"You came to this conviction, or were so convinced, because of the way the plaintiff looked. Is that correct?"

"Yes."

"And you were further convinced by the way he was using his broom."

"Yes."

"And the time was somewhere between eleven-forty and eleven forty-five?"

"Yes."

Mr. Kennon, lifting his hand and then getting to his feet, said, "I object, your honor. The witness is not being questioned. He is being heckled. Besides, if it is the credibility of the witness that is being attacked——"

"May I explain myself, your honor?" Mr. Brewer said. "Counsel is incorrect in thinking that I am trying to attack the credibility of the witness. Over my objections, your honor ruled that what the witness thought had to be admitted as material. All I am now trying to do is to make sure that we know exactly what he did think."

Judge McMasters leaned forward, shaking the sleeves of his gown to give freer motion to his arms. "That would seem to be in order. I do not think that there has been any heckling, Mr. Kennon. Overruled."

Mr. Kennon sat down, and Mr. Brewer, glancing at the slip of paper on which he had scribbled his notes, said, "You have testified, Mr. Pettibone, that what you did—the actions which you claim were taken in self-defense—were closely related to what you thought. I am not misinterpreting you, am I?"

"No, I reckon not."

"Could I have an unqualified answer?"

"No."

"In short, you did what you did because you thought the plaintiff was drunk."

"He was drunk."

"Just a moment, please. No proof has been offered on that score. All we have, as I hope the jury will remember, is a piece of circumstantial evidence that might possibly indicate that the plaintiff may have been drinking—when, however, nobody knows. A previous witness has testified that he did not think the plaintiff showed any signs of being under the influence of liquor. You say that you thought otherwise. Your position, as I understand it, is that you thought he was drunk, and that it was because of what you thought that you did what you did. Is that correct?"

"Yes."

"You felt that he was coming after you—those are your own words, Mr. Pettibone; 'I though he might be after me,' you said—and you acted in self-defense. Or what you thought was self-defense. Is that right?"

"Yes."

"Because you thought the plaintiff was drunk."

"Yes."

"Suppose you had not thought he was drunk? Would you have acted otherwise? Would you have felt it necessary to take these measures in self-defense?"

"Well, I——"

"Objection, your honor," Mr. Kennon said. "What the witness might have done under a different set of circumstances, or might not have done, is wholly irrelevant and immaterial. And I find it hard to understand why he must be hounded, over and over again, on the subject of what he thought. He has said what he thought. We all know what he thought. How long does your honor intend to let this continue?"

Judge McMasters, with a bright glint in his eyes, said severely, "You will please not to question the conduct of this court, Mr. Kennon. However, I will sustain your objection. The last question will be struck. And for my own benefit, Mr. Brewer, I would like to know why we are spending so much time inquiring into the mental processes of the witness. It might help me if I am called upon to rule further."

"Certainly, your honor." Mr. Brewer turned from Mr. Pettibone and faced the bench. He said, "I have simply been trying to find out if the witness was willing to stand on his previous testimony, that's all— now that he has shown that he is, I have no further questions. The witness may be excused. But if it please the court, I would now like to ask permission to introduce a new witness, one who was not known to me until just a few minutes before we resumed after the noon recess, and whose name does not appear on the list. An offer of testimony has been made and I ask the court to receive it."

Mr. Kennon jerked himself to his feet at the mention of a new witness—or was jerked to them; it was hard to say which—and stood with his mouth open, as if he were about to say something. What, however, he seemed unable to decide. A babble of voices filled the courtroom, accompanied by much scraping of shoes, turning around, and craning of necks, and Judge McMasters, looking furious, kept pounding with his gavel until quiet was restored. He motioned to Mr. Brewer and Mr. Kennon to come before him, still looking furious, and for several minutes there was a huddle at the bench. Anson could not hear what was being said, but he could imagine. To ask permission to introduce a new witness at this stage of the trial was most unusual. Judge McMasters would have to satisfy himself that there was some good reason for it. Ordinarily, presented with such a demand, a judge would call a recess and, in conference with the opposing attorneys, come to a decision in his chambers. However, every judge had the right to manage his own courtroom as he saw fit, and Judge McMasters was apparently not going to recess. Anson knew, having been told so by Mr. Leigh, that he was planning to go on a fishing trip that week end. The weakfish were running off Cassava Beach, and Judge McMasters hoped to get a verdict from the jury that afternoon. Those weakfish, Anson imagined, had a lot to do with his not calling a recess. They were biting at anything and it was one of the biggest runs in years.

Mr. Brewer must finally have satisfied Judge McMasters that the new witness should be called. The judge asked a final question, spoke to Mr. Kennon, who responded with a rather reluctant nod, and rapped with his gavel again. Once the courtroom was still and Mr. Kennon had returned to his seat at the defense's table next to Jay Lockhart, Mr. Brewer said, "Will Miss Margaret Higgins please come forward and take the stand?"

CHAPTER EIGHTEEN

What Midge Higgins had, Anson later decided, was a sense of style. Certainly, as she composed herself on the stand, wearing a light blue dress and a cardigan sweater of a darker blue, her shiny blond hair falling down to her shoulders from beneath a soft felt hat, no one could have looked any nicer. Set her down on the streets of New York, as he often thought later, and she would instantly be taken for one of those girls who raced down for the week end from Smith or Vassar or Sarah Lawrence. Any number of times, on those rare occasions when he got to midtown Manhattan during the daytime, he had passed some girl who reminded him of Midge, and for a few minutes he could see her as she looked that day on the stand, sitting with her hands folded in her lap and waiting for Mr. Brewer to begin his interrogation.

Mr. Brewer, using that tone of voice which all lawyers reserve for a female witness, said, "If you don't mind, Miss Higgins, I am going to start out by asking you a few questions which will explain to the court why you are being introduced at this time. It is rather unusual for a witness to be admitted on such short notice, and the court must be satisfied as to the proprieties. You understand, don't you?"

"Yes sir."

"You knew that this trial was in progress, didn't you?"

"Yes sir."

"And you've probably been reading about it in our local paper."

"No sir. Not much."

"But you must have heard it discussed."

"Yes sir."

"Well, then. Did it not occur to you that you were in a position to present the court with certain information it ought to have, and which might help the jury in reaching a just and honorable verdict?"

Midge looked as though she were beginning to get lost in this maze of formal inquiry. She hesitated an instant and then said, "No sir. It didn't!"

"You say it didn't."

"No sir. I mean yes sir. It didn't seem important."

"What didn't seem important?"

Midge hesitated again. "What happened. The thing I told you about. I practically forgot it."

"Excuse me, Mr. Brewer," Judge McMasters said, giving another shake to the sleeves of his robe. "I'd like to ask a few questions myself. Young lady——"

"Yes sir."

"What caused you to change your mind—a most sudden change of mind, apparently? And when did this change of mind take place? Yesterday?"

"No sir."

"This morning?"

"No sir."

It was now Judge McMasters's turn to look lost. Not, however, for long. Leaning forward, and with just enough exasperation in his voice to indicate that he was trying to keep his irritability under control, he said, "I'm going to have to ask you to explain yourself, young lady. You *did* change your mind, didn't you? If, as you say, whatever it was that happened did not seem important to you, that you practically forgot it, then how does it happen——"

"It was my father," Midge said. "He was in court this morning. He saw me having lunch in Spier's Drugstore and came in to talk to me. He said that they were saying that Clifford was drunk, and when I said that Clifford couldn't have been drunk——"

Mr. Kennon was on his feet again, crying, "Objection, your honor! I am compelled to object!" and through the murmur of voices that rose from the rows of spectators, Anson saw Jay Lockhart's pale eyes fixed motionless on Midge. He remembered the night when he and Midge had driven to the old rice fields near Mulberry, and he thought of the various times when, Midge's name having entered the conversation, he had spoken up for her. He wondered if Jay Lockhart was thinking of that too, and if he would try to show that Midge was a prejudiced witness. But once again there was a demand for quiet in the courtroom, and Judge McMasters, again pounding with his gavel, sat with his jaw clamped until the noise had subsided. Hearing out Mr. Kennon, he sustained his objection and then, laying down his gavel, he returned his attention to Midge. "You will please to answer only the questions that are put to you, young lady. Don't volunteer any information. You'll have a chance to tell everything you know." He looked down at her, small and severe. "So it wasn't you who changed your mind. It was your father who changed it for you. Is that it?"

"Yes sir."

"And it was your father who told you to present yourself as a witness?"

"Yes sir."

"When was that?"

"Today. During my lunch hour. When I told him that Clifford——"

"Never mind what you told him. Just answer the question. Your father told you to present yourself as a witness, and it was then, I take it, that you saw Mr. Brewer. Is that what happened?"

"Yes sir."

"And if it had not been for your father you wouldn't be here?"

"Yes sir. I mean no sir."

Judge McMasters looked as though he wanted to shake his head in despair, thinking of how small were the accidents on which the course of justice sometimes had to depend. "Very well, young lady. That is all. You may proceed, Mr. Brewer."

It began gradually to appear, as Midge told her story, that Mr. Pettibone might well be mistaken about Clifford's being drunk. The jury, which only a short time before had the relatively simple choice of crediting either Mr. Pettibone or Clifford, and of weighing the assertions of Anson's father against the nearly empty pint bottle which Phineas Bell found in the pocket of Clifford's coat, now had an infinitely harder decision to make. Midge, on Wednesday, March 6, 1935, had to go to the dentist. She awakened that morning with a slight toothache and had to be asked to be excused from work to see Dr. Lucius Sommers. His office was on the third floor of the Renshawe Building, which stood on the corner of Bay and Colonial streets. On her way back to Cornish's Department Store, Midge passed the Page Hardware Company.

"What time was that, Miss Higgins?"

"Around half-past eleven."

"Could you be more exact?"

"No sir."

"Do you think it might have been later than that?"

Midge pursed her lips, looking thoughtful. "No sir, I don't. When I got back to the store and punched the clock it was eleven-forty. If I hadn't——"

"Just a moment, Miss Higgins," Mr. Brewer cautioned. "We'll get to that in time." Returning to the plaintiff's table, he picked up a narrow, oblong card which he held up for the jury to see. Addressing Judge McMasters, he said, "I hold here, your honor, the time card of Miss Higgins for the working week of March 4 to March 9, 1935. I desire to introduce it into evidence as Exhibit A and to have it examined by the jury." He walked over to the box and handed the card to the foreman. "It will be noticed that it bears the name, on the top, of the A. B. Cornish Department Store, and immediately beneath it, in handwriting, the name of the witness. If the members of the jury will look under the date of March 6—all the dates, gentlemen, will be found running down the left-hand side of the card—they will see that Miss Higgins left the store at nine fifty-five and returned at exactly eleven-forty."

Anson could see what Mr. Brewer was leading up to. Mr. Pettibone had testified that he passed the Page Hardware Company somewhere between eleven-forty and eleven forty-five. He had further testified that Clifford looked and acted drunk, and that the broom in his hands appeared out of control. Up to the present time, nothing could be offered in rebuttal. If, however, Midge had seen Clifford only a few minutes before Mr. Pettibone arrived, and if, as she had seemingly told her father, she had reason to believe that Clifford could not have been drunk, Mr. Pettibone's various contentions would be severely challenged. Proceeding very deliberately, Mr. Brewer said, "So the time, as best you remember, was around half-past eleven."

"Yes sir."

"Now let me ask you this, Miss Higgins. What happened as you were passing the Page Hardware Company?"

"I dropped my purse."

"How did that happen?"

"I don't know. I just dropped it. It's one of those new mail-pouch purses and it's always slipping off my shoulder."

"I see." Mr. Brewer, pausing, studied the jury as though he wanted to make sure that it also saw. Apparently he decided to take no chances. He said, "A mail-pouch purse, Miss Higgins, is worn across the shoulder by means of a leather strap. Is that correct?"

"It doesn't have to be leather," Midge said. "It can be almost anything. Some of the purses are made out of imitation leather. That's the kind I have. It looks like real leather, but——"

Judge McMasters, who had momentarily relaxed in his chair, leaned forward in a way that made Anson think he was going to tell Midge that she could dispense with the fashion notes. Mr. Brewer, catching his expression, said, "The thing I am trying to get at, Miss Higgins, is that these purses, regardless of the material from which they are made, hang from the shoulder by a strap. That's more or less the arrangement, isn't it?"

"Yes sir."

"And it was this strap which slipped?"

"Yes sir."

"What happened then?"

"My purse came open and everything spilled over the sidewalk."

"Everything?"

Mr. Brewer smiled indulgently, but Midge did not smile back. She said very seriously, "No, not everything. Just nearly everything. My comb and my lipstick and some loose change. My compact too. Clifford was sweeping near the door and when he saw——"

"Just answer my questions, Miss Higgins," Mr. Brewer broke in. "You dropped your purse, or your purse slipped from your shoulder, and most of its contents fell out upon the sidewalk. Is that what happened?"

"Yes sir."

"What were some of the things that were in your purse?"

"The things I just told you about—my comb, my lipstick, my compact, and some loose change."

"Do you recall the exact nature of this loose change?"

"I don't know what you mean."

"What was it? Of what kinds of coins was it composed?"

"I don't remember. It was just some loose change."

"Quarters?"

"I don't know."

"Dimes?"

"Maybe."

"Nickels? Pennies?"

"Yes, I had some pennies. Ever since the new sales tax came in, I'm always loaded down with pennies."

A ripple of laughter came from the spectators—these days, ever since the new sales tax, everybody in town was loaded down with pennies; even some of the jurors began to smile.

"What did you do then, Miss Higgins?"

"I started to pick things up. I was in a hurry to get back to the store, seeing as how they'd been nice enough to let me off, and——"

"That we can all understand," Mr. Brewer interrupted. "Just answer the question. What did you do?"

"I just told you. I started to pick things up."

"Did anyone come to your assistance?"

"Yes."

"Who was it?"

"Clifford."

Midge was asked if she could identify Clifford, and Clifford was again requested to rise. Looking at him, Anson felt that he ought to be shaken—why hadn't he said something about Midge! And perhaps Midge ought to be shaken also; were it not for her father, she wouldn't be here. In a way, though, perhaps it was better this way. For if Mr. Brewer had known about Midge beforehand and had gone over her story with her, rehearsing it and smoothing out the rough edges, the impression she was making on the jury might well have been lost. Mr. Brewer said:

"And Clifford helped you to pick up the contents of your purse?"

"Yes sir."

Not once, however, either then or later, did Anson believe that Mr. Pettibone was guilty of perjury. It must be laid to his credit that he told the truth as he saw it. He did think that Clifford was drunk, having in part been conditioned by Clifford's own behavior to believe that he was always drunk (even Marion believed that; practically the whole town did), and his imagination needed but to take one step further for him to be convinced, when he saw the broom coming in his direction, that Clifford was "after" him—grant Mr. Pettibone his own kind of imagination, his view of the Negro in general and of the intoxicated Negro in particular, and have it further inflamed by anger, and he was bound to think as he did. But against his imagination there was now this other imagination—this younger, prettier imagination, as it were—and an entirely different complexion was being put on the face of things.

"Do you remember what it was that Clifford picked up for you, Miss Higgins?"

"Yes sir. The loose change I told you about."

"All of it?"

"No sir, not all."

"How much of it?"

"I don't know exactly."

"Did he pick up any of the pennies?"

"Yes sir. Some of them."

The whole courtroom was at last beginning to comprehend. If a man could help rescue the scattered contents of a lady's purse, and was enough in control of himself to be able to pick up pennies, then how could he have been drunk—how could anyone have *thought* he was drunk?

"Did you notice anything peculiar about the plaintiff, Miss Higgins?"

"Peculiar?"

"Yes. Did anything about him strike you as being unusual in any way?"

"No sir."

"Nothing at all?"

"No sir."

"Did he seem to be under the influence of liquor?"

"No sir."

"If he had been, would you have noticed?"

"Yes sir. I think so."

"Do you just think so?"

"No sir. I'm sure that I would have noticed."

Mr. Brewer, nodding approvingly, took a meditative step toward the jury. Anson watched him admiringly. Whatever his previous errors, he was now handling himself in a way that could hardly be bettered. He said, "To go back a little, Miss Higgins, you testified that when you reached the Page Hardware Company and dropped your purse it was around eleven-thirty. You remember saying that, don't you?"

"Yes sir."

"And how long was it before you were on your way again? After you had recovered the contents of your purse, I mean."

Midge hesitated a moment, trying to think. "About five minutes, I guess."

"What time was it when you left the plaintiff?"

Midge had to stop and think again. "Around eleven thirty-five. It must have taken me about five minutes to walk back to the store."

"From the Page Hardware Company?"

"Yes sir."

"Did you stop anywhere on the way?"

"No sir."

"You walked directly from the Page Hardware Company to Cornish's Department Store. Is that right?"

"Yes sir."

"Thank you, Miss Higgins. Your witness, Mr. Kennon."

Anson, watching Mr. Kennon get to his feet, shifted his glance toward the jury. It sat, not spellbound, since Mr. Brewer had made no effort to overwhelm it, as some lawyers tried to do even while questioning a witness, but in a kind of disturbed uncertainty; it now had to think, forced to choose between two sharply conflicting stories, and, not knowing what to think, it wanted to have its mind made up for it. Mr. Kennon did all that he could to oblige. Addressing Midge with elaborate courtesy, knowing that he must not for one instant let the jury get the impression that he would try to bully a woman, he asked a few of those throw-away questions that help an attorney get the feel of a new witness, and then said:

"Permit me to ask you this, Miss Higgins. You have told us that when you returned from the dentist and punched the time clock at your place of employment, Cornish's Department Store, it was eleven-forty. Is that correct?"

"Yes sir. That's what I said."

"And you also said, I believe, that you last saw the plaintiff at approximately eleven thirty-five."

"Yes sir. It could have been a little later, though."

"Oh, I see." Mr. Kennon rubbed his chin and draped himself in a cloak of heavy thoughtfulness; he wore it, Anson thought, like mourning. "You're rather hazy about the time, in other words."

"No sir," Midge said. "I'm not hazy. It was around eleven thirty-five."

Minutes, even seconds, were vital to Mr. Kennon. What he had to show was that enough time had elapsed between Midge's departure and Mr. Pettibone's arrival for Clifford to get himself drunk; so drunk as to justify the workings of Mr. Pettibone's imagination. As matters now stood, only five minutes separated Clifford cold sober from Clifford practically unable to control a broom—if, that is, the testimony of Anson's father was entirely to be discounted and only that of Mr. Pettibone believed. Five minutes, however, was too short a span. The jury had been led to believe that Clifford had been tippling all that morning. And since Midge's time card could not be argued with, proving that she had reported back to Cornish's Department Store at eleven-forty, Mr. Kennon's only hope was to try to gain a few minutes at the other end.

"Instead of eleven thirty-five, Miss Higgins, could it not have been eleven thirty-three?"

"Well, yes. I suppose so."

"Or even eleven-thirty?"

Midge gave a quick shake to her head. "No sir. It couldn't have been eleven-thirty. I didn't leave Dr. Sommers's office until eleven-thirty."

"Are you sure?"

"Yes sir. I didn't know if my watch was right and when I was leaving I asked Winnie McNamara—Winnie's Dr. Sommers's secretary—what time it was. She said it was eleven-thirty. That's what the clock on the Merchants & Mechanics Bank said too."

"But you admit that it could have been eleven thirty-three."

"Yes sir. It could have been."

For his pains, Mr. Kennon could show a gain of two minutes. Anson wondered if it had been worth it. What it meant was that Clifford now had seven minutes, instead of five, to reduce himself to the state in which Mr. Pettibone said he found him. And seven minutes for an old hand like Clifford to get himself looping—no, it couldn't have happened. Not even Mr. Kennon could get the jury to believe that. The only conclusion was that Mr. Pettibone had let his imagination run away with him. He stood convicted, as it were, of seeing things. Anson thought he heard a faint undertone of dejection in Mr. Kennon's voice as he turned to Judge McMasters—"That is all, your honor. I have no further questions."

Any student of the law, going over the transcript of the trial, would be certain to conclude that it was Midge's appearance on the stand which marked the turning point of the proceedings, and that it was on the basis of her testimony that the jury awarded fifteen hundred dollars damages to Clifford Small. It was only natural, then, for Meg to reach the same conclusion.

"So it was that girl," she said. "She did it."

Anson found it difficult to reply. It was indeed that girl, and most assuredly it was she who had done it, but here, again, it was considerably more complicated than Meg wanted to believe. She would have liked to see it as a triumph of righteousness, a shining victory gained by one swift stroke, and it was hard for her to understand, as it would be for anyone who had not grown up in Pompey's Head, that it more nearly represented the ascendancy of one tacit assumption over the other.

"Oh, stop talking like a lawyer," Meg interrupted as Anson tried to explain. "Say what you mean!"

What Anson meant, as he went on to say, was that if in Pompey's Head there was an unspoken agreement that a person of consequence like Mr. Henry Pettibone could do no wrong in relation to a Negro like Clifford Small, so was it understood that a lady always told the truth. If the former be maintained, so must the latter. They both went hand in hand. Therefore, when the jury was called upon to weigh Mr. Pettibone's version of Clifford's condition against the description given by Midge, it was bound to decide in her favor—not because it wanted to, or did not even perhaps resent her intrusion, but because it had no choice. Begin by doubting that a lady did not always tell the truth, and who could say how it would end? Even the guarantees that protected a person like Mr. Pettibone might eventually be called into question. So even though Mr. Pettibone was assessed the token payment of fifteen hundred dollars, and everybody understood that it was a token payment, the jury, by upholding the principle that a lady never failed to tell the truth, was upholding him as well. Obscurely, perhaps, but no less tangibly. It was simply Mr. Pettibone's misfortune to have one tacit assumption outweighed by another—a matter of density of gravity, one might say. And so it was incorrect to look upon the jury's verdict as a victory for the forces of enlightenment. Pompey's Head was simply working out its problems in its own way. The forces of enlightenment did not have anything to do with it. They had not even entered the lists. All of which did not alter the fact that Meg was right. It was that girl. But if it had been some other girl, one who had not so forcibly impressed the jury as being a lady——

"I don't believe it," Meg said. "I refuse to believe it! Do you mean to say that it was because of the way she looked!"

Anson gave up all hope of making her understand. The folklore of Hillsdale, Indiana, was too widely separated from the folklore of Pompey's Head. He said, begging the question, "In a courtroom there are times when more depends on how a person looks than on what he says. But yes—it was the way she looked. I think it was that, as much as anything, that caused the jury to pry loose that fifteen hundred dollars from Mr. Pettibone. She looked like a lady, and the jury simply couldn't question a lady's word."

Meg made a face. "Lady! You're not under the impression that I'm a lady, are you?"

"You? Don't be foolish. How about a brandy?"

288

"Can you afford it?"

"Yesterday was payday."

"In that case I'll have a crème de menthe. And so that's how it ended. Your father won, after all."

"Yes, he won."

"And that's the end of the story?"

In one sense it was and in another it wasn't. It could be taken as an illustration of the truism that nothing ever ended and that what sometimes appeared to be an ending was actually a new beginning. Anson wondered how it would be if he told what happened next. That, though, was impossible. There were some things you could not tell anyone, least of all the girl you were hoping to marry. Meg said she believed that they should always be frank and open with each other, but he did not think she would want him to be as frank and open as that. He said, "Yes, that's the end. Now it's your turn. Why don't you tell me about Hillsdale?"

"Ugh," Meg said. "That place."

CHAPTER NINETEEN

Judge McMasters read Midge a final lecture before he dismissed her—"And I hope, young lady, that the next time you have information that may be valuable to a court of law, you won't need your father to make you come forward with it." Midge listened intently, once nodding her head, and an expression of relief spread across her face when Judge McMasters said she might go. Anson could tell that it had been more of an ordeal for her than she had let anyone guess, and he was glad that it was over. Watching Midge as she walked up the aisle that divided the rows of spectator seats into two sections, he wanted to get up and follow her. It was only the thought of being conspicuous that made him decide against it. He did not care about himself, but he did not want to embarrass Midge. The least he could do, however, was to thank her. She need not have offered to testify, since her father did not have her that much under his thumb, and what she had done amounted to an act of courage. In the friendless world it had become, a world whose chief attribute seemed to be a lack of courage, he wanted her to know how grateful he was.

But when finally he left his seat to look for her, unable to restrain himself any longer, Midge was nowhere to be found. He searched for her in the hall, which was full of the hangers-on who used the courthouse as a sort of club, playing penny ante in one of the basement rooms and finding even less expensive amusement whenever the docket turned up a trial, and then, thinking that perhaps she had gone outside to smoke a cigarette, he walked through the hall to the main entrance. He hoped to find her on the courthouse steps. Midge was not there either, however, and he concluded that she must have taken her dismissal by Judge McMasters as permission to go back to work.

The courthouse fronted on Colonial Square. Although it was the least attractive square in town, partaking of some of the shabbiness of its surroundings, the grimy brick pile of the courthouse and the county jail and a couple of eating places that catered to the penny-ante trade, this was the time of year when it too had a certain charm. Masses of spirea were in bloom, white as snowdrifts, along with great clumps of oleanders, both pink and white, that had been growing there for years. Anson thought how nice it would be if he and Midge could get into the secondhand Plymouth convertible he had acquired and go for a drive in the country. At this time of year you always thought of going for a drive in the country. The way he felt, he and Midge could keep on driving forever.

Shaking off his daydream, he wondered if she had a date that night. It added to his burden of depression to think that she probably had —another Sailor Greer, no doubt!—but even so he would have to see her. He wanted her to know how grateful he was, and, besides, he was beginning to be ashamed of himself. He had been a fool to let what happened that night at the Oasis come between them. Because of Kit Robbins and his wanting to please her, to be the kind of person she wanted him to be, he had been unfair to Midge. There was nothing he could do about that now, but he would not be able to rest until he thanked her for what she had done. The chances were that he would find her at the Oasis. He was not as well acquainted with her habits as he used to be, but he understood that she nearly always went to the Oasis on Friday night.

Judge McMasters was lucky. He was late getting started on his fishing trip, but he made it. The jury received the case at twenty minutes of five and brought in its verdict shortly before ten. By ten-thirty, dressed in his roughest clothes and with his gear stowed away in the trunk of his Packard, Judge McMasters was on his way to the fishing camp on Little River to which he belonged. Anxious to get in a few hands of poker before the game broke up at midnight, he sped along at sixty miles an hour. The judge and his cronies were fishermen first and cardplayers second. Lights went out at the camp at ten minutes past midnight and everybody was on the water at dawn.

Anson, driving in the same direction toward the Oasis, had to pull over to let Judge McMasters pass. In the split second that the two cars ran abreast, the beam of their headlamps tunneling into the darkness ahead, he caught a glimpse of the judge holding tight to the wheel. Then, with an added burst of speed, the Packard roared ahead.

And him a judge, Anson thought. Let anyone else go tearing along like that and he wouldn't think twice about reporting him to the highway police! It would have been easy to excuse the judge, since he was going only ten miles faster than the speed limit of fifty—a limit, furthermore, that the highway patrol rarely bothered to enforce—but Anson had no inclination to make excuses. Could he have seen his own face, he would have noticed that it bore an expression of antagonism and resentment, the tense, drawn face of a man who is going out of his way to look for trouble. He might have denied it at the time, saying that if the thought of trouble had entered his calculations it was merely that he wanted to be prepared for it, but in later years he was able to see that he must have been looking for it as well. There could be no other explanation for his having gone home and put on his best clothes. He must have wanted to wave another blue suit in the face of the bull. Impossible though it was to settle all his scores, there was nothing to keep him from settling his score with Sailor Greer. They might have to carry him out on a stretcher, but he wouldn't turn tail again.

When he entered the Oasis the band was playing "Tiger Rag." The sound of the music rose up to the high, barnlike roof, and a crush of dancing couples packed the floor. Because of the crush, Anson could see only those who were nearest him. He began making his way through the tables, looking for Midge. Passing the soft-drink bar, about which some boys and girls who looked young enough to be in high school had gathered, he noticed Mico Higgins behind the counter. Mico, he had heard, had acquired the soft-drink concession at the Oasis. He was supposed to be making a good thing out of it. The story was that he pocketed from seventy-five to one hundred dollars a week. It was probably an exaggeration, since most such stories were, but Mico was earning enough in any case for him to be able to sport a new Ford roadster. The thought crossed Anson's mind that Mico Higgins was one of those people who knew how to make money. He had parlayed his *Saturday Evening Post* route into this concession at the Oasis, and it would not be long before he parlayed the concession into something else. Mico knew how to make money the way he knew how to play blackjack. Sooner or later he would take considerable pleasure in telling all the ribbon clerks to go home.

Picking his way through the tables along the edge of the dance floor, Anson was jarred by someone bumping into him. He turned swiftly, doubling his fists. Obsessed with the notion that he was going to have trouble with Sailor Greer, it took him a second to place the half-familiar face before him. Young and slightly flushed, it belonged to Timmy Wendover, one of the high school boys who ran with Dinah Blackford's crowd. Timmy was not supposed to be at the Oasis, and Anson could tell that he was already beginning to be worried that word of it was going to get back home. "Oh, hello, Sonny," he managed finally to get out. "I didn't mean to crash into you." Timmy was privileged to call him Sonny because Marion and Charlotte Wendover, Timmy's sister, were close friends. "I'm on my way to get some cokes," he said. "We just got here. The service is pretty terrible, isn't it?" Anson knew that the boy wanted him to agree about the service, if only to indicate that they were both members of the same club, two men loose on the town, but he had no time for Timmy Wendover. The music had stopped, and as the dancers left the floor he saw Midge sitting at a table on the far side of the room. There was a girl with her, a small brunette in a pale green dress, and two men. Anson recognized one of them as Bill Dillon, the young plumber with whom he had played blackjack in the Higginses' kitchen. The other he did not know. Much as he was prepared for trouble, he was glad that it was not Sailor Greer.

Midge was surprised to see him. She looked twice as she saw him approach, the first time disbelievingly, and then, as he drew nearer, in a momentarily expressionless manner that made him realize that she was wondering what he was doing there. The others at the table looked up also. Bill Dillon nodded when he saw who it was, slowly and uncertainly, and there was something about the look in his eyes that caused Anson to understand that they had been talking about the trial. "Hello, Sonny," Midge said. "Won't you sit down? You remember Bill, don't you?"

"Of course I do. Hello, Bill. How are you?"

"I'm all right, I reckon. Wait a second and I'll get us another chair."

"Don't bother. I'll get it."

"No. Let me."

Midge introduced Anson to her companions as Bill Dillon went off to find a chair. The brunette girl in the pale green dress was named Felicity Dubois, pronounced Duboy in Pompey's Head, and her date, a man considerably older than either she or Midge, balding, in his middle thirties, was named Nathaniel Olds. He had a long horse face and a set of big horse teeth. Something was said that established him as being in the contracting business. He pumped Anson's hand up and down, said that he was glad to meet him, and offered him a drink.

"We're roosting on the top perch tonight," he said. "It's real store-bought whisky we're drinking for a change. How'll you have yours? With creek water, branch water, or tap water? We've got coke water too. You name your own poison."

A card, Anson thought. On top of everything else, I have to run into a barbershop wit. Olds was so genial and friendly, however, beaming with such equine good will, that he found it easy to forgive him. Something was needed to ease the situation, and it could be that Olds was trying to apply the light touch.

"Sit down," he urged. "Make yourself at home. There's no need to wait for Brother Bill."

"Here comes Bill now," Midge said. "You sit next to me, Sonny. You won't be too crowded, will you?"

"Crowded?" Olds rolled his eyes. "What's the matter with being crowded, like the fellow said about having to stand behind a pretty little girl in church?" He pulled his chair closer to Felicity Dubois's, making a burlesque out of ogling her. "Why don't you try crowding me some?" he said. "See if I mind."

Giggling, Felicity said, "Honest, Nat! If you aren't the limit!" and there was a further reshuffling of chairs to make room for Bill Dillon. He glanced at Midge as he sat down and then quickly looked away— "Oh, take it easy," Anson wanted to say. "I'm not trying to beat your time." Though he could only guess what Bill Dillon was thinking, he gathered that Nathaniel Olds and Felicity Dubois were thinking it also. And what they were thinking, obviously, was that he and Midge had arranged to meet each other.

Anson wondered how he was going to get a chance to speak to Midge. He could not bring himself to say what he wanted to say with the others listening in. There was nothing to do, he decided, except to wait until the music started again and ask Midge to dance. It would not be the sort of meeting he had hoped for—what he wanted was to sit and talk with her alone somewhere—but under the circumstances it would have to do. Looking toward the platform on which the band was seated, he saw that its members were again taking up their instruments. Vicksburg, he noticed, was beginning to get gray. Anson watched him tighten the ebony pegs of his bull fiddle, bending over as he fingered the strings, and then, near the platform, moving unsteadily from table to table, he saw Sailor Greer.

More than six years had passed since Sailor Greer had faced him down, and the passage of time had not improved the other's appearance. His nose was broken and there was a patch of scar tissue over one eye. He looked like what he was, a would-be fighter who had never gone anywhere and had nowhere to go, but that gross, brutal frame was still capable of doing a great deal of hurt. Anson felt a clutch of tension at the base of his throat and a duller, tighter spasm in the pit of his stomach—now that he had glimpsed the face of trouble, he had to steel himself to meet it.

The crash of music broke into his awareness. It was a number that Vicksburg, who sang the chorus in his cracked, gravelly voice, was famous for—"Who Put the Whisky in the Well?" Anson, keeping one eye on Sailor Greer, signaled Midge an invitation to dance. She had changed from the clothes in which she had appeared at court, and was wearing a white dress and a pair of silver sandals. Anson had always thought of the Oasis as part of her accustomed environment, but now she seemed out of place. She looked at him with a thin veil of worry drawn across her eyes, and it suddenly came to him, as she nodded in reply to his unspoken invitation, that she too had seen Sailor Greer. There was no way out of it now, however. Whatever happened, he had to go through with it. Turning to Bill Dillon, he said, "You don't mind my stealing Midge for one dance, do you?"

Dillon shook his head. "It will be a break for her. All I do is to step on her feet."

Nothing was going the way Anson wanted it to go. He resented their thinking that he and Midge had arranged this meeting, especially Bill Dillon's thinking it, and he was too put off by Sailor Greer's appearance even to think of what he wanted to say to Midge. They made their way to the floor and began to dance.

"Hello, Midge," Anson said.

"Hello, Sonny."

"It's been a long time."

Midge narrowed her eyes just a little. "I'd like to know whose fault it's been."

Anson had almost forgotten how well she danced. They kept to the edge of the floor, avoiding the crush as best they could. Anson noticed that Nathaniel Olds and Felicity Dubois, glued together, were dancing not far away. Deserted, Bill Dillon sat at the table alone. He was staring absently at nothing, and his face, left un-

295

guarded for the moment, expressed the patient resignation of a man who is determined to keep on hoping despite all odds. " 'Who put the whisky in the well?' " Vicksburg was shouting. " 'Oh, who put the whisky in the well?' "

"Just listen to him," Midge said. "He's certainly feeling good tonight."

After the day it had been, it seemed strange to Anson that he should be dancing. Even stranger was that he should be enjoying it. Drawing Midge closer, he leaned his cheek on hers. He knew that Bill Dillon was watching, but he did not care. Dillon had staked out no claim that he was compelled to recognize. He said, after they had danced a few moments longer, drawing away from her, "You heard what happened in court, didn't you?"

Midge's silver sandals kept time to the music. "Yes. Your father won."

Anson started to tell her that it was not his father, that it was Clifford Small who had won, and then, as her eyes held firmly to his, that piece of fiction was no longer worth the bother.

"Yes, my father won," he said. "But you know who won it for him, don't you? If it hadn't been for you——"

"Look," Midge interrupted. "Something's happening."

It was then that Anson saw Dinah Blackford. She had on a flame-colored dress and was dancing with young Timmy Wendover—so wildly, however, with such flushed unthinking abandon, that some of the other dancers had fallen back to watch. Midge recognized Dinah the same instant as he. She lost the beat of the music and missed a step. It was that, more than her changed expression, which made him understand that she regretted having spoken.

"The little fool," he said. "Does she come here often?"

Midge shook her head. "This is the first time. I would have heard about it if it wasn't."

"From Mico?"

"Who else?"

"Does that mean he has a crush on her?"

"I suppose you would call it that."

"And she?"

"How would I know?"

Anyone else might have been suspected of dissembling, but Anson knew that Midge was telling the truth. He continued to watch Dinah. She did not belong at the Oasis, and where in God's name had she got that dress? It was far too old for a girl who was barely sixteen, still all legs and arms, and he was surprised that Mrs. Blackford would let her appear in it. Except, of course, that Dinah had probably made a commotion. As he understood it, life with Dinah these days was one commotion after the other. But at least she and Timmy were no longer calling attention to themselves. The other dancers had closed in on them and they had stopped putting on a show.

"Don't worry about her, Sonny," Midge said. "She's just having fun."

It was such a simple explanation that Anson found it hard to take in. He had always thought of Dinah as a child, roaming the fields near Mulberry, looking for arrowheads and hunting for birds' eggs, stealing off in one of the rowboats to drift on the river, and he had never stopped to consider that she might be growing up—"Child, child, child!" she had burst out in his presence only a few months before. "Oh, how I hate that word! It makes me sick! Does anybody in this ignorant family know that Juliet was only fourteen?"

With that in the background, Anson suspected that there was more behind her presence at the Oasis than, as Midge seemed inclined to believe, a search for fun. She was sick of being a child, and if Juliet could die for love why couldn't she, and so here she was, fleeing in an impossible flame-colored dress from those who did not understand her. Replying at last to Midge's caution about not worrying, he said, "I'm not worried. I was just surprised to see her here, that's all."

"You don't think that's news, do you?"

"No, I don't suppose it is. I have always been pretty transparent to you, haven't I?"

Midge drew away and looked at him. "What am I expected to say to that?"

"Whatever is true."

"Of course you aren't transparent. Is anybody? Do we ever know what people are like?"

"I think I know what you are like."

"Do you?"

"Yes."

Midge gave a little laugh. "Sonny Page, Old Pompey's favorite yogi. Knows all and sees all. How do you do it? With tea leaves or a crystal ball?"

"Haven't you heard? I read palms."

"When do we start?"

"Whenever you say. I don't suppose that I could see you alone, could I?"

He was thinking that what he wanted to say would be better said if they could be off to themselves, but Midge looked surprised. She could not be expected to know what was in his mind, and he realized how blunt he must have sounded. "I didn't mean it that way, Midge," he said. "It's only that I want to talk to you. That's what I came out here for. I know that you have a date with Bill, but I thought that somehow, perhaps later on——"

Midge looked dubious. "I don't know, Sonny. It's getting awfully late. I'm a working girl, remember?"

"All right, Midge," Anson said. "You know best. Actually, all I wanted to say——"

But then, as he started to thank her for what she had done, Dinah Blackford danced back into view. Timmy Wendover had been displaced by another partner, a blond, lanky boy whom Anson did not know. No sooner did he see Dinah than he became exasperated again. Why had she ever been permitted to wear that dress! He had to admit, however, that its color was wonderfully becoming. Dinah was growing into an unusually pretty girl. Another boy cut in on her, a stranger to judge by the way she looked at him, unmistakably one of the Bugtown locals. Anson did not think that Dinah was any too happy about it, but what did she expect—didn't she know that any girl who came to the Oasis was considered fair game? What she should have done was to decline the invitation. It was understood at the Oasis that a girl could shake off anyone with whom she did not care to dance. But this way, if she was to go spinning into the arms of every bum and loafer who came along—— Ah, the little fool!

With Midge now also watching, Anson saw two more locals cut in on Dinah. They were much older than she, grinning, all but licking their lips, and Anson knew that the word had got around—here was a little chick who didn't know what it was all about; come and get it! What made it worse was that Midge knew what was happening as well as he. He saw another man cut in on Dinah, a slender, rather short youth with a pale, thin face and a plume of wavy black hair that fell across his forehead, and he recognized him as Mico Higgins. He felt enormously relieved. At least he knew who Mico was. Also, from the expression on Mico's face, the set of his jaw and the look in his eyes, it was apparent that he had decided to become Dinah's protector. Anson could wish for a more acceptable champion, but he was grateful just the same. "The Marines arrived just in time," he said to Midge. "Things were beginning to get a little out of hand."

Midge did not answer for a moment. Then, surprisingly, in a flat expressionless tone that was unlike her, "The poor kid," she said.

"Who? Dinah?"

"No, not Dinah. It's Mico I'm thinking about. Just look at him. She's in his arms at last, little Miss Mulberry. This is as close to heaven as he will ever get."

"Is it that bad? Is he that serious about her?"

"Serious?" Midge's voice sounded grim. "You don't know my brother Mico. When he wants something the way he wants that little Miss Mulberry of yours——"

"Mine?"

"Well, isn't she? Didn't she always used to say that she was your girl?"

"Don't be silly, Midge. That was just kid stuff. Besides, she's stopped saying that for years."

Midge did not answer, intently watching Dinah and Mico, and Anson, observing that Mico was dancing most decorously, holding Dinah not so much tenderly as gingerly, as though he thought she might suddenly fall to pieces, said, "I'm beginning to see what you mean. It *is* that bad."

"Bad?" Midge's voice was still grim. "You don't know the half of it. When Mico makes up his mind that he wants something, really wants it—well, you know how the colored people talk about somebody's being 'taken,' don't you? That's Mico. He stops being human almost."

"And now he's taken with Dinah?" Anson asked.

"Now he's taken," Midge said. "He's been taken before, but never like this. I feel sorry for him."

"Because of Dinah?"

"Because of everything. Little Miss Mulberry and a kid named Mico Higgins who lives in the Channel on Frenchman Street. You figure it out."

Anson was not given time to figure out anything. Another man was trying to cut in on Dinah, and with a sinking sensation Anson saw that the newcomer was Sailor Greer. Refusing to surrender Dinah, Mico glared at him hotly. Anson felt Midge grow tense—"Oh my God!" she said. "There's that horrible goon!"—and though it flashed across his mind that Midge had come a long way if she was now able to see Sailor Greer as a horrible goon, he was thinking principally of Dinah. The world of Alwyn and Malvern streets would never recover if it became known that she had been fought over at the Oasis by Mico Higgins and Sailor Greer. "Like some common tart!" he could hear them saying. "She must have given them cause!" Sailor Greer had taken hold of Mico by the shoulder—just as he once took hold of me, Anson thought—and was attempting to spin him around. Caught in the struggle, Dinah looked pale and wide-eyed, and already a ring of faces was being formed.

"Oh, do something, Sonny," Midge said in a choked tone. "Take her home."

Anson always thought that if it had not been for Midge he might not have found the courage. He imagined that he would have waited until the fight broke out and then hurried Dinah away in the excitement. He had come to the Oasis expecting trouble, even looking for it, but he did not think that he would have met it squarely if it had not been for Midge.

"All right, Midge," he said. "Home is where she belongs anyway. But will I see you later on?"

"Come to my house. I'll be waiting on the porch."

It happened so quickly that Anson was never able to put all the parts together. There was the ring of faces, and Dinah staring at him as he shouldered his way toward her, and then, at the precise moment when Mico Higgins and Sailor Greer were beginning to square away, he stepped between them. "Sorry," he said in an unnaturally loud voice that did not sound like his own. "I've got the rest of this dance."

He did not have time to think what he was doing and he always believed that it was just as well. He put his arm around Dinah's waist and started to dance with her. Beyond the ring of faces he saw Midge looking at him. Her hair was full of highlights and her eyes were very still. He noticed that Mico Higgins was standing motionless, caught in some conflict he could not resolve, and that Sailor Greer had begun to shuffle toward them. He swung Dinah around so that he and Greer were facing each other. "We're not breaking," he said in the same loud unnatural voice. "This is our last dance."

How he got away with it, he never did know. It would be foolish to imagine that Sailor Greer had been intimidated by him, and it would be equally foolish to believe that Greer felt obliged to respect that Oasis tradition which ruled that nobody could cut in on a last dance. The best Anson could do was to put it down to Dinah's being practically a sister. A brother at the Oasis had the right to take a sister under his wing whenever the going got too rough, and there must have been something about him and Dinah, some emanation of the years of shared experience by which they were joined, that caused

Sailor Greer to believe that he was Dinah's brother. There could be no other explanation. Sailor Greer turned away, muttering some final obscenity, and then the reaction set in. Anson felt lightheaded. His knees were shaking and he could feel the erratic pounding of his heart. Dinah clung to him tenderly.

"Oh, Sonny! That awful man!"

"If you don't want to have anything to do with awful men, you ought to stay away from the places where they hang out! What are you doing out here? Who brought you?"

Dinah leaned her head against his chest. "Don't be mad, Sonny. Please don't be mad."

"Who brought you?"

"Timmy Wendover."

"Was it your idea or his?"

Dinah leaned back from her waist and looked up at him pleadingly. "Mine. But please don't be mad with me, Sonny. And you won't tell Mama, will you?"

"Why shouldn't I?"

"There's no reason, I reckon. But you won't, will you? If you tell Mama she'll tell Papa, and you know what will happen. Promise you won't tell."

Why it was that Dinah could always get the better of him Anson could not imagine. It would be impossible for him to tell on her, and she knew it. He had never told on her once in his life. He said, dancing her in the direction of the front door, "Don't you know any better than to come to a place like this? Why did you?"

"The other girls come, Joe Ann and Gaby and Margie Rhett. You come. Why shouldn't I?"

"Because you shouldn't! And don't argue. Don't tell me that you're too old to be treated like a child. The truth is that you aren't old enough to have good sense. If ever I hear of you coming here again——"

"I won't, Sonny. I promise. I'll do anything you say."

"Sure, I'll bet. You always have."

"But I will. Don't you trust me?"

"Not for a minute. Not when you start acting like a little flirt. And don't dance so close! You're supposed to be a nice girl."

"I am a nice girl."

"Act like one, then. I don't want to run the risk of getting my head knocked off because of you again."

Dinah leaned her head upon his chest for a moment and then

looked up at him. "You were wonderful, Sonny. I'll always remember how you rescued me from that awful man. Just think. If it hadn't been for you——"

"Oh, Dinah, shut up! Try to stop acting for a while." He stopped dancing and took her by the arm. "Come on. We're going home."

"Now?"

"Yes, now."

Dinah hung back. "I won't. I came with Timmy. What will he think?"

"Look, Dinah——"

"But he'll tell everybody. It will be all over school. Everybody will know that you dragged me home. I'll be disgraced."

"All right, then. Let's find Timmy. I'll get him to take you home."

"You mean you'd *make* him. You'd tell him he *had* to. You'd *bully* him?"

"Dinah, I'm tired of arguing. Are you coming with me or do you want me to get Timmy to take you home? Make up your mind!"

Dinah stared at him abjectly, wearing what Mrs. Blackford called her "sweet sorrow on the mountain" look. She said, "I didn't know you could be such a bully. But I suppose I might as well go with you. Either way I'll be disgraced, but at least I can keep you from shaming me in front of Timmy. I'll think of something to say to him. Wait till I get my purse."

"Hurry up. I've got a late date."

"Tonight?" Dinah's eyes widened and narrowed. "With who?"

It had been a slip of the tongue and immediately Anson regretted it. "Never mind who. It's none of your affair. Just hurry and get your purse."

Anson was not surprised that she did not say a word all the way home. He did not mind. Tired as he was after the day it had been, he was glad not to have to worry about making conversation. Several times he glanced toward her and he could tell that she was still nursing her grudge. When he stopped the car before the Blackford house on Malvern Street he kept the motor running.

"I'll wait here until you turn the lights on."

Dinah opened the door on her side of the car without answering.

"Are you so mad that you aren't going to say good night?"

Dinah slipped from the car, turning her back on him.

"There's nothing to be unpleasant about, you know," he said. "It's not very becoming."

He could tell how angry Dinah was by the way she held her head.

It seemed all out of proportion to what had happened, and he could not really believe that she thought she had been disgraced.

"Good night, Miss Sulky. I hope you feel better in the morning."

Dinah slammed the door. The noise hung in the air for a moment and echoed along the street.

"Have fun on your late date!" she said. "Have fun!"

CHAPTER TWENTY

It was past midnight when Anson drew up before Midge's house on Frenchman Street. There was no moon and not many stars. Between the splash of bluish light that fell from the lamps at either corner, the street lay dark and empty. Anson cut off the motor and opened the door cautiously. It seemed important not to make any noise. This was merely a late date he had with Midge, differing from other late dates only in that the night was a little farther gone than usual, but because of the darkness and the silence, the row of sleeping cottages in which not a gleam of light showed anywhere, it had begun to seem like a clandestine meeting. Midge, he saw, was waiting on the porch. Her white dress appeared from behind the tangle of moonflower vines that covered that part of the porch where the swing was, and as Anson walked up the steps he could hear a faint creaking of the chains from which the swing hung. Midge must have been sitting in it. They spoke in hushed voices.

"Have you been waiting long?"

"No, Bill just left."

"Did you tell him I was coming?"

"No, why?"

"I just wondered."

"Shall we sit in the swing?"

"Will it be all right? We won't wake everybody up, will we?"

"Not if we're quiet."

The chains of the swing creaked softly as they sat down. It was dark and intimate behind the vines. Midge steadied the swing by pressing her silver sandals against the floor of the porch.

"Those are nice shoes you have on," Anson said.

Midge held them up, pointing her toes. The swing rocked with the motion and the chains began to creak again.

"Do you like them?"

"Yes, very much."

"It's a new line the store is carrying. I bought them last week."

"You always look so nice, Midge."

"Thank you, Sonny. It's sweet of you to say so."

"Would you like a cigarette?"

"Yes, please. Did you get our little friend home all right?"

"Dinah? Yes, I got her home."

Midge's face came out of the shadows as he held a match to her cigarette. He lit his own and they were silent for a moment. Some nightbird called in the darkness and there was the closer chirping of a tree frog. It was the beginning of summer with all the beginning summer noises. A rooster crowed in one of the nearby back yards.

"You must have thought at the Oasis that I sounded mean about Dinah," Midge said. "I didn't intend to."

"I didn't think you sounded mean," Anson replied. "You just seemed to be worried about Mico."

"I'm not. Not really. He'll land on his feet."

"How long has it been going on?" Anson asked. "His feeling the way he does about Dinah, I mean."

Midge drew in on her cigarette and took her time to answer. "Ever since he first saw her, I think. It goes back to the time when he was delivering the *Saturday Evening Post*."

"But he's so much older than she."

"He's twenty-one and she's sixteen. What's five years?"

"A lot at that age."

"Not for Mico."

"He'll get over it."

Midge shook her head. "You don't know Mico. Do you remember what I said about his being what the colored people call taken? Well, it's true. What's the right word for it? Possessed?"

"He's actually that much in love with her?"

"Love?" Midge drew in on her cigarette again. "Who said anything about love? That little Miss Mulberry of yours is something he wants. He wants her the same way he wants to make a lot of money. Making a lot of money comes first, though. If he had to choose, he'd choose making a lot of money."

Earnest though Midge was, Anson could not take it seriously. Nothing could be more impossible. Taken, possessed, or whatever he was, Mico Higgins was barking up the wrong tree. He said, "Why do you keep on calling Dinah my little Miss Mulberry? I'm not responsible for her."

"I know you're not," Midge said. "It's just that you and Wyeth Blackford have always been best friends and I think of you as practically a member of the family. And I don't have anything against Dinah. I can't blame her if Mico decides to go off the deep end."

"She's a nice child," Anson said. "A brat, sometimes, but a nice child."

"You like her, don't you?"

"Sure, in a way."

"Does she always flirt with you like that?"

"Like what? When?"

"At the Oasis, when you were dancing." Midge looked at him steadily. "If I were Kit Robbins I'd be jealous."

"Kit?" Anson had to struggle to control his voice. "All that's over," he said. "Kit and I have broken up."

"Broken up?" Midge sat up straight. "When did that happen? I thought that you and Kit——"

"That's all over," he said doggedly. "It's been over a long time."

He did not think he sounded very convincing and he was afraid that Midge did not think so either. Another crow from the rooster pealed through the dark. The thin, clear call, rising higher and higher on the final note, made Anson wonder if it came from a bantam. It sounded like the crow of a bantam, but he could not be sure.

"Do you really mean it, Sonny?" Midge said. "I heard that you and Kit——"

"Oh, Midge, why do you believe everything you hear? That's the trouble with this town. It feeds on gossip the way a tadpole is supposed to feed on its own tail. That's one of the reasons why I'm going away."

"Going away? Are you going away?"

"Yes. I'm going to New York."

"For good?"

"If I can make it for good. I don't give a damn if I never see this town again."

Even as he said it, aware of the bitterness that had crept into his voice, Anson realized that it was the final step. Saying it aloud had given it a reality that it did not have before. Midge said, "It's not because of what happened, is it? That's not why you're going away?" and he thought for a moment that she must be referring to Kit. Even in the dark his confusion apparently showed because Midge said, "I mean about your father and Mr. Pettibone. Is that why you're going away?"

"Partly," he said. "When I think of some of the things that have been said about my father, simply because he wanted Mr. Pettibone to do right by Clifford——" And then, no longer caring whether he sounded bitter or not, he poured out the accumulation of grievances that had been storing up in him. He did not once mention Kit's name, but it was Kit who was foremost in his mind. He knew that if it were not for Kit Robbins he would not be going away.

"Shinola!" Midge said when he finished. "What do you care what they say? Everybody gets talked about at some time or other. It will die down before you know it. That's no reason for you to leave Old Pompey."

Anson realized that what she was saying was true. Everybody did get talked about, and even the worst kind of talk died down in time, and it was hardly a reason for leaving Pompey's Head.

"It's not only that, Midge," he said. "It's everything. I don't want to spend the rest of my life being a one-horse lawyer in a one-horse town. I want to amount to something. There's more opportunity in New York. I want to give myself a chance."

Words, words, he knew, pretending to a set of ambitions he did not have, and were it not for Kit Robbins he would not be thinking of leaving Pompey's Head. With every word, however, the more irrevocably he was committed. In a way he could not define, he had the feeling that he had already put Pompey's Head behind him. It was as though he were standing by the rail of a ship that was putting out to sea, watching the shore line recede.

"It doesn't sound like you," Midge said, "but I guess you really mean it."

"Yes, Midge, I do."

"When are you leaving?"

"As soon as I can."

Midge bent over and reached for a metal ash tray that was lying on the floor on her side of the swing. She snubbed out her cigarette and handed the ash tray to Anson.

"I'm going to miss you, Sonny," she said. "I never see you any more, except when we happen to run into each other on Bay Street, but I'll miss you. I hope you have all the luck in the world."

The shore line was receding farther and farther and it was like watching the flutter of a handkerchief waving farewell. He was setting out on a long, uncertain journey and Midge was wishing him all the luck in the world. He had often heard himself being wished all the luck in the world back in the days when he wanted to go to Burma and gather the seeds of wild plants.

"Thank you, Midge," he said. "I reckon I'll need it."

He smeared the end of his cigarette on the tray and told himself that it was time to go. He said, "But that's not why I wanted to see you, Midge, to tell you that I was going away. I wanted to thank you for what you did at the trial. Things looked pretty black before you came along. If it hadn't been for you, Mr. Pettibone would probably have got away with it. I'll never forget it, Midge. It was a fine, brave thing for you to do."

He meant it, every word of it, but Midge did not seem to believe him.

"It's my father you have to thank," she said, "not me. To tell the truth, if it hadn't been for my father——"

Anson would not let her finish. It was a fine, brave thing for her to do, and he did not want to have it tarnished. "Even so, it was you," he said. "Your father didn't whip you into it. You didn't have to. You did it of your own accord."

Midge was still for a moment. She said, "You're sweet, Sonny. You always have been," and then, noticing that he was still holding the ash tray, she took it from him. "Let me have that," she said. "It goes under the swing."

Anson watched the fall of her hair as she bent over and put the ash tray on the floor of the porch. The chains of the swing began to creak again, and from off in the distance there came the rattle of one of the owl streetcars. They were called that because they ran all night. Anson was again reminded of how late it was. He said, "I guess it's time for me to be shoving off, Midge. You ought to be getting to sleep." He rose and stood looking at her for a moment. The swing rocked gently as she lifted herself from it and held out her hand.

"Good night, Midge."

"Good night, Sonny."

"Thank you again for what you did. I'll always remember."

Her hand was in his and her face was turned slightly upward as she looked at him. He bent his head and kissed her gently. He could feel the soft parting of her lips before she turned them away. She stood still for a moment and then said, "I don't suppose I'll be seeing you before you go away, will I?"

"Sure, of course you will. I'll call you up. We'll go to a show or something."

He said good night again and added that he really ought to go, hoping that she would say he could stay a few minutes longer.

"Take care of yourself, Midge," he said. "I'll be seeing you."

"Good night, Sonny. It was nice of you to come out of your way to see me. I appreciate it."

"Appreciate it? It's I who should do the appreciating."

"Good luck, Sonny. Whatever you want, I hope you get."

He was going away again, standing by the rail of an outgoing ship and watching the diminishing shore. He was leaving Pompey's Head forever and Midge was telling him good-by. He lifted her face and kissed her again, and this time she did not move away. He put his arms around her and brought her close, feeling her legs hard against his. She curved in toward him, and then he was trying to do things he had never done to a girl before. The chains of the swing creaked loudly.

"No, no!" she whispered. "No, Sonny, no!"

"Oh, Midge."

"No, no, Sonny! Not here!"

"Where then? Where?"

"I don't know. There's no place. It's too late."

"Midge, Midge!"

"Don't, Sonny, don't! I beg you, beg you! Oh, Sonny!"

"Please, Midge, please!"

"No, Sonny, no! We'll wake everybody up! I want to do it and if I did it with anybody I'd do it with you—— Oh, heaven, heaven! No, Sonny! Oh God, no!"

Half an hour later, tiptoeing up the stairs to his bedroom, Anson was sorry it had happened. A trace of Midge's perfume still clung to his coat and he could hear her saying that if she did it with anybody she would do it with him. They had not, since Midge had finally and completely established that she was not that kind of a girl, and yet they did not have to go unsatisfied. There was something in Midge's management of the situation that he did not like to think about. He was willing to accept the fact that Midge must have kissed many men since that night in the old rice fields near Mulberry, but it troubled him to think what had just happened must have happened before. It simply must have. How else could Midge have known so well how to manage? It was his fault, he told himself, more his fault than hers, but she need not have let it happen. She wanted it to happen as much as he. He had built up all those fine thoughts about her, even to the point of being practically in love with her, and how could he square all those fine thoughts with what happened on the porch? Even though he hated to admit it, it was still true what they said about getting mixed up with a Channel girl.

PART FIVE

CHAPTER TWENTY-ONE

Driving to Mulberry along the road that led to Bugtown, Anson thought that there could not be a finer day. He had enjoyed a good night's sleep, he felt fresh from his shave and shower, old Watkins had served him a good breakfast, and he was filled with an elation that he had not known in some time. Were it not that he would soon be meeting Mrs. Garvin Wales, he felt that he would be able to forget every worry he had in the world.

He hoped his meeting with Mrs. Wales would come off well. Practically everything depended upon it. Despite the pretense of his being a free agent, John Duncan's saying that he was to handle everything as he thought best and Mr. Barlowe's advising him to ride with loose reins, he had been given a set of specific instructions. He was to arrange an interview with Garvin Wales, and the interview was to be managed through his wife. "You'll have two strikes against you before you start," John Duncan had said. "As our lawyer, just as our lawyer, Lucy won't let you get anywhere near Garvin. She'll probably insult you for invading what she calls their privacy. But if you could arrange to meet her socially, through some of those connections of yours——"

Were he able to see it dispassionately, Anson thought he might find it amusing. Those connections that John Duncan kept talking about, and that Dinah had unexpectedly provided, would at best enable him only to get his foot in the door. Nor was there any reason to believe that Mrs. Wales would hesitate to slam it. What both John Duncan and Mr. Barlowe had neglected to say, and what could not have very well been put into words, was that once he had arranged his meeting with Mrs. Wales he would then have to charm her into consenting to a private meeting with her husband. John Duncan and Mr. Barlowe might have wanted to phrase it differently, but that was what it came down to. Eventually you became used to the demands that were placed upon you as a lawyer, but this was the first time he had been called upon to imitate one of those turbaned fakirs whose photographs had fascinated him back in the days when he thought that the *National Geographic* was the most wonderful magazine in the world. It might be amusing were he not so directly involved. His trouble was that he didn't even have a flute. Even if he had, he doubted that Mrs. Wales would respond. The picture he had been given of her was that of a woman who did not charm easily, and who, when she wanted to, had more ways of being disagreeable than any hooded cobra had ever dreamed of.

That, however, was absurd. Once again he was placing himself under a needless handicap by accepting those outside points of view. Examined coldly, his business with Mrs. Wales was entirely legitimate. An examination of her husband's royalty statements had turned up certain discrepancies, and he had come down from New York to discuss the matter. That was the sum and substance. At some point or other Mrs. Wales would have to enter the discussion, since she held her husband's power of attorney, but how she could object to his seeing Wales privately was more than he could imagine. Unless, of course, he let himself be swayed by what he had heard from John Duncan and Julian Tokar. In that case he could imagine anything. The first thing he could imagine was falling flat on his face. Mr. Barlowe would pretend not to notice the bruises when he returned to the office, and neither would John Duncan when he went uptown to report his failure, and the chances were that nothing would ever be said. It would only be remembered that he blew it. The whole office would hear of it in time, and then a number of other offices, and though he was now a partner, his position was not invulnerable.

However, because of the kind of morning it was, Anson could envision disaster without believing in it. He did not think that Mrs. Wales would prove too difficult. Not because he imagined that he could win her over, but because no winning over would be necessary. He did not see how she could refuse to let him see her husband. He was not going to be influenced by anything that John Duncan or Julian Tokar had said, nor was he going to be intimidated. It was too fine a morning and he felt too good.

Driving through Bugtown and then on to Double Crossing, he turned off the highway and took the dirt road to Mulberry. In another ten minutes he was there. Except for the noises of his rented car, everything was very still, the hushed, sunlit stillness he always associated with Mulberry. A pair of bluejays flew from one of the oaks that lined the drive to the house, and he heard the raucous call of a pileated woodpecker. He could see the house as he went down the drive. It stood on the highest point of the property, facing the river, and when he came to the end of the drive he saw the well-remembered fall of the land, dropping away to the old rice fields, and then the curve of the water beyond. He stopped the car and looked around him. He had never imagined that Mulberry could be so beautiful.

Compared to some of the country residences erected during its era, Mulberry was relatively simple. It was of three stories, built in 1820 when an earlier dwelling, which in turn had supplanted the first crude structure which Percy Wyeth Blackford had raised on the property, burned to the ground. According to legend, this disaster took place when a keg of gunpowder exploded in the dining room. Nobody who knew the Blackfords ever questioned the legend. It did not seem strange that they should be keeping a keg of gunpowder in the dining room.

The new house was built along the lines of what had come to be known in Pompey's Head as a raised cottage. The first floor, well raised above the ground, was supported by a number of rectangular brick pillars. Painted white, as was the house itself, they provided a series of entrances to the warren of closets and storerooms which over the years had been built on the ground floor. Wyeth Blackford and Anson had had a club in one of them—the Sylvania Archers, they called it—and once, rummaging in another, they found an old trunk that contained the schoolbooks that Colonel Robert Blackford, Wyeth's grandfather, used when he was a boy. They also found some old metal buttons in the trunk, bearing the insignia of the Pompey's Head Light Infantry, and among a pile of old letters tied with a bit of fishing twine, the invitation sent in 1859 to Tom's grandmother, who was then Miss Cordelia Lake, requesting her presence at the Light Infantry Ball.

Like so many of the country residences influenced by the Greek Revival, Mulberry was square in shape. A divided stairway with a wrought-iron railing led to the front porch. The flat roof of the porch rested upon six wooden columns, square and slender, which, rising to the floor level of the third story, gave Mulberry the soaring lightness that was its principal charm. Anson could not think of a happier house in which to live. This was not the Mulberry he had known and which, as much as the house on Alwyn Street, had been a part of him, but the old affinity was still there.

He wondered where Dinah was. In the old days he would have sounded the horn of the car, but with this Mulberry it was different. One hesitated to take such liberties. He was starting toward the porch when, hearing voices, he stopped where he was. "So you're here," he heard Dinah say. "Why didn't you let us know?" She was coming around the corner of the house from the direction of the old herb garden, accompanied by two little girls. She wore a pair of tailored gray slacks and a white linen shirtwaist and a mannish tweed coat. Her dark hair shone in the sun and there was a crinkle of pleasure around her eyes. "This is Cecily," she said after she and Anson had greeted each other, bending over the larger of the two girls, a solemn child with eyes the color of hers, "and this"—now she turned to the other, a fair slip of a creature with a small turned-up nose and a halo of yellow curls—"and this is Julia. Wrenn, the baby, is taking her nap. She couldn't wait any longer for this old slowpoke, could she, girls?"

Anson took first Julia's hand, who looked up at him with a dubious expression, and then Cecily's, who responded with a curtsy, all the while watching him with her dark, intent eyes.

"I'm glad to see you both," Anson said. "In case your mother hasn't told you, my name is Sonny."

"In case their mother hasn't told them," Dinah said. "They know more about you than you think."

"Isn't there any school today?" Anson asked. "You're not playing hooky, are you?"

"Julia doesn't go to school yet and I have a cold," Cecily said. "It's not a bad cold, though."

"I'm glad of that."

"I caught it from Julia. She's five."

"And you?"

"I'm seven going on eight. I'm in second grade."

"I have a little girl too," Anson said. "She's five, just like Julia. Her name is Deborah, but we call her Debby."

"My friend Jane Brooks has a cat named Debby," Cecily said.

Julia, still clinging with one hand to Dinah's slacks, decided to enter the conversation. She said, "I don't like cats. They scratch."

"Yes," Anson said, "that they do. Your mother had a cat once that scratched more than any cat I ever knew. Its name was Spinnet."

"I never heard a name like that before for a cat," Cecily said, looking at Dinah. "Where did you get *that* name?"

"It was born in an old spinnet that your grandmother Blackford had down in the basement," Dinah said. "I thought Spinnet was a beautiful name."

"A beautiful name but a horrible cat," Anson said.

"I adored Spinnet."

"Yes, and so did you adore that evil-tempered billy goat you used to have. And do you know what his name was, Cecily and Julia? Lancelot! Your mother also had a pet frog named Euclid, and a field mouse named Euphrates——"

"Euphrates!" Dinah cried. "I'd forgotten all about him. I found him in his nest, girls, and Sonny made me a cage for him. And, Sonny, do you remember the time——"

"When Euphrates ran afoul of Spinnet? When you wanted to take a shotgun to teach him some manners, that adorable cat of yours?"

"You mean you wanted to *shoot* him?" Cecily said.

"That's enough!" Dinah protested, laughing. "I'll not have you undermine me with my own daughters. I just wanted to frighten Spinnet, Cecily, not hurt him."

"Hmm," Anson said.

Laughing again, Dinah said, "Stop it, I say! I was a dear, sweet child and you know it!" and then, gathering the two girls to her, one arm about each, "Oh, it's such fun to see you, Sonny! It's wonderful to have you here!" She looked at him and he looked back, and she said, addressing the children, "Let's show Sonny around the place, shall we? Then you two will have to run along to Vera. Sonny and I haven't seen each other for years and years and we want to talk."

They walked about the grounds, Dinah pointing out the various improvements she had made—the herb garden replanted; the little brick building that used to be Colonel Blackford's office repaired and painted white; the long line of camellia trees that bordered the path from the house to the office pruned and trimmed ("That's the Plain Jill," Dinah said. "That one there"); the small formal garden behind the house restored according to the original plan which Dinah found in a bundle of old papers ("I've given it to the historical society. I found the architect's drawing for Mulberry, too"); a new boathouse on the river, which they viewed from a distance—and then, with Julia and Cecily still in tow, they went through the house, entering by way of the central hall, where a curving stairway led to the upper floors and a number of darkened portraits hung on the wall, along with an oil painting of the Confederate sailing vessel *Southern Star*, a blockade runner which Captain Jeremiah Lake had commanded during the Civil War—

"Didn't that used to be upstairs?"

"Yes, in the hall outside your room."

"It's a nice painting."

"Yes, I like it too."

—And then into the library, where an early-nineteenth-century globe that Dinah had unearthed in one of the basement rooms stood on the crude wooden chest which Percy Wyeth Blackford had brought over with him when he sailed with Sir Samuel Alwyn aboard the *Swan*—

"Where did all the books come from? There didn't used to be so many."

"I accumulated most of them, I guess, but the sets I had to order. Mr. Carpenter, Gaby's father, helped me. He knows a bookseller in Philadelphia."

"How is Mr. Carpenter?"

"Fine. He looks just the same. With that snow-white hair of his, he never changes."

"Do you still read as much as you used to?"

"All the time."

"The poetry too?"

"Oh yes. Poetry's become a kind of habit."

—And after the library the dining room with its carved white woodwork and medallioned ceiling and, in one corner, hanging in a vertical line on hooks which Anson remembered as having always been there, four fire buckets, made of leather and painted red and gold—

"Where in the world did you find these, Dinah?"

"Down in the basement again."

"Why did they have them only in this room, I wonder?"

"That keg of gunpowder, perhaps? Could that have been it?"

"Maybe. But you have done it proper, haven't you?"

"Not too proper, though. You don't think I've done too much, do you?"

"Of course not. It's beautiful, Dinah. I'll like to remember that you're living here. You always loved it so much."

"And you? Didn't you love it too?"

"Sure, naturally. Let's see the rest."

—And finally, after they recrossed the hall and went into the double parlor which on ceremonial occasions could be turned into a ballroom, the woodwork white as in the dining room but more intricately carved, and over the mantel the old portrait of Percy Wyeth Blackford handsome in his blue uniform—

"My old pal! He ought to approve of you, Dinah."

"I approve of him. I love that portrait best of all."

"It has style. You have too, you know."

"Well, at last! Do you realize that that's the first nice thing you've said to me?"

—Finally, with Julia and Cecily having followed them dutifully from room to room, the tour was over. Dinah said that she would show him the upstairs part of the house later on, and asked if he cared to have some coffee. He said he would, and Dinah said fine, she'd like some too, and begged to be excused while she went into the kitchen for a moment. Little Julia tagged after her, glancing over her shoulder. Anson, left alone with Cecily, said, "Do you like living at Mulberry?"

"Not much," Cecily replied solemnly. "I'd rather live on Paradise Isle. That's where my friend Jane Brooks lives. She has a pony."

"Would you like a pony?"

Cecily shook her head. "I think I'd rather have a sailboat. That's why I'd like to live on Paradise Isle. Daddy says that we could have a sailboat if we lived on the water. The river isn't good for sailing." She looked up at him with her eyes dark like Dinah's, thin and spindly as Dinah was at that age, and then, as an afterthought, "Julia's getting a pony," she said. "She's going to call it Spot."

"That's more of a dog's name, isn't it?"

"Our dog's named Bugle," Cecily said. "He's a cocker spaniel. Julia thinks that Spot would be a good name for a pony."

Anson said, "She'll have fun with it, I know. Your mother always wanted a pony, but back in those days——" He cut himself short, realizing that what he was about to say was that back in those days the Blackfords were unable to afford a pony. It was one of the sorrows of Dinah's life not to have a pony, but that was something that this gentle, appealing child could not be expected to understand. Anson said, "Your mother didn't have a pony but she did have a mule. It wasn't hers, exactly, but she sort of made it hers. The mule's name was Jack. He was kept around to do the plowing. He kicked me once. I wasn't looking and he knocked me flat. Your mother said I deserved it. According to her, it was because I used to say such mean things about Jack."

Looking at him steadily, Cecily said, "Mummy says she loves you."

"Does she?" Anson said. "I'm glad."

"She doesn't love you as much as Daddy, though."

Anson could imagine what had happened. Dinah had been talking about him before he arrived, explaining who he was and how they had known each other forever, and Cecily, detecting some new tone in her voice, said, in the way children have, "Do you love him, Mummy?"

"Yes, darling, in a way. We're such old, old friends."

"But you don't love him more than Daddy, do you?"

"Of course not, darling. I don't love anybody more than I love your daddy. This man who is coming to see us—well, I've known him since I was a baby. Your grandmother Blackford was his godmother, and he and your uncle Wyeth were just like brothers. We sort of all grew up together. But of course I don't love him more than Daddy."

And Daddy, in this instance, was Mico Higgins. This child was Mico's daughter, as was Julia with her yellow curls and also the infant Wrenn, and it was Mico Higgins who was responsible for this splendid raising of Mulberry, rubbing a bottle called Peppo and magically summoning his private jinn. It was too much to think of all at once, and Anson was glad when Dinah returned.

"You run along now, Cecily," she said. "Sonny and I are going to have some coffee on the porch. Julia's in the kitchen with Vera. They're going to bake a cake. Don't you want to help?"

"Not much. Do I have to go?"

"Yes, this time you do. Sonny and I want to talk. We'll see you later, when I give Sonny his lunch."

"Is he going to spend the day?"

"No, not quite. He's going to stay for an early lunch and then the Camellia Club is coming, and then Sonny will be back for the party tonight. Do run along now, Cecily."

"Do I have to?"

"Oh, Cecily."

The hint of exasperation in Dinah's voice reminded Anson of Mrs. Blackford back in the days when Dinah was also always asking "Do I have to?" and when they were sitting on the steps of the porch, looking toward the river and waiting for the coffee to arrive, he said, "She's remarkably like you, Dinah. You probably don't remember yourself at that age, but I do. I must say, though, if I may——"

Dinah said, "No, you may not! I know it already. She's gentler than I was, and ever so much nicer. I don't have to be told."

"No, Dinah, not nicer. The same kind of niceness in a different way."

"Ah, she's a dear, that child."

"Yes, and Julia too," Anson said. "The one so dark and the other so fair." He leaned back against one of the pillars, thinking how often he had sat in this same spot in this same way, loafing in the sun. "Well," he said, looking at Dinah, "here we are."

"Yes," Dinah said, "here we are. Glad?"

"Do I have to say?"

"It might be polite."

"Yes, Dinah. I'm awfully glad."

A young Negro woman in a maid's uniform appeared with the coffee things on a silver tray. It was the tray Mrs. Blackford used to keep on the sideboard, Anson remembered, along with a large, over-ornate epergne. He took the tray and rested it on the floor of the porch. The maid withdrew into the house, and Dinah, pouring a cup of coffee, said, "Now tell me about yourself. How does it feel to be rich and famous?"

It was the first time Anson had ever been accused of being rich and famous and he did not know how to answer. No answer, however, was necessary. All Dinah meant was that she could see that he had achieved a certain measure of success, and that for his sake she was glad. She said, "Your wife is some senator's daughter, isn't she?"

"No, Dinah, not a daughter. Just a grandniece. She comes from Indiana and her name is Meg."

"I know that. Mama and your mother used to write each other. Do you have a picture? They say she's beautiful."

"They?"

"Do you remember the night you went to see *Oklahoma?*"

"Don't tell me you were there?"

Dinah shook her head. "The only time I've been to New York was when Wyeth was in Lawrenceville and Mama and I went up to see him. We're always saying that we will go but we never do. Things keep coming up. Do you still take three lumps?"

"Yes, I do. But what about *Oklahoma?*"

"You remember Margie Rhett, don't you?"

Since there had been a time when he and Margie Rhett had explored a few of the more innocent facts of life together, he was obliged to say, "Why, yes, of course. How is Margie these days?"

"You can judge for yourself tonight," Dinah said, passing him the cup of coffee. "I've asked her to the party. She married Marlin

Fowler, the one who used to tag after Kit Robbins when you were in love with her. Did you know that Kit had moved to Chicago?"

"Yes, I happened to run into her out there once. But I'm still waiting to hear about *Oklahoma.*"

Dinah poured a cup of coffee for herself. "Well, the Fowlers were in New York on a convention—he's now head of the local office of Fenner & Beane—and they went to *Oklahoma* the same night you did. Margie said she didn't see you until the show was over. She said that she tried to get to you to say hello, and that you got into a cab just as she was coming out of the theater. She said it was beginning to rain and that your wife had on a long yellow dress. It was you, wasn't it?"

"It could have been."

"Margie was sure that she recognized you. She said that your wife was pretty enough to be in pictures. Don't you at least have a snapshot?"

"No, I haven't."

Dinah said, "If that isn't just like you," and then, after taking a sip of coffee, "Your mother and Marion are still living in Denver, I suppose. How are they?"

"Fine. They seem to like it out West. Marion has a flock of kids and Mother appears happy enough. And what's the news of you?"

Dinah swept the landscape with her eyes. "This, Mulberry and the girls. Most people think it's boring, my living back in the country like this, but I love it. It's all I want and all I need." She took another sip of coffee, looking at him over the rim of the cup. "But what's this about you and Lucy Wales? I'm so curious I can hardly stand it. What did you come down to see her for?"

Anson told her the whole story, beginning with that rainy morning when he and Mr. Barlowe went uptown to Duncan & Company—the missing twenty thousand dollars, the various sums Phillip Greene had had transferred to his own account, the checks to Anna Jones. "But I'm sure that Wales can explain everything," he said. "I don't know why Phil Greene lent himself to this sort of thing, but the one thing I do know is that he wasn't a crook. What I know, though, isn't enough. I have to prove it. Unless I get a statement from Wales saying that he knew about those withdrawals, the goose is cooked. Ordinarily there would be no problem. A single letter could take care of it. But this way, with Mrs. Wales acting up as she has——"

"I'm not surprised," Dinah said. "I've always suspected that there was a streak of meanness in that woman."

"Why do you say that?"

Dinah reached into the pocket of her coat and took out a package of cigarettes. "No reason, really. It's just a feeling I have." She shook out a cigarette and he struck a match for her. "You hear a lot of stories, though, things that the servants say——"

"What things? Whose servants?"

"Oh, you know how it is," Dinah said. "Have you forgotten the way the colored people talk? We hardly ever know anything about them, but they know everything about us. They carry tales to one another and sooner or later everybody's business gets around."

"But what exactly is it that you have heard?"

Dinah exhaled a plume of smoke and stared at the tip of her cigarette. "Tales, just tales—quarrels, scenes, fits of temper, her threatening to have him committed."

"Committed!"

"That's what Nan Schulkens says."

"But why!"

Dinah lifted her eyes. "I didn't pay much attention to the details. I think it was something about his not being competent to manage anything any longer—something like that. Why don't you talk to Nan? I've asked her to the party tonight. Since she lives on Mungo, right next to Tamburlaine——"

Anson said, "I can't go around talking to everybody, Dinah. I was afraid even to talk with Ian. Suppose it gets back to Mrs. Wales that I've been trying to check up on her? Besides, if it's only gossip——"

"That's what it is, nothing but gossip." An ironic smile played about the corners of Dinah's mouth. "Don't forget where you are, honey." She took another pull on her cigarette, and then, serious again, said, "The truth is that nobody knows much about the Waleses. Ian wasn't exaggerating when he said that they hardly get off Tamburlaine. Not that there is anything peculiar about that, or would be, if that were all. The island people never mix much with anyone else, as you know."

"From what I gather, though, the Waleses don't mix much with the island people either."

"That's right," Dinah said. "That's what I meant. If they ran with the island crowd it would be different. But they don't. Every once in a while Lucy will appear, two or three times during the season maybe, but nobody ever lays eyes on him."

"Not even you?"

"Why do you say not even me?" Dinah asked. "Lucy comes to

Mulberry more than I go to Tamburlaine. I've been there exactly twice, once when a sister of Jerry Barbour's was visiting Nan, and once when she had the Camellia Club to tea. That was two years ago."

"And you didn't see Wales?"

"That's what I'm trying to get at," Dinah continued. "Nobody ever sees him. He might as well not exist. At first, when they moved into that modern house they've built on Tamburlaine—I don't like it, but then I wouldn't; I hate modern houses—at first, as I was saying, it was generally assumed that he wanted to be left alone. We all knew that he was an author and we thought that that was it. But now, after seven or eight years——"

She hesitated a moment, looking toward the river, and when Anson asked, "Now what?" she shrugged her shoulders. "Oh, I don't know, Sonny," she said. "There's something peculiar about the whole setup. I've often wondered just what goes on on that island. But let me ask you something. This Anna Jones you mentioned—couldn't she explain those checks for you? Have you tried to find her?"

"No luck. We put a tracing agency on her trail, but——"

"A tracing agency?"

"An agency whose business it is to track down people who have disappeared, generally those who jump town without paying their bills."

"And they haven't been able to locate her?"

"Not yet. When last I heard they had come to the end of the line in St. Louis and were trying to get a lead on her there. Everything else was a blank. I'm expecting to hear any moment in regard to what was learned in St. Louis, if anything, but I've just about given up hope. Everything depends on Garvin Wales."

Dinah put down her cup. "What can I do to help, Sonny? I'll do anything I can."

"That I know, Dinah. And thank you. But there's nothing, really, except to introduce me to Mrs. Wales. You might tell her what an honest, trustworthy soul I am, and how I have cherished you from infancy."

"Lie in my teeth, in other words."

"That's life, Dinah. It makes strange demands."

Dinah reached for the coffeepot. "Do you want another cup, or will it spoil your appetite? I can't eat with you because of Lucy's coming to lunch, but I'm going to give you fried oysters."

"Not those little ones! I haven't had any since I left Old Pompey."

Dinah, looking at him, said, "Have you missed it, Sonny?"

"What? Old Pompey? All this? You? What do you think?"

"I don't know what to think."

"I'll tell you, then. Think this. Think that there have been times when I've missed it so much that I've wondered why I ever went away."

CHAPTER TWENTY-TWO

Since things had to be done to get the house ready for Mrs. Wales's coming to lunch and the meeting of the Camellia Club, Dinah had Anson's meal served on a bridge table on the porch. She sat in a wicker chair next to him, giving an occasional instruction to a Negro butler in a white jacket who came and went. Anson had a cup of soup, the fried oysters that Dinah had mentioned, a green salad, and a plate of strawberries for dessert. "My, already!" he said when the strawberries arrived. "Are they local?"

Dinah reached for one of the berries and bit into it with her small white teeth. She said, "They're trucked in from Florida. Ours aren't ripe yet. You'll have some more coffee, won't you? You used to be able to drink it until it ran out of your ears."

Anson regarded her with pleasure. It was such little things as her remembering how much coffee he used to drink that made being with her so complete a delight. They had met as they should have met, as the good friends they were, and beyond that, going farther than friendship, there was their old, affectionate intimacy, waiting to be picked up again. "Here, have another," he said, offering her a berry, and then, as she bit into it, her teeth cutting off the stem close to his fingers, "Ah, Dinah. You don't know how nice this is. And what an elegant lunch! You're too good to me."

"Company manners," Dinah said. "Don't flatter yourself."

She poured him a cup of coffee and helped herself to another berry. Nibbling at it, she lapsed into silence, staring toward the river. Anson was reminded of those dreamy spells of hers, the way she used to go drifting off into space, but again, as when he had first seen her in the lobby of the Marlborough, he was struck by the hint of sadness in her eyes. The years may have been generous, but they had not been altogether kind. She had Mulberry and her children, and as an added reward this beauty of hers, so much a part of her and so exquisitely her own, and yet in that rich harvest there had been a garnering of hurt. He was sure of it now.

"Why so quiet all of a sudden?" he said.

"Thinking."

"About what?"

"Things."

She finished the berry and stirred in her chair. She said, "Forgive me, Sonny. What were we talking about?"

"Nothing, but I was going to ask you about Gaby Carpenter. If she is coming to the party tonight, I ought to know about her. Did I hear you say that she'd been divorced?"

Dinah shook off her own thoughts. "It was after Gaby moved to San Francisco. She finally got back to New Orleans, as I don't know if you know——"

"Yes, Mother wrote me about it," Anson said. "As long as your mother was alive and they corresponded with each other, I used to get stray bits of news."

Dinah said, "You must know, then, that Gaby married this painter in New Orleans. She was living in the French Quarter at the time, trying to be a painter herself. The man she married wasn't really a painter, he was a commercial artist, but Gaby always called him a painter. You know how she is."

"I know how she used to be."

"Well, she's just the same," Dinah said. "Everything with her is always so dramatic. According to her, this man she married was one of the greatest painters in the world. The reason he had to be a commercial artist was because the world wasn't ready to appreciate his genius. He thought so too."

"Oh, you knew him?"

"I'd hardly call it that," Dinah said. "Gaby brought him home after the wedding. It wasn't a real wedding. They were married by a justice of the peace. Gaby said that she thought a real wedding would be dull. You know how *dull* everything is for her."

"Yes, that I do."

"They just stayed here a week," Dinah continued. "I'm afraid her husband didn't make himself very popular. He told Mr. Carpenter that Old Pompey was a cultural and social backwash. You can imagine how big that went over."

"A frank chap, anyway. What was his name?"

"Joe Adams. Ever hear of him?"

"No, but that wouldn't mean anything. Did you ever see any of his work?"

Dinah lifted her eyes. "Did I? While they were here on that visit Gaby arranged what she called a 'show.' They drove from New Orleans and brought some of his pictures with them. Gaby gave a party and had the pictures all over the downstairs of her house. It was awful. Everybody wanted to be nice because of Gaby—you can't help liking Gaby no matter what she does—but those *pictures!* Really! Such blobs and blotches you never saw! And he had one portrait of Gaby that made her look like an ostrich, the neck was that long! There's some modern painting I've learned to like—Jerry Barbour, Nan's husband, goes in for it—but those things of Joe Adams! You should have heard Mr. Carpenter on the subject. He was still burned up over Old Pompey's being a social and cultural backwash."

Anson laughed. "It must have been jolly all around. But just like Gaby, I must say. And then she and this Joe Adams person moved to San Francisco and were divorced?"

"Five years ago," Dinah said. "Gaby's been living here ever since."

"With her family?"

"Don't be silly. Think how *dull* that would be. No, Gaby's back in that studio of hers on Clinton Street. She lives there all alone. She's opened a gift shop, and she's made a collection of the street cries of the colored peddlers who go selling from door to door." Dinah paused for an instant, again looking toward the river, where the haze of noon was beginning to form, making a golden glow, and then said, "But what she's most interested in now is writing a novel. And do you know about what? That Indian girl, Mary—you know the one. That Indian ancestor of hers."

"Gaby?" Anson said. "I would have thought she was too emancipated for ancestors. I would imagine they'd be too dull."

Dinah shook her head. "That's the old Gaby, not this one. She's as proud of that Indian girl as can be—she says it's from her that she got her hair and eyes. She made a copy of that portrait in the museum. It hangs over the mantel in her studio."

Anson finished the last of the strawberries and reached for his coffee. He felt mildly depressed by what he had heard. He took a few swallows of coffee and lit a cigarette. "Tell me about Joe Ann," he said. "What's happened to her? Is she coming to the party tonight?"

"Joe Ann?" The way Dinah stumbled over the name was enough to tell Anson that he needn't expect to see her. "You haven't heard?"

"Is it that bad? Is she divorced too?"

"Worse."

"What do you mean, worse? Aren't she and Jay Lockhart——"

"Jay killed himself."

Of all the people in Anson's crowd, Joe Ann Williams was always the happiest. In many ways, he liked her best of all. If there was one person with whom he would not have associated tragedy, it was Joe Ann. He said, "Killed himself!"

Dinah's face was suddenly miserable. "It was too awful, Sonny. Everything about it was awful."

"But why, Dinah? Why did he do it?"

"The fool thought that Joe Ann was having an affair with the butcher at the A & P," Dinah said harshly. "Either that or he was made to think so by that mother of his! Mrs. Lockhart didn't want Jay to marry Joe Ann, she didn't want him to marry anybody, and what with Jay's being unable to give Joe Ann a child and the way he used to drink—oh, who can say what happened, Sonny?"

"I can't believe it," Anson said. "But how——"

"How did it get started about Joe Ann and the butcher? Is that what you mean?" Dinah still spoke in the same harsh tone. "It was talk, Sonny, nothing but talk. He was a nice man, that butcher. He came from somewhere around Beaufort and used to work for the A & P in Charleston. They moved him here to be manager of the meat department. That's what they called him, but he was really the butcher. I used to trade with him when I was working in the bank and keeping house for Papa on Upton Street."

"But you still haven't told me——"

"Be patient and I will," Dinah said. "He liked jazz music, just the way Joe Ann did, and he played the accordion in one of those Saturday-night bands. They used to hire it for some of the Yacht Club dances and occasionally Joe Ann would see him there. They would talk about the new records when Joe Ann went shopping—everybody knew that; it was a joke about Joe Ann's discussing the new records with a butcher at the A & P—and maybe two or three times they ran into each other in the music department that old Mr. Gregory put in his bookstore. That was all there was to it. I know."

"Know?"

Dinah's eyes struck fire and she said, "Yes, know! Joe Ann used to laugh about it with me. You remember how Joe Ann used to be, always laughing about everything. She could see the humor in her talking about Dixieland jazz with a butcher over a cut of beef."

"But I still don't understand about Jay," Anson said. "How could he have imagined that Joe Ann, she of all people——"

"His name was Jay Lockhart!" Dinah said. "You know that family as well as I do!"

Dinah lit a cigarette and in the pause Anson thought about Jay Lockhart. Though he and Jay belonged to the same crowd, they were never close friends. Jay was in the same class with Ian Garrick at the University of Virginia, somewhat younger than most of his classmates, and after he graduated with honors from the law school and passed his bar examinations, winning one of those rare things, a personal commendation from the examining magistrates, it was agreed on all sides that Jay had brains. And it was his brains that caused his drinking to be so regretted by the members of the older generation—his brains and his mother. For Jay, left fatherless in infancy, was an only child.

He came of a legal family. Both his grandfathers had been judges of the state Supreme Court, and his father, who was also a judge, had served four terms in Congress. It was not long after Jay returned from Charlottesville and went to work for Mr. Arthur Kennon that he began to assume, because of his heritage, his brains, and his drinking, the shadowy outlines of a tragic figure.

Anson thought that it was this that began to make him attractive to Joe Ann. Everyone knew that Jay had been in love with her for years, but up till then it was Wyeth Blackford who always had the inside track. Anson first detected the shift in her affections one Saturday night about a year before the trouble with Mr. Pettibone. Wyeth Blackford had gone deer hunting for the third week end in a row. Kit Robbins was also away that week end, visiting her grandparents, and Anson and Joe Ann had gone to the movies. After the show, when he and Joe Ann were having scrambled eggs and coffee in Joe's Diner halfway between Pompey's Head and Cassava Beach, Joe Ann said, "I'm just about tired of putting up with Wyeth. He doesn't care about me. If he did, he wouldn't always leave me high and dry. Well, next Saturday night he can whistle. I'm going to the Yacht Club dance with Jay. I wish I could do something about his drinking. It's a shame, seeing him ruin himself that way."

At that time Jay's drinking—his heavy drinking—was a relatively new development. His indulgence at the University of Virginia could have been put down as part of the general college program, and before that he had never touched a drop. Ian Garrick, who was naturally full of tales about Jay, said that it was the hard-drinking fraternity he had joined that started all the trouble, but Anson's father disagreed. It was his opinion that Jay's drinking was due more to his mother than to his fraternity. It was one of those things that could never be repeated outside the bosom of the family, and only gingerly touched upon within it, but Anson's father said that Jay's mother had tried to keep him tied to her too closely.

It was easy to understand, he said, especially since Mrs. Lockhart was now an invalid, and he wanted to make it very clear that he was not implying any criticism. The fact was, though, that growing up in that big house all alone with his mother and that maiden aunt of his, Miss Emmy, had probably not been too good for Jay—Jay's drinking at the university was his way of announcing his emancipation; admittedly a wrong way, nobody could deny that, and now that Jay had graduated and was in Mr. Kennon's office it could not be called emancipation any longer; now, unfortunately, it was something else.

Marion, who was sitting with the family in the library waiting for Dr. Gaffney to call, said, "If I had to sit up every night and read to Mrs. Lockhart out of The Virginians and David Copperfield and God knows what else all, I'd take to drink too."

It was characteristic of Pompey's Head that they knew even the titles of the books that Jay read to his mother—trust his aunt, Miss Emmy, to see to that. Miss Emmy was Mrs. Lockhart's older sister, a white-haired, birdlike woman whose life was dedicated to God and gossip. What made her interesting was that she gossiped about God. It was Miss Emmy's notion that she and God were on speaking terms and she was always talking, in her chatty, innocent way, about their last conversation. "Just as though she rang Him up on the telephone with Minnie Simms putting through the call," Mrs. Blackford once said.

What Miss Emmy did not tell God, which could not have been much, she told her cousin, Miss Nedda Frothinghame, who lived in the Marlborough Hotel. From that pulsing nerve center it spread all over town, as eventually it spread that Jay had at last told his mother that he intended to ask Joe Ann Williams to marry him. According to Miss Emmy, and then Miss Nedda, this piece of information was so startling that Mrs. Lockhart had one of her attacks. Mrs. Lockhart's pet name for Jay was Mr. Micawber. When finally she felt well enough to sit up in bed again, she told him, again according to Miss Emmy and Miss Nedda, that she could not believe that Mr. Micawber intended to desert her. She knew that Joe Ann Williams was a lovely girl, even though she realized that there were people who said she was a giddy little thing who spent all her time dancing and listening to that noisy jazz music, and Mr. Micawber knew that she wanted him to be happy. It had come as a shock, since he'd been so secretive about it, but she was all right now and she didn't want him to worry about her any longer. All she wanted was for him to be happy. "It was almost her death," Miss Emmy told Miss Nedda. "It came near to being the poor thing's death. But her time is not yet. He told me."

And now, as though her thoughts had been running alongside Anson's, Dinah said, "Nobody knows what Joe Ann had to put up with, living with those two women! Mrs. Lockhart heard about Joe Ann's being friendly with the butcher, of course, and that she couldn't stand. If it had been anyone else it would have been bad enough, John Vincent or Clay Wendover or any of the men in the Yacht Club crowd that Jay and Joe Ann were going with, but a butcher, a common, ordinary butcher who cut meat—that was humiliating her darling Jay in public; she wanted it clearly understood that Joe Ann was never to set foot inside the A & P again; she made Jay lay down the law."

"Oh my God!"

"Joe Ann stopped trading there," Dinah went on. "Anything for peace, she said. But it was that, and the way Miss Emmy gossiped the Lockharts' business, that started all the talk. Joe Ann had nothing to do with it. And one day when she was in Gregory's bookstore the butcher came in. It was during the lunch hour. Joe Ann couldn't just run away from him—why should she, anyway?—and while they were talking Miss Nedda arrived. She'd come to return some books to the lending library Mr. Gregory used to run."

"And Miss Nedda told Miss Emmy and Miss Emmy told Mrs. Lockhart and Mrs. Lockhart told Jay, and by the time the telling was over it was no longer a chance meeting but an assignation. Was that it?"

Dinah said, "How right you are! And do you know what Jay did? He came home drunk the next night and hacked Joe Ann's record player to pieces. He broke every record she owned. Joe Ann was so terrified that she locked herself in her room."

"Poor Joe Ann."

"That's when she left him," Dinah continued. "It wasn't the first time, but after that she'd had enough. Even the patience of a saint comes to an end. She went back home to Dr. and Mrs. Williams and went to see Mr. Garrick about getting a divorce."

"But why did Jay——"

"He thought she wanted to divorce him in order to marry the butcher!" Dinah explained. "One Saturday night he made a speech at the Yacht Club, wild and crazy as could be, saying things about Joe Ann that you wouldn't say about one of those girls down on Liberty Street. Then he went out on the pier and shot himself. Let Joe Ann marry her butcher after that!"

Anson wanted to say, "God, what an awful town! The things it does to people!" but instead, stunned by what he had heard, he asked, "Where's Joe Ann now? Will I get a chance to see her?"

"Not unless you go up to the mountains," Dinah said in a lighter tone. "She lives up near Asheville, running a nursery and a birth-control clinic for the mountain women. Dr. Williams got her interested in it as something to do during the summers, and now she does it full time. I called her up last night to tell her that you were here and to ask her to drive down for the party. She said she couldn't, but to give you her love."

"And you give her mine. Is she all right?"

"Yes, thanks to the kind of person she is," Dinah said. "She's full of what she's doing, and she loves those kids. There's a nice widowed doctor up there who is interested in her, too. He helps with her clinic. She brought him home for Christmas, and from the looks of things I'd say that they were going to get married. I dearly hope so. It's wrong for Joe Ann not to have any children of her own."

She put out her cigarette and glanced at her wrist watch.

"It's nearly one," she said. "I have to start getting dressed."

Anson sat thinking of Jay Lockhart and Joe Ann. Dinah leaned over and touched his hand. She said, "Don't be sad, Sonny. It's going to be all right with Joe Ann. Don't let it spoil the rest of our day. You'll be going back to New York before you know it and then——"

He shifted his gaze and looked at her. "Then what?"

"Then I'll start missing you again," she said. "Why don't you take Cecily on a walk while I get dressed? She'd love to show you the boathouse, I know. Like her mother before her mother had better sense, she's developed a crush on you."

"Yes, my fatal charm."

"Only for the very young," Dinah said, "and not so fatal at that. Let's go, shall we? I really must get dressed."

CHAPTER TWENTY-THREE

Anson and Cecily were walking back from the boathouse. They crossed the old rice fields by means of a wooden boardwalk laid across an earthen dike that used to be part of an irrigation ditch. In the midst of noticing that a few clumps of rice still managed to survive amid the rank tangle of grasses and weeds, Anson saw a pair of railbirds break cover. Feeling the pull of a set of reflexes that would have brought a shotgun to his shoulder, he said, "That's a fine speedboat your father has. Do you like it?"

"Not much," Cecily replied in her grave fashion. "I like the rowboat better."

"Your mother used to like rowboats too," Anson said. "Sometimes, though, she'd be very naughty. She'd drift down the river in one of them and forget to come back and everybody would be worried to death. But you're not to do anything like that, understand? I don't want to make it sound attractive."

"Do you have a mother?" Cecily asked.

"Yes, Cecily, I have. She lives in a place called Denver."

"Is that where you live?"

"No, I live in New York."

"Does your father live there too?"

"No, my father is dead."

"Was he old?"

"Not so old."

"Was he sick?"

"Yes, he was. He had a bad cough. He wouldn't do anything about it, though, and when finally he did it was too late."

"Did they bury him?"

"Yes, up in the mountains. That's where he went to try to get well."

Cecily looked up at him, apparently meditating upon what she had just heard. "We buried Julia's redbird," she said.

"Did you?"

"It fell out of its nest. We put it in a shoe box and tried to feed it, but it died. We buried it in the garden."

"Did you?"

Anson was thinking of his father. If he had not left Pompey's Head before his father died, he would probably never have been able to get away. He would have wanted to stay and look after his mother. The house on Alwyn Street would have been too big for them after Marion and Dr. Gaffney moved away, but they could have found something else. He would have had to keep on working at Garrick & Leigh whether he liked it or not. His life would have been different and he would now be a different person.

"It's a secret where Julia's redbird is buried," Cecily said.

"Is it?"

"We promised not to tell."

"You mustn't then."

It still troubled Anson to think that after he left Pompey's Head he never saw his father again. The funeral was in the mountains. His father always liked the mountains and had asked to be buried there. Because of something he was doing for Mr. Barlowe, Anson was able to leave New York for only three days. The funeral was on a Saturday and he was back in the office on Monday.

"Do you have any secrets?" Cecily asked.

Anson brought himself back to where he was. "Secrets? You mean like where Julia's redbird is buried? Let me see. I know a place where we used to find arrowheads."

"Is it near here?"

"Yes, it's that field near the river not far from the bend. Would you like me to show it to you?"

"When? Now?"

"Well, I don't know. We may not have time. Let's ask your mother."

A shiny black car driven by a Negro chauffeur swept down the drive as they approached the house. Since no one else was expected for lunch, it had to belong to Mrs. Wales. Anson was familiar enough with these country arrangements to understand that the chauffeur, having deposited Mrs. Wales, was now on his way to Pompey's Head to do a few errands before returning for her after the meeting of the

Camellia Club. Cecily watched the car as it rolled down the drive.

"Company," she said.

"Yes, a lady is coming for lunch."

"Who?"

"Her name is Mrs. Wales."

"Oh yes, I remember. Mummy told me. She's the one who lives on Tamburlaine."

Dinah was standing on the porch, greeting a woman in a light blue dress. She saw Anson and Cecily coming across the lawn and waved to them. Anson thought that his timing could not have been better. Nothing could be more natural than his walking across the lawn with Cecily, and though he had given no thought to an entrance, he could not have perfected a better one.

"Hello, you two," Dinah said as they walked up the steps of the porch. "Where have you been?" She inclined her head toward Cecily, saying, "You remember my daughter Cecily, don't you, Lucy?" and then, as Cecily curtsied solemnly and Mrs. Wales said, "My, Cecily, how enchanting you look today," she turned to Anson. "And this is one of my oldest, dearest friends. Mrs. Wales, Mr. Page. His first name is Anson, Lucy, but we call him Sonny. You must have heard me speak of him."

Mrs. Wales had not, as her expression clearly showed, but she smiled and extended a hand. The brief formalities over, Dinah said, "Sonny used to live here but he now lives in New York. He's a lawyer, of all things. And the funniest thing——" She paused and gave a little laugh. "Sonny had to come down on business and I just found out last night that his business is with you."

"With me?" Mrs. Wales said in a cool, level voice that yet managed to sound a note of incredulity, and as she fastened her eyes on Anson, eyes of a rather chilly blue, he noticed, he wished that he had some of Dinah's grace—how well she had managed and how comfortably she had brought it off. He said, "One might as well confess one's darkest sins, Mrs. Wales. I'm John Duncan's lawyer. He asked me to come down and see you."

Mrs. Wales's eyes rested lightly on him for a moment. "But what an amusing coincidence," she said. "That you and Dinah should be such old friends, I mean. Are you visiting here at Mulberry?"

"If I had my way he would be," Dinah let fall. "I've even offered him his old room. Such a stubborn man he is, though, that he insists on staying in town at the Marlborough."

"Rather than here?" Mrs. Wales said, again striking her note of incredulity. "He must be stubborn indeed."

Anson had now had time to observe her appearance. What precisely he had expected he could not say, but he found himself mildly disappointed. Having had her earlier attractiveness so repeatedly emphasized, he had built up a picture of a woman who would still show evidences of an almost irresistible desirability. It must be assumed that once she had been desirable in more than an ordinary way—the large blue eyes set wide apart; the excellent profile; the slim figure— and it could not be overlooked that for some men of the older generation represented by John Duncan and Julian Tokar she would probably be desirable still. She was not yet fifty-five, and there remained more than a few traces of the lively sensuality which Anson had been given to understand was one of the chief sources of her appeal. She had not made a career of the arduous business of being young, but she had not let herself go, either.

Dinah rested a hand on Cecily's shoulder. She said, "Come now, it's time for your nap. Besides, I want to take your temperature." Cecily said, "Oh, Mummy, do I have to? Sonny's promised to show me where to find some arrowheads," and as Dinah replied, "Yes, dear. You're supposed to have a cold, remember," she glanced at Anson. "You and your arrowheads," she said. "You're beginning all over again with a new generation, I see," and then, after a few parting asides to Mrs. Wales, she led Cecily into the house.

"Such a charming girl, that Dinah," Mrs. Wales said to Anson. "Did you two grow up together?"

"Yes, in a way."

"I gathered as much from the arrowheads. Are they to be found here at Mulberry?"

Anson could not believe that she was interested in arrowheads. Her voice reminded him of his own when he was making conversation with Cecily.

"There's a field near the river that they say was an Indian camp," he said. "Sometimes we used to find them elsewhere too."

"How very interesting," Mrs. Wales replied. "But then everything is interesting about this old place, isn't it?" She turned on her heel with a swinging motion and faced toward the river. "I never come here without thinking that what is happening out there"—she indicated the "out there" with a light wave of the hand, a gesture so schooled that Anson thought she must be remembering it from her role in *Caesar's Wife*—"is little more than an unpleasant dream. But

337

then I would, of course. This is my part of the world. My roots are here."

A speech, Anson thought. He understood, however, that it was intended to have more than a dramatic effect. It would not have surprised him had Mrs. Wales gone on to say that she came from a family as well placed as the Blackfords. She stood looking toward the river for a few moments longer and then, "Why don't we take advantage of these few moments that Dinah has arranged for us," she said. "Wasn't it thoughtful of her?"

She spoke lightly, with no hint of displeasure. Anson gathered that she wished merely to have him understand that she had not been taken in. Seating herself in one of the wicker chairs that stood on the porch, she said, "So John Duncan sent you down to see me, did he? Did he tell you how cross I am?"

"I gathered that you were not entirely pleased," Anson said.

"Good!" Mrs. Wales jutted her small chin in what he took to be an imitation of menace. "You doubtless have it in mind to cajole me, and it is just as well for you to know that I have no intention of being cajoled. John Duncan let you know how disagreeable I've made myself, I suppose."

"No, Mrs. Wales. Nothing was said to indicate——"

"Oh, come now! Let's not play games with each other, Mr. Page. I have made myself disagreeable and I rather imagine that I shall have to continue to be disagreeable. That's your misfortune, I'm afraid. And tell me——" Another quick jut of the chin and she was looking straight at him. "Did you not have time to write, or did you imagine that it would be more to your advantage simply to drop from the sky?"

Now that the time had come, Anson found that he could not lie. He said, "I wanted every possible advantage, I admit. Considering the delicate nature of the situation——"

"Delicate?" Mrs. Wales interrupted. "Is embezzlement delicate?"

There was no mistaking her intent. Gracious she was willing to be, even friendly, but let him not forget that it was she who held the whip hand. Proceeding more cautiously, he said, "Yes, Mrs. Wales. To us it is extremely delicate. That is why Mr. Duncan felt that I ought to come down to see you."

"But why didn't you write?"

Anson hoped that bluntness might pass for sincerity. He said, "Mr. Duncan was afraid that you might not see me."

"So at last we have it!" Mrs. Wales said. "Mr. Duncan was afraid, was he? Would it shock you to know that it pleases me to hear that?" She paused briefly, as though awaiting an answer to this unanswerable remark, and then, "John Duncan has been atrocious in his neglect of us," she said. "Did he say why he was afraid that I might not want to see you?"

"Not in so many words, Mrs. Wales. I simply gathered——"

"Nonsense, Mr. Page!" Her voice, though impatient, was still not angry. "Surely John Duncan took you into his fullest confidence. If you are afraid to speak truthfully, I'm not. John Duncan was correct. I would have refused to see you. I meant what I said when I wrote that I intended to turn everything over to my own attorneys."

"I hope to convince you that that won't be necessary, Mrs. Wales."

"Do you? How?"

Knowing that he was letting himself be drawn into deep water, Anson said, "We've uncovered a few papers that might throw some light on the subject. If I had a chance to discuss them——"

What he intended to say was "to discuss them with your husband," but Mrs. Wales, with a show of interest, said, "Papers? Really? Very well, I don't want to be any more disagreeable than I have to be. Could you come to my island in the morning? You know Tamburlaine, I suppose."

"Yes, I used to fish there."

"You don't say. That's another amusing coincidence, isn't it? Shall we say eleven?"

"That would be fine."

"Good," Mrs. Wales said, closing the subject with a nod. "Now tell me more about yourself. Dinah said that you used to live here. She didn't mean Mulberry, did she?"

"No, not quite. I used to live in Pompey's Head."

"And now you're in New York?"

"Yes, I am."

"Will you be here long?"

"Only a day or two."

"Ah yes, I forget," Mrs. Wales said. "It is I who am responsible for your being here, am I not? It's too bad that we couldn't have met under pleasanter circumstances. I have no love for John Duncan. He treats my husband as though he did not exist. Has the man no gratitude?"

But John Duncan would have said that it was she who had no gratitude. He would have accused her of being responsible for any alienation. With this in mind, Anson replied, "About that, Mrs.

Wales, I wouldn't know. I do know, however, that Mr. Duncan still hopes to get the manuscript of your husband's new book."

"More nonsense," Mrs. Wales said. "He knows as well as I that there is to be no new book. My husband abandoned it several years ago."

"Is he writing nothing at all then?"

"Nothing."

A brown thrasher flew across the lawn, followed by a cardinal, and down toward the river a woodpecker drummed in the woods. Mrs. Wales said, "My husband is blind, as you know. Writing has always been difficult for him and he finds it impossible to dictate. We tried it, he and I, but the handicaps were too great. He will never write anything again, I'm afraid."

"But what a tragedy!"

Inside the house a telephone rang several times and then fell silent. Mrs. Wales said, "Yes, for him it is. Am I to take it that you are one of his admirers?"

Anson did not think that this was the time to mention his reservations concerning Garvin Wales. "Yes, I am," he said. "Aren't you?"

It was the tone of her voice that prompted the question. She appeared to be referring to a stranger rather than to the man to whom she was married.

"Admire him?" she said. "But naturally I admire him. How can one not admire a man of genius?"

Anson was glad that Dinah picked that moment to return. She came out of the house with a sulky look on her face. Anson thought that it added to her attractiveness.

"I'm sorry I took so long," she said. "That was Mickey on the telephone. He's flying to Wilmington in the morning. It has something to do with that new plant." She shook off her sulky look and said, "Lunch is ready when you are, Lucy. Did you two get everything straight?"

"Hardly everything," Mrs. Wales answered. "We're saving that for tomorrow. Mr. Page is coming to Tamburlaine to see me."

"How nice," Dinah said.

"Yes," Mrs. Wales rejoined. "Isn't it?"

She looked at Dinah and then at Anson, sweeping them both with a single glance. Anson thought that her eyes were colder than before. She gave the impression of saying that she could see through them. Since nothing could be more absurd—what was there to be seen through?—Anson felt called upon to speak. He said, "It's you I have to thank, Dinah. I'm afraid that Mrs. Wales wouldn't have consented to see me if it hadn't been for you."

"Indeed I would not have," Mrs. Wales said. "It was very clever of you to let me find you here."

"Clever? Him?" Dinah's voice was lightly bantering, and Anson knew that she was coming to his rescue. Once again he had to appreciate how skillful she was. "It was my idea to have him here to meet you, not his," she said, addressing Mrs. Wales. "The truth, Lucy, is that I used you as an excuse. I wanted to show him Mulberry and I wanted to have him to myself for a little while. He's only going to be here for a few days and pretty soon the whole town will be after him."

"Old home week, in other words," Anson said. "We expect to have to call out the police to maintain order."

Mrs. Wales consented to smile.

"Thank you for lunch, Dinah," Anson said. "It was elegant. What time do you want me tonight?"

"Around seven. Mickey said he'd pick you up at the hotel if you'd like him to."

"No, I think I'd best manage on my own. Good-by, Mrs. Wales. I'm grateful for your kindness."

"You must not confuse kindness with curiosity," Mrs. Wales said. "I'm looking forward to our little chat."

Anson did not know what to make of her. He had the feeling that she had been playing a role, trying to live up to the advance notices which she imagined he had been given of her. She had carried it off skillfully enough—the great man's wife; the injured party; the outspoken sophisticate—and yet the impression he had was that of a rather conventional woman. It was not by accident that she had gone out of her way to remind him of her family background. She might be Mrs. Garvin Wales, an identity which unquestionably held its advantages, but clearly it was more important to be Lucy Devereaux.

To understand that, however, was not to render her less formidable an adversary. Back in his room at the Marlborough, Anson moodily reflected that he had got nowhere. It had been demanded of him that he meet Mrs. Wales on a social basis, as he had, but he was as far away as ever from an interview with her husband. Much more disconcerting, however, was his blunder in saying that he had found certain papers that might clear up the matter. What papers? Phillip Greene's memos to the accounting department? The checks to Anna

Jones? What did they prove except what Mrs. Wales regarded as having already been proved, that Phillip Greene had embezzled twenty thousand dollars of her husband's funds?

Because of his own clumsiness, he had put himself under a grave handicap. Mrs. Wales would naturally expect him to produce the papers he had mentioned. How could he, though, without giving the whole show away? And if he did not, what then? He thought he knew what then. Mrs. Wales would ask him to leave and he would have had it.

It was now past three o'clock and the last mail delivery had arrived. Nothing had come from the tracing agency. Acting on impulse, Anson picked up the telephone, asked for long distance, and gave the operator a New York number. He said he wanted to speak to Mr. Adolph Mootz. He had to spell out the last name twice. The operator asked him please to wait, and he could hear her putting through the call. The New York operator also had to have the last name spelled out for her. Moose? she asked, and the local operator said no, Mootz, z as in zebra, and after a few more hums and buzzes Mootz's hoarse rumble came over the wire. "Who's calling?" he asked. "Who?" and Anson decided that there had been confusion enough. "It's all right, operator," he said. "Put Mr. Mootz on."

Adolph Mootz was a former New York City detective who had opened his own agency. Anson had never met him, but he suspected that he liked to refer to himself as a private eye. The very nature of his occupation implied a certain grubbiness—people who jumped town ahead of their bills; husbands who deserted their families; wives who left a trail from tavern to tavern and then disappeared—and though they had conversed only on the telephone, Anson gathered that Adolph Mootz took a rather cynical view of human nature. It had pleased him to get a piece of business from a firm like Roberts, Guthrie, Barlowe & Paul.

"I was going to send you a night letter, Mr. Page," he said after Anson had made known his identity. "We heard from our man in St. Louis."

"Any luck?"

"I dunno. That's for you to decide. The woman's dead."

Anson had to stop for a moment. "Dead?"

"That's right. If you want, I'll read you what we got on her."

"Wait till I get a pencil. All right. I'm ready."

Adolph Mootz cleared his throat. "Anna Jones, female, age seventy-four——"

"What age?" Anson said.

"Seventy-four. What's the matter, Mr. Page? Don't it figure?"

"I don't know. What else?"

"Last registered home address, 2061 Osbiso Street. You know St. Louis, Mr. Page?"

"No, why?"

"This Osbiso Street. It's a kind of crummy part of town."

"Go on."

"Last known address, the St. Louis General Hospital. Admitted June 28, 1940."

"When?"

"June 28, 1940."

"What was the matter with her? Do you know?"

Adolph Mootz's voice, when he replied, had a slightly aggrieved tone. He said, "Sure we know, Mr. Page. We really went to work on this job for you. All out."

"But what was the matter with her?"

"Cancer of the stomach. She had an operation. That was on June 30, 1940."

"June 30?"

"That's right. Our man in St. Louis checked the records. Then she died."

"When?"

"The next day, July 1, 1940."

"Any survivors?"

Adolph Mootz's voice hesitated a moment. "Not that our man could locate, Mr. Page. This Anna Jones lived all by herself in a rooming house at that address I gave you, the one on Osbiso Street. Best line our St. Louis man could get, she was a cleaning woman. One thing, though——"

"Yes?"

"She didn't seem to be bothered too much about cash. People like that, Mr. Page, you know how they are. They get sick and it puts them in a jam and they end up under a pile of bills. Some of them never get out. People like that, they have a hard time. Not this Jones woman, though."

"No?"

"She paid cash money all the way through, right on the line. I figured that that was the joker you were after."

"Joker? What joker?"

"The money. All her hospital bills cleaned up, her rent paid, and over five hundred dollars in cash. Where'd she get it, a cleaning woman? Maybe we can help you along that line too, Mr. Page."

"We'll have to wait and see. Did anyone claim the body?"

There was something in Adolph Mootz's voice that suggested a shake of the head. "Not a soul, Mr. Page. The hospital had to take care of all the arrangements. That's where the five hundred came in. It seems like she didn't want to be buried in no potter's field. I guess that winds it up, Mr. Page, unless you want us to keep on working. It figures that she must have got the money from somewhere. If you want us to start working along that line——"

"If I do, I'll let you know."

"I hope you're satisfied with our service, Mr. Page."

"Yes, Mootz, I am. I'll be expecting your bill."

Mootz's voice was genial and expansive. "That you got to expect, Mr. Page. There's always got to be a bill."

Anson opened his briefcase and brought out his notes. Even though he told himself that there was nothing to get elated about, he could not down a feeling of excitement. In one sense, Mootz's information only complicated matters—how had a cleaning woman become involved with one of the world's leading novelists and the most respected editor in New York? Useless though it was even to try to speculate, at least he knew something about her. He did not yet see where it was going to lead, nor could he be sure that it was going to lead anywhere, but one small corner of the puzzle was at last beginning to be filled in.

He went carefully over his notes. They showed that during the early months of 1940, from February through June, Phillip Greene had written out four checks to Anna Jones—one for $100, two others for $500, and a fourth, dated June 12, for $1,000. They came to a total of $2,100, and during that same period Phillip Greene had withdrawn a like amount from Garvin Wales's account.

The first thing that came to Anson's mind was that blackmail could be ruled out. Anna Jones was someone for whom Phillip Greene had been made to feel responsible. Though the maze into which he had been drawn seemed to have become more devious than ever, Anson felt considerably better. One thing he knew for sure. Anna Jones was no doxy Phillip Greene had shacked up somewhere. She was a cleaning woman who was seventy-four years old when she died. It did not tell him much, but it told him something. He would not be wholly unarmed when he went to Tamburlaine in the morning.

344

Through the slanting sunlight of late afternoon, the clock in the steeple of St. Paul's struck four o'clock. Looking through his pockets for a cigarette, Anson found that he had none. He went down to the lobby, picked up a couple of packs of his brand at the magazine counter, and decided to take another turn about the streets. He had several hours to dispose of before returning to Mulberry and could think of no other way to pass the time. He walked up to Monmouth Square, crossed over into Bay Street, and, remembering that he was almost out of razor blades, went to the drugstore where he had first tried to get in touch with Dinah over the telephone. He was waiting for one of the clerks to get around to him when he happened to notice a matronly looking woman sitting at the soda fountain on the other side of the store. Her blond hair was cropped in a way that seemed much too young for her, and she was having a strawberry soda that also seemed much too young, and when she turned her head to speak to a small boy who sat on an adjoining stool he saw that it was Midge Higgins.

He was not particularly surprised to find her there. He knew that if you hung around Bay Street long enough you could count on meeting practically everyone you knew, and it was just as if he'd run into her in Spier's Drugstore back when he was working for Garrick & Leigh. Though her face was much plumper, it was still pretty, even with the web of little wrinkles that radiated from the corners of her eyes, and though she seemed worn and tired, glad to be resting for a moment, she was able to manage a smile for the small boy. She finished her soda, wiped off the boy's mouth with a paper napkin, and reached down for a large shopping bag that rested against the base of the soda fountain. Anson was reminded of the night they had sat on the porch of her home on Frenchman Street and she bent over to get the ash tray that was under the swing—there still remained that much of her old grace. She slipped from the stool, followed by the boy, and Anson caught up with them as she was paying her check at the cashier's desk. "You wouldn't need a strong man to carry your groceries, would you?" he said.

Midge turned at the sound of his voice, recognizing him immediately.

"For the love of Pete!" she said, and her face looked less worn and tired. "I heard you were back in town. How are you, Sonny?"

"I'm fine, Midge. And you?"

"I can't complain," she said. "You look like the world's been treating you all right. You haven't changed a bit."

"Neither have you, Midge."

"Shinola!" she said. "I'm getting big as a house. It seems to agree with me, though. This is one of my boys, Edwin, the youngest—I've got four. Shake hands with Mr. Page, Edwin."

Edwin shook hands, looking at Anson in the slightly put-upon fashion of a small boy required to be polite, and Midge shifted her shopping bag to the crook of her other arm.

"Can't I carry that for you?" Anson said.

"No, thanks, Sonny," Midge said. "It's not heavy and the car's parked just around the corner." She held out her free hand. "It's been good to see you. How long are you going to be in town?"

"Not long, Midge. Only a couple of days or so."

"That's what I thought," Midge said. "I'd ask you to supper, but I know that you won't have time," and what she was saying, as a matter of simple truth, was that fifteen years had passed and they no longer had anything in common. She pressed his hand warmly and smiled. "Take care of yourself, Sonny."

"I will, Midge. Give my regards to Bill. I'm sorry I won't be able to come to supper."

"I am too," Midge said. "Come on, Edwin. We've got to be going."

"Good-by, Midge," Anson said. "All the best."

"You too, Sonny. Be good."

He walked to the door with her, holding it open, and after she left he went back to the counter and bought the razor blades he had come for. It was nearly five o'clock when he got back to the Marlborough. He stopped in at the bar, took his time over a couple of drinks, and returned to his room. He showered, shaved, and began to get dressed for Dinah's party. His meeting with Midge had depressed him a little and he was glad that he would be seeing Dinah again.

CHAPTER TWENTY-FOUR

Mulberry's double parlor had been thrown open into one room, all the lights were lit, and a buffet supper was spread in the dining room where the red-and-gold fire buckets were. Cocktails had been served in the parlor and the guests had now drifted into the dining room. Anson was talking to Margie Rhett Fowler, or, rather, listening to Margie talking. She said:

"I knew it was you that night at *Oklahoma*. And the trouble we had getting tickets! Marlin had to work through the New York office two months in advance. He had to go to New York on this convention—he's head of the local office now, you know—and he gave me the trip as a birthday present. That and the downstairs part of the house done over and a fur coat. I bought the fur in New York. Marlin could be there only three days, so Sally Wilkinson and I went up a week in advance. You don't know Sally, do you? She comes from Alabama and her husband is the new president of the power company. They live on the water not far from where we do. Sally's one of my best friends. When they moved here and bought their place on Paradise I thought that she might be one of those fuzz girls——"

"Fuzz girls?"

Margie picked up a plate from a pile at one end of the table and handed it to Anson. She took one for herself, passed Anson a napkin and some silver, and said, "It's a saying we have. A lot of new people have moved to town, and where they got hold of their money nobody knows. The women are always trying to splash around, especially the ones who have got into the Country Club. They never stop talking about their cars and their clothes and their fuzz. That's why we call them the fuzz girls. It's the way they say furs. Don't you get it?"

347

"Yes," Anson said. "I get it."

"But Sally Wilkinson's not like that at all," Margie went on. "She comes from Birmingham and her father is a president or a vice-president in steel. Something important, anyway. So, as I was saying, Sally and I went to New York a week ahead of Marl. We stayed in the Junior League rooms at the Waldorf. Sally and I had our pictures taken by that man on Fifth Avenue—you must know who he is; his studio is not far from Schrafft's—and we ate at Louis XIV and the Mayan Restaurant and all those other places. I was almost sorry when Marl arrived, we were having such a whirl."

"Yes, Marge," Anson said. "I can see you did."

It struck him as remarkable that Margie could convey so much information about herself in so short a time. She might be giving him her Dun and Bradstreet report. He wondered if Margie ever recalled the days when she had been willing to pay a modest price for popularity, and what she thought of the boys, now grown into men, who had exacted the payment. Did she dislike herself, or them, or did she no longer remember? Looking at Margie, who wore a long green dress and whose thin face was slightly over-rouged, he decided that she did not remember. He thought it was just as well. His own demands on Margie had always been small and had extended over a very short period, but still he thought it was just as well.

Marlin Fowler, Margie's husband, stood in line behind Anson. He had put on considerable weight. A comfortable paunch swelled out beneath the buttons of his dinner jacket, and the top of his head was completely bald. It was difficult for Anson to believe that he had ever regarded him as a threat back when Kit Robbins was the most important person in the world. It was like having a piece of folly acted out before your eyes. He heard Fowler say above the hum of conversation, "What I can't see is why don't we use the bomb? If one bomb could settle everything, why don't we use it?"

Fowler was talking to Charlie Braddock. Though Charlie and Anson had never been close to each other, Charlie was a Pompey's Head boy. He used to live on the same street as Joe Ann Williams. His family owned the thread factory and he had been Jay Lockhart's best friend. During the war he had risen to the rank of lieutenant colonel in the Army Air Corps, and over cocktails he and Anson discovered that they had been in London at the same time. Charlie had been drinking heavily, but his voice was not thick. He said, "But one bomb wouldn't settle it, Marl. That's the catch. Twenty, maybe, or thirty better still, but not one. You have to think of the target. It's not like Berlin. In a place as big as that, where there is no concentration of heavy industry, what you would have to do——" And then Gaby Carpenter, who stood in line between Charlie and Marlin Fowler, wearing a dark purple dress with many folds, broke in indignantly, saying:

"Targets and bombs! I think you're both horrible! What about morality? What about world opinion? And what about our being bombed back? They have the bomb too now, you know."

"That's just the point," Fowler countered. "Why shouldn't we hit them before they hit us? You don't think that they are worrying about morality and world opinion, do you?"

"But that's no reason——"

"You can carry this morality business too far," Fowler went on. "Don't you agree, Charlie?"

"You two heavy thinkers fight it out," Charlie Braddock said. "I want another drink."

Anson wondered if this was what they meant when they said that you can't go home again. In the old days at Mulberry the talk used to be about purple finches and cedar waxwings and what fish were running in the river and whether the ducks and quail were coming back, and now the talk was about targets and morality and whether we should use the bomb. He supposed it was inevitable. They were expressing their emotions, as everyone did, and during the past fifteen years a whole new set of emotions had come into the world.

Margie Rhett Fowler was helping herself to a slice of baked ham from a large silver platter. She turned her head to Anson and said, "When can we get you for supper, Sonny? You can't go away without seeing our place on Paradise. I want you to meet my sons, too. What about Saturday?"

"I don't know if I'll still be here Saturday, Marge."

"Certainly you can stay the week end," Margie said. "Since Mickey has to go out of town, I thought that you could bring Dinah. We might even have an oyster roast."

"If I'm still here, Marge, I'd like to."

"Dinah would enjoy it, I know," Margie said. "With Mickey away so much, she gets lonesome way back here in the country." She moved along and stopped before the salad bowl. "Incidentally," she said, "I understand that you two put on quite a reunion scene in the lobby of the Marlborough yesterday."

Scratching was such an ingrained habit of Margie's that Anson supposed she could not help herself. She always used to be scratching

349

at somebody, Kit Robbins and Joe Ann Williams and Midge Higgins most of all, and this quick scratch at Dinah was part of the same compulsion. It was disturbing, however, to realize that he and Dinah were already being talked about. There had been what Margie called that reunion scene in the Marlborough, they had spent part of the morning together, Dinah had given him his lunch, and now there was this party to welcome him home. He couldn't quite imagine what was being said, but he knew that they were saying something.

Margie piled some of the salad on her plate and looked toward the head of the table, where Dinah stood behind a chafing dish, serving her guests as they came along. "She's beautiful tonight, isn't she?" Margie said to Anson. "I hate to think, though, what Mickey had to pay for that dress. They were in Dallas not long ago and she bought it at Neiman-Marcus."

Anson wished that Margie would shut up. Knowing that she would be sure to repeat it the first chance she got, he said boldly, "I wouldn't know anything about the price tag, but the dress couldn't be more becoming. She looks like something out of the High Renaissance."

Margie said, "My, what a pretty compliment! You should tell it to her. She'd especially appreciate it, coming from you," and Anson decided to give up. It had been years since he had to contend with anyone like Margie and she was out of his class. Helping himself to the salad, he looked at Dinah. Her gown was of a shade almost the color of watermelon, and he thought that only a woman of considerable self-confidence would have risked it. He was reminded of the flame-colored dress she wore that night at the Oasis. If the one represented a kind of rebelliousness, the other spoke of the same rebelliousness finally disciplined and brought under control. Dinah's arms and shoulders were bare, and her only ornament was a little choker of pearls and diamonds and gold—he half expected Margie to tell him that, expensive though it looked, none of it was real.

Dinah was chatting with Nan Schulkens, who, small and blond and pretty, stood holding out her plate. All Dinah's warm coloring was heightened by Nan's nearness, and her dark eyes lent a sparkle to the animation of her face. Something Nan said caused her to throw back her head and laugh—"Oh no, Nan!" she said. "Not *him!*"—and when Anson finally drew up before her, a hint of merriment still lurked in the corners of her mouth.

"You break a leg?" she said. "What took you so long?"

"I was visiting along the way."

"Hungry?"

"Famished. What smells so good?"

"You wouldn't mean me again, would you?"

"No, this time I mean what's in the dish."

"Scalloped turkey. You used to like it."

"I still do."

"Here, then. Amos will be back in a second with some more biscuits, and Mickey is pouring the wine. Having fun?"

"Of course. And you?"

"The most in years."

Moving past her, Anson walked toward the sideboard, where Mico Higgins, wearing a maroon tie with his dinner jacket and a matching cummerbund, stood talking with Jerome Barbour and Ian Garrick. Barbour was the Northern man who had married Nan Schulkens. Mico was the shortest of the three. He had grown stocky in a way that reminded Anson of Mr. Higgins's slow motions and deep bull chest, and the plume of hair that fell across his forehead was lightly streaked with gray. He seemed to have had no difficulty in adjusting to more than a million dollars. It may not have been his birthright, but Anson thought he accepted it as his due. He looked relaxed and correct and sure of himself—perhaps a little too sure, Anson thought, but that was because he was remembering Midge and the shotgun cottage on Frenchman Street and the night they played blackjack and Mico developed a grudge against him. He did not imagine that anyone who did not know about Frenchman Street would think that Mico Higgins looked too sure of himself.

Mico and Jerome Barbour were talking about wine. Ian Garrick, his head cocked to one side, listened attentively. The expression on his face was not so much interested as obsequious. Anson noticed that Mico had lost his Channel accent, and that his voice had acquired the hoarse intonation that seemed to be common to the wealthy Northerners who owned properties along the coast—rich Yankees they were called in Pompey's Head, unless they happened to own islands, in which case they fell into the less astringent category of island people.

Jerome Barbour was an adequate representative of the type. Older than the rest, in his early sixties, he was a thin, narrow-shouldered man of more than average height. His carefully maintained hair was white, as was his close-cropped mustache, and he held himself with a military bearing that dated from the time when he was a liaison officer with the British Army during the First World War. So did his pronunciation. "There's a Chilean Reisling that isn't a damn bit bad," he was saying. "Y'ought to lay down a few cases, Mickey. For my money, 's a damn sight better than most. No point in being taken in by labels, don'tcher know," and then he noticed Anson. " 'Lo there," he said. "Been wanting to talk to you. Understand you know John Duncan. Used to see him all the time when I lived on Long Island, practically neighbors, but haven't laid eyes on him for years. How is the old crock? Holding up?"

Anson said that John Duncan was fine, good as ever, and Jerome Barbour began relating an incident that took place when he and John Duncan were once sailing in the Bermuda race. He said, "Now old John's a damn fine skipper, no doubt of that, damn fine, might even be able to show this Corny Shields chap a thing or two, don'tcher know," and then fell into a complicated recital so full of grunts and ellipses that Anson soon lost the thread of it. Ian Garrick went through a pantomime of attentiveness, nodding his head at what he must have thought were the proper intervals and occasionally emitting a hollow laugh, but Mico Higgins, picking up one of the glasses of wine that stood on the sideboard, handed it to Anson and ushered him out of earshot.

"I must have heard that story of Jerry's six times already," he said. "Here's Amos with the biscuits. Have some."

"Thanks, Mickey, I will."

"It's great to have you back, Sonny," Mico said. "How do you like the old barn?"

Anson found it strange that he should be hearing Mico Higgins refer to Mulberry as an old barn, and that there should be that note of deliberate disparagement in his voice.

"It certainly didn't ever look like this," Anson said. "I think it's wonderful what you've done to it."

Mico said, "So you like it, eh? Personally I'd much rather be on the water, but I suppose I can get used to living back here in the sticks. Did Dinah tell you that she wants to put those old fields back to rice?"

"No, she didn't."

"It's just one of those notions she gets," Mico said, "but we might be able to take it out of taxes. Which reminds me——" His voice changed and his eyes took on a slightly different look. "There's something I'd like to talk to you about. I'd save it for tomorrow except that I won't be here tomorrow. I have to fly to Wilmington on that cellophane deal."

"Yes, Dinah told me."

"It's too bad we won't get a chance to see more of each other,"

Mico said. "Is it true that you'll be here only another day or two?"

"I have to get back to work, Mickey."

"That's what I want to talk to you about," Mico said. "No need to waste any time. This is the proposition. Consolidated keeps on branching out and we need our own lawyer in New York. How'd you like to take us on as a client?"

All that Anson could think of for a moment was that his supper would soon be getting cold, and then he thought how decent it was of Mico to want to do him a good turn. He said, "It's kind of sudden, Mickey. I don't know."

"We'd make it worth your while."

"Yes, I'm sure you would," Anson said. "I'm not certain, though, that a firm like ours is the kind of firm you want. I just don't know."

And then he did know. He could hear Mr. Barlowe saying what he thought of a patent-medicine called Peppo, and he knew that even without Mr. Barlowe he would not want to have anything to do with it. He was no longer sure that Mico Higgins wanted to do him a good turn, either. He said, "Ours is a rather peculiar firm, Mickey. We naturally do a certain amount of corporation work, but the majority of our clients are publishing houses. We have a couple of banks stowed away, and one of the senior partners has a shipyard under his wing, but most of the time we work with publishers. I don't think we could do as good a job for you as some other firms. If you'd like me to look into it and send you a couple of names——"

"It wouldn't be a bad piece of business," Mico said. "You wouldn't regret it." He had not changed the tone of his voice, but all of a sudden there was something about him that put Anson on guard.

"I'm sure I wouldn't, Mickey," he said. "If the setup of our firm happened to be a little different——"

"Your firm wouldn't have to come into it, except for the usual cut," Mico said. "You could handle Consolidated as your own account. How would you like to start with a retainer of ten thousand a year?"

A kind of film dropped across Mico's eyes, and it was not until then that Anson understood. It needed the mention of ten thousand dollars to drive it home. Mico was trying to buy him. He had bought Ian Garrick and all the other Ian Garricks and he had bought Mulberry and in his own mind he had bought Dinah Blackford and God knows what else he had bought, and now he was trying to buy him. To buy a person was to break him, to effect a very special kind of humiliation, and there must be a lot of people whom it had pleased Mico Higgins to break.

Anson felt that he had had a narrow escape. Having himself never wanted to break or humiliate anyone, it was momentarily unnerving to think that Mico Higgins would have liked to break and humiliate him. That ancient grudge must still rankle, or, if not that, coldly and dispassionately, Mico wanted to see what happened when he turned the screws. He must have heard that every man had his price, and he must have wanted to see if the price in this instance could be set at ten thousand a year.

Across the room Anson heard Dinah laugh. If there were times when her eyes seemed sad, he thought he knew why. A will to humiliate left no room for love, and Dinah was one of those people who needed love. But you could not love anyone whom you believed you had bought, especially if in the act of buying you managed also to satisfy the need to humiliate, and Dinah must have been made to understand—in some way or other, even though he might regard her as his prize possession, Mico Higgins would have brought it home. But what mattered most to Anson was what Mico had tried to do to him. It was hard to keep the anger from showing in his voice, but fortunately he was able to manage. He said, "I could use the money, Mickey, but I don't think that I'm your man. If you want me to look into it and send you a couple of names——"

"Sure, you do that," Mico said, looking at him heavily. "I just thought that I'd give you first crack at it."

Anson fully expected him to say, "For old times' sake," which in one sense would have been true, since the present moment was but a continuation of that scene in the Higginses' kitchen, but Mico failed to follow through. Instead, he said, "Well, I reckon we'd better start circulating. Why don't you get some fresh biscuits? Those must be getting cold. And if you happen to change your mind——"

"I'll let you know, Mickey," Anson said. "You'll be the first to know."

Supper over, Anson sat holding a brandy on a couch in the parlor next to Olive Garrick. The scent of vinegar no longer hovered about her, as once it did because of the rinses her colored nurse used to give her hair, but she still peered near-sightedly through her glasses, and her blue gown hung badly on her long, angular frame. She said, "Sonny, I need your help."

"Help?"

Olive nodded. "It's about changing the name of Montague Square.

I'm getting up a petition to the Commissioner of Parks. It shouldn't be called Montague Square. It should be called Carvell Square."

"Why should it?"

"Why should it?" Olive looked amazed. "That's where the statue of General Carvell is, isn't it? Oh, I know that the statue of Sir Richard Montague *used* to be there, but if we thought so little of him that we melted him down for cannon balls, why should we perpetuate his name?"

Had Anson not known better, he might have laughed—Sir Richard dead these one hundred fifty years or more, a Tory governor who had to take to the woods in his nightshirt, and Olive Garrick still riding furiously to the attack. However, under the circumstances, he dared not even smile. Olive Garrick was worshiping at her ancestral shrine. She said, "Of course I have a personal interest in the matter, seeing as how the general was my great-great-granduncle, but I think that it's just plain silly to keep on calling it Montague Square. You'll sign my petition, won't you, Sonny?"

"Well, Olive, now that I don't live here any longer——"

"What difference does that make?" Olive said. "You *did* live here, didn't you? And didn't you write your column for the paper? Your not living here any longer simply means that you can see it objectively."

"Does it?"

"Of course," Olive said. "What I really wish you'd do would be to write a letter to the paper. That might make the Commissioner of Parks sit up and take notice. All he can think of is what changing the name to Carvell Square will do to the city maps! He's the most *stupid* man! His trouble is that he doesn't even come from Old Pompey. If he did——"

Unsuccessfully Anson tried to close his ears. Olive went on to say that if the Commissioner of Parks had come from Old Pompey he would have some understanding of the question of history involved and what could you expect of the riffraff that had taken over City Hall, and then Margie Rhett Fowler, who was sitting in a chair near Olive, broke into her monologue.

"Did you hear what the Cliftons have done now, Olive?" she said. "They've bought a Cadillac station wagon."

"A Cadillac station wagon!"

"No less, my dear," Margie said. "Marl says that they paid over five thousand for it."

Mico Higgins, sitting next to Margie with a highball in his hand, joined the conversation. "Over five thousand for a Caddy? That sounds kind of steep to me. Are you sure that's right, Marge?"

"That's what Marl says," Margie replied. "Marl, didn't you say the Cliftons paid over five thousand for that Cadillac station wagon? Marl, I'm talking to you! Pay some attention! How much did you say those Cliftons paid for that Cadillac station wagon?"

Marlin Fowler, who was being attentive to Nan Schulkens, wearing the strained yet eager look of a man who is finding it difficult not to paw, turned his bald head toward his wife. He said, "A little over five thousand, I was told. I understand that it has a lot of special features."

"Like what?" Charlie Braddock said. "A solid-gold john?"

"No," Ian Garrick put in soberly, "but it does have a complete air-conditioning unit and a built-in refrigerator. I know that I may be alone in this, but personally I like Jack Clifton. I ran into him in the bank and he told me that they are all going to drive to California to see his mother-in-law. He said that when you cross the desert——"

"But five thousand dollars!" Olive exclaimed. "I think it's disgusting, the way they throw their money around. Do they expect us to be impressed? Well, I'm not! If you ask me——"

Mico Higgins said that there was something about the lines of the new Cadillac that he didn't like, and Jerome Barbour said that when you actually came down to cases there was only one automobile worth owning and that was the Rolls, and Charlie Braddock said that though he didn't know about the Rolls nothing had been built in this country that could touch the old T-model Ford, and then everybody was talking at once about cars and money and trips to Europe and the Cliftons' new Cadillac station wagon.

"I know for a fact that when they came here from Pittsburgh——"

"It's not his money, it's hers. They tell me that her father and one of the Mellons——"

"He's not so bad, I think he tries to be a gentleman in his own way, but her and her dyed hair——"

"I didn't mind the swimming pool so much because it was nice for the children, but if we are going to have to compete with five-thousand-dollar station wagons——"

It was a long time since Anson had felt so completely out of things. He wanted to be away from those people and out of that room. It was not that he thought he was better than they, or more intelligent, or endowed with deeper sensibilities. He simply did not belong with them. He belonged with them even less than he belonged with Meg's friends from the newsmagazine and the parents whose children went

356

to Boojum's and Beejum's and the Barlowes and their circle in Far Hills. He asked himself where ·did he belong, did he belong anywhere, and then he saw Dinah watching him, perched on the edge of a chair. It surprised him how clearly he could tell what she was thinking. She was telling him simply by the way she sat there that she knew he was disappointed and that she was disappointed too. "This isn't what I wanted for us," her eyes said. "Surely you know that. But what can I do? I tried, Sonny, just as I have been trying all along. Look at me. Can't you tell how hard I've tried? And don't you know how lonely I get at times? I don't belong with these people any more than you do."

Anson finished his brandy and rose from the couch. Addressing Mico Higgins, he said, "I think I'll have another drink. May I help myself?"

"Sure thing," Mico said. "What about you, Charlie? You ready for a freshener? Jerry? Marl? You fellows look after yourselves. I'm tired of being bartender."

Anson went to a side table where the bottles were and poured himself another brandy. He was about to turn away when Dinah joined him, bearing her glass.

"Buy a lady a drink?"

"If you're the lady, yes."

"Still having fun?"

"How could I not? And you?"

"No, I'm bored. I don't give a damn about what's happening on Paradise. God, what a silly name! Shall we put on some music?"

"Yes, let's."

They went to a combination radio and phonograph that stood in a corner of the parlor's second room, and Dinah began rooting among the albums and long-playing records. Anson noticed several Beethoven symphonies, Schubert, Chopin, Tschaikowsky, and a sizable collection of Brahms—all the romantics, he thought; it being Dinah, they would be. Dinah came up with a pile of popular records. "Here," she said. "Put these on. Let's see if we can get those characters down from Paradise. I'll kick back the rugs."

None of the others cared to dance—later, they told Dinah, perhaps later on. Anson stood listening to the first record that fell into place. Someone was dancing with his darling to the Tennessee waltz, and then Dinah was back at his side.

"Ask a lady to dance?"

"This lady, yes."

It was a strange feeling that Anson had. The others were still talking and drinking a short distance away, but suddenly they were no longer quite there. Amid the tangle of voices, he and Dinah moved in a curious kind of isolation. He was aware that Margie Rhett Fowler was watching them intently, as was Gaby Carpenter, though in a fond and appreciative way, and he saw Mico Higgins give them a short, heavy-lidded glance. They all seemed far away, however. Walled off by the music, he and Dinah were quite alone.

"Now I am having fun," Dinah said. "Look at us in the mirror. And aren't we attractive!"

"It's nice you think so."

"Don't you?"

"I think you're attractive. You go well with that dress."

"Finally! I was beginning to think that as far as you were concerned I might just as well be wearing a pair of overalls."

"Speaking of overalls, do you remember the time——"

And then, as the long mirror gave back their reflection and the someone who was dancing with his darling an old friend happened to see, they were remembering again——

"Such good times we had, Sonny! They were good times, weren't they?"

"Yes, they certainly were."

"Sonny."

"Yes?"

"What time are you going to Lucy Wales's in the morning?"

"Eleven o'clock. Why?"

"Couldn't we have lunch again?"

Anson hesitated and Dinah looked at him in the mirror. "Please don't say no," she said. "I'll fix us a picnic and we can go to the beach. You can come here after you leave Tamburlaine. I want to know what happens when you see Lucy, anyway."

"It sounds fine, Dinah, but——"

Dinah stopped looking at him in the mirror and looked at him directly; that tiny bright glint shone in her eyes. "But what?"

Anson was thinking of what Margie had said about that reunion scene in the Marlborough and what else would be said when it became known that they had gone off on a picnic together. The music stopped and the voices rose into the vacuum it left and they were no longer alone. There was no reason why they shouldn't go off on a picnic, however, since it was only natural for them to want to see as much of each other as possible, and, having taken her into his confidence, it followed as a matter of course that he would want to tell her what happened when he saw Lucy Wales.

"Please don't say no," Dinah said.

"All right, I won't," Anson replied. "A picnic sounds like a grand idea."

Another record fell into place. Anson and Dinah danced through it without speaking and then rejoined the others. Margie Rhett Fowler said, "You two are not going to stop, are you? You put me in mind of *The Merry Widow*," and Dinah said, "What? Not *The Two Little Confederates*? That's who we thought we were, didn't we, Sonny?" and then Anson had to listen to the talk again. This time, however, he was better able to manage. As long as Dinah was in the room he need not feel completely alone.

CHAPTER TWENTY-FIVE

During the night it turned colder, as frequently it did at that time of year in Pompey's Head, but when Anson started for Tamburlaine Island the next day the weather was still fine. There was not a cloud in the sky and a brisk wind was blowing from the river. To get to Tamburlaine it was necessary to go to the north end of town and follow the route that led to Cassava Beach, and as Anson drove through the streets, passing first one square and then another, he wished he were embarking on a happier mission. With one part of his mind still full of last night's party at Mulberry, his error of the day before came back to haunt him. Nothing could have been more unfortunate than his having told Mrs. Wales that he had found certain papers that might clear up the matter. The papers were in his briefcase, Phillip Greene's memos to the accounting department and the bundle of checks made out to Anna Jones, but in themselves they were valueless as ever. Nor did it help to know that Anna Jones was no longer alive. Foolish though it may have been, Anson realized that he had never abandoned hope that were she able to be located she might somehow be prevailed upon to solve the mystery at whose center she lay. But now she too was dead, and of the three people most immediately involved, only Garvin Wales remained. With but a few sentences Wales could put everything straight, as Anson more than ever was convinced, but how were those sentences to be had? Mrs. Wales would expect to see the papers he had mentioned, and when he refused her, as refuse he must, his one and only chance would go glimmering.

Soon he was out of the city. He noticed that the road to Cassava Beach had been widened and that a new bridge had been built across

Little River. The old bridge, a wooden one, used to be one of the best fishing places around. When the weakfish were running—weakfish being more frequently known in Pompey's Head as winter trout—you could always count on a good day's sport. Anson once took a five-pounder when casting from the bridge, and a week later Wyeth Blackford landed a monster of nine pounds. It was said to be the largest weakfish ever taken from the waters around Pompey's Head. There was a piece about it in the News, and Nick Kerkhoff, who ran the Pompano Restaurant on Bay Street, had the prize frozen into a two-hundred-pound cake of ice which he displayed on the sidewalk. There were so many fishermen on the bridge for the rest of the season that it looked like a revival meeting.

Little River was one of a number of streams that laced that part of the country. Mostly branches of the Cassava, they helped form the various islands that lay along the coast. Washed on one side by the ocean, most of these were in part separated from the land by such streams as Little River. Appearing on the map to be arms of the sea, these passages were actually the mouths of the rivers. The islands thus formed were of varying shapes and sizes. Some, like Tamburlaine and Mungo, encompassed only a few acres. Others, like Boogooloo, which had now been metamorphosed into Paradise, were several miles long and a mile or so across.

Because of the nature of the terrain, each island had to be approached more or less separately. Crossing Little River, Anson turned off the road that led to Cassava Beach and took a smaller artery that soon crossed another road, narrow and unpaved, which, after many turnings and windings, eventually found its way to Double Crossing and the road that went to Mulberry.

Anson knew this part of the country very well. He had fished and hunted it, he had traveled it on horseback and trudged it on foot, and it was all in the background of his early experience. There was again the strangeness of having returned, a strangeness that occasionally slipped over into a feeling of unreality, as when on a dead tree he saw an eagle that might have been the same eagle he once found perched there twenty years before on a blazing summer afternoon, but he was too preoccupied with what lay ahead of him to give it much thought. Though nothing could be drawn from his one meeting with Mrs. Wales to confirm the harsh things he had heard of her, he could not imagine her being kindly disposed when he told her that the papers he had mentioned were not for her eyes. Nor could he blame her; in her place, he probably would be equally annoyed.

Crossing a second bridge, a rude wooden structure that spanned a salt-water creek called Blackbeard's River, this because it could be followed to one of the several islands in the neighborhood on which the pirate was supposed to have buried part of his loot, Anson came finally to the causeway that led to Tamburlaine Island. If privacy was what Garvin Wales was after, privacy was what he had—one came here to the very edge of the continent. Pushing his rented car as fast as its regulator would permit it to go, Anson rattled across a third bridge, also made of wood, and then he was on Tamburlaine itself. When last he was there the island was unoccupied, a forgotten, lonesome place visited only in summer when the channel bass were running off its southern point, and the large new house of modern design that loomed before him had so altered the island's appearance that he scarcely knew where he was.

The house faced the sea. Anson was not familiar enough with modern architecture to be able to tell much about it. He saw a flat roof, a sweep of large glass windows, what he thought was called an overhang, and a great number and variety of camellias, many of which were in bloom. He supposed that there could not be a better location for such a house, standing with the sea at its feet and bathed in the promise of infinite sun, and yet, in that solitude, knowing that its nearest neighbor was the Barbour residence on Mungo Island two miles to the south, he thought that it had a lost, deserted look. He heard the slow, steady roll of the surf, and when he drew up before the house he caught a glimpse of the narrow beach and the shining waters beyond.

Carrying his briefcase, he went up to the front door and rang the bell. He could hear its discreet tinkling somewhere within the house and he could see his reflection in the glass. He looked the way he would have wanted to look, a fit representative of an old, substantial firm like Roberts, Guthrie, Barlowe and Paul, and he was glad that he had let Meg prevail upon him to buy that new gray suit. He had objected to it as being a uniform, as of course it was, but during the war he had learned that there was a certain amount of camouflage value in a uniform, and he suspected that he was going to need all the camouflage at his disposal.

No sound came from within the house. The gentle roll of the surf broke upon the sand, and a solitary gull flew past, cleaving the sunlight with its wings. At some distance to the right of the house there rose a grove of pines running the length of the rest of the island. It was in these woods that Julian Tokar had overheard the conversation between Garvin Wales and Phillip Greene, and, from Tokar's description, Anson knew that the Waleses' teahouse stood at the far end of the trees.

As he was wondering if he should ring again, a Negro butler came to the door. He had a set, impassive look which must have taken years to acquire. Taking Anson's hat, he said that Mrs. Wales was expecting him, and led him through a kind of passageway which was guarded, near the door, by a small statue of a vaguely catlike animal, unmistakably oriental, which was mounted on a block of marble. Two African masks hung on the passageway's only wall, its other side being constructed of glass, and Anson imagined that these, along with the statue, were part of the loot that Wales had brought back from all over the world.

Reaching the end of the passageway, the butler showed Anson into a large, sunny room. It had a huge stone fireplace at one end and a single enormous window that looked out to the sea. Mrs. Wales, dressed in a tweed suit, was sitting on a low couch of modern design that faced the fireplace. A silver coffee service stood on a glass table before her.

"How very punctual you are," she said. "I always have a cup of coffee this time of morning, and I thought that you might like to join me. Won't you sit down?"

Anson began to feel somewhat less troubled. Though Mrs. Wales's show of cordiality was nothing more than the usual sectional emphasis upon good manners, her friendliness was disarming enough to lead him to hope that she would not prove as difficult as he had anticipated. Accepting her invitation, he sat on the couch beside her. Again he was struck by how young she looked. She was unusually slender for a woman her age, zippered and corseted though she probably was, and since he could detect a few strands of gray in her light brown hair, it could not have been dyed.

"How many lumps?" she asked.

"Three, if I may."

"Three?" Mrs. Wales gave him an amused glance. "You remind me of the Brazilians. They don't have sugar in their coffee, they have coffee in their sugar. Cream?"

"Not much."

"Enough?"

"Yes, thank you."

Mrs. Wales passed him the cup and began filling her own. "How was the party last night?" she asked. "Did you have a good time?"

363

Anson did not find it surprising that she knew about the party; some mention of it had undoubtedly been made at the meeting of the Camellia Club. Since it was impossible to confess what he really thought of the gathering at Mulberry, he said, "It was a nice party. I enjoyed seeing everybody again."

"Yes, I'm sure you did," Mrs. Wales said. "Your ears should have burned, the flattering things that were said about you yesterday afternoon."

"Were they? It's good to know."

"And your friend Dinah is so extremely attractive," Mrs. Wales went on. "No one could be lovelier to look at, as of course I needn't remind you, and yet she never seems to give it a thought. For a woman, that's no small accomplishment. There's such an appealing naturalness about her. Don't you think so?"

Anson had not expected to be drawn into a discussion of Dinah Blackford. He said, "It's hard for me to tell about Dinah. I've known her since she was a child and I'm always getting double images."

Mrs. Wales took a sip of her coffee and then, lowering the cup, said, "But that's not what you came all the way to Tamburlaine to talk about, is it? I seem always to forget that we have this unpleasant business to discuss. However, before we begin, there is something I think I should explain. You have doubtless wondered how I happened to discover those—what shall I call them; how can I put it most charitably?—those errors in my husband's royalty statements. You have been wondering, haven't you?"

"Yes, Mrs. Wales, I suppose I have."

"There's no mystery," Mrs. Wales said. "It's really quite simple. My husband is not well. During the past few years his health has failed badly. He may not have long to live, and I felt it my duty to see that his affairs were put in order. To do so, it was necessary for me to go over all his accounts."

She spoke in such a brisk, matter-of-fact tone that once again Anson found it hard to believe that she was talking about the man to whom she was married; coldness and hostility he might have understood, but this bookkeeper's approach was beyond him. Mrs. Wales said, "So that's how the errors came to my attention. And if I have taken what seems an adamant position, I ask you to consider the sum involved. Surely you are aware of the circumstances of an author's life, Mr. Page. It is true that my husband has been successful, which in the bad times we have fallen into is something for which we have cause to be grateful, but we are in no position to let twenty thousand dollars slip through our fingers."

She leveled her eyes at Anson and waited for him to reply. He said uneasily, "I agree, Mrs. Wales, that twenty thousand dollars is no small sum. And there is no question, either, that on paper these errors do appear. I think, though, that we run the risk of falling into further error if we accept what's on paper at face value. For one thing, it is unthinkable that a man like Phillip Greene——"

"Why is it unthinkable?" Mrs. Wales said, her eyes suddenly narrowing. "Let me tell you plainly that if you think you can woo me by being sanctimonious about Phillip Greene you are wasting your breath. I always detested that man!"

For Anson this was a new experience. He knew that there were various people in publishing who had looked upon Phillip Greene as a rather enigmatic fellow who was never seen at cocktail parties, authors' luncheons, and other literary celebrations, and that he had consequently been put down as being stand-offish and anti-social. This was the first time, however, that he had ever heard of Phillip Greene's being detested. He so much wanted to ask, "But why, Mrs. Wales? Why should you of all people detest him, your husband's best friend?" that it must have shown on his face.

Mrs. Wales said, "Oh, I know what you are thinking—where would my husband be were it not for Phillip Greene? Was it not Greene who first encouraged him; did not Greene worry and slave over every book he wrote? I seem shockingly ungrateful, don't I?" She looked at Anson coldly and then went on, "But what if I were to say that my husband would have been better off had he never come under Greene's influence—that would seem a hundred times more shocking, wouldn't it? But it's true; I mean it! For had it not been for Greene, my husband's work would have been more constructive, more decent, more worthy of respect. It was Greene who found 'literature'—how I have come to hate that word!—in the sordid and disgraceful. It was Greene who kept him wallowing in the mire! My husband was dominated by that man, more than dominated—hypnotized! How I laugh when I hear it said that Phillip Greene 'made' my husband! Made? He ruined him! Yesterday, like most unthinking people, you spoke of my husband's blindness as a tragedy. I couldn't disagree more. I consider it a blessing that he will never be able to write another line, a positive blessing." There was a short pause, and then she finished, "In that book he was writing—his masterpiece, he called it! —he seemed to have come to a final degradation. So foul it was that had it ever been published I would have left him! Indeed, I told him so—the demands of loyalty go just so far!"

Anson had always read of people recoiling in dismay and now he knew what was meant. He realized how precariously balanced this woman was, and that the things he had heard of her must be in large part true; he understood why she had alienated all her husband's friends, and why she had come to hate his work. Much more important, however, was that she hated Phillip Greene even more. She would be inclined to do nothing that might spare him or, now that he was beyond her reach, his reputation. In that respect, Julian Tokar had not been too far wrong.

Amazed at how freely she had spoken, he began gradually to understand that she hardly realized the import of what she had said. Just how to approach her, he did not know, but neither could he remain silent indefinitely. Shameful though it was to have to cajole her, "I can readily see why you find your husband's work distasteful," he began. "You're not the only person it has offended. And I realize, too, that your opinion of Phillip Greene may be different than mine. Moreover, it must be admitted that on the face of things your conclusion is correct. It does look as though he embezzled the money."

"I'm glad you agree to that much," Mrs. Wales said. "Does John Duncan?"

"In the absence of contrary evidence, yes," Anson replied. "Before I left New York, Mr. Duncan handed me a cashier's check for twenty thousand dollars, made out in your name. My instructions are to turn it over to you unless I can convince you that Phillip Greene is completely innocent."

Mrs. Wales looked at him quickly. "With no strings attached?"

"With no strings attached," Anson repeated, and then, thinking that he detected a slight change in the wind, "You yourself are to be both judge and jury," he added. "Either you are convinced that Greene is innocent, or I hand you the check. There the matter stands. Any courtroom proceeding would be bound to be disagreeable, and I am happy that you will not have to be subjected to it."

Appalling though it was to have to dissemble, it was even more appalling to find how readily the dissembling came; he should have felt rewarded by Mrs. Wales's changed appearance, but he did not. She said, "I must say this much for John Duncan—at least he had wit enough to employ a gentleman." She picked up her cup of coffee, drank, and set the cup down. "Very well, Mr. Page. I accept your proposition. Yesterday you mentioned certain papers. It is by means

366

of these, I suppose, that you hope to convince me that there has been a mistake."

"Only in part," Anson said. "Let me be completely honest, Mrs. Wales. The papers of which I spoke may be divided into two sets. The first shows only what we already know—that Phillip Greene caused twenty thousand dollars to be withdrawn from your husband's account and put into his own."

"Ah, I am supported then," Mrs. Wales said. "There is no argument."

"Not on the basis of that set of papers alone," Anson said. "However, there is a second set which appears to be directly related to the first. This set shows that exactly the same amount, twenty thousand dollars to the penny, was distributed by Greene over a period of years that corresponds almost to the day with the period covered by the withdrawals."

"Distributed?" Mrs. Wales said. "What do you mean, distributed?"

"Just that," Anson said, at a loss and hoping to gain time. "Twenty thousand dollars was removed from your husband's account by Greene, and this twenty thousand he in turn distributed."

"But what do you mean by distributed?" Mrs. Wales said sharply. "How? To whom? And how do I know that this is not something that you and John Duncan have invented? Where is your evidence?"

"In my briefcase," Anson said, knowing full well what would follow and having only an instant to wait.

"Produce it, then!" Mrs. Wales said. "I have no intention of letting you play cat-and-mouse with me. What are you waiting for? You said that unless you were able to convince me of Phillip Greene's innocence——"

"Yes," Anson intervened, "that I did. But please hear me out, Mrs. Wales. The second set of documents proves nothing. It was you who called it evidence, not I. The fact of the matter is that it does nothing to weaken the story told by the first. Put in the hands of a jury, it would indicate only that Phillip Greene had written out twenty thousand dollars' worth of checks——"

Before he knew it, Mrs. Wales had pounced. "Checks? Twenty thousand dollars' worth? To whom?"

Anson stared at her dully. The one error he had to guard against, and now the fat was really in the fire. Had she not stopped him, he would probably have been fool enough to mention names. It was not much for which to be grateful, but at least he could thank her for that. He said, "To whom is really of no importance, Mrs. Wales. As I was about to explain——"

"Was it a woman?"

"I'd rather not say."

Mrs. Wales gave a short, empty laugh. "You've already said, young man! So that's what happened, is it? Phillip Greene stole twenty thousand dollars to keep some floozy in caviar and black underwear—Phillip Greene, that paragon of all the virtues!" Laughing again, "It's really too delicious!" she said. "When I think of his holier-than-thou attitude, his smug rectitude—oh, it's really too much!" And then she abandoned her pretense of mirth. "No, Mr. Page," she said. "I'm afraid you've lost your wager. I shall have to ask for the return of our money. But tell me—is *that* how you hoped to convince me of Greene's innocence?"

He knew that she was not a rational woman, yet he could take only a rational approach. "Of course not," he said. "As I explained in the beginning, the checks mean nothing—taken by themselves, that is."

Mrs. Wales glanced at him suspiciously. "Why did you bring them up, then? What is your scheme?"

Anson said, "There is no scheme, Mrs. Wales. Let me review the situation, boring though it may be. Twenty thousand dollars are missing from your husband's account, and Phillip Greene wrote a number of checks for a like amount."

"To a woman," Mrs. Wales said.

"Yes, to a woman," Anson said. "That part of it, though, is beside the point. The important thing is that there would seem to be a connection between the two."

"But naturally there is a connection," Mrs. Wales said. "Phillip Greene stole twenty thousand dollars and spent it on a woman. You yourself have practically said as much. What *is* your scheme, Mr. Page? What are you after? What is it you want?"

"Only this," Anson said. "We feel that your husband may have known about those withdrawals. We think that Greene may have made them with his knowledge and consent."

"Preposterous!" Mrs. Wales said. "Utterly ridiculous!"

"Perhaps," Anson said. "Under the circumstances, however, merely in order to eliminate the possibility, I would like to put the question to your husband."

"Impossible!" Mrs. Wales said. "My husband is not well and cannot be disturbed. You are wasting your time, Mr. Page—your time and mine. You might as well know that I have discussed this matter with my husband. We have gone over each and every one of these 'withdrawals,' as it pleases you to call them, and he knows nothing about them. Nothing at all! If it was your idea to let me find you at Mulberry and then worm your way into my graces merely in order to invade our privacy——"

"It was my idea to do my job, Mrs. Wales," Anson said. "I'm a lawyer. I work for John Duncan. And in order for me to do my job, it is necessary for me to speak to your husband. Five minutes would do. If Mr. Wales tells me that he knows nothing about those withdrawals, and that Phillip Greene actually embezzled the money, my job is done."

"But why must you speak to my husband?" Mrs. Wales asked. "I have already told you that he knows nothing about it. Do you doubt my word?"

It was no time to grow tired, but Anson felt infinitely weary. He said, "You don't know me very well, Mrs. Wales, but I think you know me better than that. As a lawyer I have a job to do, and part of my job is to get a statement from your husband. So far as the law is concerned, as governed by the courts——"

"But you said that you did not intend to go to the courts."

Though there was nothing more in her voice than irritation, Anson saw that the mention of the courts had affected her as it did most people. Like them, she saw not an effort toward justice, but a conspiracy in shenanigans. It was not much of a breach, but he thought that he might be able to widen it. He said, "I remember what I said, Mrs. Wales. Either I convince you of Greene's innocence or I hand over the check. However, by the law I am required to have a statement from your husband, or, rather, by my responsibility as a lawyer. I would like to get such a statement here in private. If not, I may be compelled to ask for it in court."

Mrs. Wales said, "You're not threatening me, I hope?"

"Threaten?" Anson replied. "How could I threaten? You hold all the trump cards. Let us assume that this gets to a jury. Let us further assume that your husband declares on the stand what he is apparently prepared to declare now. What good would that do me? But you must realize that some kind of statement from your husband is necessary. All I'm trying to do is to wind up this affair as quickly as possible."

Mrs. Wales had narrowed her eyes again. She said, "Let me see if I understand. You say that in order to come to a settlement you need a statement from my husband—I don't see why, but let's agree that you do. However, should my husband tell you that he knows nothing of these withdrawals, you stand prepared to pay us our money. Is that correct?"

"Yes, Mrs. Wales, it is."

"Without any further ado?"

"Yes, without any further ado."

Mrs. Wales looked thoughtful for a moment, and outside the big glass window Anson could see the gentle rise and fall of the surf. He was thinking how peaceful it looked when Mrs. Wales spoke again. "But the real reason that you would like to see my husband," she said, "is that you think he may have been a partner to those withdrawals. Perhaps you are even convinced of it. Is that not the truth of the matter?"

"No, Mrs. Wales," Anson said. "I'm not convinced of anything. I merely have an idea that your husband may know something about those withdrawals. It's no more than a suspicion, if that."

"But enough of a suspicion to make you want to question him," Mrs. Wales said. "You think that, if nothing else, he may be able to tell you who the woman was. Is that it?"

Anson felt so drawn out that he could not evade her any longer. He said, "Yes, Mrs. Wales, in part it is. I'm a lawyer, not a detective, but it's my responsibility to try to clear up this matter. Give me five minutes with your husband——"

"Alone," Mrs. Wales said. "You naturally want to see him alone."

"It would be preferable."

"Yes," Mrs. Wales said, "that I can understand."

She looked away for an instant and there was a faint, indefinable movement of her lips—a subtle trembling of which she appeared to be wholly unconscious—that caused Anson to be uneasy. She said, "Very well, Mr. Page, I won't stand in your way. I'm afraid, though, that I must ask you to return tomorrow. My husband cannot be disturbed now, and after lunch I am taking him for a drive. Would tomorrow morning be satisfactory?"

"Yes, of course," Anson said. "What time?"

"Shall we say eleven again?"

"That would be fine."

"Very well then," Mrs. Wales said briskly. "Let's consider it settled. And it may please you to know that I shan't even be here tomorrow. I have a previous engagement. If it's a nice day, you will find Mr. Wales taking the sun on the beach before the little teahouse we built on the point. If not, he will receive you here in this room. I shall tell him to be expecting you."

370

"I'm most grateful, Mrs. Wales."

"There's no reason why you should be," she said. "Like you, I feel that the sooner we bring this to a conclusion, the better. And now, if we have nothing further to discuss, I must look after my husband. You'll forgive me if I don't see you to the door. I enjoyed our little visit, Mr. Page."

Back in the sunlight, Anson's first reaction was a feeling of relief; he wanted an interview with Garvin Wales and now he had it. Then, however, as he started his rented car and drove off, he began to wonder why Mrs. Wales had gone out of her way in an apparent effort deliberately to arrange what he wanted arranged. Somehow or other it did not seem natural. He was no longer above thinking that she might have some trick up her sleeve, but why should she want to trick him, and what kind of trick could it possibly be? It was not until he had almost reached Mulberry that he thought he understood.

CHAPTER TWENTY-SIX

"It was enough to baffle anyone," he said to Dinah, "but it seems pretty clear to me now. She'll tell her husband what to say and he'll oblige by saying it. She just wanted time to brief him. I'll have my interview, but what good will it do me?"

They were in Dinah's car, on their way to Cassava Beach. Dinah was driving. She wore a short flannel skirt that fell to her knees, a candy-striped shirt cut like a man's, and a pair of scuffed loafers. The tweed coat in which she had first appeared at Mulberry the day before lay on the back seat, along with a picnic basket and a flowered silk scarf. Keeping her eyes on the road, she said, "I don't see why you blame yourself. You will have done everything that could be expected of you."

"Hardly," Anson replied. "I'll only have gone through the motions. John Duncan will be out twenty thousand dollars, and there will always be that shadow on Phil Greene's name. John Duncan can afford the twenty thousand, but Greene was innocent! I could prove it, too, if Wales would only tell what he knows. Damn that woman!"

"She gave you a bad time, didn't she?" Dinah said.

"That makes no difference," Anson said. "I expected a bad time. The important thing is the kind of person she is—there's no hope of dealing with her reasonably. In case it has never occurred to you, Lucy Wales is a first-class neurotic. The way she hates her husband is enough to give you the creeps. All because of the books he has written; all because he has offended her parochial pride!"

"Are you sure that's all?" Dinah said.

Anson thought that Mrs. Wales could not have indicated the cause of her antagonism to her husband more clearly, and it had not entered his mind to seek any further. He said, "What else could it be? You haven't been holding out on me, have you?"

"As if I would," Dinah said. "I've been thinking, though, and I've begun to wonder if it might not be more than her husband's work. Which reminds me that he's not so bad at hating either. I've read most of his books and it runs through them all. He seems to hate everything, even himself. Haven't you ever felt that?"

"No, not quite," Anson said. "Not so far as hating himself is concerned. I know a man in New York, though, a fellow by the name of Julian Tokar, who would more or less agree with you. But you said that you thought it might be more than Wales's work. What else do you think it could be?"

"What about Anna Jones?"

"Well, what about her?"

"Isn't it likely that Lucy may suspect something?"

"I don't think so," Anson said. "Anything is possible, of course, especially in that household, but I feel that if she were in any way suspicious, she would have given herself away. No, I think you're wrong. The way she forced me into admitting that there was a woman involved would indicate that she was stumbling onto something for the first time."

"Yes, I suppose you're right," Dinah said. "What I was thinking was that if there really was some connection between Lucy's husband and this Anna Jones, and if it was kept alive all those years, as you seem to believe—well, had I been in her position I think I would have sensed something. There's bound to have been a tenseness in the air. And if you add that to the way she feels about his books——"

"You have a pretty good explanation of how she got to be the way she is," Anson said. "But what do you say to changing the subject? I've had enough of her for one day."

"All right," Dinah said. "See if I care."

They were not far from Cassava Beach now, and Anson could begin to smell the sea. The woods grew thinner and thinner, the land more unbrokenly flat and sandy, and soon they were passing the line of summer cottages that served as a refuge from the heat and humidity of Pompey's Head. Boarded up and shuttered, they were strung along the far side of the road, facing the beach. They had the rather forlorn look that Anson remembered as being characteristic of them in winter, as if every memory of last summer's voices and laughter had been carried away by the wind and the tide, as if summer would never come again, and a few of the old landmarks were gone.

373

"What happened to the roof garden?" he asked.

"It blew away in that big storm we had nine years ago."

"And the hotel?"

"A fire. It wasn't worth repairing. They tore it down."

"That's where it used to be, isn't it? What's the new building?"

"A kind of combination hamburger stand and juke-joint. The high school kids like it."

Theirs was the only car on the beach. Sometimes during the winter a few of the cottages were occupied on pleasant week ends, but otherwise the beach was nearly always deserted. Dinah stopped the car near a break in the dunes. "Hand me that scarf, will you, Sonny?" she said. "I want to tie up my hair. And I guess I'd better wear my jacket too. Shall we eat now, or would you like to take a walk?"

"Let's walk. I'll get the basket."

"You look so dressed up," she said as they started off. "Why didn't you wear a sweater?"

"I forgot to bring a sweater. I didn't plan on any picnics."

"I'm not used to seeing you so dressed up."

"I don't wonder. Is there too much wind for you?"

"No, I love it this way."

They left the basket in the shelter of one of the highest dunes and started walking down the beach. It was several miles long and made a gentle curve. Beneath the touch of the wind they could feel the warmth of the sun, and the sand was hard and wet from the tide— they left a trail of footprints, walking close together. Dinah slipped her arm through his, and the trail of footprints lengthened. The waves broke softly, curling into foam, and the wind fluttered the ends of her scarf.

"This is nice, isn't it?" she said. "I never get to walk on the beach any more."

Neither did Anson, but it hardly seemed worth mentioning. There were a lot of things he did not get to do any more, and he found it rather strange to be walking on a beach on what would ordinarily have been a working day. For fifteen years the whole emphasis of his life had been on work, one working day after the other, and though it was not altogether the kind of life he would have chosen for himself, it was easy to see how he had fallen into it. It began with Kit Robbins and how much she had hurt him, and if it had not been for Kit he would never have thought of leaving Pompey's Head. He wondered if he should have. He knew all the faults of Pompey's Head and the things it could do to people, and yet, since he knew, he might have been able to work out his own solution; Pompey's Head was the only place he ever belonged, and not once since he left had he felt that he belonged anywhere.

"You really should have a sweater," Dinah said. "I don't want you to catch cold."

"I won't. Don't give it a thought."

And where had it got him, those fifteen years? When he left Pompey's Head he told himself that he wanted success, first because he was anxious to be a credit to himself and to his father, since part of his psychology could be likened to that of a man who regards his father as a failure, and also because he accepted the equation that linked success with security. But how much security did he actually have? He was a partner and should consequently feel confident of his footing, so why, then, did he envision himself being overtaken with disaster if he returned to New York empty-handed? Was not that indicative of his true state of mind? Was he still not back in his cubbyhole, anxious as ever to please Mr. Barlowe and fearful of getting a black mark beside his name?

Dinah tugged at his arm and they turned in the direction from which they had come. The wind was to their backs now, catching the loose strands of her hair and blowing them about her face, and they walked with their shoulders touching. "Look at our footprints," she said. "They seem as though they belong there, don't they, yours and mine all mixed up together? I'll hate when they're washed away."

The hardest thing in the world is to explain impulses, or at just what point a human relation begins to change, especially one between a man and a woman. They were walking on a beach, and he could feel her arm within his and the pressure of her shoulder, but it must have been the footprints more than her nearness. He must have read a kind of intimacy into them, just as she had, and they both must have turned toward each other at exactly the same moment. Her eyes were wide open and she had a waiting, startled look, and the first time he kissed her he thought that he was being unfaithful to Meg. Her lips parted and she gave a soft, muted cry, and when he kissed her a second time he thought of nothing. He let his arms drop when she twisted her mouth away, but then suddenly she pulled him close again.

"Oh, Sonny," she said. "Why ever did you take so long, darling? Why did you?"

He started to say that he didn't know, and then without having to think about it he did know. It was because of their footprints in the sand and because he had never felt more defenseless or exposed. She somehow represented the lost security of the house on Alwyn Street, together with all else that was lost, the whole lost world of Sonny Page, and she promised comfort and release.

"I guess I was sort of carried away, Dinah," he said. "I hope you don't mind."

"Darling, don't say that," she said. "Can't you tell I wanted you to? Don't be sorry."

"I'm not sorry. There wasn't much I could do about it. Only——"

Her eyes were still wide open and she was looking straight at him.

"It had to happen, Sonny. Don't you know how much I've always loved you?"

"You've certainly wasted a lot of time, then," he said. "You should have had more sense."

"Don't say that either," she said. "Just tell me that I'm still your girl."

"Of course you are, Dinah," he said. "I guess you always have been," and although he wasn't sorry, he could begin to worry about the consequences. Certain things had been in balance and now they were not, and he did not want to be in love with Dinah Blackford. He could not help loving her, since in a way he always had, but to be in love with her, easy though that would be, would present more difficulties and complications than he cared to face. He said, "Has it entered your head that all of those cottages may not be empty? It would be a fine thing, wouldn't it, if by some chance or other our friend Margie Rhett happened to be watching? Can't you imagine the field day——"

"Oh, let them talk, Sonny. Who cares?"

Anson understood that it was not because she was indifferent to gossip, or considered himself immune to it, or that she was unaware of the damage it could do, and he thought he knew how she felt. She too wanted comfort and release. They shared the past together, and all that was in the past, and in that moment, because he had always been on her side, taking up for her as they used to say, he represented the same kind of security that she did for him. He said, "I care, Dinah. I can't let you get talked about. You know how people are," and what he was saying, taken with the desire to hold her again, was that under no circumstances must he let himself be in love with her. "Let's eat," he said. "I'm hungry."

They walked to the place where they had left the basket, and

Dinah looked at their footprints again. The sun was past its zenith, and their shadows fell close together upon the sand.

"Oh, Sonny," Dinah said. "If only——" And then she paused an instant. "I wish——"

"At this moment so do I, Dinah," he said. "I wish it more than anything. But you know as well as I do——"

He could have gone on indefinitely, but it was better not to say any more. "Let's not talk about it, Dinah," he said. "It doesn't do any good."

"What does?" she said. "Tell me what does."

She seated herself on the sand and reached for the picnic basket. Bringing out a large thermos bottle and some sandwiches wrapped in waxed paper, she said, "What do you want? There's ham from last night, and peanut butter and jelly. You weren't expecting fried chicken, I hope."

"I wasn't expecting anything."

"You're a wise man," she said. "It's best never to expect anything. Besides, fried chicken is what we're having for supper."

"Supper?"

"It's Thursday, help's night out," she said. "Fried chicken's the easiest. While I'm in the kitchen you can amuse the girls. Cecily's looking forward to it."

Nothing had been said about supper before, and he was not sure that it was a good idea, and yet somehow it was settled. It was as if they both understood that he would be staying for supper all the time.

"You'd rather have ham, I suppose," Dinah said, handing him a sandwich. "Don't just sit there. Make yourself useful and pour the coffee. You'll find some paper cups in the basket."

The heat of the sun reflected itself from the sand, and it was warm and comfortable in the shelter of the dune. They had talked so much the day before, and again during the drive to the beach, that they had nothing to say. They watched the sea; they followed the flight of the gulls; they finished their lunch and stretched out on the sand. Dinah curled herself on her side, and Anson lay on his back beside her.

"Why can't it be like this always?" she said. "This is all I'd ever want."

Once again their thoughts seemed to be running side by side; he too was thinking why couldn't it be like this always and that it was all he'd ever want. He said, "Do you know our trouble?"

"Trouble?" she said. "Us? There's no trouble. I think we're wonderful."

"Be serious."

"I am serious. I keep remembering us in the mirror. I thought we were divinely attractive."

"Be serious, I say. Our trouble is Mulberry."

"Mulberry?"

"Yes," he said. "It's a kind of never-never land, everything about it—the moss in the trees, the way the sun sets, the haze on the river and those fogs we get just before dawn, the magnolias in the moonlight and sometimes not only the magnolias but the mockingbirds as well—it's not real, only there it's real, and so the true reality is somehow lost and nothing seems improbable but the world as it actually is. We had too much of it, I think. It led us astray. It somehow got us to believe that all day you can lie in the sun——"

"With me, I hope."

"With somebody."

"No, not somebody. Me!"

"All right, then. You. But always to lie in the sun, doing nothing, thinking nothing, wanting nothing——"

"Nothing?" she said, looking at him with half-closed eyes and smiling very faintly.

"Oh yes," he said. "There's always that, the man and woman thing. But even that is colored by the unreality, the moonlight-and-magnolia dream—for that's what it is, you know. And life isn't. It can't afford to be. It never could, except down here in this one place for that one short time. It's over now, dead and gone forever, but Mulberry betrays you into thinking that it isn't. And that's our trouble, I repeat. Because of Mulberry, we're sort of anachronisms, you and I. You weren't too far wrong last night when you called us the two little Confederates. But life——"

"Ah, life!" Dinah said. "How it fascinates me!" And then, stretching into a new position, " 'Lift not the painted veil which those who live call life,' " she said. "Or, if that isn't enough, 'Thus with the year the seasons return, but not to me returns day, or the sweet approach of morn and evening, or sight of vernal bloom, or summer's rose, or flock, or herds, or human face divine.' Shall I recite some more?"

"No, not now. Besides, what does that have to do with it?"

"More than you know, my good man," she said. "Someday, when I have time, I'll take you off to some quiet corner and explain."

"Do, by all means. But shouldn't we think about going?"

"No, not yet. Don't spoil it by talking about going." She scooped up a handful of sand and let it drift through her fingers. "May I ask you something, Sonny?"

"Sure, of course."

She scooped up another handful of sand and watched the grains as they fell. "Why did you leave Old Pompey? Why did you go away?"

At some time or other it was bound to come up, the same inevitable question, and still he did not know how to answer it, even though she was the one person in all the world with whom he was most at home.

"Was it Kit Robbins?" she said. "Was she the reason?"

"Yes, Dinah, in a way."

She began tracing a pattern in the sand and continued tracing as she spoke, making a series of spirals. "Didn't you know that she'd never be right for you? And didn't you know that I, if you'd only given me half a chance——"

"No, Dinah," he said. "You're letting Mulberry run away with you again, don't you see? It was your being the Lady of the Lake, and Juliet, and Isolde, and all those other creatures it pleased you to think you were. It was the time when Wyeth and I had the Sylvania Archers in the basement, and nothing would do but that you must tie a scarf on my arm. It was all that daydreaming of yours. You really didn't——"

"Oh shut up!" Dinah said, sitting up abruptly. "You make me want to hit you! You were stupid then and you're stupid still! And maybe you're right. Maybe I was a fool! But fool or not, child or not, I would have been better for you, then and now and always——"

She jumped to her feet and stood staring at the sea with a set, still look, and her eyes were wet and shining. He rose and stood beside her, and despite how impossible it was, in that moment he was able to believe what she said—she would have been good for him; there was a sympathy and a closeness that he had never found in anyone else; if any two people belonged together, they did.

"All right," he said, surprised at the roughness in his voice. "Have it your own way! Perhaps if I hadn't gone to New York——"

"Why did you?" she said. "I'd have made you be in love with me, I know I would have! And why did you have to come back? I was doing all right until I saw you again. Damn you, damn you! I hate you for coming back!"

"Don't, Dinah, please," he said. "Can't you see how difficult we're making it? I know you believe what you say, and right now I can believe it too, crazy though it seems. Do you think that I don't love you? Don't you know that in my own way I always have?"

"Why didn't you wait for me then?" she said. "Why did you run away?"

"It's too hard to explain, Dinah," he said. "We're talking about then, not now. I'm different and so are you. Things have happened to both of us, all those years. Then I was hurt and wanted to hide. I didn't want anyone to know how hurt I really was."

"Fool!" Dinah said. "Didn't you think I knew?"

"No, I didn't," Anson said. "And I can't truly say that, had I known, it would have made any difference. For that was the then of it, not now. Now I know I love you and I'm trying to keep myself from being in love with you. And I still think that if it hadn't been for Mulberry——"

"Mulberry, Mulberry!" she cried, turning on him. "Let me tell you about Mulberry, you think you know so much! You've been wondering why I married Mico, haven't you? It's been in the back of your mind all the time. Well, I'll tell you! 'Swear, fool, or starve, for the dilemma's even; a tradesman thou! and hope to go to heaven'—and someday I'll explain what *that* means, though I hope to God that I never see you again until you're so wrinkled and horrible that I can laugh myself sick over ever having been in love with you!"

"Look, Dinah, so far as you and Mico are concerned, I'd rather——"

"No, you wouldn't!" she said. "You *wouldn't* rather! You're as bad as the rest of them. Why did she do it? What did she see in him? Did she marry him for his money? All right then, I'll tell you! That too was because of Mulberry! We were living like trash on Upton Street and Papa had made a fool of himself again and the whole town was smirking behind our backs, and I thought I wanted Mulberry more than I wanted anything—it's not a house, a place; it's me; it's in my bones; I've always loved it and I always will! And Mico kept asking me to marry him. He'd been asking me for years and so finally I did. I was tired of living like trash and I wanted to be back where I belonged."

Anson took her by the shoulder, saying, "Dinah, Dinah," but she pulled herself away. She said, "And him, poor man! I wasn't in love with him, but I respected him for what he had done. I admired him, too, and I thought that I might be able to love him in time. And I tried, Sonny, God knows I tried! But almost immediately I found out

380

that he neither knows how to give love nor take it. In that respect he isn't there; he doesn't even exist. It's something that the Channel did to him, his fighting to get out of it and the way he thinks he has to get back at everybody, not himself to knuckle under but to make the others knuckle to him. And that much he's done; that much he can show. But me, his wife——" And suddenly, dropping her head, she began to weep.

"Don't do this to yourself, Dinah," Anson said. "I was a fool. I never should have——"

"What did you do?" Dinah said, the tears rolling down her cheeks. "Do you think you made me want to talk to you, or that it's because you kissed me? If I can't tell you, who can I tell? Wyeth? Papa? Them? But it wasn't only that Mico didn't want or care for love—I have to be fair. It was me too! I shocked him. I was a lady, and a lady is supposed to be different from those girls on Liberty Street. A lady shouldn't want to do it that bad! He thought he'd married a lady, and when he found out that what he'd got was someone——"

"I absolutely insist that you stop!" Anson said. "I won't have you doing this to yourself!"

"And then it was awful," Dinah went on unheedingly. "He felt that if I was like that when I married him, I must have been like that before. And done something about it! Spent my whole life doing something about it, dear God! I had to be rotten through and through, like all the rest of what he calls us broken-down snobs; I just *had* to! Everything got thrown up to me, the boys I used to go with, the men in the bank, Wyeth's friends when he was selling ice cream, and you too—oh yes, you above all! I think he would have divorced me long ago if he wasn't afraid of divorce and if it wasn't for the girls—that I can't take from him; he is proud of the girls— and because he is obsessed with wanting to get into the Light Infantry Club. He won't feel that he's completely out of the Channel until he belongs. And without me he can't; he needs Percy Wyeth and all the rest of them. And meanwhile, as my reward, I have Mulberry. So I got what I wanted, you see. Aren't I the lucky one! And aren't you proud of me! 'Swear, fool, or starve, for the——' "

She choked up with sobs and began crying so hard that Anson again had to take her by the shoulder. He could feel her trembling, and some of her trembling communicated itself to him. He said, "Dinah! You've got to stop! Look at me."

"No, I won't," she said. "Let me go, Sonny. Oh, why must you see me like this? I didn't want it to happen, it's the last thing I wanted. Please let me go."

"No, not yet, not until you're yourself," he said, putting his arms around her, and when he spoke again he had to fight down a catch in his voice. "Enough is enough, Dinah. I can't see you like this. I love you too much."

"Because you're sorry for me? Because you pity me?"

"Don't be a fool! Because I love you."

He lifted her face, and for a moment she tried to turn it away, and then, with a stifled cry that was half a whimper and half a moan, she brought her tear-stained lips up and around to his. The sea faded, the sky faded, and when finally he was able to speak again, he said, as so often he had said before, though never with this kind of huskiness, "Come on, now. I'm taking you home," and then, hours later, after supper when the children were asleep and the house was still, the huskiness became almost an impediment to his speech. "Dinah, baby," he said, and she said, "Oh, darling, I love you so much," and led him to his old room. The brass bedstead in which he had slept was still there, and the dresser with the scars he had made, and when at last he possessed her, in a wholeness of possession he had never known or dreamed, past and present came thundering together and he was master and owner of it all. He seemed to have been released of a burden under which he had unknowingly labored all his life, and somewhere, as again she wept, burying her face in his shoulder with the sheet half drawn across her narrow loins, and her hair dark as the shadows the moonlight made—somewhere, because it was Mulberry, where nothing was ever altogether real, not even this, a mockingbird sang either in irony or celebration beyond the window. "That damned bird," Anson thought. "That damned impossible bird." He did not want to be in love with Dinah Blackford, but now, hopelessly, he knew he was.

CHAPTER TWENTY-SEVEN

Anson awoke next morning shortly after dawn. He had not gone to bed until nearly two o'clock and had slept badly. He tossed first in one position, then another, and finally decided to get up. Sleep was plainly impossible, and since he had eaten practically nothing at Mulberry the night before, he felt hungry. The dining room of the Marlborough was not yet open, but he knew that there were several all-night cafés near the station on Lafayette Street, and the walk would do him good. He had to do something to clear his mind. This was the day when he was going to see Garvin Wales, and he could not think only of Dinah Blackford. Going into the bathroom, he stripped off his pajamas and turned on the shower, letting the cold water beat down upon him until he was numb all over.

Half an hour later, when he stepped from the elevator into the lobby and walked past the desk, the young night clerk who had admitted him into the hotel gave him a cheery good morning.

"You are an early riser, aren't you, Mr. Page?" he said. "You slept well, I hope."

"Yes, thanks. There's nothing in my box, is there?"

"Not yet, sir. The morning mail doesn't get here till half-past eight. Are you enjoying your visit? Have you seen all our points of interest?"

"Yes, I have, but I shan't be here much longer. I'll be checking out tonight, as a matter of fact. Does the Special still leave at nine?"

Without having given it any thought beforehand, he knew it was time to leave. By that evening he would have had his interview with Garvin Wales, and there was no use in hanging around any longer. To be in the same place as Dinah and not be able to see her was more than he could bear.

"Yes, sir," the clerk said. "The Special pulls out at nine o'clock exactly. I'm sorry that you're not staying longer with us, Mr. Page."

"So am I," Anson said. "I would like to be staying indefinitely. Something's come up, though, and I have to get back to New York."

"Not an emergency, I hope."

"No, not an emergency. Just one of those things."

A pile of the Morning News lay on the counter, and Anson bought a copy. The clerk said, "There's a real piece of news this morning. It seems like we may get that cellophane factory. Old Pompey is looking up."

"Yes," Anson said, "apparently it is."

The chill of morning hung low on the earth, and when he began walking toward Lafayette Street he was glad he had worn his topcoat. The streets near the Marlborough were gray and deserted, and though it was too early to tell what kind of day it would be, it looked as though the spell of sunny weather may have ended. Turning off Independence Street, on which the Marlborough stood, he walked down a narrower thoroughfare, known as Prince Street, which, twelve blocks away, came out before the railroad station; he had decided that while he was about it he might as well buy his pullman space back to New York.

Prince Street had no connection with royalty. It had been christened in honor of a local educator, Dr. Themistocles Prince, who in 1789 opened the first institution of higher learning in the state. This was known as the Pompey's Head Classical Academy. Housed originally in a one-story frame dwelling, the academy moved into a new and larger building in 1826, at which time it became known as the Classical College of Pompey's Head. Its new headquarters, a gray-painted brick building of early Republican architecture, stood on the present Prince Street, two blocks from the site now occupied by the Lafayette Street station. The Classical College continued in existence until the Civil War, when, like so many other institutions of a similar nature, it was forced to close its doors. The fine brick building thereafter fell on hard times—it became a rooming house for river boatmen, a different kind of house, a storage place for cotton and other freight, and finally, toward the turn of the century, when its interior walls were ripped out, a livery stable.

During Anson's boyhood it stood unoccupied, an empty shell of a building in a part of town that had gradually turned into a Negro neighborhood. Much to the regret of those who thought that it should have been purchased by the Historical Association and restored, the structure was torn down and the site turned into a parking lot. Now, however, as Anson saw when he drew near, the parking lot had been supplanted by a one-story wooden building, not much more than an enclosed shed, that looked as though it too should be pulled down, streaked and grimy with the soot that had drifted over from the railroad tracks. Though it was too early in the morning for the building to be open, a crude sign identified it as the Jubilee Farmers Market.

Had it not been for the *News*, Anson was not sure that he would have given it another thought. After buying his pullman ticket, he went into a café on Lafayette Street directly across from the station. He was the only customer. He sat on a stool at the counter, ordered some ham and eggs, and looked through the *News* while the counterman busied himself at the stove. The counterman was a thin rack of a man with a long neck and a large adam's apple that moved up and down. One of the headlines on the front page of the *News* said that a multimillion-dollar cellophane factory was being sought for Pompey's Head, and according to another, two people were dead and two were injured in an automobile accident not far from Double Crossing. The weather was to be partially cloudy with probable rain that night, the State Jaycees were in convention, the Seventh Annual Show of the Pompey's Head Camellia Society opened today in the old armory on River Street, Miss Jacqueline McDowell had been the guest of honor at a miscellaneous shower, and a compromise farm bill had been approved in Washington. There were the usual deaths and funerals, in the notices of which there appeared many of the familiar Marlborough County names, the well-known and the obscure, Cone, Drew, Harris, Peeples, Pettigru, and Watts, and Mrs. Zelma Bryan, of Crystal City, had reached her one hundred and third birthday. A complete line of dancing taps could be had at Wilson's, the latest summer dresses had arrived at the A. B. Cornish Department Store, *All about Eve* was playing at the Bijou, and on the next-to-last page, beneath the crossword puzzle, the Jubilee Farmers Market stood ready to buy, barter, or sell.

Farmers Market, Farmers Market, Anson's mind said, and then, in a way that he would never be able to explain, it found the connection for which subconsciously it must have been groping. The counterman brought first Anson's coffee and then his breakfast, placing the plate on the counter before him, and for a moment Anson stared at it blankly. The first check endorsed by Anna Jones had been cashed at the Farmers Market in Ransome, Alabama, Cleon Pyle, prop., and here was the Jubilee Farmers Market where the old Classical College used to be, and if anyone other than a colored person ever traded regularly at a farmers market in any Southern town with a sizable Negro population, he had yet to hear of it. The trail that could be followed by the checks, Ransome to Detroit to St. Louis, now led to a startling conclusion. For was not Detroit one of the terminals of the new underground? Together with Chicago, was it not the place where each year hundreds of light-skinned persons with a modicum of colored blood crossed over the line—"passed," as they said? And once crossed over, hazardously established as whites, did they then not drift off to some part of the country as far from their original homes as they could get: could not St. Louis, nearly half a continent away from Ransome, Alabama, be seen as a place of ultimate refuge?

It could not be true and yet it was true. It stood written out in the black letters that spelled the name of the Jubilee Farmers Market. To some degree Anna Jones had been a colored person, and, no doubt of it now, she stood in some intimate relation to Garvin Wales. Furthermore, if she was seventy-four when she died in 1940, she had to be either fifty-three or fifty-four, depending on the exact date of her birthday, when she received the first check from Phillip Greene in 1919, and Wales, now in his sixties, would have been in his twenties. Greene was out of it completely. It was extremely doubtful if Greene, in 1919, at a time when he too was in his twenties, only a few years out of rural New England, had known a colored woman during the entire course of his life.

"You want toast, sir?"

"What?"

"I asked if you wanted toast?"

"No, never mind."

Unable to eat the night before at Mulberry, Anson was now unable to eat again. He had to force himself to swallow, washing down each mouthful. Paying his check, he walked back to the Marlborough as fast as he could. When he reached his room he opened his briefcase, brought out his notes, and studied them carefully. Though he had no proof of anything, he knew he could not be wrong. Mr. Barlowe would say that he was rushing his fences, but this was one time when he could forget all about Mr. Barlowe. This was no guess, no surmise, no hunch. He knew. It was the one clear gain he could show for having grown up in Pompey's Head. There was much that he still did not know, but with the one piece supplied by the Jubilee Farmers Market, the puzzle was beginning to take shape.

The phone rang, causing him to jump. It was Dinah, calling from Mulberry.

"Hello, Sonny. I didn't wake you, did I?"

"No, how are you?"

"I'm all right, I guess. I had to call you. I haven't stopped thinking, not for a minute."

"Neither have I. I was going to call you a little later on."

"I knew you would, but I couldn't wait. Have you had breakfast?"

"Yes, sort of. And you?"

"No, just a cup of coffee. I was hoping that we could have breakfast together. Don't say it's impossible. I know it is. I know how impossible everything is. Are you sure that you're all right?"

"I'm as all right as you are, put it that way. There were no reverberations from the servants, were there?"

"No, they didn't get back until long after you left. It seemed long, anyway. It's all beginning to seem so forever long. Will you come to lunch today, after you've been to Tamburlaine?"

"No, I won't. It wouldn't only be lunch, and you know it. If I should see you today, alone——"

"Oh, Sonny, why——"

"Let's not ask why, Dinah. It's too late for whys."

"So you won't come for lunch?"

"I want to, you know that, but——"

"Or supper either?"

"No, not supper either."

"We'll be good."

"Yes, I can see us being good. Besides, who wants to be good? I don't. Do you?"

"You know what I want. But does that mean that tomorrow is out too? What about that oyster roast at the Fowlers' tomorrow night? Shall I accept for both of us?"

"I won't be here tomorrow, Dinah. I'm leaving on the Special tonight."

There was a long pause. Outside the window a few blue patches began to show in the sky, the sun shining weakly, and her voice was different when she spoke.

"Tonight? You're leaving tonight?"

"Yes, it's best that I should. If I stay it's going to be impossible for me not to want to see you alone, and if I do——"

"But am I not going to see you at all before you go? I have to tell you good-by like this, over the phone?"

"No, of course not. How could I let you?"

"What, then?"

"Why not have supper with me here at the hotel?"

There was another pause, and again her voice was different.

"All right, if that's the way it has to be. I can drive you to the train. Do you need me to help you pack?"

"No, but come early. Around seven. That will give us time for a drink. Don't be late."

"I won't. Does the Special still leave at nine?"

"Yes, so if you get here at seven——"

"I'll be there a little before. Meet me in the lobby?"

"Yes, where you were sitting the other day."

"Good luck on Tamburlaine."

"What?"

"I said good luck on Tamburlaine."

"Oh, that. Thank you. See you at seven. Be beautiful."

"I'll try. Take care of yourself."

"You too."

He hung up, still hearing the sound of her voice, and there was a feeling of emptiness in the room. He told himself that he'd best start getting used to it, this feeling of emptiness, since it was going to be with him for a long time. Lighting a cigarette, he went to the window and looked at the sky. The patches of blue had widened and the sun was gaining in warmth. It looked as though it would come up to Mrs. Wales's definition of a nice day, and that he could expect to find Wales sitting on the beach before the teahouse.

It was not yet eight o'clock, however, much too early to start for Tamburlaine, and he had to do something to get rid of his restlessness. Beneath his excitement he knew he was tired, dead tired, but he could not stay caged in his room, tormenting himself over Dinah. He went out into the streets again, walked down Bay Street as far as the river, stopped in a diner near the waterfront for another cup of coffee, took a roundabout route back to the center of town, and eventually, shortly after nine o'clock, found himself before the Pompey's Head Historical Museum on Montague Square.

The statue of General Carvell stood in the square, subject as always to the discourtesy of pigeons, and the doors of the museum were open. Entering the building, which at this hour of morning had not yet completely rid itself of the stillness of night, he nodded to the solitary attendant, a small, white-haired woman who sat at a desk near the front door and looked at him curiously, and then, seeing that nothing had changed, that the likeness of George Washington woven in silk still hung framed on the wall beneath the storm flag from the Confederate cruiser *Shenandoah*, he was again back where it all had started. He remembered the day when the eighth grade visited the museum with Miss Harrington, and how he was jealous because Ian Garrick had been paired off with Midge Higgins, and he stopped for several minutes before the glass case where the diary of Sir Samuel Alwyn was displayed. He wandered idly through the other rooms, and as he was leaving, going past the attendant's desk, she asked him if he wouldn't like to sign the visitors' book. He said yes, he would, and as he inscribed his name in the register with the pen she handed him, noticing that the last visitor had been a Mrs. Gracie Foxx from Milledgeville, Georgia, he thought that it was something like dropping a coin in a box and then lighting a wax taper, the way they did in churches of the Roman faith. He returned the pen and left the building. He had now done everything he should have done, and there remained only Garvin Wales.

Like practically everyone else involved with publishing, Anson had often seen photographs of Garvin Wales. The most famous of these, which at the height of his reputation had frequently appeared in the literary publications, was taken when Wales was living in Jamaica. It was a head-and-shoulders portrait, and he was looking almost straight into the camera. Instead of wearing one of those flamboyant sports shirts that are more or less essential to the well-dressed man in a place like Ochos Rios or Montego Bay, he was as conservatively attired as a Manhattan banker. Though his appearance could not have been more correct, it seemed to Anson, possibly because he had found it advisable in the line of duty to reread a few of Wales's books, that the dark suit and decorous four-in-hand went a little oddly, not only with the man as revealed by his work, but with the outer, visible man himself.

A famous motion-picture actress, imported from Hollywood to appear on Broadway in the dramatization of Wales's *The Night Watch*, once described him in an interview in the New York *Times* as being treacherously handsome. From Wales's picture, Anson could guess what was being hinted at. The long, narrow face gave the impression of a kind of aggressive masculinity, the bold chin, the high cheekbones, the rather heavy nose bearing the indentation of a slight break, and there might be suspected a latent brutality, not vicious, more on the order of a willingness to slug it out in a barroom brawl, were it not for the suggestion of extreme sensitiveness imparted by the dark, intense eyes.

But no photograph of a well-known person stands alone. It is always given a further dimension by his personal legend. Driving to Tamburlaine and remembering Wales's likeness, Anson saw a ragged figure hunting for gold in the jungles of Nicaragua, a sweaty seaman chipping rust from the decks of a dirty tramp steamer, a youthful warrior in puttees standing before an old Wright Whirlwind, and, in the years that followed, a handsome, confident man, secure in his reputation and commanding the best that the world had to offer.

For an instant, then, before his mind could clear itself of its preconceptions, he could not believe that the huddled figure who sat in one of two striped canvas chairs that stood on the beach of Tamburlaine Island was the man he had come to see—so wasted he was, so gaunt, so apparently sunk in lassitude and dejection, that the tone of Anson's voice was that of one who enters a hospital room where the patient lies dangerously ill.

"Mr. Wales," he said. "Mr. Wales."

Whether or not Wales had heard him approach, he could not say. After he left his car parked before the house, his footsteps were muffled in the sand. And even now the huddled figure did not move. Wales sat facing the sea with a steamer rug thrown across his knees. Bareheaded, his sparse white hair thin on the crown, he wore a yellow flannel shirt, a tan cashmere sweater, gabardine trousers, and a pair of heavy shoes. Immediately behind him was the small teahouse which he and Mrs. Wales had caused to be built, standing at the edge of the pines. It was a one-room structure with glass windows on all sides.

"Mr. Wales," Anson repeated. "Mr. Wales."

For another moment, perhaps longer, Wales sat motionless and then turned his head. His eyes groped blindly, still with the intense look that stared from his photographs, and Anson saw that the slow ravages of optic atrophy had left them unmarred. Wales appeared to have some difficulty in detecting the direction from which Anson's voice came. He moved the focus of his eyes past the place where Anson was standing, and then turned his head in the opposite direction.

"Mr. Wales," Anson said, "my name is Anson Page. John Duncan sent me down to see you."

"I know who you are," Wales said. "My wife told me all about you. I have nothing to say," and he turned back to the sea.

"Nothing?" Anson said, studying him carefully.

"No, nothing," Wales said. "You're wasting your time. Why don't you pay my wife her twenty thousand dollars and go?"

Standing where he was, Anson could look past Wales and see the place off the point where he and Wyeth Blackford used to go fishing. The channel bass always seemed readier to bite on a day of sunshine and cloud like this, in the windless calm that so often preceded a rain, and he would not have been surprised to see Wyeth come round the point at that moment, bending over the oars of the old rowboat they used to keep hidden on the south side of the island.

"All right, Mr. Wales," Anson said. "I'll go. But first let me ask you just one question. Is it actually your wife's twenty thousand dollars, or yours? Did Phil Greene really steal that money? Are you saying that he did?"

Wales groped with his eyes again. "Why did you come here?" he said. "Why did you talk to my wife?"

"I had to," Anson said. "She would not have let me see you otherwise. But what about it, Mr. Wales? You haven't answered my question. Did Phil Greene embezzle the money? Say that he did and I'll leave at once."

Wales did not answer. The sun faded for a moment, leaving a dark patch on the sea, and then shone brightly again. Anson said, "I think you know better, Mr. Wales. I think we both know better. I had hoped not to have to appeal to you in the name of friendship——"

"I have nothing to say," Wales said. "You've talked to my wife and that's enough. Good day."

Anson looked past him at the water off the point. On a day like this, still as it was, you might even be able to pick up a few sheepshead, even though they did not often take a hook in open water, preferring to feed around the barnacled pilings of old piers and wharves. Glancing back to Wales, he saw that he had partially clenched his fingers. It was one of those telltale signs that you looked for if you were a trial lawyer, and he was beginning to understand how a trial lawyer felt.

"Who was Anna Jones, Mr. Wales?" he said.

"In Christ's name!" Wales cried, turning swiftly. "Don't mention that name aloud! My wife may be listening. Are you sure she isn't hiding somewhere back in those trees?"

Anson looked toward the pines. Seeing nothing but the shadows of the grove, he said, "No, Mr. Wales, your wife isn't listening. The butler said she was out. I called first at the house, just to let her know that I'd arrived."

"Why did you tell her that there was a woman involved?" Wales said. "Didn't you know that she'd try to get it out of me, putting me through hell?" His eyes stared emptily, and then, in a quieter tone, "How did you find out about Anna Jones?" he asked. "Who told you?"

"Nobody told me, Mr. Wales," Anson said. "I learned of her through those checks that Phil Greene sent. He kept them all."

"And that's all you know?" Wales said. "Nothing else?"

Anson had always known that there were some men in the law who gained a sense of power by breaking a witness over the wheel, and never had it seemed more distasteful. Here was another witness who would have to be broken, put on the rack until every last nerve gave way, and he wished it were someone else who had this hateful duty.

"No, Mr. Wales," he said calmly, "that's only the beginning of what we know. We know, for instance, that when Anna Jones received her first check from Greene she was living in a place called Ransome, Alabama. That was in 1919. We know that she lived in Ransome for sometime thereafter and then moved to Detroit. She remained in Detroit for four years. Then in 1929 she left Detroit and moved to St. Louis. We know that she lived in St. Louis until she died. That was ten years ago, in 1940."

Wales sat very still. "What else?"

Knowing that the moment of crisis had finally arrived, and that on this one turn of the screw depended either the breaking of the man before him or his own downfall, Anson had to steel himself. He said, "This is what else, Mr. Wales. We know that Anna Jones was a colored person, so light of skin that she might easily pass for white," and the way Wales went rigid told him that he had not been mistaken. He had expected a sense of triumph, a feeling of having overcome innumerable odds, and not once had he imagined that he would be ashamed. However, despite his shame, he must go on. The victim had to be kept on the rack until he broke completely.

"It wasn't Phil Greene who helped support Anna Jones, Mr. Wales," he said. "It was you. Phil was doing you a favor, perhaps the greatest favor he ever did. Why don't you admit it? Why do you want to brand him as a thief?"

Wales did not answer and Anson forced himself to continue. He said, "Think of what will happen if we have to bring this to court, Mr. Wales. Everything will have to come out, you know. Your relation to Anna Jones is bound to be established. It will have to be shown that she was someone whose identity you wanted to hide, and that Phil Greene, whose only motive was to help you, to whom you went for help——"

"Why don't you come out with it!" Wales cried hoarsely. "Why don't you say that you've found out that Anna Jones was my mother!"

Sightless though Wales's eyes were, Anson had to look away. A choked, broken sound came from Wales's lips, and then, as Anson noticed that the sun had gone under again, nothing was worth it any longer—not John Duncan's twenty thousand dollars, not Phil Greene's reputation, not the severest damage that failure might do to himself. "I beg your pardon, Mr. Wales," he said. "I humbly beg your pardon," and something in his voice caused Wales to lift his face.

"So you didn't know," Wales said. "You suspected, but you didn't know. It was just a courtroom trick," and he sat motionless again, the tide curling softly on the sand.

"I'll be leaving now, Mr. Wales," Anson said. "I will tell them in New York that you had nothing to do with those withdrawals, and beyond that I'll say nothing."

"No, wait," Wales said, holding out a hand. "You understand why I can't do anything to help Phil, don't you?"

"Yes sir, Mr. Wales," Anson said. "I understand."

"It's my wife," Wales said. "I can't explain about those withdrawals without explaining about Anna Jones. And if ever my wife found out——"

Anson did not want to listen to any confession. He said, "I think, Mr. Wales, if you don't mind——"

"You have the right to know about Phil," Wales said. "Sit down. Isn't there another chair here?" He waited for Anson to settle himself, and then said, "I did go to him for help, as you suspected. I had no one else to go to. It was a good many years ago, in 1919. Were you alive then? I can't see to tell."

"Yes sir," Anson said, "I was alive then. I'd been alive for over nine years."

"I'd been alive for some years longer," Wales said. "I was thirty-one. I'd published my first book, a thing called Cenotaph, and made my first money. Enough money to marry Lucy. She was a Devereaux, you know. Her people have always been prominent in this part of the country. They came over with the first Huguenots."

"Yes sir," Anson said, "I know about the Devereauxs," thinking it strange that Wales should pause to emphasize his wife's family background. "This is my part of the country too."

"So I understand," Wales said. "But that's how things stood with me in 1919. I thought I had everything I wanted. I had finally climbed out of that mudsill world I had been born into—white trash you'd call it, being who you are; my father was a cropper—and I knew that I could be a writer. That, though, was due to Phil. *Cenotaph* was the turning point. Had it not been for Phil it wouldn't have been published, and had it not been published I was ready to forget the itch of being a writer and take to a pick and shovel if I had to."

His thoughts turned inward for a time, and Anson watched the incoming tide—a tiny sea creature raced across the sand, housed in a spotted shell; it burrowed frantically and disappeared. Wales said, "What's happened to my conscience, you ask? Owing so much to Phil, why don't I offer to help him? I have no conscience. I never did have much—it's a luxury, a conscience, and in the flour-sack world that I was born in you learn to do without—and what little I had I lost. Even then I couldn't have been much good." He stopped for a moment and then went on. "I stopped having a conscience when I found out that Anna Jones was my mother. I grew up without a mother, not knowing I ever had one. She dropped me in a corn patch and ran. I mean that. I wasn't born, I was dropped. Dung, you might say. And as soon as she was able to run, she did—not that I blame her for that, God knows. My father was a brute. I was only eight years old when he died, but I would have murdered had I dared. I had one thing that was mine, a bantam rooster, and one Saturday night, drunk, he wrung its neck—that sort of thing doesn't happen in your world, does it? You people never know. And by Christ I hated you for not knowing! I wanted to rub your faces in that dirt and filth, just as mine was!"

Again he paused and then, "So for running away I couldn't blame her," he said. "I tried it myself when I was seven. But then, later, after I came back from the war and *Cenotaph* was published, I began to forget. The things that had happened to me began to seem as though they must have happened to someone else. That wasn't me, that white-trash kid shunted from one cabin to another, four and five to the room—I was the author of *Cenotaph* and the husband of Lucy Devereaux. I was a war hero. They'd even given me a medal. So I tried to forget and gradually I did. If you want to forget something bad enough, there is always a way. And then I found out about Anna

Jones. How? The itch, the writing of another book. Do you know Demopolis, Alabama?"

"No, I've never been there."

"I had only one subject," Wales said. "The South. I had the war, too, every man who's been in a war has that, and I also had that time I was in Central America and my two voyages as a seaman. But my real subject was the South. To follow up *Cenotaph*, I wanted to write a book that would be laid in the past. Not a historical novel, such as Lucy wanted me to do, but a book that would be something on the order of *The Red Badge of Courage*. Something, I say. One man and one act and the psychological consequences of that act. I must have had Conrad's *Lord Jim* in mind too. And it seemed better to place it in the past. What I wanted to do was to take a man from one of the older civilizations, a man of some cultivation, and set him down in the wilderness of the new world. Then let there be that one act— treachery, I had in mind. What happens to him then?"

A light breeze sprang up, rippling the surface of the sea, and the tide rolled in a little stronger. Wales said, "I talked it over with Phil Greene, and he told me about those Napoleonic exiles who arrived in Alabama in the early 1800s—Demopolis was the town they eventually settled. They called themselves the Association of French Emigrants for the Cultivation of the Vine and Olive. I grew up about two hundred miles north of Demopolis, if what I went through could be called growing up, but I didn't know anything about those French people until Phil put me onto them. You know how interested he was in American history, don't you?"

"Yes sir," Anson said, "I do," thinking of his first lunch with Phil Greene and how Greene had insisted on his telling the story of Mary, Chief Tupichichi's daughter.

Wales said, "I hadn't been back to Alabama since long before the war. When I left I told myself that I never wanted to see it again, it or any other part of the South, but I was wrong. I missed it. I couldn't believe it at first, but I did. Before I started writing that book I had in mind, I wanted to see it again. Lucy was hoping to get a part in a new play and didn't want to leave New York. I went to Demopolis alone."

He fell into a spell of silence that so prolonged itself that Anson thought he had been forgotten. Then, "By that time I was Garvin Wales, remember," Wales said. "I'd had my pictures in the paper and I'd married Lucy. Our wedding was even in the newsreels. I was somebody, a celebrity, a man of letters. And how I wallowed in it! If a reporter from the Demopolis paper hadn't called up for an interview, I probably would have gone to the office and demanded one. When you have the itch as bad as I had it then, there's never an end to scratching. Art, literature!" He gave a dry, scornful laugh. "What a joke! The itch, ringworm, Indian fire, that's what it is! When will the stupid bastards ever learn?"

The soft noises of the tide lapped into the ensuing silence, and Anson, looking at Wales, said to himself, "The truth is that this man doesn't believe in anything. Perhaps he once did, but not for a long time. It's been a kind of vengeful nihilism he's lived for. And Dinah was right; he does hate himself. Julian Tokar was right too. It's not his wife who destroyed him. The real destruction came from within."

"So I got what I wanted," Wales said. "They put my picture on the front page. Garvin Wales, noted Alabama author. Not trash any more, you will notice. Garvin Wales, noted author, son of Robinson Wales, member of a distinguished north Alabama family. And why not? Aren't they all distinguished families, out of the mudsill? Don't they all have pedigrees and ancestors, every last damned member of the boardinghouse aristocracy? Don't they all trace their lineage back to Mary Stuart or the first Duke of Norfolk or even Eric the Red? And wasn't my father fifth cousin to the biggest landowner in Fayette County? Wasn't he? And hadn't I married a Devereaux? Should I have gone out of my way to claim I was trash?"

Anson found himself shaking his head. "No," he thought, "not you too! I can understand about the others, but that you, the angry naysayer, that you should be caught up in it too," and then Wales was speaking again.

"You must have guessed the rest of it by now," Wales said. "A woman called at the hotel in Demopolis where I was staying and asked to see me privately. An octoroon. I knew it the moment I laid eyes on her. Lighter than most, even lighter than I, but still I could tell. And my mother! Oh, she was my mother all right. She was clever enough to have brought along proof. She showed me her marriage certificate and she knew the birthmark I have in the small of my back. I'd got out, I'd managed to climb from that white-trash mud, and now I was back in it again! But worse! Now I was nigger into the bargain, trash and nigger as well!" He turned to Anson and said, "You try being nigger someday. Find out what it does to you. See what happens to your conscience," and a look of torment twisted his face. "I was in love with Lucy," he said. "I had just married her and I was proud of her. I didn't want to lose her, as I knew I would.

Oh, it's easy for you to stand there and condemn a man! It's easy to say that he shouldn't deny his own mother! But what about her? Did she think twice about denying me? And what did she want except money? What else did she ever want? Her husband was sick, her new husband, Rufus Jones, a black man—was I to go back and tell Lucy that I had a black man for a stepfather, dear Christ!"

"I think I'd better leave, Mr. Wales," Anson said. "These things that you're telling me——"

"If it hadn't been for him I would have made her leave that part of the country right away," Wales went on. "She was light enough to pass for white anywhere, even in the South, and I wouldn't have gone through the agony of waiting every minute to hear that someone had discovered who she was. It wasn't until Jones died that she went to Detroit. I planned it all out with her before I left. I didn't dare go anywhere near Ransome, which is about fifteen miles out in the country from Demopolis, and I didn't want to run the risk of having her come back to the hotel. I gave her the money I had in my pocket and told her to meet me the next night in the bus station. She was afraid of going into the white waiting room, but I made her do it. I told her that I would send her some money regularly, two or three times a year, and that she mustn't ever come near me. I told her that if ever she did the money would stop. I said that in return for the money she would have to go to Chicago or Detroit and cross over the line. In the back of my head I had the idea that if ever it was learned who she was, at least I could say she was white. I told her that I couldn't send her the money myself, lest somehow it give me away, but that I had a friend I could trust, a man in New York, and that she would get the money through him. I told her——"

The sun went under again, disappearing behind a wall of cloud, and Anson no longer listened. He at last knew the whole of it, and he needn't be told how Phillip Greene had consented to help. There was a smell of rain in the wind, and now that the sun was gone the sea looked cold and gray. Nobody, he thought, ever completely escaped. His father had called it Shintoism, which was as good a word as any, and what it offered was a kind of ready-made identity, something that could be slipped into as one slipped into a coat. Did it not explain them all? For what would Olive Garrick be without General Carvell, or Gaby Carpenter without that Indian girl Mary to whose comfort and shelter she finally returned, or Dinah Blackford without Mulberry? Yes, Dinah too—much as he loved her, he had to see her plain. "I was tired of living like trash on Upton Street," she had said, "and I wanted to be back where I belonged." And all the others: did it not explain them as well?—Mr. Pettibone who wouldn't have Clifford sweep dust into his face, Kit Robbins who wanted so frantically to belong, Ian Garrick's social cowardice, Mico Higgins's desperate ambition to become a member of the Light Infantry Club, Jay Lockhart's killing himself because he could not bear the humiliation of thinking that Joe Ann wanted to divorce him in order to marry a butcher, and Mrs. Wales's hatred of her husband's work— was it not the secret and the key?

And was it not also the key to Garvin Wales? If it could be said of the others that they had been crippled, was he not the most injured of all? The contempt and bitterness that inked his pages, the mockery, the rape in the attic and the miscegenation in the cotton fields, the adultery in the graveyard and the incest in the kitchen, the feuds, the murders, the fratricides, the swarming coilings as in a snake pit— what was the whole body of his work, relieved only by a love of landscape, the earth itself, but a wild, senseless striking out at that which he had always longed for, even in the depths of what he called the mudsill, and which he had been driven to realize, because of Anna Jones, that he could never have?

And one thing more—what of he himself: what, at last, of Sonny Page? Why had he assumed that he alone had escaped unharmed, simply because he had gone to New York? Why had he needed this agony of Garvin Wales to make him see things as they were? He had always thought that he had left Pompey's Head because Kit Robbins had hurt him in his pride, but now he knew better—it wasn't his pride that had been hurt, it was his gentility. That which crippled the others had crippled him also, and if he wanted to know just how crippled he had been, he need look no farther than Midge Higgins. The truth was that he was afraid of Midge—not because she was a Channel girl, but because he was an Alwyn Street boy; if he hadn't been afraid he would have let himself be in love with Midge, as he always wanted to be; he would have accepted what she had to offer, and he might even have asked her to marry him—it was easy to see that if she had not come from the Channel his thoughts would have turned in that direction. Though he had found it convenient to blame Kit Robbins, she was actually blameless—long before she appeared on the scene he must have been walking with a limp. And it was true what he said to Dinah about their trouble being Mulberry: it was Mulberry that lay at the bottom of it all. He was drawn to Mulberry as a place, and by the happy times he had known there; but more than a place it was a symbol, and it was to the symbol, more than the place, that he had always aspired—now he could see it whole and plain, the view from Pompey's Head.

"My wife would commit me if she knew any of this," he heard Wales say. "She's already threatened to, saying that I can't manage any longer. And it's true. I can't manage. I'm blind and I'm getting old. I don't want to be put off somewhere to die alone."

Anson barely heard.

"It looks like it might start to rain at any minute, Mr. Wales," he said. "Don't you want to go back to the house?"

Wales did not answer. Anson waited a few moments and then said, "I think I'll be leaving now, Mr. Wales. Good day, sir," and started walking up the beach. Halfway to the end of the grove of pines he turned, and when he turned he saw the flash of a woman's dress behind the teahouse. It was Mrs. Wales, and he knew she had heard every word. Shocking though it was to find her there, it was even more shocking to realize that she had arranged his interview with Wales in order that she might also arrange to eavesdrop—he was too stunned to feel more than a sudden chill. Still, though, he broke and ran, and did not stop running until he reached his car. He wanted to get away from that horror and he was sick at the thought of what he had done to Garvin Wales. Murder would have been a gentler crime.

CHAPTER TWENTY-EIGHT

Driving from Tamburlaine Island as fast as he could, what Anson wanted most was to see Dinah. He could never tell anyone the whole story of what had happened, not even her, but at least he could have the comfort of her presence. What he was going to say when he got back to New York he did not know. He had made Garvin Wales's secret his own responsibility and now he would have to live up to it. Had he not seen Wales he would be infinitely better off. He would then be able to say that Mrs. Wales had taken so firm a stand that he had been unable to budge her. John Duncan would be out twenty thousand dollars, and he a considerable amount of face, but he would not have placed himself in this hopeless position. John Duncan and Mr. Barlowe would naturally expect some kind of explanation, and how was he going to say that although he had learned that Phil Greene was innocent Mrs. Wales would still have to be paid off? If you wanted to make gestures you ought to be able to afford them. He could not expect John Duncan to pick up the tab, not when it came to twenty thousand dollars, and neither could he expect Mr. Barlowe to place much confidence in him in the future. The first thing you learned in law school was that a lawyer's first obligation is to his client, and it was this obligation that he had elected to put aside. His only way out would be to resign. He did not see what else he could do, and it wasn't much to show for fifteen years. He was too old to make a fresh start in some other firm, assuming that some other firm would be willing to take him on, which in itself was most unlikely, and in a place like New York City it was foolish even to imagine that he could open his own office. A kind of panic took hold of him, for what would happen to Meg and the children, and thinking of Meg made him think of Dinah again—better to keep away from Mulberry; better not to do any more damage than was already done.

When he crossed the bridge at Little River it began to rain, and it kept on raining until he reached Pompey's Head. He found a place to park near the hotel and hurried through the rain into the lobby. It was shortly after one o'clock, and the dining room was beginning to empty. Old Watkins was checking hats and coats, and when he saw Anson his face brightened.

"No, now," he said. "It's Mister Sonny again. How you, young man? I didn't see you for breakfast this morning."

"I had to get an early start, Watkins," Anson said. "Do you think you can find me a table?"

"Yes sir," Watkins said. "No trouble at all. Did you get your message?"

"What message?"

Watkins shook his head. "That I don't know, sir, but one of the boys was paging you a while back. He was after getting you to take a call on the telephone."

"You don't know who it was, do you?"

Watkins shook his head again. "No sir, that I don't. I reckon there's a slip under your door, and in your box at the desk. Do you want to look into it before you have your lunch?"

"No, Watkins, it can wait."

He imagined that it was Dinah who had called, wanting to find out how he had managed on Tamburlaine. He would have to call her back, but there was no hurry. He did not want to hear her voice right at that moment. He wanted to be with her more than he wanted anything, and he knew that if he heard her voice he could not keep from going to Mulberry. He had reached the end of his endurance and he could think of nothing more blessed than being able to go back with her to his old room in the rain.

Watkins left his post to show Anson to a table. "It sure came down in a hurry, didn't it?" he said.

"Yes, Watkins, it sure did. Do you think it will keep on raining as hard as this?"

"No sir, that ain't likely. This time of year, it's more'n apt to come down in one big bust and then spend the rest of the day showering in and out. You have a good lunch now. The London broil is good today. Why don't you try that?"

"Thank you, Watkins, I think I will."

He found that he was hungrier than he thought and ate his meal with satisfaction. The prospect did not look any brighter, but he felt considerably more fortified. He was drinking his coffee when the phone rang in the dining room. The headwaiter answered it and came to Anson's table. He said that it was Mrs. Higgins calling from Mulberry. Anson followed him back to the phone and picked up the receiver. There was a note of urgency in Dinah's voice.

"I've been trying to reach you, Sonny. Where have you been?"

"Here, for the last half hour or more. What's up?"

"Did Lucy Wales get hold of you?"

Anson felt a sinking sensation. "No, she didn't. Has she been trying to?"

"Apparently. She called to find out if you were here."

"What gave her the idea that I might be?"

"I don't know. She said that she'd been trying to reach you at the hotel."

"What does she want? Did she say?"

"No, only that she wanted to see you immediately. What happened this morning?"

Anson hesitated before replying. "Nothing that I'd care to talk about over the phone. Does she want me to go back to Tamburlaine?"

"Yes, right away. I told her that you were leaving tonight and she said it was essential that she see you."

"Essential?"

"That's her word, not mine. Nothing went wrong, did it?"

"It all depends on your definition of wrong. I didn't get what I went for, if that's what you mean."

Now it was Dinah's turn to pause. "I'm sorry, Sonny. I've been keeping my fingers crossed all morning."

"Well, now you can uncross them. Didn't she give you any idea of what she wants?"

"No, she didn't. All she said is what I told you, that it was essential that you see her immediately. Are you going to?"

It was just that which Anson was trying to decide. "Yes, I suppose I have to. There's no way out. I'm getting damn tired of hacking back and forth all the way from town, though, especially in this rain."

"You don't have to hack back and forth all the way from town, you know."

"Yes, I know."

"Don't drive too fast when you go back there. That causeway gets slippery when it's wet. Be careful, won't you?"

402

"I will."

"And, Sonny——"

"Yes?"

"I love you."

"And I you."

"Be careful on that causeway."

"I will."

The rain amounted to a deluge when Anson drove back to Tamburlaine Island. Crossing the bridge at Little River, he could see that the waters were rising swiftly, as they always did in one of these rains, and when he reached the island and stopped before the house, he had to sit in his car for a few minutes, waiting for a break in the downpour. He could not imagine why Mrs. Wales wanted to see him and did not much care. It was more curiosity than anything else that had brought him here, and now that Mrs. Wales could harm him no further, now that he knew her for what she was, he felt none of the apprehension that had hampered him in times past—of that burden, at least, he was free.

Taking advantage of a momentary lessening of the rain, he dashed from the car and ran to the house. Mrs. Wales herself opened the door before he had time to ring, and he understood that, having seen him drive up, she had been waiting for him. She looked at him for a moment without speaking, wearing a flowered silk dress, and shook her head in a manner that was almost affectionate.

"You poor man," she said. "You're soaked. Come into the living room by the fire. I won't like to think that I am responsible should you take your death of cold."

Ready though he thought he was for anything, Anson was not ready for that. Were this his first encounter with her, and were it not for that terrible memory of her lurking behind the teahouse, he might have been misled into believing that she was genuinely fond of him. This was one time, however, when he was not going to let down his guard; he had had enough of her being the elegant lady and he knew the ruin she could do. Following her into the living room, where the rain was streaming against the window and a fire was burning in the hearth, he could feel himself grow tense. So far outside her reach he stood, so disassociated, that he could view not only her but his own emotions with detachment—this was the first time in his life, he realized, that he had ever thought anyone was actually repulsive.

"I talked with Dinah," he said. "She told me that you wanted to see me."

Mrs. Wales nodded. "Yes, I did," she said, "and you have every right to be cross with me for making you come out here in all this rain. Would you be less cross with a drink?"

"No, thank you, Mrs. Wales," Anson said. "It's a little early for a drink. If you'll tell me what you want to see me about——"

"Of course," Mrs. Wales said. "You're a busy man and I can't expect you to spend the whole afternoon gossiping. I fear that I have been much too much of a botheration already. But why didn't you *tell* me, Mr. Page? Why did you think that you had to go to my husband?"

Anson tried to make some sense of what she was saying but could not—he stared at her dumbly. Moving to the hearth and standing with her back to the fire, Mrs. Wales said, "Or was it because you thought that I might not understand? I can't say that I blame you, though, considering how disagreeable I've made myself. And don't contradict, please—I *have* been disagreeable, and I can't say that I like myself very much. But how was I to know that Garvin borrowed that money from Phil Greene—that he wanted it to take me on that trip around the world, and that Phil was generous enough to let him pay it back in installments? Why didn't you *tell* me, Mr. Page?"

Anson stood there staring: was this some new piece of unbalanced deviousness, or had the woman taken leave of her senses completely? How could she even attempt this fantastic about-face? Mrs. Wales, however, could not have been more delightfully poised; her air was that of a woman who has made an unfortunate, but at the same time amusing, mistake. Spreading her hands behind her, she said, "I knew Garvin couldn't afford that trip. Successful though *The Alien Sky* was, there was not a trip around the world in it—I should have known that he must have borrowed the money somewhere. He isn't very careful about the way he handles funds, I'm afraid, but then none of us Southern people are, are we, Mr. Page? And in that respect I do believe that Garvin is one of the worst of the lot. I sometimes suspect him of thinking that he still lives in the time when his people were among the largest landowners in Alabama, and when there was all the money in the world. Did you know that his grandfather and Jefferson Davis were closely connected?"

"No," Anson said woodenly, "I didn't."

"What the exact connection was I don't remember," Mrs. Wales said, "and it's certainly of no importance. What *is* important is that I caused you to have so little faith in me, and that I behaved so badly that you felt you had to go to my husband. And he was furious with me after you left this morning, as you can imagine! Oh, how ashamed you two have made me." She gave her head a little shake and looked at him contritely. "And another thing, Mr. Page—when you mentioned those checks of Phil Greene's, why didn't you tell me the whole story?" For the briefest instant, as her eyes met his, she was forced to look away. He had the feeling that she was tottering precariously, that she stood on the very edge of a scream, but then, with a solemn look in her eyes, "I find it very touching that he was sending those checks to one of the Greenes' old family servants who needed help. By not taking me fully into your confidence, and by letting me think those dreadful things, you let me fall into a most undignified position—those things I said about Phil: how were you to know that they were nothing but a bad-tempered woman's pique?"

She turned away from the hearth, swinging her hips in the girlish way she had, and opened her blue eyes wide. "Shall we call it quits, Mr. Page?" she said. "Will you accept my apology?"

"Certainly, Mrs. Wales," Anson said. "Of course I will."

Relief, as he looked at her, was mixed with incredulity. It was not deviousness and it was not madness. Eavesdropping behind the teahouse, she had found the truth too unbearable to face, much less to act upon—she had not said a word to her husband, and never would, lest she be compelled to confront it squarely, and now she was turning her back on it forever. By pretending it was not true, she would in time find it possible to make it not true. Soon it would be gone from her mind completely, and she would never have heard of a woman named Anna Jones. It was not deviousness and it was not madness. It was simply that she was Lucy Devereaux and that, as Lucy Devereaux, she could not have been married all these years to the man whose mother was Anna Jones. What she was saying, and what she was asking him to join her in saying, was that there was no such person as Anna Jones, that she never once existed.

"I suppose you're right, Mrs. Wales," he said. "I guess I should have told you the whole story. I should have known that you would understand."

"Ah, it's kind of you to say so," Mrs. Wales said. "You make me feel a little better. But I know how busy you must be, and I don't want to keep you any longer. I have written a little note that explains everything, which I have here for you to read." She went to the low table that stood before the couch and picked up a piece of blue note paper and a square blue envelope. "All it says is that my husband told me that he borrowed that money from Phil Greene, and that those withdrawals, as you called them, were Garvin's way of paying him back. Will that be satisfactory?"

"More than satisfactory, Mrs. Wales," Anson said, reading the note hurriedly and slipping it into the envelope. "Thank you very much."

"No, Mr. Page," she said, resting her hand lightly on his arm. "It is I who should thank you. And I do, most gratefully." She looked at him for another fleeting instant and removed her hand. "Had it not been for you and your patience, I would have let my bad temper place me in a most undignified position. But now, again thanks to you, none of us need ever give a thought to this silly misunderstanding again. The rain seems to be letting up a bit, and I know you want to go. The next time you come South to visit, do remember that we will always be happy to see you. And give my love to Dinah. Until the next time, Mr. Page."

The remainder of the day passed quickly. The rain had settled to a steady drizzle by the time Anson reached Pompey's Head, and when he returned his rented car to the U-Drive-It agency it was after three o'clock. One of the men at the agency drove him back to the Marlborough, and when he went up to his room he stretched out on the bed and fell asleep. He awoke with a start a little before six o'clock, hurriedly shaved and showered, dressed, and packed his things. His gray suit was damp when he folded it into his suitcase and he supposed he should have had it pressed. He was about to leave when the telephone rang. It was Dinah, waiting in the lobby. He said he'd be right down.

She was sitting in the same chair where he had found her the first time, and the usual collection of elderly people had gathered before the hearth. She was wearing a fur coat over a black dress and hadn't bothered with a hat. She rose from the chair when she saw him step from the elevator, and they met in the middle of the lobby. They stood for a moment facing each other, and he tried not to think that he was going away. "My, don't you look lovely," he said. "Are you ready for a drink?"

"Yes," Dinah said. "I could use a drink."

They went down to the bar, which was more crowded than usual, and sat in the same booth in which they had talked a few days before. Waiting for their drinks to arrive, Dinah said, "What did Lucy want? Did you see her?"

"Yes, I did."

406

"What happened?"

Not having rehearsed any story, Anson had to invent as he went along. He said, "Not much. I saw Wales this morning, and after I left they must have had a conference. We finally got everything straight."

Dinah's face lit up. "You did!"

"Yes," Anson said. "It seems that Wales borrowed that twenty thousand dollars from Greene to take Lucy on a trip around the world. It was more than he could pay back at once, so he had to return it in installments. That accounts for those withdrawals. It turned out that Wales knew all about them."

Dinah studied his face. "But what about that Anna Jones person?"

"Oh, her." Anson faltered for an instant. "Those checks to her were more or less a coincidence. She was just somebody that Phil Greene wanted to help out."

Dinah did not move her level gaze. She said, "You're not telling the truth."

"Aren't I?"

"No, you're not," Dinah said. "I can always tell when you're making things up, and I know that there's more to it than that. I won't ask any more questions, though, since I can tell that you don't want to talk about it. But it's all settled then. You got everything you came for?"

He looked at her and she looked back.

"Yes, sure," he said. "Everything."

They had a second drink and then went up to the dining room. Anson had not thought to reserve a table, but they were lucky enough to be seated by the line of windows that looked out into the garden. The rain was over now, nothing more than a mist. They were neither of them hungry. Dinah wanted only a shrimp cocktail and a small green salad, and these she barely touched—Anson did no better with the lamb chops he ordered. It was a relief when the time came for them to go.

Dinah had her car parked before the hotel and she drove him to the station. The mist put yellow rings around all the street lights and hung in the trees like fog.

"It looks as though it's rained itself out," Dinah said.

"Yes, it looks that way."

"Tomorrow ought to be a pretty day. I guess the Fowlers will be able to have their oyster roast."

"Are you going?"

"No, I don't think so. They'll have that same old crowd and it won't be any fun. Did I tell you that all my daffodils were blooming?"

"No, you didn't."

"I wanted you to see them. It's too bad that you couldn't stay longer."

"Yes, it is. It's a good thing that I didn't get hung up, though. Things would have backed up on me at the office."

Reaching Lafayette Street, Dinah drove to a parking place behind the station. The parking place adjoined the tracks, and the Special stood ready to leave. Plumes of steam came from beneath the cars, and some of the passengers were already boarding.

"You wait here," Anson said when Dinah parked the car. "I'll find a redcap."

"No, I want to go with you."

"In that case I might as well carry my bag."

"Don't forget your topcoat. It's on the back seat. And your briefcase too."

After checking the number of his pullman, which was 241A, Anson and Dinah walked down the line of cars—when they came to 241A, he saw that it was the same one in which he had arrived, *The Marshes of Glynn*. The amiable porter, the one whose name was Thomas McElroy, recognized him. He nodded politely, including Dinah in the greeting, and took Anson's things into the car.

"Well, Dinah," Anson said, "I guess I'm on my way. Thanks for everything."

"It was wonderful to see you, Sonny," Dinah said. "Come back soon and bring your family. Make it a real visit the next time."

"I'll do my best. I'd certainly like to. And you try to get to New York. I forgot to give you my address, but you can always find us in the phone book."

The porter stepped from the car and walked a short distance away, turning his back. His white jacket was fresh and spotless and his shoes were newly shined. Up toward the front of the train a voice called, "All aboard, all aboard," and the porter, turning, repeated the warning. Anson took the collar of Dinah's coat and lifted her face and kissed her. She kissed him back, harder and harder, and then pulled away.

"You still smell good," Anson said. "I can't say anything, but I'll always remember. Keep on being my girl."

"I will, always," Dinah said, "and I hope it breaks your heart. I hope you'll be miserable as I'm going to be miserable. Kiss me again,

408

quick," and then a bell was clanging somewhere and the porter was telling him that he had better get aboard. "Don't forget to get that lipstick off your face," Dinah said. "Do it right away."

Anson lifted himself onto the car after the porter and leaned from the steps as the train began to pull out. Dinah stood bareheaded on the platform beside the track, and as the gap of distance widened, already lengthening into separation, he saw that her eyes were wet and shining, the way they were on the beach. She simply stood there, not waving or moving, and he leaned from the steps until the train swung on a curve behind the station and he could not see her any longer. He went into the car, found his way to his roomette, and wiped off his lips with a towel from one of the racks, looking in the mirror. He had brought a faint drift of her perfume into the roomette with him, and for a moment, turning from the mirror to dispose of the towel, he had to bend his head. He took out a cigarette and was hunting through his pockets for a match when the porter returned. The porter struck a match for him, holding it steady until his cigarette was lit, and then blew the match out.

"Well, sir," he said, "how did you find things in Old Pompey? Just the same?"

"Yes," Anson said. "Just the same."